Joanna Bourne has always loved reading and writing romance. She's drawn to Revolutionary and Napoleonic France and Regency England because, as she puts it, 'It was a time of love and sacrifice, daring deeds, clashing ideals and really cool clothing.' She's lived in seven different countries, including England and France, the settings of the Spymaster series.

Joanna now lives on a mountaintop in the Appalachians with her family, a peculiar cat and an old brown country dog. Visit her online at www.joannabourne.com, and connect with her via Twitter @jobourne, www.facebook.com/joanna.bourne.5, or www.jobourne.blogspot.co.uk.

Irresistible reasons to indulge in a Joanna Bourne historical romance:

'Joanna Bourne is a master of romance and suspense' Teresa Medeiros, *New York Times* bestselling author

'Bourne is an undeniably powerful new voice in historical romance' *All About Romance*

'Destined to be a classic in the romance genre' *Dear Author*

'Exceptional characters, brilliant plotting, a poignant love story' *Library Journal*

'Unusual, resourceful, and humorous heroines' Diana Gabaldon, *New York Times* bestselling author

'Distinct, fresh, and engaging' Madeline Hunter, *New York Times* bestselling author

'Addictively

By Joanna Bourne

Rogue Spy

Joanna Bourne

headline
ETERNAL

Published by arrangement with Berkley,
a member of Penguin Group (USA), LLC,
A Penguin Random House Company

First published in Great Britain in 2014
by HEADLINE ETERNAL
An imprint of HEADLINE PUBLISHING GROUP

1

Cataloguing in Publication Data is available from the British Library

ISBN 978 1 4722 2251 0

Offset in Times Lt Std by Avon DataSet Ltd, Bidford-on-Avon, Warwickshire

Printed and bound by CPI Group (UK) Ltd, Croydon, CR0 4YY

Papers used by Headline are from well-managed forests
and other responsible sources.

HEADLINE PUBLISHING GROUP
An Hachette UK Company
338 Euston Road
London NW1 3BH

www.headlineeternal.com
www.headline.co.uk
www.hachette.co.uk

To Rowen

Acknowledgments

I am deeply grateful to my wonderful beta readers, Sophie Couch, Madeline Iva, Mary Ann Clark, Jan Burland, and Laura Watkins. Their wisdom and good sense have kept me out of trouble more times than I can count.

I'd like to thank Fabienne Camille and Catherine MacGregor for help with the French language used in the manuscript and Zan Marie Steadham for help with the Latin. My thanks also to Deniz Bevan for helping me with edits. Any correct usage is the fruit of their effort. The mistakes are all my own.

As always, all my gratitude to my knowledgeable and patient editor, Wendy McCurdy, and my wonderful agent, Pam Hopkins.

One

When you must run, carry nothing and never look back.

A BALDONI SAYING

THE END OF HER OWN PARTICULAR WORLD ARRIVED early on a Tuesday morning, wrapped in brown paper and twine, sealed with a blob of red wax. She found it at the bottom of the pile of the morning's mail.

She sat at her desk in the library, pleasantly full of breakfast, opening letters, ready to be brisk with the contents. Camille Leyland—Cami—dutiful niece, British subject, codebreaker, French spy, ready to deal with the morning post.

The Fluffy Aunts didn't believe in opening mail at the breakfast table. "A barbarous custom," Aunt Lily called it.

Books filled the room she sat in and most of the rest of the substantial cottage. They ran floor to ceiling along every wall of the front parlor, the entry hall, the back parlor, what had originally been a bedroom, and this little study at the back of the house. Books, plump with pages of notes and bristling with bookmarks, stuffed the shelves two deep and wedged in every available space on top.

In the next room Aunt Lily and Aunt Violet bumbled back and forth, trailing scarves and arguing amiably about . . . something to do with Gnostic symbology. In any case, they had wandered deep into the maze of academic dispute. Any decoding done today would fall in her lap.

The window at her back was open to the morning. Sun fell across these nearest shelves in the pattern of the window-panes, eighteen trapezoids across the books. The leather bind-ing was mellow brown, red, and blue. The gold lettering on the spines turned to curls of fire.

To work, to work. She'd get the pesky small business of the day out of the way first. It was an old relaxing routine to cut a fresh nib on the pen and unstopper the ink. She slipped her shoes off and cuddled her stockinged feet under her, comfy as a cat. Her desk was bare as the deck of a ship at sea. When one codes and decodes for diplomats and the secret agencies of the British government, one keeps a tidy desk.

"I can't find . . ." Aunt Violet leaned in at the door. "Cami, did you move the Norbert manuscript for some reason?"

"Try the boxes on the table." That answer usually worked.

"I have it here." Aunt Lily's voice came around the corner. "I was consulting it last night. Fanshaw is wrong. Incorrect citations. Sloppy scholarship. No real knowledge of his sub-ject. He is quite simply wrong."

"Ex scientia vera," Aunt Violet said.

Half a lifetime of Latin over the dinner table made the translation automatic. "From knowledge, truth." Herself, she'd always thought one could have too much truth.

Aunt Lily crossed the door to the front room, coming in and out of the line of sight, carrying a large manuscript. "Stupid as *owls*. Not the Hungarians. Stuffy old fools and their Cambridge politics." That was obscure, but probably true, the Fluffy Aunts being shrewd in such matters.

A serene, blue and gold morning filled the sky outside the window to her left. The air was full of academic infighting and the scent of late roses. This first letter . . . she glanced at the postmarks. That was from Aunt Lily's man of business. She could set it aside, unopened. The Fluffy Aunts invested in cog production and rope inventories and God knew what and didn't seem to go bankrupt.

She slipped her letter opener under the seal of the next letter and loosed the news that Mr. Owens, owner of the Sparrow

Bookshop in London, had located a copy of *De Componendis Cifris*, exhaustively described herein. How much would they authorize him to bid on it? That went to the pile on the far left, for Aunt Violet, who collected. A bill for a hat slid into a drawer with other bills to be paid next time she was in London. A letter from Germany, in German. That was for Aunt Lily.

Paper by paper, she sorted order out of chaos. It was not unlike decoding, in its way.

Aunt Lily stalked about, muttering, in the other room, "Not Ogham. Not Welsh. Next he's going to spout nonsense about Aramaic."

The letter opener was an antique dagger from Italy, honed to a killing edge. But no one would wonder why she kept a deadly weapon in the house. Lay it gently in a desk drawer and the knife became unremarkable as a goose quill.

It was beautiful in a spare, serious way, the sort of knife one of her Baldoni ancestors would have used to commit murder. She'd bought it in London eight years ago for that purpose, and it worked. She hadn't killed anybody with it since.

The knife was also perfectly good at opening letters.

The next offering of the mail was a note, elegantly addressed and hand-delivered from the manor. There would be a tea next Tuesday. Would the Misses Leyland care to attend?

Tea and tittle-tattle, chatter of King Charles spaniels, flooding in the lower fields. The Fluffy Aunts would love it. She set that aside to write a bright, cheery answer later, because the bottom of the pile held something more interesting. Her last but not least of the morning was a square packet wrapped in clean brown paper, tied with string. It was wider than her hand and not much thicker than an ordinary letter. Some object about the size of a shilling weighted the center.

Because of what she'd once been, because of what she'd once known, she saw the dozens of small details and tried to fit them into a pattern. Shopkeeper paper, suitable to wrap Byron's poems or a ham. Ordinary twine. Unremarkable red wax for the seal. That seal slopped over the flap of the paper and the knot in the twine. It would be hard to lift undetectably, if anyone took a notion to engage in that sort of behavior. The signet could have been the letter *L* or a boat. Or a duck.

The aunts had an eclectic network of friends spread to every corner of the map. Sometimes their friends sent curios. But when she turned the little package over, it was addressed to her, not one of the aunts. Educated writing, probably in a man's hand. The postmarks showed it had been sent from London four days ago.

She cut the string and smoothed the wrapping back to reveal a sheet of cream-colored writing paper inside, folded in thirds, then folded inward at the sides. When she picked it up, a ring fell out to spin in a long, small clatter and wobble itself flat.

A gold ring. Her fingers told her it was real gold and worth far too much to send in a letter through the post. The band held a pearl the size of a pea. She slanted it to the light. It was set in a circle of ten very nice little rubies. Well matched, square cut, excellent color, about a carat all told. Very nice indeed.

A child's ring. She'd seen this somewhere.

Her body recognized disaster before her mind did.

She read the first lines of the letter and distinctly, crystal by spiked crystal, she felt herself turn to ice.

My dear Camille,

We are not yet acquainted, so I enclose this small token as introduction. You will have seen this ring in the portrait that hangs above the fireplace in the parlor of Wythe Cottage. Hyacinth Besançon, née Leyland, toys with a brown-and-white spaniel named Felix, called Lix-Lix. The child to her left, the genuine Camille Besançon, wears this ring.

She is here with me now. I foresee great awkwardness when this somewhat more authentic Camille returns to her aunts' house. The Leylands might forgive your deception. The British Service, Military Intelligence, and the Foreign Office will not.

If you try to run, they will pursue you mercilessly.

Make some excuse to travel to London. Meet me at the Moravian church in Fetter Lane on Friday at noon. Bring with you the key to the Mandarin Code. Do so, and you may continue your comfortable life with the Leylands. I

will present you with the inconvenient remnant of the past
I hold. You may do with her as you will.

A friend

Snakes of fear slithered along her bones. She had not forgotten how to be terrified, even after many years of safety.

Outside the window, in the garden, a few house sparrows had come to hop about in the grass. The brightest color was the quince tree, yellow against the brick. The hollyhocks were seedpods now, all their leaves brown, looking disgruntled with autumn. Even in early September frost nipped them at night. She could see beyond the wall to the wood on the other side of Dawson's field. Tree shadows flickered against the sky.

It was really a beautiful day.

For ten years she'd been safe in the village of Brodemere, playing the part of the Leylands' niece. But before that, she'd been one of the Cachés, one of the terrible, well-trained children sent to England by the fanatics of the Revolution. She'd been a French spy, placed in an English family. Placed with the Leylands, because the two dithering, scholarly old ladies were the codemakers and codebreakers for the British Intelligence Service.

The British Service would not be forgiving. They could not allow a French spy who knew so much to escape. It would not matter to them that she had never stolen secrets. That she had long since shaken free of her French masters. She'd read thousands of documents as she ciphered and deciphered. The British Service couldn't afford to let her live.

She let her breath out unevenly, accepting this truth. One must know when it is time to run. When she was a child, her parents had died because they stayed one day too long in Paris, playing a role that was too profitable to abandon.

She lowered the fluttering letter to the blotter to cover the ring. Rested her hands on the desk so they wouldn't shake. She would not alarm the Fluffy Aunts. Would not bring them to her desk, worried and curious, full of sharp, shrewd attention.

It had been a long, fine game, being Camille Leyland. She'd played it so thoroughly she had almost forgotten it was a lie.

Aunt Lily stood at the table in the corner and leafed through a folio book, exchanging opinions through the open door with Aunt Violet . . . something about the Hermetics and Rosenkreuz. They'd slipped into speaking German.

At any moment either of them could look in her direction and know something was terribly wrong.

Become smooth as an egg. Placid as tea in a cup. Show nothing.

She bent over the desk as if she were reading the letter. Nothing in the poise of her body betrayed fear. Nothing, nothing showed on her face.

I have not forgotten what it is to be a Caché. At the school in Paris—the Coach House, it was called—she'd learned to recite the English kings, to play spillikins and Fox and Geese, to make small bombs, to dance the Scotch Reel, to kill with her hands. She'd had a different name then. Memories of that time spun and tumbled in her head like a pack of cards, tossed in the air, falling.

When she looked up, the world was changed. The books beside her desk, the mail in its prim stacks, the big lamp, the copybooks and quills, the sharpened pencils in the Etruscan cup felt strange, distant, trivial. The woman she was becoming, second by second, no longer belonged in this quiet village, in this small house where two harmless old women argued about Finnish vowel sounds.

The Fluffy Aunts knew the Mandarin Code as well as she did. The man who sent this disgusting letter must be well aware of that. If he couldn't get the code from her, he would come to acquire it from them. Her first task, before all others, was to lead his attention away from this cottage. Away from the aunts.

She slipped the letter opener into her sleeve, where it stopped being harmless and turned into a dagger again. She put her palms flat on the desk and made herself think.

From the next room, Aunt Violet called, "So vexing. He agrees with Johnson."

"Then they are both wrong." Aunt Lily snapped the volume she was studying closed. Emphatically, she pushed her glasses back up the bridge of her nose.

"Huncher is very unhelpful. I'll try Middleton."

"I'd accept Middleton," Aunt Lily stepped briskly from the room, "*cum grano salis.*"

. . . with a grain of salt. She would miss them so much.

She folded the letter, feeling the texture of it acutely, seeing every nuance and shade of the wood grain of her desk. The pearl ring was light in her hand when she picked it up.

For ten years, she'd lived in this safe, pretty cottage in the place that belonged to Camille Besançon. At night, in her room up under the slope of the roof, in the narrow bed beside the window, she'd looked out over the fields toward the mill pond and imagined the child who'd died. That child, her parents, and the young brother had been murdered so a Caché could be placed in the Leyland household. So many murders committed so a French spy could live in the cottage in Brodemere with the Latin and tea cakes, German, algebra, Hebrew and Arabic, the intricacies of code, the calculus, Spanish, Polish, chess, good wine . . . "There is nothing worse than inferior wine," Aunt Violet always said. "One might as well drink ditchwater."

I couldn't have saved that child. I was a child myself, and helpless.

But in the silence of the night, all those years, she'd felt guilty.

Could Camille Besançon have somehow escaped the slaughter? Could the little girl who'd worn this ring possibly be alive?

"Whyever am I holding this Von Herder book?" Aunt Violet's voice receded toward the parlor. "What was I looking for?"

"Middleton. It should be on the shelf behind you, next to the Asiatic Register. To the right. The other right, dear."

They'd given her so much. She'd been able to give them so little.

Now she could protect them. She could make certain this blackmailer never, ever came near them. If Camille Besançon had somehow survived, she could give the Fluffy Aunts their niece. Their only blood relative. It would be a small repayment for the lies she'd told.

I'll never see them again. I can't even say goodbye.

She slipped the ring into her pocket. It was time to go. She turned in her chair and dropped the blackmail letter on the fire. It blackened and became ashes. No one would be surprised to see her burning it. Codemakers burn every scrap of paper they're not using.

The man who'd written that sly, lying letter could have bribed some villager or one of the servants to report to him. Even now, someone might be standing in the wood spying on them with field glasses. From this moment on, she'd assume someone was watching.

She'd always known that one day, without warning, it would be time to walk away. But she wasn't ready. She would never be ready.

She'd made her preparations. Two miles past the parish pump, under a great flat stone at the end of an old stone wall, money, warm clothing, and sturdy walking shoes waited, wrapped in oilcloth. She'd help herself to the muff pistol and kit from the drawer in the hall when she went by. Then she'd stroll down the front walk carrying nothing but her reticule, as if she went on some ordinary stroll to the village. She'd stand up and walk away. It was as simple and as hard as that.

In a minute of two she'd get up and do it. When she was quite certain she wasn't going to cry.

It didn't matter how determined and clever you were. When the sword of Damocles falls, there you sit, stupid as a chicken, with your skull cleaved neatly in half.

Two

Many a man has woven his own noose from parchment. Put nothing in writing.

A BALDONI SAYING

PAX STOOD AT THE WINDOW OF THE DANCING Dog, holding a mug of ale, looking out at Braddy Square. He'd come back to London, to duty undone and promises broken. To men he'd betrayed. Back to where it began. Back to Meeks Street. There were no decisions to make. No work left undone. He was just putting off the inevitable. Strange to discover this late in the game that he was a coward.

Stop thinking. He'd slogged the leagues across France, crossed the Channel, and made the long ride from Dover to London by not letting himself think.

He set his mug lightly to one of the windowpanes and didn't pretend an interest in drinking ale. Nobody in the tavern bothered him. He found himself watching a woman who stood in the open space of the square. At this distance she was just a brown cloak, making a line of dark sienna against the light behind. He couldn't see her face under the hood. Something in the sweep of cloak from shoulder to ground when she moved said she was young. She'd brought bread to scatter for the birds. A couple dozen pigeons and sparrows had formed an attentive circle.

He hadn't slept for a long time. Hadn't tried to. He'd

ridden . . . how many horses had he ridden to exhaustion? He'd pushed on through the night, not because what he had to do was important but because he'd rather spend the hours riding than lying down, staring at the ceiling in some French inn. He was almost sure he hadn't slept since he left Paris.

This last quarter mile, within sight of Meeks Street, was the hardest. He couldn't make himself go on. He'd washed up at the Dancing Dog, dropped his valise, and stuck.

The woman in her dark cloak had a quality of waiting, as if she were meeting somebody. Maybe that was what caught his eye. She stayed motionless while everyone else passed through the square on business that took them elsewhere.

The wide front window of the Dancing Dog was made of old, thick, wavery panes of glass that distorted the world. A man in a blue coat passed the tavern, west to east, carrying a parcel. His image thinned and stretched from pane to pane. It was like watching him through water.

They knew Thomas Paxton at the Dog. A decade ago, when he'd been doorkeeper and messenger boy at Number Seven, he'd raced in and out of here every day, fetching meat pasties and beer to the agents, rattling through at a run, returning empty jugs to the counter in back.

Ten years ago he'd kept an appointment with a traitor in that dim and shadowy back corner to the right. He'd handed over a sheaf of secrets and become a traitor himself. A milestone in his life.

He snuffed out that thought the way he'd pinch off flame to save the candle for another day.

The battered valise at his feet held two changes of clothing, money, and a spare knife. His gun was packed on top, loaded. Carruthers had handed it back when he rode out of Paris, probably hoping he'd use it to suicide. That might be the simplest solution for everybody.

Damned if he'd make it that easy for them.

In the false bottom of the bag he carried a dozen letters, correspondence from Paris to the Meeks Street headquarters. They'd made their resident traitor the courier on this trip. The ways of the British Service were mysterious indeed.

Maybe Carruthers knew this particular burden was the best

way to get him to London alive, and as fast as a horse could travel. That might be what she had planned. The British Intelligence Service worked five or six levels of subtlety deep.

He was carrying a copy of his confession with the other messages. That last week in Paris he'd written out a lengthy account of his life, with particular attention to the ways he'd betrayed the British Service. He was also delivering a final report on the whole matter from Carruthers, Head of Section for France, to Galba, Head of the British Service.

He could have opened that. He could have lifted the seal and replaced it undetectably when he was eight. Twice, he'd taken that report out from the other letters and thought about reading it.

Snare after snare. Temptation after temptation. Maybe Carruthers advised a swift and final end for the man who called himself Thomas Paxton. What did a man do when he opened that letter and found his death warrant?

He'd never know. Both times, he'd put the report back with the other letters and repacked the bag. He hadn't taken the bait, if it was bait. He didn't have much honor left   just a patched-up, threadbare rag of it—but he would have used the gun on himself before he lost the last of it.

He ran the back of his fingers across the window glass, feeling the ripple in it, feeling the cold. Trapped inside the glass, pinpoint bubbles glinted silver.

Galba wouldn't be content with killing him. Galba would want to pry the top off his soul and drag every one of his slimy secrets out into the sunlight.

Mugs clicked behind him. A chair scraped on the floor. The barman cleared tables. Two plump women walked past the Dancing Dog, side by side, one neat in dark green, the other in dark blue. They leaned together, their heads close, their handbaskets bumping, steps matched, a picture of old friendship and a lifetime of confidences shared. He'd have sketched them in quick slashes of watercolor, then stacked up ink in a blunt, dark splotch on the pavement at their feet to give them a single shadow.

On a bench in the square, a man unfolded a cloth across his lap and took out bread and cheese, enjoying an early lunch.

The woman he'd been watching tossed another wide circle of crumbs and her cloak flowed like water falling. Sparrows hopped and scuttled madly left or right around her feet. He'd do that lone, self-contained figure in chalks, the sweet curve of her cloak laid in burnt sienna over indigo. He'd thumb in one soft smudge of pale amber under her hood, where the plane of her cheek showed. He would have liked to see her face.

There. That was her last handful of bread. He watched her dust her fingers and motion to the boy lounging on the step at the mercer's. Sam, floor sweeper, delivery boy, holder of horses, one of the fixtures in the neighborhood, ran over to conduct business. He took coin, accepted a letter, and headed down Meeks Street.

She wasn't here to feed sparrows, then. The calculations that always churned in the bottom of his mind broke the surface. Why would a woman send a note from the middle of Braddy Square instead of from her own front door? Why not drop it in the post? Why was she wearing her hood up on a fine day like today?

Life was full of mysteries he'd never solve. Maybe that was a love letter she was sending. Maybe she'd spend the afternoon naked in the arms of her man.

Enjoy yourself, pretty lady. His own afternoon would be less pleasant. Time to get on with it.

His mug of ale was still full when he slid it onto the nearest table. He set a coin beside it and picked his bag up, taking it left-handed so he'd have his knife hand free. Nobody looked up to see him leave. It was a point of pride to him that nobody noticed.

He checked to make sure he wasn't followed out of the Dog. It was habit. Just habit. He had all the habits of a spy.

CAMI trailed her messenger lad to the top of Meeks Street and stood watching him strut down the pavement. He was brisk as any boy who knew eyes were on him.

The church bells finished up the count of eleven. Her flock of birds flew away to do bird errands now that she had no more bread for them. Probably their lives were full of whatever troubles birds fell heir to and all that cheery chirping and hopping about was a deception. She was something of an expert in deception.

When she paid the boy tuppence to deliver the letter, she'd pressed a shilling into his hand on top of it. "If they ask who gave you the letter, describe someone else. If they ask where I went, point the other way."

Her family—the Baldoni—used to say, "Prepare for many evil eventualities. Some of them will arrive."

The air settled around her, still and heavy. The sky over London was white, opaque and dull as cheap crockery, full of bright sun. Her boy turned at Number Seven, tripped up the stair, and stood waiting for an answer to his knock. She waited also. She'd stay to see this letter delivered. There was too much at stake to take that for granted. Inside the shell of calm she'd closed around her was a chaos so loud she couldn't think. It was fortunate she'd made her plans beforehand and needed only to follow the path she'd laid out.

From the corner of her eye she saw the shift of light. A man walked toward her across Braddy Square. For a sharp instant, she was afraid.

But no. She wasn't in danger yet. She had an hour before she walked into the trap laid for her.

She turned away, not sharing her face with this man passing by, being careful. In the long, soft years since Paris, she hadn't forgotten the rules.

She collected only a glimpse of him as he walked past her and continued down Meeks Street . . . a tall, long-limbed man, dressed in dark traveling clothes, somewhat dusty. He wore well-scuffed riding boots, riding gloves, and a soft, broad-brimmed felt hat that shaded his face. He carried a valise and moved fast, with the clean grace of an athlete. Something about him made her think of a man trudging uphill with no end in sight. If she hadn't been supplied with a sufficiency of troubles of her own, she would have been curious.

Far down Meeks Street, her messenger boy delivered the letter, gave a cheeky salute to the house, and was down the stair before the door closed behind him.

That was done. Whatever happened to her in the Moravian

church on Fetter Lane, that message was safe. There should be no repercussions. She'd timed its delivery so the men of Meeks Street would decode it only after she'd completed her business with the blackmailer.

She crossed Braddy Square in the direction of a godly church where an ungodly meeting would take place. She looked back once. She wasn't really surprised to see the man with the valise climb the stairs of Number Seven Meeks Street.

Three

Many buckets of quarrel are filled from the well of ignorance.

A BALDONI SAYING

PAX PUT ONE FOOT IN FRONT OF THE OTHER FOR the last thousand steps, not letting himself slow down.

Meeks Street hadn't changed. Ugly prosperous houses lined both sides of the street, the doorknobs polished and the steps well scrubbed. Some houses were shut up tight, keeping the air out, but most had the window sashes up. Muslin curtains rippled, lipping in and out over the sills. The linden trees were turning yellow. Gray smoke from the kitchen fires slanted off the chimneys and spread out to disappear.

Number Thirty-one was still ruled by the sleek black tomcat that played sentry on the garden wall. Number Twenty-three had added five stone urns along the front, carrying five yew trees shaved and clipped within an inch of their lives. At Nineteen, a dog stuck a yapping muzzle through a gap in the iron gate.

All familiar. He didn't belong at Meeks Street anymore, but it felt like coming home.

Down the street, Sam had delivered that woman's message to Number Seven.

He glanced back over his shoulder. The woman in the dark

cloak was gone. She'd waited just long enough to see her letter delivered. Gone . . . and she left the air behind her shimmering with intention and planning.

I don't like this.

Young Sam swung away from Number Seven, errand completed, and headed back to the square, running his fingers along the iron palings, whistling, pleased with himself.

Why didn't she want to come to Number Seven? He took the steps fast. For the first time in two weeks, he had a reason to be in a hurry.

He pounded the knocker and left his hand spread flat on the door, willing it to open. The door was painted Prussian green with a little black in the base. The knocker was brass, in the shape of a rose. Forty years ago they'd picked the rose knocker out of the ruins of the old headquarters after it burned. The plate to the right of the door read, *The Penumbral Walking Club.*

He didn't have a key. Nobody got past the front door of Number Seven unless somebody let him in.

He pounded again. Where was Giles?

The lock disengaged. Giles, a sturdy, open-faced sixteen-year-old, opened the door, letter in hand. He said, "Pax." Nothing but surprise and pleasure in his voice. "You're back. Hawker said you'd be here in a day or two. Grey's landed in Dover—"

"Give me that." He took the letter from Giles, dropped it on the table, and brushed his fingers on his coat.

"It just came," Giles said. "Sam brought it. It's addressed to Galba."

The door on the other side of the ugly front parlor opened. Hawker, compact, dark haired, deadly as a snake, dressed like a gentleman, strolled in. "I didn't think you'd be fool enough to show up. There's still time to turn around and run."

"No, there isn't. Hawk, look at this. Don't touch it."

"I wasn't going to." Hawker approached, feline and inquisitive. "Communication from the greater world."

The folded paper was addressed to Anson Jones. That was Galba's real name, not the name he used when he was Head of Service. *Mr. Anson Jones, Number Seven, Meeks Street.*

"What's wrong with it?" Hawker took his knife out, twitched the blade under the note, flipped it over.

"It's from a woman."

"Not, in itself, a bad thing."

In fifty words he told Hawk how the note had been sent. "And . . . I know the handwriting. This *e* with the sharp corner, tilted up. The bar on the *t* slanted down. I've seen that."

"Where?"

"Not recently. It's . . ." He shook his head. "A long time ago. Somewhere."

"Part of life's eventful journey."

"It'll come to me." He pulled his knife and helped himself to Hawker's. He steadied the note and slit the seal without touching the paper at all. "Don't breathe." That was for Giles. Hawker had already stepped back.

Hawker murmured, "You do realize we're prying into the private correspondence of the Head of Service."

"I know." He laid the page flat, using the knife point to push the edges back. On the paper, line after line of numbers and letters. "And we have code."

"Do we?" Hawker bent forward. "How dramatic."

"A Service code."

"A Leyland code." Hawk's finger hovered over the inkblot that marked it as Leyland code. "I don't recognize the identifier."

"One of the old ones. Before you came to the Service." Code. Something about code . . . and that handwriting.

Then he remembered. He'd been thirteen or fourteen, sitting at a long table in the cold, bare schoolroom of the Coach House, painstakingly disassembling a code. The dark-haired girl beside him leaned over her slate, scribbling down the sharp little *e* and the slanted *t*, deciphering as fast as she could write. None of them could touch her when it came to code breaking.

Vérité. Vérité's handwriting. Ten years ago, when he'd had a different name and Vérité had been his best friend. "I know who she is. I knew her when she was a child." A particularly deadly child.

Hawk said, "A French spy, then. One of you Cachés."

"One of us. Yes." He flipped Hawk's knife to hold it by the blade and handed it back to him. "I have to find her. Giles, go wash your hands. Don't touch the letter again. Don't let anyone get close to it till I come back."

Giles said, "Why not?"

Hawker answered for him. "Because Galba opens mail addressed to that name with his own hands. There could be poison in the paper. Or smallpox. I saw that done once. We may be playing host to a weapon of the assassin's trade. The woman who sent it is Police Secrète."

"At one time, she was. I don't know what she is now." He wondered what else to say and couldn't think of anything. "Tell Galba I'll be back."

"Giles will tell him." Hawk was already grabbing his hat from the hideous sideboard.

"Hawk, you can't help me with this. You know why."

"Because you're Thomas Paxton, infamous French spy." Hawker's dark face was inscrutable, his eyes cool and assessing. "I'd better keep an eye on you."

"You're on the sick list. You have a bullet hole in you."

"Not a large one. We'll argue about it as we walk. Lead the way."

The hell of it was, he needed Hawk. He made the only decision possible. Somehow he'd make it right with Galba when they got back. "Then come on."

Four

The eagle is uplifted by air. The fish is supported by water. The Baldoni are sustained by subtlety.

A BALDONI SAYING

A DOZEN PEOPLE DAWDLED THEIR WAY AROUND Braddy Square or sat on the benches. Vérité was gone. Pax swung in a circle, looking for any sign of her.

Hawker caught up with him. "She has five minutes' head start. Will she break into a run?"

With her training? "She won't even walk fast. She's gone three or four hundred yards."

He and Hawk had worked together so long they didn't have to discuss strategy. Hawk took off to the left, following the perimeter of the square, clockwise.

One person in Braddy Square would have noticed which way Vérité had gone. Sam was back at his accustomed post in front of the mercer's, meditating on the distant clouds. He was willing enough to point to the corner where the Dancing Dog did its trade. "She went down there. In a hurry, she was."

Wouldn't it be nice if life were that simple? He fumbled a half crown loose from his pocket and held it up. "There's two of these if I catch up with her."

He made to tuck the coin back in his pocket.

"Down there. Morte Road." The boy's eyes shifted east. "She give me shilling to say she gone t'other way."

Now they had a chance. He flipped the coin to Sam and said, "If I catch her, come find two more of these tonight at Number Seven," and left the boy with a grin on his face.

He ran east, hearing Hawk behind him. The first corner gave no sign of her. No dark cloak. No woman alone. No woman the right size and shape.

"This is exceptionally futile," Hawk said. "Except for Sam, who had a profitable morning. You bribe large."

"Always bribe large, close to home."

"A rule to live by. What are we chasing?"

"Long, dark brown cloak with a hood. Dress under it is dark blue. The woman's thin, medium height, a bit more than twenty. Brown eyes. Black hair, short and curly. She's pretty." He corrected that. "She's probably pretty. I didn't see her face."

"You didn't bother to angle over and get a good look. You are a waste of balls, Mr. Paxton."

"I didn't let a woman put a bullet in my shoulder, Mr. Hawkins. We go left."

They ran the next street without a glimpse of Vérité. At the corner, this time, he chose the right hand. There were more people on the street in this direction. Then, sixty feet ahead . . .

He slowed. "You see?" He shifted aside to let Hawker get a good look.

"Do we follow her, or do we collect her now?"

"We follow. You take the lead. And keep your face covered. If she makes a habit of watching Meeks Street, she may know you."

"A joy shared by feminine multitudes." Hawk stripped off his neckcloth and stuffed it in his pocket. He pulled a thin black neckerchief from another pocket and tied it in place around his neck, a fashion for laborers and small tradesmen. "Who is she?"

"French."

"Not precisely a crime. More what Doyle would be calling a social solecism." Hawk unbuttoned his jacket. Crushed the lapels tight in his fists and let them hang rumpled and slightly crooked. What had been fashionable now looked like a cheap imitation. "Hold on to this for me." Hawker handed his hat over and ran a rough hand through his hair, putting himself another step downward on the social ladder.

"She may be armed. Don't get close."

"I never take chances," Hawk said. He probably even believed it.

"I'll signal when we need to change places."

Hawk nodded, his eyes on the dark flick of a cloak in the distance. He reset his coat on his shoulders and hunched in on himself, losing an inch in height. Unrecognizable, he faded into the crowd.

TWENTY minutes later, inconspicuous behind a handcart stacked with bales of newsprint, Pax watched Vérité open the door of a small church on Fetter Lane, just off Fleet Street. He was fairly sure she hadn't spotted him. Ten years ago she'd been skilled in the game of follow and be followed, but he and Hawker had used every trick in the book to stay invisible. They were skilled, too.

An empty church. This looked like she was meeting somebody.

He picked a rectangular slash of shade at the doorway of a stationer's across the street from the church, a spot just made for a man to be patient in. Fetter Lane wasn't as busy as Fleet Street, but it was full enough of printers and booksellers, newspaper offices and taverns, that a man might stand here awhile, waiting for a friend and an innocent meal of chops and ale. Playing his part, he pulled his watch out and checked it. Still well short of noon.

He'd been carrying a newspaper for the last little while. Now he shook it open to hide his face. He signaled, *Come here,* by holding the paper with the first two fingers on his left hand spread and his thumb up.

A minute later, Hawk stopped at the stationer's window and became absorbed in boxes of nice letter paper, a blotter with green felt, and a gold-plated pen set. He said, "The Moravian church. How religious of her. May I assume our quarry is a dedicated Christian reformer with a grim face and abominable taste in clothes?"

"Our quarry is a dedicated French spy." Under cover of the newspaper, he slipped his pistol out and checked it. Everything in order.

"Doubtless she's expecting others of her ilk," Hawk said. "Or they're already inside. And me with only two knives concealed about my person. If I'd had some warning, I'd have dressed for work."

"Don't kill anybody. Don't put knife holes in her."

"Right. No killing," Hawk said. Then, "And largely unhurt."

"Yes."

They considered the church. He, over the top of a stiff newspaper. Hawk, in the reflection in the shop window.

Hawk said, "Do we call for reinforcements, which is my own personal favorite in situations like this, or do we pop in and join her?"

"You wait here." He folded the newspaper. "I'll go talk to her."

"Or I could deal with her, which won't ruffle my pinfeathers a bit, and you could while away the idle minutes out here."

"If you hear shots, that's not a signal to engage. Stay out of it unless I call you. Follow anyone who leaves."

Hawker said, "You're giving orders for some discernible reason? Last I heard, you were a French spy and a traitor."

" 'When two Independent Agents undertake a joint operation,' " he quoted, " 'the senior agent shall command.' "

"The hell with that."

"You took the words right out of my mouth. Circle round the right of the church and stay in place. I'll go pay a call on an old friend." He crossed Fetter Lane, dropping his newspaper in the back of a goods wagon on the way.

Five

One cannot walk straight when the path is crooked.

A BALDONI SAYING

THERE ARE NO CONGENIAL PLACES TO MEET A blackmailer, Cami thought. The Moravian church would do as well as anywhere.

Fetter Lane headed north from Fleet Street, being stingy in width and less than straight about it. It was a street of printers and bookshops, with an inn that had been serving pork pie since the time of Good Queen Bess. Samuel Johnson had lived on Fetter Lane and Thomas Hobbes and Dryden. Even nowadays you couldn't lob a rock without hitting somebody bookish.

She knew Fetter Lane well. She couldn't count the times she'd tagged along behind the Fluffy Aunts from bookshop to bookshop, carrying their spoil of carefully wrapped commentaries on the Babylonians and histories of the Scythians. She'd never paid any attention to the Moravian church, though.

She'd passed it three times yesterday, studying the outside but not getting close. Now . . . the door swung open, unlocked. That would be her blackmailer who'd arranged that. How helpful of him.

She pulled her hood up over her hair to be respectful,

stepped across the threshold, and closed the door behind her. It was quiet here, a private, muffled-up place to kill somebody, when you came down to it. She was surprised there weren't more murders done in church.

She swatted the thoughts away and they came buzzing back, like flies.

She was fairly safe. If the French wanted her dead, they'd have drowned her in the duck pond in Brodemere. If they wanted to kidnap her, they'd have done that in Brodemere, too.

She walked corner to corner to corner of the church, feeling cold seep out of the stone of the floor, smelling tallow candles and soap. There were four tall windows on the right side of the church, but they'd built a gallery with extra benches up there, right across them, blocking most of the light. The only thing worse than meeting a blackmailer was meeting one in all this gloom.

A thin descant warbled behind her thoughts listing all the ways she might die in the next hour or so. She ignored it.

The windows were clear glass. The walls were whitewashed, utterly unadorned. The stiff, upright pews were unpadded. At the front, rising high and dominating everything, was a huge pulpit of dark wood, devoid of carving or ornament. It said much about the blackmailer that he held his rendezvous in a church. Such contempt for God, to choose this place. He'd picked a cold, ugly church, too.

She slid into a pew on the left-hand side, along wood worn smooth by many backsides, and straightened her clothes. She touched the hard shape of her knife, safe beneath her skirt. Touched the pistol that rested in the pouch sewed inside her cloak, over her heart. She was comforted, as one always is by concealed weapons.

She'd been born in the hills of Tuscany, into the great, rich, noisy household of the Baldoni, in the town of San Biagio del Colle. In the church there, the carved stone soared to heaven and the pillars unfurled at the top to bloom like lilies. At the feet of the old statues, there was always a garden of lit candles, sending prayers to heaven. The windows told stories in jewels of light.

She'd never understood why the English thought God did

not like this. But then, even after a decade among them, there were many things she did not understand about the English.

It wouldn't be long now. She felt afraid around the edges, but the core of her was vibrating with excitement. Soon the game would be in play. She'd missed this. She was Baldoni, and scheming was in her blood.

She pressed her hands together, knuckle to knuckle, and steadied her breathing, building strength for the confrontation to come, clearing her mind, setting the little voices of fear to rest. She laid row upon row of certainty in walls around her heart and lungs, until she made of herself a fortress.

It was hard to work alone. Hard to be without anyone to guard her back. Without family. The aunts had been—

She cut off the thought before it formed and resolutely laid her hands, one in the other, loose in her lap. Her hands would whisper, *I am not worried. I'm prepared to deal with you.* It was an old saying of the Baldoni that lies are not words only. One deceives with every fingernail and toe.

The latch clicked. The door opened and sounds of the street spilled in.

He was early. What did it say about her blackmailer that he'd come to the meeting early?

The boot steps told her it was one man who walked toward her, taking a long stride. There was no scrape or sound of breathing to indicate he'd brought accomplices. He'd decided this was not a transaction to share with the multitudes.

She stayed as she was, seated, head bowed, making him come to her. When he was close, she turned to see him.

He stalked toward her, a tall, lean man, not hurrying. He walked like a fighter, graceful, balanced forward on his feet. Walked like one of the larger predators, entering a dangerous patch of jungle. Nothing about him called attention, and yet the threat of him coalesced from the dimness like one single, pure violin note from noise.

His eyes hid in darkness under the wide brim of his hat. He hadn't bothered to remove it in this poor excuse for a church. Then he lifted his head and light found his features. High-bridged nose, wide lips, angular jaw. A face of spare bones with the skin tight across.

She knew him. Shock hit like cold water. "Devoir . . . ?"

"Vérité." He said her name calmly. Her old name. The name from the years in Paris.

"What are you doing here? How did you find me?"

"I followed you."

She tried to match this man with the brilliant boy she'd known, a boy on the edge of manhood, angry inside, tightly controlled, given to long silences, self-contained, secret as a closed watch.

He took hold of the carved wood at the end of the pew. In that simple act, he demonstrated, beyond doubt, that this was, indeed, Devoir. She would have recognized his hand anywhere, in all its familiar machinery of long fingers and the jutting bony knob of his wrist. His hand was like the rest of him—spare, enduring, the flesh and bone stripped to the essential, the necessary, the irreplaceable.

He wore his hair long enough to tie behind, out of his way. Strands of it, uncooperative, marked sharp white lines from his temple, across his cheek. She said, "You haven't changed."

"You have. I passed a dozen feet away from you and didn't recognize you." His eyes were the same emphatic blue, so dark it was almost black. Devoir's eyes. "I barely know you even now."

The cold voice didn't belong to the boy she'd known ten years ago.

Why was he here? Devoir wasn't the blackmailer. Not possibly. The boy she'd known might have grown up to lie, kill, commit great crimes and treasons, but he could never have framed the sly melodrama of that note. Why had he followed her? Not to exchange cheerful reminiscences, apparently.

Her blackmailer would arrive at any minute. *I can deal with only one debacle at a time.* Then she thought, *I know that coat.*

He wore a dark greatcoat, cut for riding, the sort of anonymous garment a man could buy in any town from London to St. Petersburg. At the Coach House, they'd been taught to dress plainly when they were working.

That coat had passed her in Braddy Square. She'd noticed it because it was dusty and the man who wore it walked carefully and deliberately, as if he were very weary indeed. He'd made his way down Meeks Street a minute after she sent her messenger boy in that direction. The man wearing this coat had climbed the stairs at Number Seven, looking very much at home.

The Service had found her. Or the French. Either way, it was disaster.

Six

If the box is opened even a crack, all the secrets escape.

A BALDONI SAYING

IN THE COOL DARK OF THE CHURCH, PAX LOOKED down at black, black curls and skin that glowed like a wash of ochre over rose madder. Vérité never lost that gold color to her skin, even in the middle of winter.

He'd said, "I barely know you," but it wasn't true.

Ten years had fined down her features and taken the childish plumpness from her cheeks, but the set of the eyes was the same, girl or woman. The long, strong planes of that stubborn face hadn't altered. The bones are immutable.

Some indefinable interior quality of Vérité remained as well. An unflappable toughness. An ironic intelligence. Whatever it was, it looked up at him from behind the same familiar brown eyes.

There was no better place to confront her. It was private as a tomb in here. Without preamble, he said, "You sent a letter to Meeks Street. Why?"

"Is that where you saw me? In Braddy Square?"

"Feeding birds. You made a pretty picture."

Her shoulders lifted a fraction of an inch. "That was a mistake, then. Another mistake was waiting to see the message delivered. One can be too conscientious. Next time, I'll wrap the letter around a spontaneous rock and throw it through the window."

"That works, too. You sent a letter to Galba. What did you put in the paper, Vérité?"

A moment passed. "It's not about the words. You're asking if I sent poison in that letter."

"You had a certain skill with poisons, once upon a time."

She looked at her hands, there in her lap. "And having that skill, I must use it . . . as if I were an amateur musician, eager to sing a ditty in the drawing room after supper." Her voice was empty as wind whistling through a crack in the window. "I put that note into the hand of a young boy. There's another, not much older, who answers the door at Meeks Street. And you ask if I poisoned the paper."

"The child I knew in Paris wouldn't have. You aren't that child."

She lifted her eyes to meet his.

A decade peeled away and he was back in the Coach House in Paris, learning to be a good, obedient French spy. Vérité, in the schoolroom, head tilted to the side, deciphering code on a slate. Vérité lying to the Tuteurs, her face innocent as an up-turned daisy. Vérité, grinning, reaching her hand down to hoist him up over the wall of the Coach House for an expedition, stealing pastries for everybody. Vérité, sharing her dinner with a stray cat.

They'd been friends.

She said, "You opened the letter and saw code. Do you know, a great many troubles in this world would be avoided if we all stopped reading each other's mail."

She gathered her cloak around her and slid toward him across the place she'd left empty. She wore drab, practical clothing. Spy's clothing. No jewelry. Nothing about her to attract attention. Nothing to flash a warning if she moved quickly.

He hadn't expected to find Vérité still deep in the Game. When he thought of her in the years between, he'd hoped she'd slipped into an ordinary life. Sometimes, lying in a shepherd's hut on the side of a mountain, looking into a fire of pinecones and dried moss, he'd remember her. She was a piece of his past he wanted to remember. He didn't have that many. He'd pictured her dancing at a country ball or running her fingers down the row of books at a lending library. Painting bad watercolors of some English countryside. Taking music lessons. He'd imagined what she'd look like without any shadows behind her eyes.

She wasn't wearing a wedding ring. He'd thought she'd have a husband by now.

Why didn't you get out of the Game, Vérité? The Tuteurs went to the guillotine and the French lost track of us. You could have been free.

When the records in the Coach House burned, most of the Cachés faded quietly into the populace and became English. Vérité was still a spy, still working for the French.

As he'd chosen to work for the English. Damnable that his last act as an agent would be turning an old friend over to the Service. "How did you get that code?"

"You'll figure it out." She sat looking at the back of the seat before her, face closed and intent, as if she were reading something written on the wood there. "We missed you, you know. It was hard at the Coach House without you. We fell apart for a while, me and the other Cachés. We depended on you."

"I told you not to."

"We did anyway."

The Tuteurs always took the boy or girl without warning, from a meal or in the classroom. They'd say, "You have been chosen to serve France," and march them away with nothing but the clothes on their back.

He'd known it would be his turn, sooner or later. He wasn't exempt. He'd never been treated specially.

When the Tuteurs came for him, Vérité stood at her bench, looking stricken, scattering gunpowder and tangled fuse from a half-made bomb. He'd worried what would happen to her—the youngest, the smallest of them—when he was gone.

"We voted Fidélité leader after you left." She ran her fingertip around the post at the end of the pew.

"Good choice."

"He did well enough, but he wasn't you. When we parceled out your things, they gave me your blanket." Laughter flickered across her face, under the soberness. That was pure Vérité, that glinting, elusive spark that lit up in the middle of some desperate business. "For a week, I went to sleep holding on to it and crying . . . till everybody got tired of that and tossed it out the window. It took me two days to wash the mud out." She shook herself. "I haven't thought about that in years."

"A lot of water under a lot of bridges."

"And some bridges burned forever." She sighed and stood up, turning so she ended up facing him. Every instant of movement was graceful. Unstudied. She could have been a leaf twirled in the wind. "This is like . . . it's like when Alexander burned his ships on the shore so his army couldn't run away. We have our backs to the sea. Neither of us can retreat."

"No retreat," he agreed. In a few moments, one of them would hurt the other. They shared that knowledge without having to say it aloud.

"I'm sorry it's come to this," she said. "I owe you so much. I would have died of despair in those first days in the Coach House if you hadn't been yelling at me."

"I never yelled."

"You became ironic. We were all in awe of you when you were ironic." She leaned against the end of the pew. Her cloak was weighted on the left side of the front. That would be where she carried a small, reliable pistol. She'd always loved pistols.

It surprised him to find himself looking down at the top of her head. He'd grown since he was fourteen.

"I cared for you, Devoir, with my whole heart, as only a child can care for another child." She spread her hands, empty, palms up. "Yet here you are and here I am, very close to enemies. I have a sudden urge to say something significant about Fate and Inevitability."

That sounded like the too-old, too-wise girl he'd known. His Vérité still lived inside this sleek brown stranger with the eloquent hands and the measuring eyes. It wasn't only bones that stayed unchanged year after year.

He wished he didn't have to arrest her. Men like Galba, Grey, and Doyle wouldn't blame her for being a French agent, but they couldn't let her run loose, either. She'd go to imprisonment in one of the escape-proof houses the Service kept in remote corners of the kingdom. They'd treat her as well as they could.

She took a casual step to the left. "I didn't feel you following me from Braddy Square. You remain an expert at being invisible."

"Thank you."

"I'm going to pay dearly for sending that letter. The funny thing is, I meant it for the best. I've stumbled into something the Service needs to be warned about. And two old women are in danger. I was afraid of being killed and taking my knowledge with me across the River Styx." She edged left again, luring his attention away from the door and whoever was coming here to meet her. Nicely done.

On the training field at the Coach House, they'd been matched for fighting sometimes. They'd signaled cues to each other for the next strike, the next feint, planning a game of attack and defense, keeping the Tuteurs happy with a showy fight, making sure neither of them hurt or got hurt.

They were studying each other now, giving no signals. No clues.

She shifted position along the wall and he matched her, step for step.

"So." She retreated a little. Retreated again. "The Tuteurs put you into Meeks Street. Does the British Service know you're a French spy?"

"I told them I'm Caché." *They've known for a couple of weeks now.* No reason to tell her how long and well he'd lied to them.

"That's unfortunate." She caught her lower lip in her teeth. Hard white teeth making a dent in a soft lip. "I'd hoped to talk my way out of this encounter by threatening you with exposure."

"Not that easy." He took a step that ate into the space she'd made between them, driving her left again. Now the sun was in her eyes. His advantage.

"I could tell you how loyal I am to England. Would that convince you to walk out of here and stop making trouble for me?"

"I'll let you sort out your various loyalties at Meeks

Street." He wished he didn't have to take her there. But Vérité hadn't been playing patty-cake for the last ten years. That ingenious mind had been busy. She'd been acquiring English codes, for one thing.

"My problem"—she gestured, inviting his attention to her problem—"is that you may not have become English. You could have remained loyal to France. A Caché from the Coach House, placed in the belly of the British Service, would be the most valuable agent France could have in England. You may be Police Secrète."

"I'm not."

"You'd deny it, of course, to lull me into a false sense of security."

"It isn't working, is it?"

They'd ended any pretense. Now they circled each other openly in the narrow confines of the aisle between the pews and wall.

Her voice remained calm, her step fluid. "If you've become English, you will arrest me. If you're still French, we've mislaid our recognition signs and you must extinguish me ruthlessly and hide my body under one of these uncomfortable benches. Unless I kill you first. Or we might kill each other like a pair of cocks in an ill-managed cockfight."

"Nobody's going to kill anyone." He made it an order.

They faced each other in the empty church, each of them judging the distance between them. It was the length of a single lunge with a knife or a blow with the fist. It was inescapable death from a fired pistol. This was a fighting distance that left no room for retreat or defense. Advantage would go to whoever was first to attack.

Neither of them attacked. Nothing simple was happening here. Nothing straightforward.

She stilled. The lines of her drab clothing hung quiet. The strength of her determination glowed vivid as fire inside her skin. She could have been a candle lit in this churchy gloom.

That was the way she always looked when she fought. Doubly alive. Daring the world to aim a blow in her direction. Dodging it quick as an animal when it came.

The child he'd known had been skinny as a whip, vibrating

with energy, her arms and legs too long for her body, her features too big for her face. Now all the disparate, unsettled, unfinished parts of her had come together. Then, she'd been dangerous. Now she was deadly.

But her voice was full of laughter, same as always. "What do they call you at Meeks Street? Not Devoir. George? Clarence? Percival?"

"Thomas Paxton. Pax."

"Pax." She mumbled the syllable around her mouth, tasting it. "Latin for peace. It seems an odd name for a spy."

"I've always thought so. I don't want to fight you, Vérité."

"We agree, then. And I'm Cami. I've been Cami for a long time now."

A thread of recognition spun from the name "Cami." He couldn't grab hold of it. "Will you come with me to Meeks Street? Come quietly? I don't want to hurt you, Cami."

"I don't want to hurt you, either."

Slowly, she ventured a single small step into the space that lay between them. And then the next step. She kept her hands in his sight, held before her, unthreatening. She said, "I'm sad for the memory of an old friendship, lost forever. I owe you a tremendous debt from those days in the Coach House." They were very close now. Hesitantly, as if her hand made the decision all by itself, she reached toward him. "I come from a family that never forgets debts. I wish . . ."

"There is no debt."

She touched his cheek. It shocked like a spark from cat fur. She whispered, "I wish . . ."

An awareness of Vérité as a woman had been hovering in his muscles and blood since he'd walked into the church. He'd pushed it away. Ignored it. Denied it.

Now it crashed over him like a hot wave. Heat everywhere. On his skin. Pooled in his groin. Hunger for her became a massive tug, as if his heart were being pulled from his body.

He was used to mastering his emotions. Making himself cold. But he was angry when he snapped out and manacled her wrist and held it away so she wasn't touching him.

He said, "No." Just the one word dropped between them.

She stared at him with eyes like dark jewels. "I wish we hadn't met again."

"So do I."

"I would have liked to remember the boy I knew once upon a time."

Her hair fell in rings that gleamed like polished ebony. How would it feel to fit his fingers into those curls? They'd just fit.

She didn't try to free herself. That was the worst of it. This close to him, where he could feel her breath on him, she didn't fight to get away.

He said, "I haven't become a fool . . . Cami." Deliberately, he used the name of a stranger, one that didn't belong to the girl he'd known. "Step back a bit."

"You think I wish to seduce you?" A wry smile. "Even my great folly doesn't stretch that—"

The door of the church creaked open. A man stood framed by the doorway, backed by a dazzle of daylight. A middle-aged man, taller than most, strong featured, with brown hair cropped short. He held himself very straight, very proud.

It can't be. Before the name formed in his mind, before he recognized, before he believed, he felt coldly sick in his belly.

It was a trick of light. It was imagination. Madness. He whispered, "No."

The bastard had died six years ago, burned with a dozen others in the house on rue Jacob. What was left of the charred body had been identified beyond doubt from old scars. Men came from all over Paris to see the monster thrown into the lime pits.

He said, "You're dead." Could he kill a nightmare? He let go of Vérité. Pulled his gun.

Her cloak swirled a sharp confusion. Metal glinted in her hand. She tossed a dark cloud in his face. Her fist slammed into his belly.

He gasped. And the air was red agony. Fire in his lungs. Hot knives in his eyes.

His gun clattered at his feet. He grabbed for Vérité and felt her slip beyond his reach. He staggered and fell to his knees on the cold stone.

He couldn't breathe. Couldn't see. He groped on the floor, trying to find his gun.

Blackness and pain, endlessly, everywhere. Worlds of it. No air anywhere. *Damn. I'm going to die.*

Over the roaring in his head he heard Vérité running away down the aisle.

even

*When the choice is between boredom and danger, a
wise man chooses to be bored.*

A BALDONI SAYING

CAMI JERKED BACK. THE CLOUD OF SNUFF AND HOT
pepper spread like a black exhalation, floating bright in the
light from the windows, dark in the lines of shade. Devoir
grabbed at her, blind and clumsy with pain. His fingers
slipped in the folds of her cloak and she was free. After years
of soft living, the old dance of attack and retreat still lived in
her muscles.

He doubled over and fell to his knees, choking. She kicked
his gun, clattering, across the stones.

Devoir was down. Another betrayal to mark on her slate.
She was a Baldoni, after all.

The *mélange de tabac*—the snuff mixture—was a Caché
weapon. On the sparring field of the Coach House they'd been
trained to survive it. The Tuteurs would throw the powder
suddenly and follow it with kicks and punches. "Get up. You
are a soldier of France," they'd say. "Fight like a soldier. Get
up. Fight."

Devoir always staggered up again. He'd been the toughest
of them all.

He was tough now. He scrubbed his mouth and nose into

his sleeve, snarling and cursing, his hat lost under the pews, his pale hair wild over his face. He didn't rub his eyes. The Cachés taught each other these useful skills in whispers in the cold dormitory at night. Never touch your eyes.

She headed toward the blackmailer, who stood squinting in the gloom. His right hand was thrust deep into his coat pocket, almost certainly because he was carrying a gun there. She'd just as soon it stay pocketed. Men didn't like to draw a gun and put it away without using it. There was an old Baldoni saying to that effect.

She rounded the last pew and put herself in the line of fire between that gun and Devoir. Not a tranquil place to be.

She went forward, making every step an interval, individual and distinct, hoping the blackmailer would avail himself of these moments to make wise choices. If he was experienced and controlled and intelligent—a professional, in short—they might avoid gunfire and death in the church today. That was a worthy goal in the great scheme of things.

Or the man might shoot her, reload in a brisk fashion, and then shoot Devoir. If she'd misjudged how important she was to this man's long-term plans, she would be dead and never get to tell the lies she'd crafted. That would be a great pity because they were very good lies.

In the background, Devoir blundered against wooden pews that screeched and scraped. She could hear him panting, almost feel the pain of air pushing past a tight, burning throat. She didn't look back to see whether he was up on his feet, being concerned with the important matter of not getting shot in the next little while.

In a minute or two, Devoir would retrieve his own pistol. She was almost sure Devoir wouldn't shoot her. She had no such sanguine expectations of the man she walked toward.

Close up, the blackmailer was a fellow of pleasant features, brown hair, and washed-out, light-colored eyes. He was well groomed and well and comfortably dressed, even fashionable. Over it all, like a slick surface, he carried an air of conscious superiority. She placed him in his fifties, of an age to be one of the bitter dispossessed fanatics who'd ruled France during the Terror. A few of them had escaped the guillotine when Robespierre fell. Since he knew an uncomfortable lot about her, he was, or had been, Police Secrète. Maybe even one of the men who'd created the Coach House and pulled the strings of the Tuteurs. She might even have seen him, long ago in Paris, which would explain the uneasy twinge of recognition plucking at the back of her mind.

He eased a nasty little cuff pistol out of the pocket. She said, "Put that away. We have to get out of here. Now. Before his friends show up."

"I told you to come alone."

"In your informative letter. Yes. I didn't bring him. He followed me."

"Who is he?" He peered into the obscurity of the church.

She collected the last step that lay between them. "He's an unforeseen complication and I've dealt with it. Get out of my way."

He didn't budge. He didn't send the gun back into hiding. These were not good signs. He said, "Did you blind him? What did you use? Poison? Acid?" He had a surprisingly melodious voice.

"I employed methods sufficient for my purpose." Let him think she was armed with poison. Always let an enemy overestimate one's ruthlessness. "He won't interfere again."

He lifted the pistol and appraised it briefly. "I'll make certain of that." His voice was perfectly genial. His gaze, emotionless as the stare of a doll.

There are men who chill the blood when you glance into their eyes, passing them on the street. There are reptiles who walk in human form. Monsters with no soul looking out of their eyes. This was one of them. It amazed her that most people did not recognize them at once.

She said, "You're wasting time and I have none to spare. The man is nothing."

Nothing. She had called Devoir "nothing."

The wind from the street blew in and skipped across her and lifted the smell of snuff from her clothes. For a vivid instant, she was back in the sparring field of the Coach House.

It had been one of the very bad days. The Tuteur had thrown the snuff mélange in her face and beaten her till she collapsed in the mud. They called this training, but its purpose was to break her spirit.

When the Tuteurs put their coats on and left, Devoir took her up into his arms and carried her to the pump. He held her head tight against his belly through the cold, drenching shock of bucket after bucket the others drew from the pump. His muscles were hard as a wall and warm under her cheek. His fingers, careful, parted her eyelids and he dribbled water across. He said, "Open your eyes, Vérité. You have to do this."

The pain and helplessness didn't break her because Devoir was there. For her. For all of them. The Tuteurs had never understood Devoir.

Today, ten years later, she betrayed him. "The man is nothing," she repeated. "Get out of my way."

The blackmailer's eyes went from her to the dark of the church. "He's seen me." His gun leveled past her, toward Devoir.

"Dozens of men saw you walk in here. They're watching you through the door this minute, wondering who we are and why we're standing here. I intend to become less conspicuous." She jostled his gun aside and pushed past.

If she wanted to kill a blackmailer, she could do it now. She could draw knife from sheath, press it to his kidney as she passed, and slip it home. It would rid the world of some moderate amount of evil. But it wouldn't protect the Fluffy Aunts from this man's colleagues. It wouldn't lead her to Camille Besançon.

She let the moment for murder pass. One does not seize all opportunities.

At the door, she said, "Shoot him, slit his throat, smother him with a pillow. Please yourself. I leave you to deal with the corpse and these interested onlookers."

"Don't turn your back on me."

She ignored him. She wrapped her cloak tight and strode off, taking his attention with her, out of the church. Before she got to the iron pickets that separated the sacred of the church from the profane of the street traffic, her blackmailer abandoned the church and followed her.

Devoir would not die today.

* * *

THROUGH the roaring in his ears, Pax heard Vérité talking to the Merchant at the door of the church. He couldn't catch the words over the noise he made strangling on his own breath.

That son of a bitch wouldn't hesitate to shoot her. Death was nothing to him. One death or twenty. The Merchant sowed it wholesale.

Gasping, sweeping his hands in circles on the cold stone, he found his gun. Took up the dark, familiar shape.

Air knifed his throat and raked in his lungs. He grabbed the end of the pew. Pulled himself to his feet. He forced his eyes open to splinters of shattered color and indescribable pain. The doorway was an empty rectangle of agonizing light.

He staggered toward it.

They were gone. Vérité and the monster. The Merchant was out there somewhere. Alive. Loose in London. Had to find him. Had to—

Someone ran toward him, a dark shape against the light. His fingers were so clumsy it took both hands to cock the gun.

"It's me," Hawker said. "Don't shoot. Where are you hit?"

"Not . . . Not hit." He choked. He couldn't get the words out. He pointed the gun to the ground and let it hang loose in his hand. It wasn't doing him any good.

"Bloody hell." Hawker pulled him forward, down the steps. Three steps. "She threw something in your eyes. Gods in hell. Your eyes."

"Follow him. The man . . ." Words were fire and ground glass in his throat. "Go after him."

"Right."

The stones of the path tripped him. Hawk was under his arm, keeping him from falling.

"Water. Ten more steps. Hang on." Hawk dragged him the last of the way, pushed him to his knees, and thrust his head into the horse trough.

He breathed water. Came up gasping. "Follow him."

"She's poisoned you. That bloody bitch of a woman did this to you."

"You have to—" Coughing racked him. Twisted his lungs inside out. "The man. Go after him. Now!"

"One of my priorities has always been doing what you tell me." Hawker raised his voice. "I need a bucket here."

"He's . . . French spy. Important."

"Keeping you alive is important."

"Kill him." The explosion of coughing was a poker of hot iron in his lungs. He dropped the pistol, shut his arms tight around the pain in his chest, and spoke through fire and vitriol. "Find him. Kill him."

"I'll just do that. Kill him out of hand. Damn. And they say I'm bloodthirsty." Hawk was talking to somebody in the crowd, giving orders. Saying, "Here's money," and "Take care of him."

Hawk's hand clasped his shoulder. "I'll be back. If she's blinded you, I'll cut her fucking eyes out."

He'll do it. He had to say this. Had to get it out before Hawker left. "Don't hurt her! An order. That's an order."

A dark shape blocked the hideously bright light. Hawk stood over him one last minute. "Hurt doesn't begin to describe it."

Eight

Do not consort with men who carry guns.

A BALDONI SAYING

CAMI INSERTED HERSELF INTO THE NOISE AND CON-
fusion of Fetter Lane, slipping between stout workmen who
were stolid and oblivious and nearly as good as a solid wall
for concealment. The blackmailer followed her, fuming.
She'd get well away from the church and its many opportunities for unpredictable violence before she talked to him.

Devoir needed—

She pushed Devoir out of her mind.

Fetter Lane was a fine noisy place to weave in and out of,
smooth as a fish among waving weeds. She tossed tendrils of
attention to left and right, to the traffic passing, to the laborers
wheeling barrows, to men who lingered in doorways and
chatted in front of shops. Under a fold of cloak, her right hand
with its little knife, *cum cultellulus* as it were, was ready to
slice or stab. She intended to be a difficult woman to hit on
the head and haul away in a private carriage.

She'd given considerable thought, lately, to the business of
daylight kidnapping in London. She wouldn't attempt it on
Fetter Lane, herself, but there was no reason to assume this
blackmailer was equally cautious. Many things could go

wrong in the next half hour. She was prey to a variety of qualms.

Her blackmailer had qualms and imperatives of his own. He caught up with her. "We've left a witness alive behind us. A wiser woman wouldn't have stood in my way."

She summoned up a Baldoni smile. "A wiser woman would have ignored your letter altogether. You write nonsense about a 'genuine Camille' and a code you've taken a fancy to. You—"

"Enough. We can't talk in the open street."

"On the contrary, this is a perfect place to trade confidences."

"I did not come here to—"

She left him talking to empty air and continued toward Fleet Street. He followed, as she had known he would.

It had been a long time since she'd bamboozled a dangerous man face-to-face. She hoped she still had the knack of it. This was, after all, what she'd been born to do. To lie, befool, and cheat. If she was afraid, she'd press that fear into a small, coldly pulsing ball and set it aside from her. "Fear is meat and drink to a Baldoni. We eat fear. We thrive on it." How often had Papà said that?

She wouldn't think about what she'd done to Devoir.

A small boy, weighted sideways with a bucket, crossed the pavement and slopped some mess in the swale at the side of the road. A horse and rider passed on her left, trotting. The smell of cooked meat expanded from the kitchen of an inn.

She glanced back to see a man dodge horses and wagons and run to the door of the Moravian church. She could only hope he was a friend of Devoir's and not one of the blackmailer's confederates, taking a detour into the church with a sharp, silent knife.

She'd left Devoir easy prey.

Walk away. Don't look back.

She matched the steps of one man, then another, hiding in the flow of the crowd. One bird in the flock. One herring in the congregation of herrings. It was a dark satisfaction to keep the blackmailer trailing after her.

He caught up. "Where do you think you're going? I don't plan to chase you across London."

"Fleet Street. Just around the corner." She didn't pause. Didn't bother to look at him. That would anger him, and angry men made mistakes.

Past the old inn, past half-open doors that smelled of fresh paper and held the creak of printing presses, she turned onto Fleet Street. The pamphlets and newspapers of the kingdom were printed here. Every fourth building was a bookshop. The taverns were filled with men who had ink on their hands.

She'd come here yesterday, as soon as she arrived in London, to assess possibilities and consider tactics. No actor, rehearsing a part, had ever walked the stage more carefully than she'd walked Fleet Street.

Franklin's Bookshop set an enticing table of books just inside the front door, right beneath the big plate-glass window. She ducked into the shop to the sound of the bell above the door, walked to the far side of the table, slid her knife into the pouch beside her gun, and selected a volume at random.

The blackmailer followed. "What are you doing? Why are we here?" But he was no fool. He already knew why.

"You wish to talk in private? So do I. But I feel safer with witnesses." . . . Even if the witnesses were the shopkeeper, absorbed in inspection of an elderly volume, and a square, sturdy woman working her way down a row of books on botany.

"You're overly cautious." The words were mild enough. Underneath, she heard his anger like a nail scraped across a slate.

She said, "One cannot be overly cautious."

She lowered her eyes, as if she were reading the book she held. She could look out the wide window and see all of Fleet Street. But this time of day, no one outside could see past the reflection on the window and discover her. She'd investigated this thoroughly. "Will you give me a name to call you by?"

"I see no reason to do so." He chose his own book. "It adds to your danger, the more you know about me."

He must have thought she was very stupid. "So awkward to think of you as 'that man who writes threatening letters.' "

From this carefully chosen vantage point inside Franklin's Bookshop she could watch the corner of Fetter Lane. Anyone following her would walk just there, beside the streetlamp. Unless he'd been supremely well trained, he'd pause and look both ways on Fleet Street and betray himself utterly. Very few men were trained as she had been at the Coach House.

He said, "You may call me sir. Where is the Mandarin Code?"

She wished to appear the smallest bit stupid. A stupid woman would be insolent right now. Besides, she was angry. "The squire in Brodemere has a pair of mastiffs. He's always yelling, 'Sit, sir!' and the closest one plops its hindquarters on the floor and slobbers. I shall think of that when I call you sir."

The narrow, pale, intellectual face froze. The lips tightened. "You may call me Mr. Smith."

She turned a page. "I expected more originality from the man who sent that letter."

"I leave a foolish cleverness to amateurs, Mademoiselle Molinet."

So. The Police Secrète knew more about her than she'd realized. She'd come prepared for unpleasant surprises. The day was delivering them.

In the Revolution, in Paris, Papà had been Philippe Molinet for a while, a banker, a man of many financial schemes. The *sans-culottes* who helped themselves to the wealth of the dead aristos had been endearingly gullible when it came to investments. That had been Papà's last role.

So strange that the French had assumed she would spy for them after they sent Papà and Mamma to the guillotine. Perhaps they thought children forgot. Baldoni do not forget. She shrugged. "Mademoiselle Molinet belongs to the past. One sheds a dozen such names, Mr. Smith, as snakes shed their skin."

"Shall I call you Vérité? They must have been feeling humorous that day at the Coach House when they called you that."

She didn't like him holding that name in his mouth so soon after Devoir had said it. She returned her eyes to the book she held, which appeared to be about rocks. Why would anybody want to read about rocks? "Not Vérité."

His nod was amiable. She saw him chalk that up as a trifling victory. "Camille, then."

"We'll save 'Camille' for the merchandise you offer. Call me Miss Leyland." She licked her index finger and slipped another page of smooth, dense paper from right to left. There were many drawings. Drawings of rocks, apparently. Under lowered eyelids she watched the corner of Fetter Lane and Fleet Street. Where were his henchmen? She said, "Tell me about this Camille you have acquired."

He made her wait. Deliberately and slowly he slipped his watch out of its pocket, left-handed, and clicked it open. "She is considerably more genuine than you." The hour and minutes satisfied him, apparently. He put the watch away. "She lived in Lyon. An orphan, like you. Another lost soul of the Revolution."

"How sad."

"The Besançons died when they attempted to flee France, all of them, except for her. Life is fragile."

"Some lives, certainly."

"She survived riot and war unscathed"—his voice showed regret for riot and war—"only to fall into my hands. Ironic, is it not?"

"So ironical it strains belief."

Across the street, men unloaded bales of newsprint from a wagon. A boy carried a pair of brown jugs out of a tavern, across the street, and into one of the shops. And at the corner, a man emerged from Fetter Lane. He was blessed with bristling stubby hair, large ears, and an odd, forward-jutting posture that would mark him in a crowd. Not prepossessing. He looked up and down Fleet Street, hesitated, and ambled off to lean at the doorway of a shop.

One of Smith's minions, awaiting events.

Waiting for her, as she'd been waiting for him. It was one of many precautions and expectations strewn about the street today.

Smith murmured, "Poor young Camille Besançon. So many narrow escapes. It's as if a kindly providence has been taking care of her all these years. I will regret her death." He tapped the book he held against the edge of the table, then shoved it into the pile he'd taken it from. There was something very final about that small shush of book on book and the sudden cessation of sound. "I would regret yours, if it comes to that. Were you able to copy the key to the code?"

I wrote the code. "The Leylands didn't hide it very well. They trust me."

"Where is it?"

"Safe. Well hidden."

A slight nod. "I congratulate you on your caution."

Do not attempt to flatter a Baldoni. She smiled. "Thank you. I've brought you a taste."

She tucked her own book down neatly into a row with others—*A book about rocks. Really*—and steadied herself with one hand on the book table. What she wanted was inside the halfboot she wore, between shoe leather and stocking. No one in the bookshop was paying them the least attention.

She'd been carrying the piece of rolled paper there for a while. It had become limp. And damp. And convincing. "This is half of one page written in the Mandarin Code. It's the first page of a five-page key."

Using two fingers, she dropped it into Mr. Smith's hand.

Not one person in a thousand would have caught the flash of rage that snapped through him and was suppressed. Mr. Smith was skilled in his role of reasonable man.

He unrolled her scrap of paper. The hasty writing and raggedly torn edge were corroborating detail. The scrawl of letters across the page looked genuine. Given a few hours, an expert codebreaker might hazard a guess as to whether this was code or nonsense. No one could know whether it was the Mandarin Code. Mr. Smith of the Police Secrète should have retained skepticism.

Instead, he looked pleased. She really didn't like that.

She wrapped her arms around her under her cloak, where her pistol made a comfortable weight against her belly. In a simpler world she'd have been considering which of several inconspicuous alleys would be the best place to shoot Mr. Smith.

In a simpler world, she wouldn't have thrown snuff and red pepper into Devoir's face.

Across the street, Smith's minion had taken to shifting

from one foot to the other. Perhaps he was a minion rethinking his strategy.

Two minutes ticked by. Mr. Smith studied the paper she'd bestowed upon him. Then he folded it into an inner pocket of his coat. "You've done well." His thin lips created an affable smile. He leaned across the table of books, closer, to keep their conversation private, and his breath on her face was like a fly crawling on her lips and in her nostrils. "You will bring me the rest of this key."

"After I talk to your unlikely Camille." He wanted her to retreat a little, so she didn't. She stayed exactly as she was. "Bring her to me tomorrow, at the rope walk in—"

"I will name the time and place," he said.

Even a very foolish woman does not walk into an ambush. "You've sent me a trumpery pearl ring anyone could buy in a jewelry shop. I need considerably more evidence of your Camille Besançon before I fetch the Mandarin Code from where I've hidden it."

"Do not try my patience."

"Then don't assume I'm an idiot. This fabulous Camille you threaten me with, who survived so miraculously and comes forth so conveniently. Do you think the Leylands will accept her? I've had ten years to establish myself. I hold those old biddies like this." She closed a fist under his nose. "This tight. They wouldn't believe your impostor if she cried tears of diamond."

It worked as she'd hoped. A little crude boasting, a little vulgarity . . . and he was contemptuous of her.

His voice became both smug and threatening. "It's not the gullible Leylands who will believe her. It's the British Service. And Military Intelligence."

"I am not afraid of—"

"Once exposed, you will not escape England. I doubt you'll ever see trial. They're hasty men at Military Intelligence and the price of spying is . . ." He sketched a smooth line with his thumb, mimicking the slitting of throats, demonstrating the ruthlessness of the British intelligence establishment, in case she had somehow overlooked it.

"It's a pretty display of threat," she said. "But the sting in the tail of your wasp is a convincing Camille Besançon. I doubt you have one."

Smith lifted his head suddenly, poised as a hound when a bird flutters in the bush. "You ask for proof? Wait. Wait one minute. I will give it to you." He'd been counting the minutes, watching for something on the street. Now he saw it. "You wish to see Camille? Turn and look at her."

It was impossible to travel at speed on Fleet Street, but the carriage that approached was skillfully maneuvered between wagons and horses and made good time. A young woman, one hand on the lowered glass, leaned out the window. She had a fine-boned, pretty face and long, black hair elaborately arranged. Her bonnet was decked with ribbons and cherries. Her pouting, discontented mouth was red as those cherries.

That was the Leyland family face. The Leyland hair. The Leyland cast of features. A true match for the painting in the parlor of the Leylands' cottage. If that were an impostor, she was an extraordinarily well-chosen one.

The driver on the box had pulled a hat low over his face, letting her see only his mouth and nose and the shape of his jaw. Two men rode inside the coach with the woman. There was an impression of their size and dark coloring, but no glimpse of their faces.

The coach rolled past and turned at the corner at Fetter Lane. Smith said, "Camille Besançon."

"Perhaps. Perhaps not." But certainty fell like cold lead into her stomach. The woman in the carriage was the Fluffy Aunts' niece. Their blood kin. That woman must, somehow, be rescued and restored to them. She felt traps close around her. From some obligations there is no escape.

Smith spoke softly, persuasively. "When she is dealt with, you will return to the comfort of your accustomed life. Why should you not? Who else will challenge you after so many years? On one hand, imprisonment, questioning, and almost certain death. On the other, your placid village and the life you have earned for yourself. The life you deserve." Smith let that sink in for a moment. "One code. I will never approach you again."

She let time pass, as if she were thinking the matter over. "I need to talk to her."

"That's understood. You will have your chance to trade girlish confidences with the amiable Camille. When you are satisfied, we'll make the exchange. The woman for the code. But I choose the time and place."

"You give me no choice." She put on a sullen expression, held it for several seconds, then let her shoulders slump. "Where?"

"Semple Street, outside Number Fifty-six. Eleven o'clock in the morning, three days from now."

Three days. That left almost no time to prepare. "I need—"

"Your needs do not interest me. You will come to Semple Street, as ordered. You will bring the key to the Mandarin Code. You do not want to face the consequences for disobedience."

She made a muscle in her cheek twitch. She'd practiced. "You'll have your code."

"Do not disappoint me, Miss Leyland," he said quietly.

She gave a sharp nod. She didn't touch him as she walked around and past, her hand under her cloak, on her gun. The shop door jangled as she pushed it open and stalked out into Fleet Street, away from him.

Little glances behind told her that Smith had stayed where he was, studying the selection of books in Franklin's Bookshop. But his henchman abandoned his lackadaisical perusal of the passing scene and followed her.

ine

The man who plays with fire will be burned.

A BALDONI SAYING

PAX PUSHED BREATH PAST THE STRANGLING KNOT in his throat. *Breathe in. Breathe out.* Air clawed its way into his clenched chest. *Don't cough. Control the need.* Fire tore at his mouth and lips. Raked his throat all the way down to his heart. But especially, fire burned his eyes.

The blur of a woman held the bucket while he sluiced water again and again over his face. He sucked it into his mouth and nose. Spat down onto the street.

He cupped water and held it against his eyes. Everything else was just pain. He could live through pain. But his eyes . . .

The jabbering, shuffling crowd let a voice through. ". . . no more sense than a gaggle of molting pigeons. *Out* of my damned bloody way. You there—yes, you—hop it!"

Hawk wavered into his line of vision, back too soon to have done a job of murder. Even Hawk needed a few minutes.

He's lost the bastard. God damn it. He's lost him. Pax steadied himself on the edge of the horse trough and pushed himself up to his feet. His voice came out in a croak. "Did you kill the son of a bitch?"

"Couldn't find him."

The monster had slithered away to his hole. He could be anywhere in London. "Go back. Try again."

"I can't catch smoke. I never got a look at him." Hawk waved somebody forward. "Give me those." And there were white towels. "Take this."

A wet towel and a dry one. Breathing through the wet cloth helped. "Get back and track the woman. She'll lead you to him, sooner or later. She's pretty. Somebody'll remember which way she went."

"Later. I'll find her again. I saw her face."

"Follow her. Don't hurt her." *Hawk's planning to forget that part.* "Won't tell you anything . . . anyway. Police Secrète."

"And will remain silent under all but the more melodramatic tortures. So I kill the man and leave that pustulant excrescence of a woman alive. You made yourself clear. How bad is it?" Hawker's hand, shadowed and huge, came toward him and lifted an eyelid. Exquisite, precise pain stabbed.

"Damn it. Let be."

"Your eyes are swimming in blood. Can you even see?"

"I see fine."

"You're not lying well. That's worrisome. I'll get you to Luke. No—Maggie's in town. I'll get you to Maggie. She'll know what to do. And these upstanding citizens have found us a hackney." Hawker dropped coins into an outstretched hand. "My tips are making Fetter Lane rich today. Let's get out of here before somebody puts a bullet in you."

He sopped water out of his hair with the dry towel. Tossed it aside. "Need my coat. Gun's on the ground someplace."

"Not even stolen. I have collected your various belongings. We will now depart. This way." Hawker got under his arm and steadied him.

"I can walk." He stumbled, saying it.

"You can dance an Irish jig as far as I'm concerned. Never known such a bloody-minded, damn-your-eyes bugger. And will you cod-sucking idiots get out of my *way*!" Hawker shed his upper-class accent and let himself drop into deep Cockney when he wanted to make a point.

Pale faces, the solid brown of a horse, bright dresses. When he blinked, the street was lines of color that shattered and broke. He'd paint this with mad, slapdash color. Lay down thick, writhing rivers of paint, like the man El Greco. He'd seen three El Greco canvases. Two in Paris. One in Venice. It needed searing color to capture this mad derangement of vision, this street. He'd paint it with—

If I can paint again . . .

Don't think about that. Do the job. Everything else comes later. Tell Galba about the Merchant. Start the hunt.

He had a single clear view of the square block of the hackney coach, till he blinked and blurred it. His sight was coming back.

He needed enough sight to kill a man.

The monster walked under the sun. The French called him Le Marchand, the Merchant, but he was every dram and inch of him a monster. Even the Police Secrète were glad when he died.

I got roaring drunk the night they brought news the Merchant was dead. I was in Paris with Carruthers and Althea and the others in the house on the Right Bank. The kitchen filled up with agents and friends and we celebrated till dawn. I thought I was free.

He's alive. He's been alive all this time.

Rage set him shaking. Or maybe he shook with cold. *And maybe I'm afraid.* "I'm wet clean through. That woman kept slopping buckets over me."

"Workmanlike job of drowning you," Hawk agreed. "Let's get to Meeks Street before you catch pneumonia."

A half dozen paces to the coach. Colors jostled madly, detached from meaning. Faces floated against the gray-brown buildings. Shirts, dresses, and coats flowed and rippled white, umber, cinnabar, indigo. And, in the confusion, one streak of dull sienna brown stood still.

That exact and particular burnt sienna.

Vérité. She'd made a mistake and they had her. *You know better than this, girl. Never look back. Weren't you paying attention when they taught us that?*

No reason for her to be here, except that she was worried about him. Damn Vérité.

He lowered his head so she wouldn't see his lips move. "She's twenty feet away. To my left at ten o'clock."

He didn't have to say, "Don't turn and look at her." He didn't have to say who "she" was. Hawker knew.

There was too much anticipation in Hawk's voice when he said, "I'll follow her. We get in the coach. I'll spill out of the coach after we start."

"I'm coming with you."

"You can't see."

"If I don't keep up, leave me behind." He pulled himself up, through the door, into the coach while Hawk gave instructions to the driver.

Hawk climbed in behind him, already sloughing off his own coat and reversing it. "He'll slow down past the corner."

"You take the lead. She knows me."

"That goes without saying. It takes somebody who knows you well to want to kill you."

"She wasn't trying to kill me." It wasn't easy, dragging his coat on over the wet shirt.

"Could have fooled me." Hawk pulled off his hat and tossed it over. "Switch hats. You put this on."

"Let me tie the hair back." He found a thin black ribbon in his pocket and hobbled his hair back in a club under the hat.

"Next time, dye your damned hair. A babe in arms could spot you at a hundred yards with your hair hanging down."

It was too hard to explain the reasons he'd come to Meeks Street without disguises. "It's not that bad."

"Yes, it is."

The coach rolled to a stop and they swung out, fast, Hawk on one side, him on the other.

CAMI joined the thin outer edge of the crowd, well back from the unfolding drama. Men pushed a way behind her or in front of her and stopped to satisfy curiosity or strode on impatiently, going about their business. Glimpse by glimpse, she watched Devoir deal with the damage she'd done him.

A man—a colleague from the British Service, doubtless—jostled past her and elbowed through the onlookers, swearing at them in a ripe city voice. He was brown skinned, black haired, quick moving, and annoyed. That was another face worth adding to her memory.

Devoir staggered to his feet, dripping wet, eyes slitted against the sunlight. He moved like one of the great predators, wounded but not clumsy, like a tiger who'd fallen a long way and landed on his feet, jarred and dizzy but ready to fight. She was immeasurably glad she didn't have to face him at this moment when his inner nature was so close to the surface.

She was one of the few dozen people on earth who knew this truth about his deadliness. His Service comrades would have seen it. Cachés who'd been in the Coach House with him knew. Maybe he had enemies who'd fought him and somehow survived. Nobody else.

The two men talked, heads together, words emphatic. They were friends, then.

In the glare of midday, Devoir stood in wet shirtsleeves and an unbuttoned vest. The linen of his shirt was almost transparent where it stuck down tight to his skin. Distinct, clearly defined muscles wrapped his arms and strapped long lines across his upper chest. He didn't have the body of one of those hearty gentlemen who rode to the foxes or took fencing lessons and sat down to a comfortable dinner every night. She knew, in some detail, what the strength of such men looked like. Devoir was muscled like a workingman—a sailor, a soldier, a bricklayer, somebody shaped by unrelenting labor. The strength of him had been formed in days of work without respite and nights with too little sleep. He was, inside the drab, ordinary clothing, inside that tanned skin, a professional, a spy to the bone.

Devoir dried his hair with a white towel, vigorously, and talked to his friend. A hackney coach drew up to the curb. The crowd parted. The two men got in and it drove away.

Devoir would go back to whatever plans and schemes he pursued at Meeks Street. She'd go about her own business. They wouldn't meet again. She would sink into memory. He'd call her to mind once in a while, when someone mentioned betrayal.

She knew nothing of his long-ago past, but she knew this

much—before he'd been taken to the Coach House, everything weak in him had already been burned away. He must have survived terrible things to become a metal, like silver, like steel, that you could hammer upon or put through the fire, and it emerged unchanged. The Tuteurs had never broken the strength at the center of him.

She watched the hackney till it turned at the corner and was lost from sight. Then she walked briskly toward Holborn, Mr. Smith's minion sneaking along behind, surreptitious and easy to spot. With luck, he'd never notice when she circled around and started following him.

en

Allies are found in unexpected places.

A BALDONI SAYING

PAX KEPT HIS EYE ON WHAT HE COULD SEE OF Vérité, which was a six-inch swath of her cloak, a gin bottle, and the line of her shadow on the cobblestones. She'd curled herself on the steps leading down to a cellar, holding the bottle balanced on her knee. She was perfectly unobtrusive. Perfectly patient. Sixty paces beyond that, the furtive man who'd followed her out of Fetter Lane was behind the door of a tavern.

"We could take her," Hawk said.

"Not yet."

"I could scoop her up all by myself." Hawk's eyes unfocused for a minute. That was Hawk, thinking. "I'll walk around back and come up the street behind her. You count two hundred, then make some noise. I set a knife at her throat and talk to her persuasively till she decides to be sensible. We truss her up and tuck her in an alley, quiet and neat. Then we pick up the Frenchman."

"You'd hurt her or she'd hurt you."

"I don't mind hurting her some."

"I realize that. You don't get to do it. And none of that would be quiet. She's Caché."

"Not the first Caché I've met." Hawker scratched his forearm through his coat. "Not the first one I've fought with, if it comes to that."

Thirty yards away, Vérité lifted her gin bottle out of his sight, pretending to take a drink, then set it back on her knee. On a grimy little street like this, anyone—man, woman, or child—could find a corner and settle down with a bottle and be ignored. Folks didn't strike up conversations with the drunken, who tended to be belligerent and less than clean. The bottle itself was a handy weapon.

"She acts like you do," Hawker said. "Holding a bottle of gin is one of the tricks you taught me. She stalks her target with the same . . . I guess you'd call it the same flavor."

"We were trained by the same men."

"At the Coach House. Almost makes me wish I'd gone to school sometime or other."

"You didn't miss anything."

"Latin."

"There's that." He had a sudden memory of Vérité and Guerrier out on the training field, waving the stubs of broken bottles at each other, leaping around, dancing, making faces, acting like the children they were. They'd have been ten or eleven years old. Guerrier making jokes. Vérité laughing. Everybody in a circle around them, shouting encouragement, clapping.

Deadly, deadly children.

He said, "Be careful when you face her. She's dangerous, even for a Caché."

"I'm dangerous myself," Hawk said mildly. "I'll accuse you of the same."

" 'But yet I could accuse me of such things that it were better my mother had not borne me.' "

"Not the Bible." Hawker frowned. "Shakespeare?"

"*Hamlet.*"

"Jolly fellow, Hamlet. I'm surprised it took five acts for somebody to kill him. I could have done it in three."

He and Hawker leaned, side by side, against a damp, slightly gritty brick wall that was crumbling, flake by red ochre flake, to the dirt of the alley at their feet, powdering into dissolution. Give London five or six hundred years and it would reduce this wall to dust and wash it into the Thames.

He was eroding, himself. His eyes hurt. His mouth was dry as bone dust. Each breath was a long, stinging ache right down to his chest. The undercurrent of pain scraped away at his concentration. Every breath and blink was a distraction.

Ignore it. Set it aside.

He kept his eyes on Vérité. Hawker ran his attention up and down the street, into all the blind corners, across the windows that looked down on this road, and up to the rooftops. They'd worked together so long, in so many places, they didn't have to settle how to divide up the duty.

Hawk said, "I am officially disgusted with this slinking along the byways of London, hoping your erstwhile female colleague leads us someplace interesting. Let's drag somebody back to Meeks Street and be rudely inquisitive. I vote we start with the woman."

"We're not voting. And I don't crack eggs by slamming them with a hammer."

"That's profound, that is." Hawker began picking coin from his pockets and spreading it across the palm of his hand. "I like that word 'erstwhile.' I've been trying to work it into conversations. Right. Not the woman. We'll go to the tavern." He studied his hand. "Where I will carelessly set ten shillings, thr'pence, ha'penny spinning across the floor. While the assembly scrambles for coinage, we drag your Frenchman off to Meeks Street."

"And warn off the man I really want."

"The one yonder maiden went to meet in the church. The fellow you want dead."

"That one."

The man in the tavern belonged to the Merchant. They were always the same type—men who wore the dull skin and heavy, subtly stunted body of workers from the starved, laboring *quartiers* of Paris. Men who obeyed without question. Men with the angry, shrewd eyes and stolid, obstinate faces of fanatics.

He's one of the Merchant's men. He knows where the monster is.

Hawker sighed and put his money away. "They know we're following, even though you're reasonably skilled in the art and I am extraordinary. Hundred percent likelihood on the woman. Fifty-fifty for the man."

"They know."

Hawk pulled out his watch, heavy, embossed silver, worn dull, and opened it. "Two hours till dark. We can continue our tour of the public houses of Soho, pausing at intervals to let the Frenchman piss in alleys on the way between. After that, we won't be able to see him clearly. No loss, in my opinion." He put the watch away. "Are we learning anything at all from this peregrination around the capital?"

"We've seen a face. One of the men in one of these taverns came to carry a message."

"We've seen one hundred and seventy-two faces. Half of Soho."

"We'll know him when we see him again." He took a deep breath and didn't think about the pain. Wouldn't think about the pain. "When it starts to get dark, we'll collect the woman."

Hawker said, "That gives me something to look forward to."

Grab Vérité. Get her to Meeks Street. Help question her.

He wiped his mouth and leaned on the wall, unobtrusive enough that nobody glanced at him as they went by. Ahead of him, Vérité crouched on her cellar stairs and watched the tavern like a cat at a mouse hole. Like him, like Hawker, she'd be memorizing every man who went in and out. They were looking for the end of a string that might lead to that bastard.

Whatever she knew about the Merchant—and she knew something—she didn't know his lair.

Hawk looked up suddenly. "What have we here?"

At the far end of the street, three men left the tavern. They fell in, side by side, walking in step. The door of the tavern swung open and another two followed them.

Men with a single purpose. A gang.

Vérité. He straightened and tensed, about to run in that direction. Instinct shouted—She's alone.

But this wasn't years ago in the Coach House. This wasn't Piedmont. Not Tuscany. She wasn't one of his men, left in a forward position, vulnerable, unprotected, about to be surrounded.

And she didn't need his warning. Vérité's shadow vanished. Her cloak whipped away and was gone. None of those five men glanced in her direction. They headed for Hawker and for him.

"Soho Square." He rapped it out fast. A place to meet if he and Hawker got separated. "Follow the man, if you have a chance. I'll follow the woman."

A grunt from Hawker. Then there was no time for talking. More men came from the alley behind them and suddenly they were fighting six, seven, eight men.

Now seven. Hawk had kicked one in the groin and stooped to scoop up a knife, saving his own blades for future use.

Damn. They were young. Younger than Hawker. Not one of them as old as twenty, armed with walking sticks and knives and—*God help us*—fists.

Hawker muttered, "Amateurs," being contemptuous and also warning him, in case he was about to kill one.

He'd seen the same thing. So he didn't draw a blade. He ducked under a cudgel aimed at his head, plowed his fist into a belly, and cracked the man's jaw against his knee as he went down. Satisfying.

Hawker was shaking pain out of his hand, snarling. "He had a book under his coat. What kind of man walks around with a book under his coat?"

"Then don't use your fists. Kick him in—" He grabbed another boy by his lapels and swung him around to crash into the brick wall. Hard to say what part of the lad hit first, but it made a satisfying thump. "Kick him in the bollocks."

A dark shape ran in from the left, behind Hawk, fist raised, holding a brown bottle. It blurred downward.

Gunshot cracked and everybody froze.

I'm not hit. It took a second to decide this.

Hawker wasn't hit, either. It was another man who'd started bleeding from his forearm down his sleeve and dropped his wine bottle and dropped the idea of fighting as well. He fell back against the wall, looking amazed.

He knew what he'd see when he turned around. Cami hovered in a slant of shadow ten feet away. She slid her gun back to its accustomed secrecy.

Damned if she didn't smile. A conspirator's smile. Rueful. Guilty. She swirled her cloak and slipped around the corner, gone. He heard her running away.

Then a fellow he thought he'd already discouraged got to his knees and picked up a brick. That was somebody who needed to be kicked in the belly to discourage him some more. Hawker obliged.

"She missed," Hawk said, "if she was aiming at you."

"She wasn't."

"Well, she missed if she was aiming at me."

The man—the boy—who'd been hit was yelping about having a bullet in him. "She shot me," he said. "Shot me." All amazement.

The last three, the ones who hadn't engaged in combat and hadn't sustained any damage, edged shoulder to shoulder and slowly backed away. Scared boys. Damn it, who sent scared boys out to attack somebody like him? Like Hawker?

This was a distraction, a misdirection, a delaying tactic. The man they'd been following had paid these boys to attack or lied to them.

Maybe he could salvage something. He said, "Soho Square. I'll meet you or send a message. Get some men." Then he took off after Vérité.

leven

Every man contains a multitude of men.

A BALDONI SAYING

MR. SMITH HAD LONG AGO ABANDONED ANY PAR-
ticular name for himself. A warrior of the Revolution
needed no name. "Smith" would do as well as any for the few
days he remained in London. He arrived at the inn through
various and secret ways, circling in as a spider spirals in upon
his web.

The inn made the right noises. The innkeeper scolded one
of the maids in the front hall. The men in the taproom murmured and coughed. The clank from the kitchen was just
right. Not too loud. Not a dangerous silence.

Upstairs he checked the hall from end to end, drew his
pistol, then pushed open the door of the private parlor. He
stood in the doorway and flicked his gaze side to side across
the room. Two of his men sat at the table. So did the tiresome
woman he'd brought from France.

Everything was as expected. He uncocked his pistol and
set it on the mantelpiece, ready and loaded. The woman began
complaining loudly even before he dropped his hat on the
back of a chair and pulled his coat off to lay over the seat.

"Where have you been?" She had a peculiarly piercing

voice and a provincial accent. "What is the use of sending me for a drive when I am not allowed to go into any stores or talk to anyone? Why didn't you come with me? Why didn't you tell me you'd be gone this long?" There was more in that vein.

She had not seen him on Fleet Street when she passed in the carriage. Good. It saved explanations.

He nodded at the end of each sentence she said and caught the eye of Jacques, his second-in-command.

"Everything proceeds." Jacques tilted his bowl and wiped it round and round with a piece of bread. "No one has shown interest in us."

"Good." An approving nod to Jacques. At the same time, he expended a reassuring smile upon the woman Camille. He was patient with women. They required that homage to their weakness. To Jacques he said, "The work on the carriage?"

Jacques chose his words. "They have almost finished . . . preparing it. The shipment from Thompson will arrive . . . in the proper place, tomorrow."

"Hugues is on guard?" He went to the window and pulled the curtain back an inch and looked down into the ugly, cluttered courtyard below. There was no reason to expect trouble, but he was alive today, when many men wanted him dead, because he took precautions.

Gaspard dunked bread in his soup and took a sopping bite. "I will relieve him when I have eaten." They were good republicans, his men. No complaints from them about the inn's swill. They ate to give the body sufficient fuel to serve the cause. "I've hired the wagon we—"

"I am mad with boredom." The tiresome, inevitable woman rose from her chair and flounced across to confront him. "Since we returned from the carriage ride, Jacques has stopped me from going outside. Not even for one little walk."

You break into a conversation where men speak of serious matters. "They obey my orders. I regret if they have been impolite."

"You said there would be theater in London. Opera. Music. You said there were shops more beautiful than anything in Lyon and I would see them all. Instead, I cannot go to the pastry shop twenty paces down the street."

He'd promised any number of things. "It is not possible today. Perhaps tomorrow."

"I am sick of this tomorrow and that tomorrow and I am sick of this place. You bring me racing along your foul English roads until I am bruised. Now you ignore me. I stay here and stay here, day after day, and you do not take me to my family." She stamped her foot like a child. "You promised to take me to my aunts."

His men ate in silence. Gaspard, who lacked Jacques' intelligence, smiled derisively around his bread.

"My poor Marie-Claire. You have been very brave for so long. So strong through all these difficulties." He flattered her back to her place at the table. "I have explained the danger. Your enemies are everywhere. You must be wise as the serpent."

She was wise as a pig's intestine.

Once this fool of a woman had been Camille Besançon. Now she was Marie-Claire Gresset, pampered foster daughter of the watchmaker Gresset, a man of some importance in Lyon. She had escaped the fate of her family, rescued by one of the smugglers and given to the Gressets to take the place of a daughter who'd died.

He'd known of her survival. Of course he'd known. In those days he gave the execution order for every man, woman, and child who died to allow the placement of Cachés. He chose each death as carefully as a jeweler selects the next pearl in a necklace.

It had seemed profitable to let a member of the Council of Lyon cheat the Revolution and effect his petty rescue. Who knew when he might want to destroy Gresset?

"You leave me all day with servants," the woman whined, as all women whine. "Ill-bred, impolite, poorly trained servants who ignore my orders. I don't even have a maid."

Useless herself, she wanted another parasite to wait upon her. "I will see to it," he murmured. "A day or two and all will be arranged."

"Not a day or two. Now! And tell these dolts to obey my orders."

As if men would leap to do the bidding of a woman. It wasn't even the blind arrogance of the aristocracy. Marie-Claire

Gresset had almost forgotten she'd ever been a Besançon. She was petite bourgeoisie now, with all the pushing, busy vulgarity of the class. The aristocrat lived inside her only as a residue of resentment, a certainty that she should be better treated than she was.

Even now, she believed no one would dare to hurt her.

He patted her shoulder. Like all women, she was gentled with a few strokes. "I wish only to keep you safe. Be patient."

"I am done being patient. This is intolerable. You keep me prisoner in this hovel where the coffee is pigswill."

"I share your annoyance. These pigs of Englishmen should not be allowed in the kitchen. They know nothing of the art of cooking. Let me send for tea."

"The tea is worse. You complete all your tiresome business. You hire wagons. You buy horses. You receive shipments. But you never take me to my aunts!"

"Soon." He gave no sign of impatience. He did not resent the expenditure of time necessary to soothe this idiot to complacency. "I promise you, by this time next week you will be in the beautiful chateau of your ancestors. I swear it. You will take your place as Lady Camille de Leylands. You will attend the opera wearing the Leyland jewels. There is a parure of rubies red as blood and every stone bigger than your thumbnail."

Ridiculous fairy tales for a gullible, greedy child. He spun the pretty story for her because it was easier to deal with a docile woman than to keep her trussed in a closet. Either way, she would serve her purpose.

She said, "Now. Today. Take me to my aunts now!"

"Soon. They are ready to alter their will in your favor, but the impostor who has stolen your place is very clever. Very dangerous. We must meet with them in secret. We must proceed carefully." He constructed a gentle smile. "In a very few days we will celebrate your return to your proper place."

Under the blade. That is your proper place. We guillotined your kind.

He made more murmurs and vague promises. Then he motioned Gaspard to engage her in conversation and retreated across the room to the peace to be found on the rough benches that flanked the hearth.

Her complaint continued like dripping water and was no more important. Sensible discussion with Jacques became possible. "Édouard has not returned?"

Jacques shook his head.

"I set him to following the Caché woman. He will be busy with that. And we have a small success. This." The paper he'd taken from the Caché bitch was still faintly damp in his coat pocket. He didn't hide his distaste as he dropped it on the bench. "English code, or something that is a good counterfeit of it, written in her own hand."

Jacques unrolled the half sheet, flat on the bench, holding it from index finger to index finger. "Useful. I'll drop pieces of this along Semple Street the night before."

"Burn the edges, just a little. It will be more convincing." The scraps would be found. More proofs for the British press, in an assemblage of many small proofs.

"It is a nice addition. You've eaten?"

"Not yet."

A pot warmed on the hob. Jacques scraped to the bottom of the pot and filled a bowl he took from the mantel. "The meeting with the woman? It went well?"

"There was one complication that resolved itself. Nothing important." He accepted the bowl and a pewter spoon and put them on the bench beside him. "You were right about her. She's gone soft and stupid. She's forgotten everything she learned in the Coach House."

Jacques fetched the stub end of a loaf of bread under his arm and the wine bottle and two glasses. The bread he tore in half and set both pieces next to the bowl. The wineglasses took the last of the space on the bench. "She lived in a household of women. Books everywhere. Tea parties."

"The vaporing of the female intellectual is universal. Their salons and their politeness and the endless, pointless arguments were the curse of the Revolution. They destroyed more good men than bullets. Come. Sit with me. We must talk." And he took up his soup and began to eat.

A year ago, when he first planned this operation, he knew he'd need an expendable agent. Best would be an unquestionable French spy, known to the British Service, easily identifiable, eminently expendable. The Cachés came to mind. There were dozens left up and down England, hidden, weak, self-indulgent men and women who'd abandoned their loyalty to France. They were deserters as surely as if they'd run from the battlefield. They were traitors to the ideals of the Revolution.

He was, perhaps, the only man left who knew where they were. If he had not had other concerns, he would have arranged the assassination of each one.

He'd remembered the Gresset girl was still alive in Lyon. The genuine Besançon would be a threat or a lure or a bribe for the Caché who'd taken her place. The aristocrat and the traitor Caché would, at last, make themselves useful.

He'd sent Jacques and Charles to Brodemere to study the Caché planted in the Leyland household.

"She'll do, then, this Caché?" Jacques poured sour wine for both of them, then pulled a rush-bottomed chair near the hearth and sat in it.

"Admirably. As you said, she's soft as a new cheese. Promise her imprisonment and death, she'll obey from fear. Threaten the old women, she'll obey from a sickly, puerile sentimentality. Offer her a chance to dispose of the proof of her imposture, and she will shed the trappings of morality like a scratchy coat." His eyes slipped to the Besançon. "They're alike, those two, the spoiled aristocrat and the failed spy. One fool is lured to England by promises of rich old aunts. The other will do anything, including murder, to stay in her fat, safe, comfortable life in Cambridgeshire."

"The Caché . . ." Jacques drank and wiped his lips on the sleeve of his coat. "If Édouard finds where she's staying, can we just reach out and take her? We could hold her here with this other one. Or keep her in the cabinet shop, in the basement." He topped off his glass. "Why not?"

Jacques could ask this. They had survived, mission after mission, because every one of his men felt free to sit with him like this and speak to him as an equal.

Sometimes it was good, in the quiet leading up to an operation, to explain plans and the reason for decisions. "We are six. One must stay here with the Besançon. One at the cabinet shop. One driver. That leaves only three men to subdue a Caché who is armed and must not be killed at that time and must not escape. That is too few."

Jacques drank more wine. After a minute, he said, "You're right. It is a chance we cannot take."

"She has obeyed me so far. She came to London on my orders. She met me at the time and place designated."

"True."

"Those are good indications she will come to Semple Street. When we find her hiding place, we will keep watch. On the appointed day, if she disobeys orders, you may kill her then."

Jacques nodded. "That's good, then. Good. There is always the possibility that—"

The Besançon raised her voice. "No, I tell you. No and no and no! I will *not* be trapped in this room another day. If you try, I will—"

He rose and went to her. "But of course you are not trapped. Did you think that? Then I have been remiss in my care of you." He made one of the graceful, meaningless half-bows men made in homage to women. "Tomorrow we will amuse ourselves. Do you know, I saw a delightful hat in a shop window today. Only a short walk. A delightful walk. We will go shopping tomorrow, you and I."

She simpered. Now they would discuss hats. He settled himself beside her and pretended to listen.

Jacques retrieved the bowl of soup and dry, tasteless bread for him. English food. It did not make him homesick for Norfolk. A true revolutionary has no country but the Revolution.

welve

*Malevolence is sold at a bargain. One pays full
price for stupidity.*

A BALDONI SAYING

PERHAPS I MADE MISTAKES. CAMI CONSIDERED THIS
possibility while she picked the lock. She worked by touch
because it was midnight and the moon had no chance against
this wet fog.

Her mistake—if it was a mistake—lay not in letting Mr.
Smith's minion trail after her. That was according to her plan.
What she'd done next was not. It had been self-indulgent to
return to Fetter Lane when she had all of London at her disposal. It had been an error in judgment.

She'd gone to make certain Devoir was up and cursing,
snarling, furious with her . . . able to see. She couldn't walk
away and not know.

It was a very Baldoni decision. Nothing is more important
than friendship. Baldoni do not haggle like shopkeepers over
the cost.

Devoir . . . oh, Devoir was all he'd been at the Coach House,
and more. Coughs racked him, he gasped for breath, but he got
stubbornly to is feet. Half-blind, surrounded by bumbling confusion, he'd spotted her thirty feet away. She'd seen him do it.

She'd seen him catch the sleeve of that dark-haired man and give chopped, vehement orders.

Devoir had attached himself to her like a cocklebur and followed her up and down London all afternoon and evening. In the end, though, it had turned out well enough. Here she was where she'd always intended to be, breaking into Braid's Bookshop.

London is ungenerous. The night does not willingly offer up free lodging. Every park, every thin alley, every backyard shed, even the protected overhang of a front doorway, is locked and watched. The shop owners and householders of London no more wish to shelter people who walk at night than the landholders of Cambridgeshire wish to provide coverts for foxes.

She was invading an institution of sorts. Braid's had bought and sold books in this brick house on Paternoster Row for two centuries. There were castles in England with lesser pedigrees. Probably an antique Marcus Braidus had traveled to Rome on donkey back, brought home Latin scrolls for homesick centurions, and sold them in a mud hut on this site.

The Fluffy Aunts always came here when they were in London.

She concentrated on the padlock on this gate, which might have deterred a toddler with a jackstraw. Otherwise, it was a waste of iron.

She would take this new knowledge away from the day. Devoir no longer fit in the box her memory had made for him. She saw him . . . differently. She saw him as he must appear to a stranger. He'd stood in the center of that yammering mob, his coat discarded and him wet through to the skin, the linen of his shirt being revelatory about his anatomy.

He was still stringy as wrapped leather on that long frame, still thin and drawn out, but he had broader shoulders now. He'd become hardened and steady in his body. Somehow harmonious. The awkward bones and angles of Devoir, the boy, had become this swift, sleek predator, muscled like a man. It unsettled her to see him looking like a grown man.

In future she would avoid Devoir like one of the biblical plagues.

The lock grated open to her. Only imagination made the scraping loud in this empty alley. She pushed the gate slowly inward, balancing it delicately on its hinges so it wouldn't squeak in an unseemly manner.

Her intrusion onto the Braid's property was accompanied by a satisfactory silence. No one looked out any of the windows up and down the alley. Behind the board fence of the house next door, the vocal little dog was tearing away at the stale loaf she'd tossed him. Like most dogs he was inclined to bark madly at every wandering cat and let a sneaking invader like her pass unannounced.

She was more tired than she'd expected to be at the end of this day and more wet and less successful. She didn't begrudge the afternoon spent following and being followed by the bristly head and large ears of a Frenchman. She only wished he'd been more careless. She'd hoped to follow him back to wherever they were keeping Camille Besançon. If that woman was Camille Besançon.

The henchman had not, unfortunately, taken his bristly head back to report to Mr. Smith. Instead he'd wasted his day, and her own, lounging his way from one Soho tavern to another.

So her first plan hadn't worked. Tomorrow she'd try something else.

The yard behind Braid's was full of rough sheds and the bins waiting for the rag-and-bone man. None of that showed as even the ghost of a shape in this darkness. The windows were dim red rectangles, upstairs and down. Braid's left a low fire burning, safe behind a grate, in every room. Books don't like the damp.

At home they left fire on two of the hearths downstairs and—

Not home. That wasn't her home.

She pushed away those thoughts. They were painful and unprofitable and there was no going back, anyway.

She had not liked being followed by the skillful, nearly invisible Devoir. Her awareness of him was spun from tenuous glimpses of a hat in a crowd or a face reflected in a shop window. It had taken hours to snip him loose from her trail. The squire back home . . . the squire in Brodemere used to claim the fox enjoyed the hunt as much as the huntsmen did. Piffle.

She eased across the flat, unevenly set stones of this yard. They were slippery in this wet, solid mist, which seemed an unnecessary complication to the evening. If London hadn't been enjoying such a wet night, she would have had some moonlight to see what she was doing.

Nowadays Baldoni made their living in comfortable salons, cheating at piquet or dealing in meretricious copper mines. But they never forgot they had once been mountain bandits. They still taught their children the not-so-gentle art of tracking prey in city and countryside. How to avoid becoming someone else's prey. Concealment is a skill with wide applicability.

And she'd been trained in the Coach House. Truly, she had a solid grounding in the robust arts of sneakiness.

The window of Braid's book storage room, warm looking and welcome in the dark, was a dozen feet away. She'd dry this cloak by the fire and—

She kicked into a pail some nameless fool had left in the middle of everything.

It thudded loudly and rolled down the paving stones, clattering. Every dog up and down the alley took to yapping its head off.

She held absolutely still and counted two hundred in Latin.

A proper Baldoni wouldn't stub a toe against a wooden bucket, regardless of how dark it was. A good Caché wouldn't, either. Maybe she should stop congratulating herself on eluding the British Service and pay more attention to what she was doing.

The heavy, foggy air drizzled on her, determined about it. Stubborn. She could have done without such firm decisiveness. She counted to two hundred in the Tuscan of her childhood.

The dogs became bored with inciting one another to frenzy. One final deep bark some distance away ended it. No windows lit up anywhere along the alley.

The count in Spanish was not strictly necessary, but she did it anyway. Patience separates the amateur from the professional.

She whispered, *"Doscientos,"* before she limped her way forward, feeling ahead of her with cautious, intelligent feet.

There were no more obstacles. The lock on the window yielded to the logical argument of a thin blade. The window-sill, when she hiked herself up to it, was slippery with the wet and full of splinters. She swung her feet inside, into the ground-floor storeroom, and was in an old familiar place.

Books on every side, shelves and shelves of them. Crates stacked at the far end. A sizable pile of clean straw, tidy in the corner. More books, a roll of brown paper, scissors, and a ball of twine on the table. The half-open door was full of reddish light from the little fire on the grate in the main shop.

The shop cat, a long, languid tom named Pericles, curled his way around that door and padded over, prepared to welcome her with his usual indiscriminate affection. This was a quiet, contemplative room to break into, filled with the smell of book bindings and glue, warmed by the buzzing purr of Pericles the cat.

She didn't close the window at once. She set her hands against the frame on either side and looked out, pleased she wasn't being rained on. The fabric of the night stretched around her . . . sky and streets, wet brick, dark smells, the random sounds of London.

Men were looking for her. She felt it as a tiny prickle on the skin, a touch on the mind. They wouldn't give up. She was in danger every day she stayed in London.

Pericles jumped to the windowsill and bumped at her hand with cold nose and feathery whiskers. Nothing more comforting than a cat.

The night was empty except for a mist that didn't quite become rainfall. When she was as sure as she could be that she was alone, she removed Pericles from the sill and closed the window, shutting out the damp and the darkness. For tonight, she was safe.

Thirteen

Even an honest man may walk abroad at night.

A BALDONI SAYING

PAX WALKED THROUGH DARK RAIN THAT DIDN'T
so much fall as hang suspended in the air. It condensed on his
face and formed droplets that fell from the brim of his hat. He
had the feeling that if he stood still he wouldn't get wet at all.

Goods wagons rumbled past, making deliveries in the
empty streets long before dawn. A few laborers plodded
toward the fish stands and vegetable markets, head down, enduring, and the mist ate up their voices when they passed.
There were almost no women out.

He'd sent word where to meet him. He'd wondered if
they'd come. If they'd let Hawker come.

They were waiting outside St. Paul's.

The hackney stood in the circle of wet paving lit by a
streetlamp. Thin, bright lines traced the brass railing of the
coach and the stippling of worn gilt on the window frame.
They'd lowered the carriage lights to coin-sized points of red.
Walking toward it felt like approaching a huge animal crouching in the dark. Up on the box, Tenn slouched inside his driver's coat, dozing, leaned back, the reins slack in his hand,
playing a black coachman hoping for one last fare of the

evening. Thirty feet away the steps of St. Paul's led into black mist.

Hawker, in a shabby jacket and cap, held the cheekpiece of the right-hand carriage horse, stroking the long nose and verbally abusing the pair in broad Cockney. They were right nodcocks, weren't they, letting somebody talk 'em into dragging a coach around? Then he switched to his beautiful, educated Parisian French, misquoting Rousseau. *"Le cheval est né libre, et partout il est dans les rênes."*

Hawker made a convincing groom till you heard him speak French.

The horse is born free, and everywhere he is in reins. Rousseau wrote some of the books he'd used to teach Hawk French. It had seemed a good idea at the time.

How many meetings like this, in how many open fields and dirty alleys? How many welcomes by old friends, a circle joined together by a hundred shared dangers in the past?

This would be the last time. Even now, he wasn't one of them. They just acted as if he were. They all knew better.

He said, "Where's Doyle?"

Hawker switched from his fluent French to his fluent Cockney. "If I kept the estimable Mr. Doyle in me pocket, I'd inform you of his whereabouts. As it is—"

Hawk hadn't finished before Doyle appeared out of the dark. Large, ugly, imperturbable Doyle, wearing a scar on his cheek and the clothes of a shopkeeper.

"We been asking each other if you'd show up in London," Doyle said mildly. He ambled over to lean against the big wheel of the coach, letting the drizzle fall on him and around him without any sign he noticed it. "And here you are, right on time. Seems you've brought a bit of excitement with you."

"To brighten our otherwise dull lives." Hawker came up to make the third corner of the triangle. "Stillwater is watching Paternoster Row. McAllister is down Ludgate. We are alert on all points of the compass, as usual. You lost that damn woman, didn't you?"

"He don't have her tucked under his arm, so we will assume she slipped away," Doyle said.

"Solely because he wouldn't let me sneak up on her and

lay a knife at her jugular, which, if I had done, would have discouraged her from wandering off *and* made it less likely she'd take a shot at me."

Doyle, Hawker, and him. It felt like the three of them, on the job, running an operation together. When he was fresh come to Meeks Street, it had been Doyle who trained him. Doyle who took him out on his first field work. Who brought him home between assignments to be fussed over by Maggie and play knucklebones with their offspring. He couldn't number the lies he'd told Doyle.

He didn't want to meet Doyle's eyes, so he talked to Hawker. "She didn't shoot at you. She shot a man before he could brain you with a bottle of wine. You should be thanking her."

"Oh, I will. I will," Hawker said. "The minute I meet her, I'll do just that."

"Then let's arrange it." He turned away from St. Paul's, putting the faint push of damp air in his face. The great dome of the church loomed above, invisible, blocking the wind. He'd been in the high mountains of Italy long enough that he could sense the shape of the countryside from the way the wind blew.

Vérité was out there in the soft night, hidden as only a Caché learned to hide. If he didn't find her in the next hour or so, he might not find her at all. "I followed her out of Soho, going back and forth, but generally in this direction. She knows the streets—didn't hesitate—and this is where she was going." He sliced a line to the west with his hand. "I lost her there, in Fisher's Alley."

Doyle followed that line with his eyes. "How did she lose a fine old tracker like you?"

"She had a cutout in place. A classic. She ducked in a shop and out the back, slick as wet ice."

"I do appreciate a woman who understands the fine art of the chase," Hawker murmured.

The shopgirl had blocked his way long enough for Vérité to wriggle away like an eel, out a window, into the maze of alleys. "She paid them to delay me. It was arranged yesterday."

Tell them the last of it. She deserves appreciation for the joke. For the sheer audacity of it. "She went through a corset shop." The memory of his search of a corset shop would stay with him awhile. "There were customers in the back."

Hawker grinned.

Straight-faced, Doyle said, "There would be." He searched in his pockets and found his silver toothpick case.

"She's toying with you," Hawk said. "That is sarcasm. Pure sarcasm."

Doyle said, "You'd recognize that."

Hawk paced to the front of the hackney, then turned and came back again. The horses kept a watchful, interested eye on him. "She set up her cutout yesterday, so whatever she's up to is recent. Or else . . ." He raised his hand. "No. Don't tell me. If she lived in London, she'd have a dozen cutouts in place. She only just arrived in town."

"Within a day. Maybe two. She hasn't had time to do anything elaborate. Her escape plan will be basic, simple, stripped down. Classic procedures."

"Classic is she'll run straight from that shop to her hiding place. Spend as little time as possible in the open." Hawk said what they all were thinking. "That means she's not far from Fisher's Alley."

"Gone to ground." Doyle flicked open the toothpick case with his thumbnail. "She's got some bolt-hole. Someplace safe."

"Not far from here," Hawker said. "Where she will spend the night warm and dry. Unlike some of us."

"Ain't you a delicate flower all of a sudden." Doyle's scarred smile was pure, amused villainy. "You stand there and grow moss for a bit while Pax and me figure out where she is."

"I'm not complaining," Hawk said. "Just pointing it out."

They stood in an island of light, floating in a dark sea, facing west, toward Fisher's Alley.

"She won't break cover till morning, when the streets get busy," Doyle said.

"At which point we'll lose her, even if this fog lifts," Hawk said.

The Merchant was alive, loose in London, running like a rabid dog. Vérité was the key to finding him. There was no chance in hell he'd let her escape. He squared his thumb and fingers and held them up to frame the west, spreading north and south from Ludgate. A space seven or eight streets wide. "She's in there."

"Well, that's useful." Hawk removed his cap and shook some of the rain off. "I cannot tell you how excited I am at the prospect of searching the neighborhood of St. Paul's, house by house. We'll go up one side of the street and down the other, picking locks." He peered up to where the dome of St. Paul's couldn't be seen. "Maybe I can break into the church. That's a sin I haven't committed recently. There is not a boring minute in this life."

"She's not in the church." Hawker was capable of invading St. Paul's if he wasn't stopped. "That's too public, too open, too few doors, no defenses. She was trained . . ." *Say it. No more lies. Not to Hawker. Not to Doyle.* "We were trained in the Coach House to avoid places like that."

"Some of the best spies in the world came out of that school in Paris." Doyle took out a toothpick and considered it. "You Cachés."

That answered a question. Doyle knew he was a traitor and he knew the details. But he'd come to help. No questions asked.

A considering silence fell. To all appearances, Doyle was in deep meditation upon the black mist in the direction of Paternoster Row. Hawker had gone back to pacing.

After a minute, Hawker said, "I'm getting tired of chasing this fox all over London."

"Vixen," Doyle corrected mildly.

"Right. I know that," Hawker said. "This vixen. Tell me her name. I'm annoyed at her."

"Vérité." It felt odd, telling them her name, as if two parts of his life were colliding, breaking to pieces, falling into each other. "You've been annoyed at her all day. You keep offering to kill her."

"Earlier I was irked when she tried to blind you. Now that she's aimed gunfire in my direction it has become my own personal ire." Reaching the end of his chosen path, Hawk turned and paced back. "Why here? Why this place?"

Doyle rolled the ivory toothpick between his fingers. "A friend nearby? Somebody in trouble goes to a friend."

"This quarter's crawling with Frenchmen," Hawk said. "Émigrés, spies, royalists, the scaff and raff of the Revolution."

But it didn't feel right. "That's not why she's here." He ran his sleeve across his face, feeling the grate of leather over his eyelids, smelling the rain. "She's on her own. She wouldn't drag a friend into this business. It's treason."

"Treason's a hanging affair." No way to tell what Doyle was thinking.

Was Doyle warning him not to pull Hawker down with him when the reckoning came? No need. He wouldn't let Hawk do anything stupid.

Hawker paced, digging a trench in his ten or twelve feet of the pavement, arguing with himself. "Not hiding with a friend, then. Not the church. Nobody's going to hide in St. Paul's, it being full of churchmen. Who knows when one of them will take a notion to ring bells or start praying? She's not crouching in somebody's coal shed because we have determined she planned this all out in advance. Lodgings?" Hawk answered himself immediately. "We might find her that way. She'd be remembered. She's pretty. Always a nuisance, being pretty."

"You'd know," Doyle said.

Hawker ignored that. "She doesn't know the city." Hawker had the Cockney's sense of superiority over people born in the hinterlands outside the sound of Bow bells. "She'll know bits and parts of it. She'll have favorite streets. That's what she led you through. That's where she's hid herself."

"And she's near Fisher's Alley." Doyle plied the toothpick awhile. "There's a chance I can narrow this a little. A while back I heard dogs barking up and down Paternoster Row, not far from the market. I didn't get there in time to pin it down."

"You think that was her." Possible. Very possible. Nothing so discreet as nighttime breaking and entering.

"Dogs. The curse of an honest thief." Hawk went back to pacing and discussing matters with himself. They could set flame to a pile of trash, yell "Fire!" up and down the street, and catch the woman when she came running out. They could set the dogs barking again and try to recognize a particular yap . . .

The fog skirted back under a forward line of wind. A streetlight showed the name over a shop. Morrison Bookseller. What had Hawker said? *She'd know some streets well.* "You come to Paternoster Row for books. Half the booksellers in London are here."

Hawker, being Hawker, had to say, "She's a dedicated reader. She wants a nice novel to lull her to sleep. We'll find her burgling one of the bookshops along Paternoster."

"When I was chasing Vérité, we kept passing bookshops. She knows the streets with bookshops."

"What else?" Doyle watched him.

Vérité, with her head bent over a slate in the schoolroom at the Coach House, scratching out codes, counting under her breath. Vérité filling her long bench with papers full of numbers, letters, charts. "She's a codebreaker, the best they'd ever seen at the Coach House. Back in France they got excited about that and trained her. They would have placed her where she could get hold of codes."

"Books. Code. Book codes," Doyle muttered.

Hawker, still now, pulled at his lower lip. "Bookshop. Get out of the rain in a bookshop. Fine. Good." Behind his eyes, he was like a tiger pacing. That alert and impatient. "Which bookshop?"

"I know where she has to be." He'd added everything together, clicked the last puzzle piece into place. "She said she's called Cami. That has to be Camille. She used one of the old Leyland codes in the letter she sent to Meeks Street."

Doyle saw it in an instant. "Great gibbering frogs. Camille Leyland."

"They didn't slip her into the home of some general or Foreign Office drone, hoping she'd come across a code once in a while. They were more ambitious. She went to the top codebreakers in England. The Leylands."

Doyle said, "They put her right under my nose."

"Couilles du diable," Hawker whispered.

"She played me for a fool," Doyle said.

"Consistently and with panache," Hawk said. "She comes from France. She miraculously washes ashore in a shipwreck. She just happens to be the Leylands' niece. It was always too much of a coincidence. Why didn't I see that?" Hawker kicked at something in the street.

"Because I told you she was genuine." Doyle grimaced. "A hundred witnesses saw the girl stagger ashore. She was half-drowned and bruised head to foot from tumbling on the rocks. When I questioned her, I saw a little girl, shaking with fever, letter perfect, and innocent as a rose. I believed her."

The Tuteurs were meticulous when they made a placement. His own story had been just as good. "You could have talked to her for a week and never caught her in a lie. At the Coach House we were trained to resist interrogation." He stepped off the pavement into the street. "You can't imagine how well we were trained."

Hawker fell into step beside him. "You know where she is."

"I know where a Leyland would be and she's been a Leyland for the last decade." Vérité had become Cami. He knew where a Cami would be.

Doyle, with no break in the appearance of good-natured indolence, was at his other side. "She was ten years old. Even the French didn't send ten-year-old Cachés."

"She was twelve and scrawny as a twig."

"She didn't sell secrets." Hawk found another rock on the street to kick. "We'd have spotted her the first time we lost a Leyland code. What the hell has she been doing all these years if she's not selling English secrets?"

Hiding. "If that bastard gets his hands on her, she'll spill every code she's ever seen. Every secret she's read. He could make stones talk." They'd reached the top of Paternoster Row, looking down the line of streetlamps. "That's what the bastard's after. The Leyland codes. She's gone to ground at—"

"Braid's Bookshop," Doyle said. "Specializing in the literature of France, Germany, and Italy. The Leylands shop there when they come to town."

"They shop everywhere," Hawker said. "When I was door-keeper at Meeks Street they used to send me all over town, looking for some Greek commentary on horseradishes."

Doyle said, "But Braid's for the code books. Cheap editions printed in Paris or Vienna. Inconspicuous. Replacements available everywhere. And the owner's apartment at Braid's is empty."

They were walking away from the streetlamp, stepping on their shadows. None of them made any noise except the soft words, back and forth.

"Now, that I didn't know," Hawk said.

"You been in France." Doyle loosened up his coat, making it just that one bit easier to get to his gun. "The finer points of life in this great metropolis have escaped your attention. The old man's wife died . . . it must be six months ago. He moved in with his daughter and I don't think they've rented out the upstairs. They hadn't last time I went by."

They stopped, together, at the alley that ran behind the houses on this side of the street. Braid's was six houses ahead, marked by a glow of light in the shop window. Wind reshaped the mist, revealing the street for twenty yards, then taking it back again. They were all getting wet.

"I love unoccupied premises." Hawk patted his chest, checking knives, following Doyle's example. "As the professional milling cove among us, I suggest we call in Stillwater and McAllister to watch the shop. You, Pax, and I go in the back way. We—"

"I go in alone."

A long pause.

"You want to do that?" Doyle asked. "She's already attacked you once."

"I'll be more careful."

Silence. Waiting.

He said, "I may convince her to talk. We were friends once. No." He cut off what Hawk was about to say. "This isn't as simple as dragging one more Caché out of hiding. We need the information inside her." He glanced at Doyle. "It's important."

Doyle didn't point out that a traitor took a lot on himself, giving orders. "We could convince her to talk at Meeks Street."

"Not by any method you'd be willing to use. She knows how to keep silent. As I say, we were trained."

Doyle took another half minute, then nodded. "It's your decision."

His decision. He imagined the moment of capture. Overwhelming fear and then a fight she had no chance of winning. His gut kept saying it was wrong to give Vérité to the Service. He couldn't remember a time he'd had to push himself forward on one path when every instinct badgered him to take another. "Give me time with her."

"Some time. Then you need to report to Meeks Street. Galba's patience is not infinite." Doyle paused and said, "Don't let her get behind you."

"I won't." He pulled his mind to the last details that had to be arranged. This game could end in a lot of different ways. "Put McAllister and Stillwater on the front, left and right. You, if you will, take the far end of the alley, watching the back of Braid's. Hawk takes this end. That corner, where he's out of this wind. This isn't the weather for somebody with a bullet hole in him."

"Bullet wounds are no match for my well-practiced stoicism," Hawk murmured.

"I'll go in the window up there." It was an upper-floor window on the front. Almost certainly, Vérité was sleeping in the back of the shop, near a fast escape. With luck, she wouldn't hear him breaking in.

Doyle studied him for one more minute. "You're sure you want to do this?"

"There's a good chance she'll talk to me if I'm alone." He buttoned his coat so it wouldn't get in his way.

Hawk said, "Going by past behavior, there's a good chance she'll slit your throat."

The window was fifteen feet up. "I will hold that thought in mind."

He clamped his throwing knife in his teeth and backed down the pavement. He ran, hit Doyle's cupped hands, and took the leap upward. Caught the windowsill with his fingers and hung. Found a toehold in the brick and pulled himself up.

ourteen

It is not enough to know how to ride. One must know how to fall.

A BALDONI SAYING

SHE SLEPT DARKLY AND DREAMLESSLY. SOMEONE touched her shoulder.

She came up clawing. Hitting out with the heel of her hand. Then he had her wrists trapped, caught, pushed to the straw she slept upon. A ton of solid muscle held her down. Her legs tangled in the wool of her cloak, kicking uselessly.

Shadows resolved into a face leaning over her. He said, "Don't fight me."

Devoir. It was Devoir.

She froze.

His fingers settled to a better grip on her wrists. He said, "Hello again, Vérité."

She could curl upward, ram her head into his face, break his nose . . .

And that was an exercise in the futile. Even if he didn't know exactly what she was planning, and she was quick enough to batter him raw, he wouldn't let go. You could grind Devoir neatly into sausage and he wouldn't let go.

His body pressed like rocks. His breath blew hot on her face. Strands of his colorless hair hung between them. Her gun, loaded and ready, hidden under the rolled-up dress she was using as a pillow, could have been in Northumberland for all the good it did her.

She considered this abrupt reversal of fortune from every possible angle and didn't like it. "I wasn't expecting you."

"You should have." For a minute, his eyes glittered, fierce and unreadable. Abruptly, his weight was gone from her. He curled to his feet and stood looking down. "We didn't finish talking."

The British Service had found her. Her long deception was finished. Time to pay the piper. Icicles of panic shivered in her muscles.

Slowly, she pushed herself up to sitting. Her fingers brushed the pistol grip.

"Don't," he advised.

There are opportune moments for violent ambush. This did not seem to be one of them. She stretched her arms out, resting her elbows on her raised knees, on the cloak she'd used as her blanket. She intertwined her fingers, looking harmless.

He said, "Get over by the wall. Leave that cloak where it is. I want to see your hands the whole time."

"I'm in my shift."

"I've seen you naked."

They'd all seen each other naked in the spartan dormitory at the Coach House. When they were Cachés. When they were children, spies in training, miserable and deadly. When they'd been friends. "I was twelve. Nobody was interested."

"I'm not interested now. Get up." The words scraped out of his throat one by one. If he still hurt, so many hours after she'd thrown the *mélange de tabac* at him, he wasn't going to be in a forgiving mood.

She drew herself together against the cold, feeling hollow and weak. Once, she'd been questioned by men from the British Service. They'd been gentle with her because she looked like a child and they believed her well-practiced lies. The men who came for her this time would not be gentle. They wouldn't believe her and they wouldn't forgive her for deceiving them.

If they were in this house, they were quieter than smoke.

Devoir said, "Stand up. Get back against the wall."

Not Devoir. Paxton. She would think of him as Pax and remove the last familiarity from her mind. Pax, the stranger. Pax, the unknown and unknowable. Dangerous Pax.

She kneed out from under her cloak, stood, and backed away till her spine encountered bookshelves. She was a model of docility.

"Very wise," he said.

Thin red firelight leaked through the open door from the front of the shop, the half-banked fires that kept the damp out of the books. He crossed the room like a tall shadow, uncannily silent, and knelt on the pile of packing straw she'd slept in. He kept a prudent eye in her direction.

She said, "You're safe from attack. You're four stone heavier than I am and expecting it."

"I'm glad we both realize that." He pulled the pistol from under her makeshift pillow. Fluid, shifting gleams ran up and down the barrel as he inspected it. "Nice gun." He weighed it in his hand. "It's light."

"I hollowed out the stock." The first shock was ebbing away. She tucked her hands under her armpits to keep them warm. It also hid her breasts. She was shaking. In the most dire of her nightmares, she'd never imagined facing Devoir as an enemy, having given him so much cause to be furious with her. "I wasn't going to shoot you."

At least, she didn't think so. She hadn't considered the matter in depth. "I don't shoot old friends."

He tapped the pistol butt on the floor to knock the powder out and make the gun useless. "That's reassuring."

"If I did, your colleagues would be on me like a pack of wolfhounds. Where are they, by the way?"

"Here and there." Pax wore the same dark clothes he'd had on in the afternoon, inconspicuous in the night. His hair was undisguised, pale as old ivory. He laid the gun aside. "Let's see what other deadly things you're carrying."

His voice was deep and gravelly from the slight damage she'd done to it earlier with the *mélange de tabac*. He set about plundering her cloak with intent, efficient motions. He was not, she thought, merry hearted and forgiving.

"Knife," he said, finding one. "And surprise, surprise, another knife." He slipped that one from its sheath, admired it, then tossed both of them down beside the pistol. He began pulling four-inch pins from the seam of her cloak. "You're a walking armory."

"I'm not generally. Weeks go by and I'm innocent of anything but one little penknife to cut package string. Most days, I couldn't menace a stalk of asparagus." Not being obvious about it, she felt along the shelves behind her. Books were of no use in this situation, but perhaps someone had left a pair of scissors. "I'm no longer carrying a little silver box full of ground pepper and snuff. That bolt has been shot, so to speak. There's some wire you haven't found yet. It's in—"

"Stop that." He didn't look up. He meant, stop searching the shelves, which he had somehow noticed her doing.

There probably wasn't anything to find anyway. She hugged herself close and awaited events. Was it a good sign that no one else from the British Service had popped in? Could Pax possibly be working alone? "How did you find me?"

"I asked the pigeons." He located the wire in the hem of her skirt and drew it out.

"That's not a weapon. Merely useful. And it's the end of your discoveries. I don't expect you to believe me, though."

"I don't."

She was chilly with nothing but her shift between her and the night. Her nipples had drawn up tight, making little peaks against the linen. Cold and a bit painful. Also immodest. She covered up as well as she could. It was silly to think of modesty and impossible not to.

He'd finished investigating her rolled dress and moved on to the pockets, showing no interest in breasts. "You have a penknife." It hit the pile of knives and metal darts with a musical chink.

"I'd forgotten that. Can't think why. You never know when you'll have to penknife somebody to death." She could, in fact, kill someone with it if she had to. As Pax knew. "My father used to say the most deadly weapon is the human mind. I agree in principle, but I'd rather face a hundred philosophers than even one gun."

Pax was silent in response, a silence she'd call hostile and problematic.

"Nice set of lockpicks." He added them to the pile. "So. You weren't quite disarmed."

"Picklocks aren't weapons."

"You could poke my eyes out."

"I don't need little iron sticks to do that." She'd use her thumbs, as they'd been taught. They'd learned those lessons, the two of them sitting side by side, cross-legged in the dirt, in the courtyard of the Coach House.

"I hope that completes the arsenal. I'm going to be irritated if I search you and find something else." He pushed her clothes away and uncoiled upward and came toward her.

He was fast. There was nowhere to retreat. He pushed her back against the shelves, his arm across her chest like an iron bar. Lines of wood dug in, up and down her spine.

He snapped, "What does he want?"

"Who?"

"Try again." His arm pushed the breath out of her. "What . . . does . . . he . . . want?"

Smith. He meant Smith. "I don't know."

"Keep lying and this will be a very short conversation. We'll finish it at Meeks Street."

"Wait." Her voice wavered at the edges. She steadied it. "Just . . . wait."

"Where is he? Why is he in London? What game are you two playing?"

"No game. I'd rather stuff live rats in my shift than play games with that man. I've seen him precisely once. We didn't exchange addresses."

"Why did you meet him?"

His back was to the door and all the light. His face was hidden, utterly. She spoke to darkness and she told the truth. "About a week ago, I got a letter, a nasty little missive full of threats and blackmail. I came to London to meet the blackmailer. When you walked into that church, I thought it was you."

"Really?" The word fell like ice, arctic cold.

"For six seconds. Acquit me of more stupidity than that. If you wanted something from me, you wouldn't write letters.

You'd track me down to a storeroom at the back of a book-store and bark questions into my face. You'd half choke me while you were doing it."

He stopped pushing his arm into her chest and took her shoulders instead, shaping his hands to get well acquainted. "What's he doing in London? What does he want?"

This was not, perhaps, the moment to explain how much she knew about England's secret codes. So she said, "I have no idea."

Pax's thumbs twitched in the delicate indentation where collarbone met the bones of the shoulder. They'd been taught how to torture captives, starting there, where unbearable pain lay just below the surface. Their teachers had made sure they experienced that pain.

She felt him carefully, deliberately, loosen his grip and slide his hands downward to manacle her arms.

"Here's good advice," he said. "Don't trust that man. Don't believe anything he promises. And don't lie to me."

She could feel anger inside him, like the dark orange coal in a hearth that flares into fire unexpectedly, all at once. She knew him in this mood. In the Coach House, Devoir used to sit up at night, staring into the dark, brooding, radiating this kind of tightly wrapped rage.

He'd never let it loose. She wondered if he'd do so now. "Let's talk first. You can hurt me later, if you still want to."

"I'm not hurting you. I'm not even making you nervous."

"I beg to differ." Held this way, she couldn't shrug, but he'd feel the twitch.

Somewhere in the long years, Pax had become tall. She hadn't needed to look so far up to talk to him when they were children. He'd been thin then. Now he had the stripped-down frame of someone who'd pushed himself relentlessly, too hard and too long.

What did it say of a man that his hands were callused from fingertip to palm? That his forearms were wire-hard muscle under the skin? She read years of self-discipline in his body where it weighed, honed and hard, against her. There was no hint of compromise anywhere in the compendium of him.

She'd fought Devoir on the practice field when they were

children. He was stronger. She was faster. Sometimes he won. Sometimes she did. They'd slap the ground and stand up and begin again. If they fought now, she wouldn't win without hurting him badly. She might not win even then.

London was filled with amiable fools. It was a pity one of them hadn't waylaid her. "This is pointless. You don't have to extract information from me like a toothdrawer pulling teeth. Everything important is in that letter I sent to Meeks Street. Read it."

"It's in code."

"Decipher it." When the Fluffy Aunts came, they'd have it worked out in ten minutes. She wriggled inside his hold, against his body. "I haven't been benign to you recently, but if I promise to be inoffensive for five or six minutes, will you give me enough space to scratch my nose?"

"Bear the discomfort."

Supportez l'inconfort. C'est votre sacrifice à la Révolution. She remembered cold days, hungry nights. Hours in the bare training field, hurting with a dozen kinds of pain, body and mind. The Tuteurs said, "Bear the discomfort. It's your sacrifice to the Revolution."

In those days, Devoir had been a rock of strength for all of them, endlessly strong, endlessly patient. She missed him. This stranger was no substitute.

Paxton—most definitely he was Paxton, not Devoir—wrapped himself the whole length of her body, reading the tension of her muscle, ready to predict any attack before she made the first twitch. He was nicely graded force, intelligently applied. One must applaud.

But any man on earth can be persuaded. A judicious mixture of lies and truth could work wonders. "You're expecting great revelations. I'd rather you didn't."

He made a disbelieving exhalation between his teeth. That eloquent, familiar noise. That was Devoir's comment on so many of life's small happenings.

His grip loosened slightly. There was room to breathe.

She said, "I will spill out everything I know in your lap in the hope you will lose interest in me. Shall I tell you the man you seek favors a British gun? A Mortimer, I think. He sounds like an Englishman and dresses like one, but he's probably French. Police Secrète would be my guess. He knows too much about the Coach House for him to be anything else. He calls himself Smith."

"That's not his name."

"My well-trained intellect had already come to that conclusion. Do you know your coat is wet?"

"A little damp."

"You're soaked. And now I am soaked. We'll both catch pneumonia." She shifted in the close confinement of his coat wrapped around her, aware of the edge of a lapel, the round buttons on his waistcoat, the smooth cloth of his trousers. His chest barely shifted with his breath. Otherwise, he was motionless as a wall. She was the one restless against him.

She wasn't wearing enough clothes to protect her from too much knowledge of his body. She felt everything through the linen of her shift. Her breasts, sensitive with the cold, shocked when she rubbed against his coat. Old friendship, old memories rose up. She knew him too well. Every touch against him was just on the edge of being familiar and feeling safe.

There's too much silence. I have to say something. But she was awash in sensation. It was a hot river flowing under her skin.

I don't want this. But part of her did.

ifteen

A wise man comes to a negotiated truce with
his cock.

A BALDONI SAYING

PAX'S HANDS CLOSED CONVULSIVELY. NOT BY HIS will. Not by his intent. He couldn't help it.

Vérité explored the confines of the hold he had on her, being irritated, talkative, and close to naked. Where she wasn't soft skin, she was the slide of the thin cloth that barely wrapped her up. Her breasts grazed his chest, swift and startling. Her belly slipped across his. She was everything womanly—strength, softness, mystery. Since she was Vérité, she added a good dollop of deadly to the mixture.

He had a cockstand the size of a pine tree.

You don't think of her that way, a voice inside him said.

But he did.

She's not twelve anymore.

He wanted her in the most straightforward, simple, earthy way. Maybe it had started when they stood facing each other in the church. Maybe before that, when he watched her cross Braddy Square in a long, lithe sweep of brown cloak. Maybe when she became exquisitely lethal and attacked him.

Her hair brushed his face, tightly curled, glossy, feather soft, smelling of wood smoke and snuff. It grabbed him and pulled him into memory, into the years of the Coach House. In the stark dormitory under the rafters, two dozen starved, savage, brilliant children slept on mats on the floor, huddled together in the cold dark, sharing blankets. Vérité used to fit herself beside him, snuggled up to keep warm, her hair tickling his nose.

The way it was doing right now. If he chose, he could lower his head to that bedlam of curls and breathe her in. He could sort through the waves and semicircles with his lips. He could drop his hold on her arms and put his hands to her breasts and run his thumbs across her nipples, back and forth, learning them by touch, feeling a miraculous response in them.

He'd painted women clothed, naked, and at every stage in between. This was different. Vérité was more than an image made with pigments and brush. More than blended color and the fall of light. She was touch and smell and taste, breath, life, pulsing blood.

He'd seen the dark fuzz between her legs through the linen of her shift. The image filled his mind. He imagined stroking that soft kitten. Touching Vérité, pleasing her, enticing her. Persuading her down into the straw.

The unbearable sensuality of the image climbed out of his groin and plucked at every nerve in his body. His body tightened like iron bands.

That wasn't for him. Not with Vérité. Not with anyone.

She gave an impatient, determined shove at his chest. "I can't talk like this. You're just bullying me. I'm not trying to run." Her voice came up, muffled, from the region of his cravat. His coat was pushed aside where she twisted against him. Any minute now, she was going to brush up against his cock.

Then she did exactly that. She gave one startled jerk and went absolutely still. He felt her vibrate with her heartbeat.

She whispered, "Let me go. I said I'd tell you what you want to know."

If he didn't let go of her now, he might not be able to.

He opened his hands and stepped away and away, keeping an eye on her, till he felt the storeroom door at his back. He reached behind him to open it and let more light in.

She didn't try to hide herself. She kept her arms at her sides, her fists clenched. Her skin was pale as milk in this weak light, a sketch in pastel, laid down in thin shades of color. She looked scared and sneaky and determined. A warrior maiden, utterly indomitable in a shift that didn't cover half of her.

She was beautiful. Add that to the list of complications.

She was also cold. He'd dragged her out of her warm nest and left her shivering in the damp air.

He gathered up her cloak from the floor and tossed it to her across the space between them.

"Thank you." Gravely, she organized it in her hands, turned it right side out. "There are some complications it is better to ignore."

That was Vérité, being direct.

"I intend to," he said.

"Then we both shall. Why are we still alone? I keep expecting your friends to arrive in a great thumping vehemence. I don't hear them."

"They're waiting outside."

"So you came to take me alone. That was either a mistake or very subtle. I don't think you make many mistakes." She circled the cloak around her and was enveloped in darkness. Only her face showed and her feet, white and vulnerable against the wood floor. "This is better. Ask your questions."

She didn't look at where his cock was hidden under his coat, being obstreperous.

It wasn't that easy for him to ignore what his body demanded and demanded.

He thought, *You can't have her.* But the corridors of his mind were crowded with old choices, clamoring to be reconsidered. The rules for every other woman on earth didn't apply to Vérité.

I want her. That was the path to madness and beauty. *I could convince her. She knows what I am and I could still convince her.*

He knew he wasn't thinking clearly.

Deliberately, he ran his hand into his sleeve and found the old burn scar on his forearm. The skin was thin there. The surface of the scar felt nothing. Beneath that, there was no protection against pain. It lurked there, waiting for the slightest touch.

He dug his nails in deep, found pain, and held on to it till he was in a place clean of thought and feeling. Till the universe narrowed to a single cold, spiked, dark point.

When he stopped and pain receded he felt empty. It hadn't helped at all. Vérité was still beautiful and he still wanted her.

He said, "Tell me what you know about Smith."

Her eyes, wide and dark, didn't waver. "Almost nothing. There. That was simple."

"Tell me this nothing."

"What do you need to know? I can tell you that he tells lies the way other men breathe." Her fingers made a knobbly half-moon at the front of her cloak, keeping it closed around her. "I don't think I got ten words of truth out of his mouth the whole time I was chatting with him."

Vérité had seen to the root of the Merchant. He was a man constructed of lies. "What else?"

"He wears London tailoring, expensive tailoring. His gloves are French. I didn't notice that when I was talking to him, but I see them now, in my mind. London boots. London hat. Good, solid quality. Almost new. You could hunt down his bootmaker and his tailor if you have the time to fritter away. It won't lead anywhere."

"Probably not." The Merchant liked good clothing. One of his vanities.

"I will point out what you have already figured out. He set only one man to follow me through London, so he doesn't travel with multitudes."

The Merchant was a weaver of grand schemes, but schemes he could accomplish with a few like-minded fanatics. He'd have a small band with him, loyal to the death.

She was stalling for time, and he didn't have a lot of it. Doyle would get impatient after a while. He said, "Tell me more."

She reached up and rubbed her nose, buying another second or two. "I wish I could be sure you aren't working for the French."

"There are no guarantees. Tell me about Smith."

She didn't answer directly. "The problem is, we're both lying about some things. We're lies within lies within lies, you and me, like Chinese puzzle boxes. Boxes within boxes."

She shifted from one foot to the other. "You're loyal to somebody. That's your nature. Loyalty. I just wish I could figure out which side you're on."

She didn't know him as well as she thought, if she believed he was loyal. The last person on earth he'd been honest with was facing him right now, across this chilly storeroom.

In her bare feet. He said, "The floor's cold. Go stand on the straw over there."

"Excellent idea. Thank you." As she walked across the room, she ignored the pile of guns and knives and lethal instrumentation tucked away under the table. Of course that entirely convinced him she'd forgotten their existence. "My toes thank you as well."

They were pretty toes. He wouldn't think about kissing from one toe to the other. Sensitive toes and pink as seashells.

She sank to her knees in the straw, wriggled to sit cross-legged, and pulled the cloak around her, doing a good imitation of a hen settling its feathers on the nest. She picked an angle where the light fell on her face, demonstrating that she didn't have a thing to hide.

He hoped he hadn't missed a weapon or two, hidden in the straw. Not that Vérité needed weapons.

She was still talking to herself. "I will entertain the hypothesis that you turned English. If you were Police Secrète, I'd already be dead, killed in my sleep a minute ago. All this breathing I'm doing is the argument you're not French anymore."

He crossed the room till his boots touched straw. "I never was French. Let's go back to that meeting in the Moravian church."

"It has not wandered far from my thoughts. As I say, I came to be blackmailed. Aside from the surprise of meeting you, all went as expected. I met Smith, who threatened to uncover me to the Service. Treason was mentioned. And the slitting of throats. Also torture and imprisonment and the futility of panicked flight."

"Many and varied threats."

"One could almost believe you were there, eavesdropping. Yes. Many and varied. After the threats and dire predictions,"

she set her hands free of the cloak and gestured out a dire pre-
diction, "we discussed blackmail like civilized people."

He said, "Smith wants the Leyland codes."

He caught the split-second hitch in her breathing. "You've
deduced a great deal." She said it calmly enough. "Yes. I was
placed with the great codebreakers of the age, the Leylands,
my impractical, dithering old ladies. It's been an education
living with them in Brodemere, though not a terribly useful
one. Did you know I can now speak four dead languages?"

He caught something in her voice. A sadness around the
edges of the words. "You can't go back to them again."

"Do you think I don't know? The note I sent to Meeks
Street contains my goodbye." She held her hands out like
cups and turned them over with a dreadful finality. "That part
of my life is finished."

The Tuteurs at the Coach House used to rap her knuckles
with a cane when she talked with her hands. Un-English, they
called it. *Pas suffisamment anglais.* They never broke her of
the habit.

He said, "I'm sorry."

"There are inevitabilities." She turned her head away. "I was
always packed and ready to run. I had longer than I expected."

"Smith promised you could go back, I suppose."

"For a mere soupçon of a treason I can remain Camille Leyland, he says. The British Service will remain in blissful ignorance, he says. A single code and I'm free of him forever."

The cynicism in her voice was reassuring. "He lies."

"I wouldn't believe him if he recited the alphabet. He
wants the Mandarin Code."

He searched his memory. "Not one I know."

"At some point you may turn your attention to how Mr.
Smith knows about it. I suspect Military Intelligence, myself." She patted the straw next to her. "I wish you'd sit down."

"So you can attack me more conveniently?"

"There's no convenient way to attack you, Devoir." She
shook her head sharply. "No. I'm calling you Pax now. Pax,
you have friends outside. You have the British Service at your
disposal. I can't fight all of you. I'm trying to negotiate a
truce. For God's sake, sit down and talk to me."

"A truce?"

"Some semblance thereof. I'd give you promises of good behavior if it would do any good."

"I wouldn't believe them." But he folded himself down next to her, his shoulder beside her shoulder. Nothing could be more platonic and uninvolved than the two of them, side by side, not touching.

She said, "This is better. You aren't Devoir, but in a poor light I can almost fool myself into thinking you are."

It was just as well she couldn't see into his head. Right now he was imagining how easy it would be to slip that cloak away from her shoulders. In this light, her skin would glow white as the moon.

His mind took off like a runaway cart. Vividly, he saw himself pulling her down beside him in the straw. In his imagination, she was more than willing. He saw himself stroking her shift up and up her thigh, revealing the soft, dark tangle between her legs. Hidden at the center, carmine and rose madder.

Enough. He wasn't going to touch her.

He slowed his breathing. Wrenched his mind back from the brink of some madness. Curled his hands on his knees, relaxed and harmless.

He was in control. Always. That didn't change no matter how many damned, beautiful, half-naked old friends he sat next to. "Tell me about Mandarin."

Starkly, simply, she said, "Mandarin replaces Peacock."

That was a drench of cold water in the night.

It replaced Peacock. That made Mandarin the new code for private communication between Galba, Head of Service, and the twenty-four Heads of Section across Europe. Code for the most secret of secrets.

He swung around in the straw and knelt, confronting her. "You aren't carrying that around, are you?"

"Not being mad, no. Even Smith—who thinks I'm stupid as an owl—didn't expect me to arrive with Mandarin in my pocket. I'm to bring it to our next meeting." She gave one of her almost shrugs. "Where he intends to kill me. Or possibly kidnap and torture me. We will see."

She knew the importance of what she'd just said. She watched him, hiding the ferocity of her attention under half-closed lids.

The next meeting. This was why he'd followed her across London. This was why he'd come into Braid's Bookshop alone. She could tell him a time and place where the Merchant would be. "You have your own plans for that meeting," he said. "He won't realize that. He underestimates women. You, he wouldn't understand at all."

"I am opaque and mysterious. Tonight, however, you will see my forthright side. Ask your questions."

They were inches apart, with shadows and silence around them. Her pupils were huge. The chaos of her curls fell across her forehead and around her cheeks, making her look ridiculously young. Under her cloak, she pulled her knees to her chest, becoming small, emphasizing how slight she was. How unlikely it was she'd attack anybody. Nobody could be more harmless.

He said, "Why did you meet Smith in the church?"

"The blackmail letter—"

"—Would send you racing to the nearest port, not trotting tamely up to London. You've been ready to run for years."

He watched her decide what to say, thinking it over carefully. Vérité had been rash sometimes. Cami was older and wiser. She picked out a few words. "He offers me something I want."

"You must want it badly to come strolling under the nose of the Service." He let impatience into his voice. "What could be that important?"

"You don't need to know." A sharp shake of her head. "It's something the British Service would toss away without regard or interest."

"What?"

"Consider this instead." She raised her index finger. "He still wears French gloves. He hasn't equipped himself head to foot in English clothes. That argues he hasn't been in England long."

"Reasonable assumption."

Two fingers. "He wants Mandarin. Only Mandarin. He's

gone to remarkable effort to get it. Do you see what I'm saying?"

"One specific code implies one very specific need."

"One operation. Perhaps the Service can imagine what it is. I cannot." He heard the small clicking sound of Vérité tapping her teeth together. She used to do that when she was adding facts up, seeing patterns in them. Her mind had always fascinated him.

She held up a third finger. "I have one last conclusion about Mr. Smith. He's not only newly come to England, he's working on a tight budget of time. A strict, short allotment of days. Maybe even hours. He was fussy about when and where we meet. It's important. He was angry. I saw one flash of it in his eyes when I tried to change the place and day."

He knew that anger. No raised voice. No warning. It only showed in the eyes and in the curl of a lip. To a child, it had been terrifying. For an instant his flesh shrank under old pains. Memories of old beatings. The monster had possessed a heavy, self-righteous fist. "He gets angry easily."

"You know him well, then. I thought so, from your voice."

There were spies of skill and training. Spies of intuition. Cami had become both. She tilted her head to the side and studied him. "You hate him."

He didn't answer her.

For what the Merchant had done to his mother, he would die. Bare hands, gun, knife. It didn't matter so long as the Merchant lay dead on the ground at his feet. This time, he'd be sure the job was done right.

" 'It is better to be the rider of a great hatred than to be the one ridden.' My family says that and I share it with you. They have a great many wise sayings." She let her hand drop to her side. "The meeting place is the last important thing I know. The only secret I'm withholding. If I tell you where and when the meeting is, will you let me go free?"

"No."

"I see." She closed her eyes and put her forehead down on the cloak where it covered her knees. She sat that way, breathing quietly, her eyes closed. When she spoke again, it was in the most ordinary tones and her voice was muffled against her cloak. "If I don't walk down a certain street, on a certain day, at a certain hour, Smith will turn into smoke and blow away. You'll lose him."

"Tell me the meeting place."

She looked up to study the straw and floorboards in front of her. "My head is so full of secrets it rattles when I walk. Your Service will lock me up like the Crown Jewels. They'll send a substitute to that rendezvous or try to ambush Smith on the street. And it won't work." She met his eyes. "You have to let me go so I can meet Mr. Smith."

"So you can pursue some private exchange with him."

"If you let me go, you can make sure he dies. You, yourself. There will be no political bargaining that trades a French spy for an English one. No imprisonment he can escape from. No bribes that open doors for him. If you let me go, here and now, I will give you his death, into your own hands."

"You've found a way to tempt me." Wise little Vérité, with her pithy sayings, had most certainly grown up. She'd emerged as Cami, with a cynical, supremely clever understanding of her fellow man.

She said, "If you take me to Meeks Street, your superiors will tell the Foreign Office and Military Intelligence. The Police Secrète will know within a day. Military Intelligence is riddled with French spies. Maybe the Service is."

"I don't think so."

"I know two French spies placed right in the heart of the Service." She grinned suddenly, a wry, feral twist of the lips, and he saw the old Vérité again, inside this new Camille. "We were good, weren't we? Except, I never spied. I committed a thousand lies, in every way, right and left, but I swear I never passed code to the French."

"I believe you."

"It doesn't matter. I'll pay for all the spying I didn't do. If the Service doesn't kill me—regretfully and humanely, the way you'd put down a good dog—they'll keep me locked up till my secrets cool. Years and years. Unless the French dispose of me. Unless Military Intelligence gets me, which they will, because my crimes fall within their authority. Then I am dead." She reached her hand out from under the brown wool and laid it on his arm and watched it there, as if she wasn't sure what it might do. "Do you remember what we swore, all those years ago, in Paris, in the Coach House? The Oath of the Cachés?"

"Childish drama."

"Your idea. Your words."

"I was dramatic in those days."

When he'd come to the Coach House, the Cachés were preying on each other. The strong ones took food and blankets from the weak.

He'd put a stop to it. He wasn't the biggest. He wasn't even the best fighter. But he was used to getting hurt and he had nothing to lose. He fought with a ferocity none of them could match. In a week, he had most of them behind him. In a month, he had them all.

The Oath of the Cachés turned a dozen vicious, broken children into a wolf pack, faced outward against the world. "I made that up because we needed something to believe in. We needed magic."

She recited softly, "'To the last extremity, I will never betray another Caché. We are one blood.'" She said it in French, the way they'd said it, crouched in a circle on the floor of that cold attic dormitory.

He hadn't thought about the words in a long time.

She said, "So far as I know, none of us broke the oath. Will you give me to the British Service?"

"I have an oath there, too."

"I'm no danger to England. I swear it. I'll come to the meeting place with you. I'll be the bait in your trap. I'll give you Smith's head on a platter." Her fingers tightened. "But don't give me to the Service. Let me go. I'm asking for my life, Pax."

ixteen

The obligations of friendship are set in stone.

A BALDONI SAYING

SHE SAID, "I'M ASKING FOR MY LIFE, PAX."

She called him Pax, the name of the man he'd become.

He loosened the grip of her fingers but kept hold of her hand. When he turned it over, there were shadows in the hollow of her palm as if she held darkness there.

She was the one to speak. "We were friends once. I would have trusted you with my life. You would have trusted me."

"Not recently." But she'd picked the right argument. It was unsettling how well she understood him and he understood her. In the long, lying years in the Service, he'd missed having someone to talk to.

He'd already decided what he'd do.

On her palm the lines of fate and fortune were strongly marked, but imperceptible to his fingers. The tendons under the skin were invisible, but he could feel them with the lightest pressure. So many differences between seeing a woman and touching her.

Vérité knew what he'd been and what he was capable of. She'd seen him curled on the ground, shaking, exhausted, and beaten. She'd seen him commit murder. *She's the one woman I don't have to lie to.*

He didn't so much make a decision as accept an inevitability. He might have been waiting ten years to sit across from Vérité in this pile of straw, talking about friendship and trust, the two of them a bare inch from attacking each other. He knew what he was going to do. Some part of him had planned it before he climbed in the window of Braid's Bookshop. He said, "I can say anything to you."

"You're armed and I'm not. You can recite Dante in the original Italian if you want."

That made him smile. "Or I can do this." He kissed the hollow of her hand. Maybe it tickled.

She drew in a breath, sharply. He had her attention.

She said, "Pax?"

The inside of her wrist was filled with the pulse beat. He ran a touch up and down the side of her fingers, between one finger and the next, where it was soft. Sensitive, he thought. She'd be sensitive in lots of places.

"What are you doing?" She frowned down to where he explored her hand.

"This."

They knelt in the straw, facing. He set two fingers under her chin, lifted her attention up to him, and considered the woman who'd grown from the child Vérité. A tilted nose. Raphael would have put that nose on an impudent cherub. Dark eyes making some realizations. The curve of her cheek that held the sensuality of a Caravaggio.

She looked startled all the long moment he leaned to her and convinced her lips open with his and went into her mouth.

"And this," he said. He felt her surprise. Her lips were full of tiny shocks and a disbelief that held her still, and then the softening. He pursued that softening, demanded it, gave neither of them time to think or plan. He wasn't in the mood to trade calculation with her.

"Now this." He nuzzled across warm smoothness of cheek and forehead and the planes and valleys of her nose. Into the silly, frivolous ears lost in the ocean of her hair. He'd drawn the geography of a face a thousand times. This transformed shape, line, light and dark, all shades of color into texture. It overwhelmed thought.

He sucked her lower lip. Softness and slickness. She was . . . oh, she was remarkable. A thousand distinct complexities of her mouth came to life under his tongue. *This is the way it should feel.* Every discovery of shape and taste robbed his brain, tugged at his cock, wound the tension inside him tighter and tighter.

After the first surprise, she wasn't reluctant. She licked into his mouth. Nibbled at the corners of his lips where the skin went thin. Little teeth held his lips, anchoring an instant, stretching, pulling, letting go.

She grabbed her fingers into his jacket. Stretched upward to him. Kneeling, pressed against him. Her mouth became passion incarnate. She was heat and quick breathing and her arms went around him. Under the wool she wore, her shoulders were naked. He pushed the cloak away and put his hands on her and felt her thin bones shaking. Vérité, the great schemer who planned everything, wasn't scheming this.

He drew back. She was breathing fast, lips slack, eyes open but empty of thought.

He wondered if he looked like that. Stunned.

Awareness crept back into her gaze. He saw the absolute puzzlement, the amazement. Then she blinked and laughter welled up everywhere inside her till it spilled out into the dim air of the storeroom. Deep, husky laughing. That was pure and simple Vérité. Her unquenchable delight in all of creation.

She said, "Why did we do that?"

Because I wanted to. You wanted to. Because I've made my choice of betrayals. "You tell me."

"Are we seducing information out of each other?"

"If we had all night, maybe. But we don't. We'll do that next time." He got up to standing, clumsy about it. Aroused. Vulnerable to attack and knowing that he was. The brush of his trousers across his cock struck like hot lightning. "Think about this. Whatever I am, whatever I've done, you know I wouldn't kiss somebody I was about to turn over to the Service."

"I am . . . I'm bewildered."

"We both are. We'll learn to live with it." His muscles were dense and heavy, roaring with the need to hold her and get inside her. Looked like his days of being in charge of his body were over. Here and now, with this woman, when he couldn't afford to be distracted.

Just damn it. He reached his hand down to help her to her feet. It'd be nice to think she wasn't entirely steady inside her own body right now.

She stood still beside him, cloak discarded, probably cold again, looking suspicious, radiating sensuality and competence. Beautiful.

"I'm supposed to trust you," she said, "because you kissed me."

"It worked. Check through your private opinions when you have a spare moment. Right now . . ." Right now, get her covered. Get her skin out of sight. Get those breasts hidden where they didn't drive him mad.

Her clothes were shoved under the table, out of the way. He retrieved them and tossed them in her direction. He laid her weaponry out on the tabletop, bit by bit, in a line. "You get dressed. Put your arsenal back in its accustomed places. Then we sneak you past four of the best agents in the world, who are waiting outside, alert and suspicious. Don't use your arsenal on me and don't kill my friends."

She burrowed into her dress and emerged. "You left me behind five or six thoughts ago. You're letting me go. Why are you letting me go?"

"Because you're going to give me Mr. Smith's head on a platter. Remember?"

She ran the length of a stocking through her hand, straightening it. Then she stood on one leg and slipped it on. Her garters had fallen on the floor so she stooped to pick one up.

"Meet me tomorrow, at noon, outside Gunter's." He looked at the window. It was wholly dark. No sign of dawn. "Or maybe I mean today. About ten hours from now, anyway."

"I'm a fugitive in London, armed to the teeth, engaged in desperate enterprises, pursued by the British Service. You want me to eat ices with you at Gunter's, in Berkeley Square, in public, in the middle of London. Perhaps we will share a pot of chocolate. My bewilderment is unbounded."

"A woman can sit alone in a confectioner's. Same principle as a church or a public square, but with chocolate and little cakes. And you won't get rained on."

"I understand that much." She sounded annoyed.

"The Service won't be looking for you there. If I don't show up at Gunter's, go to the confectioner's on Barr Street at five and wait. Tomorrow, the same."

She wore the expression of someone thinking furiously. "Why would I do this?"

"Because you're alone, Cami. You have a plan and you need help with it. I know a great deal about Mr. Smith that you need to hear. I'll share it with you tomorrow, when you show up."

No expression on her face, but he knew he'd made his point.

He said, "And if you don't show up, there'll be broadsides on every street corner with your face on them."

She maneuvered into the second stocking and slowly tied the garter. "You're persuasive."

"But you'll come to meet me because you trust me."

"You're sure of that?"

"Cachés trust each other. They never betray each other. Somebody told me that recently. Let me do up the buttons in back. We're in a hurry."

Without hesitation, she turned and presented him the nape of her neck, the white triangle with her backbone running down into her shift, the curls above interlocked, every one with a tiny half-moon of light trapped in it. He wanted to close his teeth on her and bite down and hold her there like a tomcat on his tabby.

Her skin drew up and twitched where his fingers ran across, doing up the buttons. Seven buttons. He closed them from bottom to top, working his way upward. There were levels of hell that provided less torture.

He said, "You'll leave by the front. There are two agents keeping an eye there. The two dangerous ones are at the back."

"They'll know you let me go."

"Not right away. That's the last of the buttons. Pack up. We're in a hurry." He pulled his wrist knife.

She flinched, but he'd already flipped the blade and cut himself high on the shoulder.

She hissed, "Stop that."

The cloth of his coat and shirt split cleanly. He'd got to the skin underneath, making a fine, long cut that looked authentic.

"What the devil—"

"Distraction and explanation." He felt the pain and ignored it. He was bleeding down his sleeve. "More blood than I was aiming for."

She was already pulling a handkerchief from her pocket. "You should have asked me for my knife. Here. Clean your blade. No. I'll do it. You might leave blood on your cuffs and everybody'll know what you've done."

He let her clean his knife and slip it back in the sheath on his arm.

She said, "You're going to lie to your Service."

"I won't have to say much." There'd never been much chance of staying in the Service. Now there was none at all.

"Hold your arm out. Left arm. Turn it a bit." She picked one of her knives from the table and used it, delicately, to make two long slashes in the sleeve over his forearm. Obvious defensive wounds. "You're letting me go."

"This is supposed to make you trust me. Is it working?"

"Yes." She stashed her knife and shivered, a tremor that ran all through her. Fear and excitement. Maybe other emotions.

While Cami gathered up her extensive collection of weapons, he let himself bleed onto the floor of the storeroom, scuffling the drops around as if there'd been a fight. Then it was through the front room of the shop, walking in a red glow past a thousand books. Cami was behind him, filled with silent concentration. He said, "I'll stagger out the front door and keep my friends busy. You sneak out behind me." He smeared his blood on the doorknob. "Ready?"

"Ready." She patted from one lethal device to another, making certain they were all secure. "First the *mélange de tabac*. Now they'll think I've stabbed you. Your friends are going to chop me into dog meat."

"Make sure you don't meet them on your way out."

"There she goes," Doyle said.

"Where?" Hawker used a thread of whisper. "Ah. I see."

They shared the shelter cast by the bay window of a print shop, across the street, thirty paces from Braid's Bookshop. From this excellent vantage point they observed the drama Pax enacted with Stillwater and McAllister. Not the details, but the import and tenor of the conversation. While that was going on, a shadow flitted lone and surreptitious from the bookshop to the street and progressed from one pool of dark to the next.

"You going to take the lead on the follow or should I?" Hawk said.

Doyle said, "I'll rest here."

Small fractions of time passed. "Looks like Pax wants her to get away," Hawk said.

"Looks like."

"There's a number of good reasons we should interest ourselves in Cami Leyland." Hawker's eyes tracked their quarry, shadow to shadow to shadow. He was motionless himself.

Staying invisible was largely a matter of staying still. Pax, the leading practitioner of the art of invisibility, had taught him that.

Doyle nodded. "I can't recall when I've come across someone who needed dragging off to Meeks Street in a more firm and immediate fashion."

"I'd like a few minutes alone with her, discussing that incident with the snuff in his face."

"And there is the vexed matter of her knowing all our codes. There. Off she goes, with our Pax covering her retreat. Enough to make a man wonder what Mr. Paxton is up to, unless he's a French agent, of course, and engaged in treason."

"Oh, that's likely, that is."

They waited. They didn't see her slip around the corner. They just ticked off enough time to know she must have covered the requisite ground.

"And she is out of sight." In the dark, unseen, Doyle managed to convey the impression of a nod. "I'd say it's time to get our boy back to Meeks Street."

"Let's go do that."

eventeen

A man who says he tells no lies is a saint or a liar.

A BALDONI SAYING

PAX JERKED ALERT. AN INSTANT OF CONFUSION AND he knew where they were. He'd fallen half-asleep in the hackney.

"We're here." Doyle kicked the coach door wide open. "Everybody out." He swung from the door, hooked his boot into the back wheel spokes to climb down, and walked off to wake up the house, not seeming to hurry but somehow covering the ground fast.

"Back with us, I see." Hawker scrambled past him, out of the coach, onto the ground. He flipped down the stairs and stood, casually keeping an eye on things.

Streetlamps staked out a series of twenty-foot claims up and down Meeks Street. At Number Seven, they'd lit the lanterns at the door.

He was expected. The prodigal had returned. He didn't anticipate a fatted calf.

He steadied himself on the coach door getting down. The half hour of sleep had disoriented him. The paving stones seemed to catch at his feet all the way up the walk. The stairs were unfamiliar under his boots, the railing strange in his hand.

He was stupid with weariness, and he still had lies to tell.

The door opened before he got all the way up the stairs. Giles was fully dressed, holding a candle. He'd have slept on the couch in the study on a night like this, when agents were out working. He said, "Galba's in his office," and added, lower, to Hawker, "He's annoyed."

Giles stood back to let them in. Doyle went first and took the candle from Giles's hand to light one of the lamps lined up on the table.

"Well, that's coincidental. I'm annoyed, too." Hawk walked through the door. "Damn if it does anything but rain in this city. Give me the key and I'll lock the weather outside."

I'm wet. He knew that in some distant, unimportant way. He was stiff with cold and just on the edge of shivering. They all were.

He left his hat on the ugliest sideboard in Europe and followed Doyle from the parlor through the door into the hall. He'd been ready to face Galba a dozen hours ago and lay down all the truth he had in him. Now he was going to lie.

Giles locked the parlor door and caught up behind them in the hall. "Food? A bath? Do you want to change?"

He shook his head. "Just Galba."

Nobody who held the position of doorkeeper was a fool. Ten years ago it had been his work. Now it belonged to Giles. This wouldn't be the first time Giles opened the door in the middle of the night to an agent, tired and dirty with travel, who needed to talk to the Head of Service.

Probably the first time he'd let in a traitor.

Galba will send the boy away on errands if I have to be killed. They won't let Giles know about it till it's over.

He wondered how they'd get rid of the body. That was the kind of job they'd have given him, if he hadn't been the one getting killed.

Doyle said, "Tea. Food. A dry blanket. Bring them to the office." Giles took off running, headed for the kitchen. Doyle's eyes went to Hawk. "You go upstairs and change."

"Later," Hawk said.

Doyle said, "Now. That's an order." When Hawk just kept

walking, he added, "Galba's going to say the same thing. You're not part of everything that goes on at Meeks Street."

"I'm part of this," Hawker snapped.

"Laisse tomber." He didn't realize he'd spoken French till it was out of his mouth. "Let it rest." He must be staggeringly tired to make a mistake like that. Or maybe he just couldn't play a part anymore. Not with Doyle. Not with Galba. Not with Hawker. He went on in French, "I'm a spy. I'm a traitor." Hawk had to understand where they stood. "You can't help me. Step away."

"Oh, that's good advice. A veritable fount of wisdom is what you are. Having failed to get yourself killed in Paris, you come riding in from France like a bloody migrating sparrow to see if they'll do it here." Hawker spat that out. "You couldn't just walk over to the Police Secrète and let your erstwhile employers do the job, because they might not make you suffer enough. No. You come to let the Service do it. God, if I ever met such a pigheaded cully."

Doyle used his teeth on a fingertip to take his glove off. " 'Erstwhile.' I like that."

"My never-ceasing endeavor to expand my grasp of the King's English," Hawk said. "What'd you grow up speaking, Pax? French?"

"Danish." A relief to tell some truth. He was tired of lying to his friends . . . to the men who would have been his friends if he'd been honest.

Hawk said, "Not my first guess. We are in for some interesting revelations, aren't we?" And to Doyle, "Do you know what Galba's planning to do with him?"

"No idea." Doyle switched the lamp to his other hand to take off the right glove. "He'll do it whether you're there or not."

"So I should wander off and warm my feet by the fire while you and Galba gut him like a mackerel. I think not."

Doyle, imperturbable, stuffed the gloves into the pocket of his coat. "I won't kill him at headquarters, will I? Not when I got all London to be murderous in. I'll let you know what's decided. Trust me with this."

"I do. I'm coming in there anyway. You'd have every agent in England in that room if they could fit."

"Which would serve no purpose, except irritating Galba." Doyle's eyes slid toward the office of the Head of Service at the end of the hall. "I'll speak for you, Hawk."

His friends. He'd wondered where Doyle would stand in the matter of punishing the traitor in the British Service. Now he knew. Doyle and Hawker were going to fight for him. Madmen, both of them. Legendary madmen.

They'd picked the wrong battlefield. They didn't know how much he had to confess. They didn't know he had more lies to tell.

Doyle said, "What Pax has to say will be easier if you're not hearing it."

"Embarrassing revelations in the spy trade. We'll all be awkward together." Hawker hadn't even slowed down.

The mirror at the turn of the hall showed their approach, Doyle a little behind him, Hawker a little ahead. When they got there, his reflection pulled the knife from inside his coat and laid it on the table. His gun went beside that. Then the wrist knife from its sheath. The boot knife came next. The wire in his sleeve. A pointed steel needle eight inches long. Vérité wasn't the only one who walked around armed to the incisors.

Doyle caught the significance at once. Hawker, a second later. An agent goes armed. An enemy under parole doesn't carry weapons into the office of the head of the British Intelligence Service.

Doyle set his hand flat on the door of Galba's office. "You ready?"

The house was silent. If anyone was awake upstairs they were staying out of this. He was acutely aware of Galba, on the other side of the door, listening and waiting for him.

He caught a last glimpse of himself in the mirror. *This is what a man looks like when he walks out to face a firing squad.* "Let's get this over with." He pushed past Doyle into Galba's office.

ighteen

The width of a blade separates saying too little and saying too much.

A BALDONI SAYING

IT WAS AS HARD AS PAX HAD EXPECTED. HE WALKED through the door Doyle held open, took three paces into Galba's office, and faced the Head of Service. "I have a report to make. You have to hear me out."

Galba sat at his big desk, a wide-shouldered, massive man with a mane of white hair, wearing a red banyan and an expression of impatience. "Let us not be dramatic. I have always trusted your sense of what is important, Mr. Paxton. I doubt that has changed. Sit down."

"I'd rather stand."

Galba said, "I didn't ask what you'd rather do. I said, 'sit down.' You're bleeding."

"It's not important."

"That's something else I didn't ask you. Will," Galba turned to Doyle, "why is he in this state?"

"He fell asleep on the way here and he needed sleep more than he needed fixing a minor wound." Doyle divested himself of his greatcoat and looked around, deciding where to put it. He chose a straight-backed chair under the window. "It's barely leaking by now."

"Other injuries?"

"None."

"I need not have asked." Galba shifted mail from the center of his desk to the side. "Adrian. It appears you expect to join this conference. Why?"

Hawker had planted himself in the doorway. "I am an ornament to any conversation. And while I'm here, you won't dispose of him."

"It's too late at night to deal with this," Galba said. "Will?"

Doyle eased himself into the shabby, comfortable chair to the right of the desk and stretched his legs out long. "Let him stay."

Galba said, "Paxton?"

It took him a second to realize Galba was asking him whether Hawker should stay. "He's not necessary."

"Well, that's duly noted." Hawker walked past him and put his hand on the back of a chair, looking down at Galba.

Galba's eyes were chips of blue ice when he contemplated Hawker. "Let me sum this up for you, Adrian. Over the last four days, with considerable effort on everyone's part, we have closed your bullet wound and brought your fever under control. You were ordered not to leave the house until Luke pronounced you fit for duty. Was there some part of that order you didn't understand?"

Hawker shook his head. "No, sir. But I—"

"You not only disobeyed my direct orders, you did so at Mr. Paxton's behest. No one is better aware of Paxton's anomalous position than you, yet you went without hesitation when he called. Do you expect to be rewarded?"

Hawker never did have the sense to stay quiet. "You'd do the same."

Galba's eyes didn't waver. "That is the sole reason you're in less trouble than you deserve. Go. You may return here after—" He interrupted the objection before it was spoken. "After," he repeated, "you've changed clothing and dried your hair. I'm the one who will have to face Doyle's formidable Marguerite if you die of fever."

"I'm not going to die of—"

"Did I express a desire to discuss this? Go."

Hawker left without a word. The hall outside was silent,

but he was probably running upstairs, rather than lurking and eavesdropping.

"Mr. Paxton." Galba's eyes shifted to him. "I told you to sit down."

"I'll stand. It'll keep me awake."

Ten years ago, he'd faced Galba across this desk, with Doyle sitting in that same chair. He'd been fourteen and he'd told them he was Thomas Paxton. His life in the Service began with that lie. Tonight, in the same room, before the same men, that life ended. He'd come full circle.

Ironic. "I'm not Service. I don't have to obey orders."

"An interesting argument. I'd expected a somewhat more penitent return." Galba removed a packet of papers from the drawer of his desk. "This doesn't contain a resignation. Does Carruthers have it?"

"She didn't ask for one." His eyes no longer held a scorpion sting from the snuff mixture, but they felt gritty from tiredness. "I'll write it out when I'm done here."

Galba fanned the papers out across the blotter on his desk. "This is thorough."

His confession was in tight-written, neat script, inclusive, detailed, and damning. "Carruthers kept me locked up for a week, writing that and making copies. You could call it house arrest. Then she sent me to you."

Galba said, "I wondered if you'd show up here. Doyle said you would."

"Where else would I go?"

"You'd see it that way, of course." Galba selected a page. "Ten years ago, when you first came here, you stole secrets and turned them over to the French. Is that correct?"

"Yes."

Galba looked up. "Expand on that."

He fixed his eyes on a point in the bookcase behind Galba, on a red book next to a blue book next to another red book. "I was trained as a French spy in the Coach House in Paris. I came to Meeks Street pretending to be Thomas Paxton, son of James Paxton, British Service agent. You took me in. I used that position of trust to steal confidential information."

He'd written that in every copy of the confession. Now the

words clenched in his throat when he said them out loud. He had to tear every syllable loose from his gullet and guts. Strange that it came out emotionless and dry as dust.

"You stole the documents listed here." Galba slid a dozen pages to the center of his desk.

"I may have missed some. It's been a long time."

Doyle leaned back in his chair, closed his eyes, and clasped his hands behind his head. "Twenty-year-old naval deployments. Gossip from the Russian court. Receipts for hiring horses." Doyle snorted. "Vital secrets, that lot."

"I took old files from the basement. It's still treason. I've admitted everything." He swung back to face Galba. "This is more important. Today, I followed the woman who sent the coded note, to the church in Fetter Lane. I saw—"

Galba raised his hand and cut him off. "Is further action required between now and daylight?"

Nothing could be done, no questions asked, no searches made, in the middle of the night. "No."

"I have given you four agents and twelve hours to deal with that." He touched Cami's coded note where it waited on the side of the desk, still undecoded. "Do you need to return to the streets at this time?"

"Tomorrow. In daylight. I'll make sketches." Sketches of the Merchant. Not Cami. He didn't want them to find Cami in whatever refuge she'd run to this time. And he had to sleep. He was swaying on his feet . . . and dripping blood. He tightened his hold on his upper arm.

"Then we will set that aside for the moment," Galba leveled his hands on either side of the pile of papers that held his history, "and return to your deeds ten years ago. You admit that you met a Frenchman—your *surveillant*—over a period of five months and gave him various, largely worthless documents. You killed him," Galba consulted a page, "with a single stab wound under the sternum, on the morning of May fifth. You were fourteen."

He nodded. He'd written everything down. There was nothing else to say.

Doyle opened one eye. "That was the man they found in Swan Alley, a decade or so back. I wondered about it at the time. Nice, professional work if I remember correctly."

It hadn't been his first kill. "We were well trained."

"I'll give the French that," Doyle said. "They produce deadly fourteen-year-olds."

Galba turned a half dozen pages facedown and went onward. "After that, did you provide information to the French?"

"Never." He was expressionless. Anything on his face, any nuance of his voice, was there because he allowed it. It could be just another lie. When you lied as well as he did, even the truth was a calculation. "That was the end of it."

After he'd killed his *surveillant* he'd waited, month after month, for the Police Secrète to reach out from France and kill him. No one came. In the end, the Tuteurs had been the ones to die. When Robespierre fell, they fell with him. Their lines of command were broken. Their records burned. They took their secrets and the location of their Cachés to the guillotine.

Galba said, "Did you lie to me or to your other superiors in the British Intelligence Service?"

"I lied about who I was."

"Other than that." Galba was impassive.

"I spotted Cachés twice and didn't tell you." He swallowed again. "They'd gone English. I judged they were no threat."

"Other than that."

They'd come to tonight's lies and disloyalties, still ongoing. "An hour ago I had a Caché trapped, and I set her free. She's Camille Leyland, niece of *the* Leylands. But I need her loose in London." He shook his head, trying to clear it. Trying to say enough and not too much. "Don't bring her in."

"You will doubtless explain why, eventually." Galba continued, "Is there anything else you have done in the last ten years to harm British interests or the British Service? Any more lies I should know about?"

This room, this office of the head of the British Service with its untidy shelves and hundreds of files and reports, the violin case, the matched knife and sword that Galba had carried on assignment thirty years ago—this room held the center of his whole adult life. He'd made himself someone with a right to be here.

He closed his eyes. Galba and Doyle were both looking at him when he opened them again. "When I reported, I reported as if I were working for you. As if I were an agent. I didn't edit the truth."

"I never caught him at it, if he did." Doyle slid ink bottle and penholder to the side, clearing a space on the desk. "When Hawker's reporting, on the other hand, any resemblance to the facts is pure coincidence."

The dumbwaiter rumbled in the dining room, coming up from the kitchen. Giles would be here in a minute with tea.

He turned to the sound and felt the almost weightless burden he wore around his neck. Sometimes the small lies are the hardest to let go of.

The twine caught in his hair as he pulled it over his head. He'd put the ring under his clothes before he left Paris. He hadn't felt right, wearing it after he'd been found out.

He set the ring on the desk. It was solid, heavy gold, bearing a shield with two chevrons and three stars. He'd used it for sealing letters. Everybody in the Service knew it. He'd worn it on his little finger because it couldn't get past those bony knuckles of his.

Galba studied it soberly. "James Paxton's ring."

Say it. Just say it. "I took it off his hand. In Russia. When he was dead." He tasted smoke and death in his mouth again, remembering. The Merchant and his men had brought him to the dacha they'd burned down and the family they'd murdered. They made him bury the bodies and heap rocks on top, so he'd be convincing when he described the scene. They'd held him down and burned his arm. Then they pointed west and told him to walk to England. It had taken him six months. "I didn't kill him and I couldn't have stopped it. I'd send it to his family, but there isn't any."

Doyle said, "The Service is his family."

That was what Galba had said, ten years ago, to the boy who walked into Meeks Street claiming to be James Paxton's son. Galba had said, "Now the Service is your family."

Doyle leaned across the desk to pick up the twine. He let the ring hang a moment, turning. "We'll take charge of this." At the bookcase beside the hearth he took down a plain wood box, put the ring in, and closed the lid quietly. "He was a good man.

A good agent. We'll find a use for that signet someday and re-member him."

"He wouldn't begrudge it." Galba gathered the pages of the confession together and squared the edges. "We must now deal with this deplorable situation. You should have come to me, voluntarily, years ago. Did you really fear retribution for crimes committed when you were fourteen?"

"Hawker's still alive." Doyle settled back into his chair. "I'd call that better-than-average evidence the Service has vast tolerance."

"You have made serious errors in judgment, Mr. Paxton," Galba said.

A rattle of cups—that had to be deliberate—sounded out-side the door. Hawker carried in a tray with bread and ham, teapot and cups.

His arm ached. His eyes burned. But he couldn't let that pass. "I'm not Paxton."

Doyle snorted. "Like to know who you are, then."

"Do you consider yourself Dalgaard? After your mother?" Galba drew in the corners of his mouth. "According to these extensive self-revelations you've never lived as Niels Dal-gaard and your mother deserted you when you were nine. I doubt you want to answer to the ridiculous name 'Devoir.'"

"He could use MacIntosh. Or Ambleside. Dalrymple. Hig-gins. Widding-Smythe." Hawker set the tray in the space cleared on the desk. "Or Jones. There's something reassuring about a Jones." He lifted the lid off the pot and looked in.

"Or he could stop trying my patience." Galba found an empty folder in a pile behind him. "You are not the first man to take a *nom d'espion* as his own. You have been Thomas Paxton all your adult life. Continue. I have better things to do than cater to your sudden qualms of conscience." Galba dropped the folder on his desk. "As you seem to have been working for the British Service for the last ten years, you are still my agent and under my orders. You will therefore sit down."

The moment stunned him. Tore all his words away. Left him unable to think. He sat abruptly in the straight-backed chair beside the desk.

Hawker put a cup of tea on the desk in front of him. "Drink this, since I went to the trouble of carrying it in. Not my job, I will just mention."

The tea was warm, full of milk, and sugared till it was syrup. He took a sip, then drank the rest in one long swallow.

"For the moment, Adrian, your job is to be silent. Now . . ." Galba set his hands together. "Mr. Paxton, you do not fail in your assessment of the important. Tell me what we've been chasing across London."

He was tired so it came out simple and blunt. "The Merchant is alive."

ineteen

*A man who looks only at his goal is blind in
one eye.*

A BALDONI SAYING

GALBA PICKED UP THE TEAPOT AND WEIGHED IT
in his hand. "Do you want the last of this?"

"None for me. I'm sloshing with tea."

"Something stronger?" Galba tipped the teapot toward the
bottle of twenty-year-old brandy that inserted itself into a row
of books. A general in Napoleon's army repaid an old debt by
keeping Galba supplied.

"I wouldn't do it justice. I'm tired and I'm headed home to
Maggie." A warm thought on a cold night. Doyle folded his
hands across his waistcoat and leaned back, savoring it.
"There's a couple hours of night left. I'll pluck my wife out of
bed and we'll watch the sun come up."

"I envy you, Will. You spend too much time away from
home. Go to her." Galba gathered papers together—Pax's
confession, Carruthers's letter, Pax's service record, the
coded note that had set everything off, still undecoded—and
slid them into a file with a red stripe on the lip. "This mess
will still be here in the morning."

"I'll put people on the street in Soho as soon as Pax makes
us some sketches." Doyle scratched the fake scar that ran the

length of his cheek. It didn't come off in the rain, but it itched. "I'll pull in everybody who's worked Paris. If the Merchant is using any of his old crew, one of our men might spot them."

"Keep Paxton away. If he knows the Merchant, the Merchant knows him." Galba frowned at the chair Pax had been sitting in. "I applaud Mr. Paxton's attention to detail, but he's left his blood in my office."

"And most likely a trail of it down the hall. Any slice he cuts in himself is going to bleed for a while. He has a genius for authenticity."

"One of many reasons he is supremely useful to the Service. I will not lose Paxton as an agent because he was a French agent first." Galba sat scowling a moment longer. Abruptly he slapped his hands flat on the desk, scraped the carved oak chair back, and levered himself up. "This is a damnable business."

"Couldn't agree with you more."

"He allowed a Caché to walk out of a trap he set for her."

"Using some considerable ingenuity to do it." Doyle stretched his legs out comfortably. "I'll just mention that I'm the one who let her wriggle out of the bookshop tonight."

"I realize that."

"I backed Pax's instincts."

"Those instincts have him lying to us about that woman." Galba swept the Paxton file into the top drawer of the desk and locked it with a key from the ring in his pocket.

"An exercise in futility, locking things in this house," Doyle said.

"Adrian stays out of my office. We have an agreement, which he has not yet breached." When Galba crossed the room to open the door to his office, no one lurked in the hall.

"Hawker's upstairs, getting Pax bandaged." Doyle pushed himself to his feet and followed Galba into the hall.

"I don't have agents. I have a menagerie." Galba took the lantern from the table outside his office, frowning at Pax's gun and knives, still piled there. "A French menagerie."

"Technically, Pax is Danish. Hawker's Cockney to his fiendish core, so that's one Englishman. Fletcher claims to be the descendant of Cornish kings. Ladislaus—"

"They planted a spy on me, Will, and I didn't see it."

"I had him underfoot for years and didn't catch it. Makes me look a right fool. If I had any particular faith in my own judgment, Pax would have pulled the bung on it tonight."

Side by side, down the hallway, they passed old maps on the walls and the bureau at the front that held the gloves and hats of everybody currently sleeping in Meeks Street.

Doyle began to pick his scar off. It left a thin, shiny line where the glue had held it. "I sent him on missions when he was sixteen. Dogged, cold as ice, ingenious, utterly fearless. I could walk off and worry about something else, knowing he was on the job. The perfect agent."

"We have arrived at the end of that fiction," Galba said testily. He took the stairs upward.

Doyle followed. "I should have asked myself why that boy came to us knowing how to kill. That's not what James Paxton would teach his son." The false scar came off as a thin skin, pale and stretchy. He rolled it between his fingers, making tacky little balls he dropped into the pocket of his coat.

Removing the scar was getting out of disguise. For him it was becoming the man who'd go home to Maggie and the kids.

The second-floor hallway was cool silence with a single candle left burning in a glass chimney at the end. One bedroom showed a bright strip under the shut door and there were low voices inside. No words leaked through, but the tones were clear. Hawker exasperated. Pax determined.

Galba didn't pause there. He waited till he was halfway up the next flight of stairs to say, "Paxton knows where the Caché woman is, or how to find her. He knows more about the Merchant than he's saying."

"We're all of us founts of mystery and intrigue when you delve deep enough." The last of the scar was off his face. Doyle rubbed the rough place it left behind. "One of the things he's not saying is that he plans to kill the man. When Pax was hurt, he sent Hawk to kill the Merchant. Not follow or capture. Kill."

"It is not his decision to make. I'll give orders tomorrow."

"You'll give orders. Well, that's the problem solved, then."

The third-floor hall was another dim, silent corridor, this one hung with lithographs from a manual on the art of the duello. Swordsmen saluted, lunged, parried, riposted. Agents on long-term assignment to London slept here. They were asleep now, or at least staying quiet as men walked past.

The door to the attic was halfway down the hall. Galba pulled up the simple latch and the attic stairs were revealed, steep, narrow, and utterly black. A draft of chilly air hit their faces.

"Either Pax is a Service agent taking my orders or he doesn't belong under this roof." Galba lifted the lantern as he climbed. "I have uses for the Merchant alive. Alive, I can question him. I can trade him to the Austrians. I can give him to Military Intelligence and buy future cooperation. Dead, he's just an embarrassing corpse. I will not have an agent who kills without orders. That is intolerable."

"He hasn't done it yet." Doyle waited till they reached the top of the stairs, beyond range of anyone's ears, to say the rest. "We didn't do well by the boy, putting him to the work we did."

"We have dirty work to do." Galba's face was set in a grim expression. "Paxton seemed strong enough."

"He was nineteen when he began."

"It wasn't his first death."

"It was too many kills," Doyle said. "Twenty-six in Piedmont and Tuscany. Five more in France, for Carruthers. Hawker said those assignments were tearing at Pax's entrails like mythical Greek vultures. I should have stopped it long since."

"If an assassin doesn't have bad dreams, we've created a monster. We've both done that work, Will."

"They can be very bad dreams," Doyle said.

"We learned to live with them. Paxton will, too."

The floor creaked underfoot as they walked the narrow hall of the attic. Light from the lantern reached out to hit odd angles of ceiling beam and door frame.

They walked through the long single storeroom that ran the length of the front of the house. Smaller rooms lined up on the other side. Here, everywhere, the Service kept weapons and an eclectic array of clothing and traveling gear. All the bits and bobs a man would keep in his pocket or carry in his valise. The accouterment of a spy.

"I don't have to tell you why I kept him in place too long."
Galba frowned his way past stores of clothing made in Paris
or southern France or Austria. "We sent an assassin to Piedmont and ended up with an Italian folk hero. I ordered a few
strategic deaths among the French officers and Paxton attracts
a band of Merry Men and rouses up the countryside against
Napoleon. Even now, he could whistle a hundred men out of
farmhouses from Genoa to Switzerland."

"Don't know where he learned to run a secret organiza-
tion, but he has a genius for it." Doyle smiled. "We'll use that.
I can always find killers."

"I agree." Galba added tartly, "Paxton may celebrate re-
tirement from the trade of assassin by not killing the Merchant."

They'd come to a door at the end of the passageway, a
sturdy door with a grille in it. It looked like it would lead to a
prison, and it did. Meeks Street had played host to many un-
willing guests.

Doyle said, "Is this what you plan for the cuckoo in the
Leyland nest? Put her here?"

Galba fingered the cold iron of the key before he put it in
the lock. "She's a French spy, Will."

"So is Pax."

"Pax is ours." The lock was noisy and stiff. The lantern
tossed shadows around while Galba turned the key. "He's
been ours since he walked into my office ten years ago,
starved down to a skeleton, with burns festering on his arm.
We made him what he is. You made him what he is."

"Right now, he's lying up one side and down the other to
protect the woman. He doesn't trust us with her. And he's
right."

"I am not the archfiend."

"How hard are you going to question her? Can you promise
we won't turn her over to Military Intelligence? Or let the
Foreign Office put her on trial?"

"Not unless I have no other choice whatsoever." Galba
sounded impatient. "I intend to have other choices."

The prison cell was painted stark white and held a bed,
dresser, basin and pitcher, desk, and chair. When they had

prisoners, they hung a lantern outside the grille of the door and built a fire on the hearth in the main attic.

Doyle said quietly, "This is what Pax is afraid of."

"There are worse fates for a spy than comfortable detention." Galba pushed the door all the way open and brought the lantern inside. The light revealed more detail but didn't make the space less spartan. "I'll bring some books up. Paper. Quills."

"Oh, that'll be a comfort to her."

"Cervantes wrote *Don Quixote* in prison. Maybe she has a book in her. I'll have George put on fresh sheets and light a fire. It'll take a day to get the chill out of the plaster."

Doyle ran his fingers into the grille in the door. "Is this what we're planning? Because I'll tell you right now, it's a bad idea."

"We are prepared for all eventualities." Galba studied the room, one side to the other, his eyes unrevealing. "I like this no better than you do."

"Are you prepared for Pax to break her out of here?"

Galba frowned. "It is more than fellow Cachés, bound by oath, then. Is he *épris*? Has she seduced him? He's not indifferent to women, even if he lives like a monk."

"He's not thinking of her as a friend who happens to have breasts. And it's past time he made a fool of himself in that particular way." Doyle checked the hinges of the door into the white cell. Checked the lock. "When he came out of the bookshop, he looked like a man who's been with a woman."

"That is a complicating factor," Galba muttered.

Doyle gave the lock one final shake and stepped back. "I hate dealing with Cachés in every particular and all directions."

"It's just as well you let her leave the bookshop. It delays the moment Paxton is forced to choose between the Service and the woman."

"When he does, we've destroyed him," Doyle said. "Or we've lost him for good."

Twenty

London-living Lazarus,
The Dead Man risen and risen again,
Your hand in an L just like this
Brings you to his trusted men.
If you want to see his face
The second sign brings you to his place
First finger up, three fingers down,
The thumb just touches the littlest one.

A BALDONI CHILDREN'S RHYME

NO MAN, AS JOHN DONNE POINTS OUT, IS AN ISLAND, but some of them are very slender peninsulas. Cami had felt like a stretched and thin extension of the great continent of mankind since she'd cut herself off from the Fluffy Aunts to adventure upon the lonely business of rescue and, quite possibly, murder. Maybe that was why Paxton could wrap her so quickly in so many strands of old friendship and new obligation. Because she had made herself so alone.

How would she free herself of him when this was over?

She walked, listening for any sound behind her. The last small mists of the drizzle had disappeared an hour ago. Here and there a piece of the night sky opened up above the city, holding a moon. Sometimes she could have counted the bricks in the wall she was passing and the moon reflected in every pane of glass. Sometimes the details were frankly obscure.

She felt vulnerable under the sky in this huge, ugly city, driven from her bookshop lair like a fox from its earth. Predators grow fat on animals turned out of their accustomed places. London was full of predators.

A little wind pushed at her back like an encouraging kitten.

She should be safe enough. Men who wanted to hurt and terrify women would take their custom to Seven Dials and amuse themselves with impunity among a rich selection of prostitutes. The tethered lambs under the streetlamps were her best assurance of safety. And she was close to Bow Street. Men didn't like to cudgel and rob right on the doorstep of the magistrate's office. Really, she was as safe as any woman out on the night streets of London could expect to be.

Besides, she was armed. Extensively so.

She watched the night alertly and wondered what to do about Pax.

Because of Pax, she was damp, weary, and free, instead of dry, warm, and imprisoned. He'd lied to his friends for her. He'd stabbed himself in that coldly accurate way and used his blood to paint more lies inside that bookshop. He'd bled for her. She might have fallen into the middle of an Elizabethan stage drama.

Now she owed a blood debt and must find a way to repay it. What could be more traditional? More Baldoni?

Maybe Englishwomen didn't think that way, but the women of Tuscany did. In all the years that lay between this night in London and her Italian childhood she had never become anything else but Baldoni.

Pax seemed to have become as Italian as she was. He hunted this Mr. Smith, this blackmailer, with a determination like cold iron. Hated with the poignancy of needles of ice. Pursued with the ferocity of Nemesis. Whatever this Mr. Smith had done, Pax would avenge. The Baldoni understood vengeance.

She took a left turn and a right, avoiding men not yet in sight who did not sound entirely sober. Carriages rolled past, taking the fashionable home after the ball, after the opera, after a light, select supper, after the assignation with a secret lover. A more prosaic wagon clanked along a side street, heading the same direction she was, but slower.

Blackmore Street crossed Drury Lane. Ahead of her, two women carried heavy baskets and chatted companionably. She was getting close to the market. To the north, not close, a night watchman woke everybody up, telling them it was three o'clock on a cloudy Saturday morning. "All's well," he said.

All was well. The Fluffy Aunts slept safe in their flowered bedrooms in the cottage in Brodemere. In a day or two, when Meeks Street sent word, they'd learn what had become of her. They might even be glad the impostor was out of their house. With luck, their niece, their blood kin, would be under their roof in a week or two. That would balance the scales.

Nothing is more important than family. No one knows this better than the woman who has none.

Avoiding chummy little knots of gentlemen strolling from ballroom to brothel, she came at last, by roundabout ways, to Covent Garden.

At three in the morning London's great market buzzed like a hive of bees. Yellow light licked faces bent over the fires lit on the cobblestones. Yellow lanterns hung from the poles that lifted the awnings over the stalls. Under the smell of greenery and apples, rotten vegetables and garden dirt, the night smelled of those oil lamps. There were less pleasant smells, too, though some of the worst had been washed away by the rain.

It was yesterday's rain now. She'd walked her way into to-morrow, a day that inherited a number of old problems and would grow a fine crop of new.

She would meet Paxton today at noon in the square outside Gunter's. Whenever she tried to think about the logical reasons for doing this, she thought instead about long fingers gentle on her face, persuading her mouth upward for the glide of his tongue into her. Thought of the brush of white hair on her cheeks, smooth as silk. He'd kissed her with the care and attention usually given to the creation of a work of art. Kissed her as if he had all the time in the world. As if that were the most important event of this sharp-edged and dangerous night.

That was not a foolish reason to trust him. Men reveal themselves at such moments.

Besides, if she didn't meet Pax at noon, he'd tear London apart looking for her. And he might be useful. Perhaps his plans to destroy Mr. Smith and hers to rescue the niece of the Fluffy Aunts could bump along comfortably, side by side, on the same road.

She entered the market and almost immediately nipped back to let a handcart roll past. Thus she did not get knocked to the stones, bruised and dirty. It was a reminder that "Any worthwhile enterprise is filled with hazard." She heard that wisdom inside her head in Tuscan. The English would perhaps say, "Nothing ventured, nothing gained," but that lacked the flavor of the Italian.

The more substantial stalls on the far side of Covent Garden were closed and shuttered, but the long tables in the middle of the square were busy. Men and women were purposeful there, unloading baskets from wagons, stacking beets and apples. She made her way through the crowd, jostled by wicker baskets, pushed aside with a brusque, "Watch it, girl," from men who rigged their awnings in the dark, ready to shelter vegetables from a sun that wouldn't come up for another two hours.

She'd come to Covent Garden to send a message and required a particular sort of messenger to carry it. Not the hackney driver yawning and scratching on his seat behind the horses, there at the door of a brothel. Not that laborer hunched under a sackful of turnips. Not the farmer with a load of cabbage. Her man or woman belonged to the market itself.

The water pump was across the square, just south of the church, neatly placed in front of the watch house. She pumped and caught the stream in her hands, so cold it made her hands numb. It was a shock when she burrowed into it and washed face, neck, ears, and up and down both arms. It was ice cold to drink. Good water, tasting of iron.

Nearby, two girls sat cross-legged on the curb, skirts drawn up over their knees, washing watercress in a bucket. Another, this one older, tied the leaves into plump, practiced little bundles and arranged them in rows in the flat basket at her side.

Children of the market. Natives of this dangerous jungle, sweet-faced and hard-eyed. They'd know.

She wandered casually toward them, not meeting eyes but

just looking out over the square. She held her hand, thumb and index finger making an *L*, in the shadow of her cloak so that only those three girls could see. She said, "I want to buy a service," as if she were asking about green beans. The words had been the unvarying formula of request for more years than anyone could count.

The *L* was for *Lazarus*. Magistrates and bailiffs enforced the law of the land elsewhere. In Covent Garden the King of Thieves ruled. Through the rookeries of St. Giles, along the docks of Wapping, even in considerably more respectable places, no barrow wheeled, no booth hawked its wares, no prostitute inveigled a customer into her room upstairs without paying a pence to Lazarus. To the ruler of London's own horrific underworld. He was threat and brutality and a kind of rough justice.

One watercress girl looked at another. Eyes shifted to an old woman twenty paces away.

That was all the direction needed, a nod being as good as a wink.

The watch house was surrounded by a low wall and iron railings with spikes on top. It was well lanterned down the walk to the door and inside the windows. At this hour it was quiet as the grave. Nothing less than riot would open that door and call out the watch.

She'd send her message to Lazarus within spitting distance of the watch station. Her world was compounded of irony and discomfort this fine morning.

The woman sat on the little wall, wearing shabby black, her back to the rails and the light. She held a basket of apples in her lap. This time the signal of introduction brought no reaction, except that the woman took an apple out of her basket and began to polish it on her skirt. That went on for perhaps half an apple before she said, "Wotcher want?"

"I need to buy a service. Can you send the message?"

"Mebbe."

So. She'd found the first link in the chain, one of the legion of street sellers, pickpockets, peddlers, and beggars who occupied the fringes of Lazarus's realm.

"Wot service?" The woman spat on the apple, regarded it

dispassionately, and polished some more. Not a woman spendthrift with her words, the apple seller.

"You don't need to know." She gave another hand sign, then, this one old and powerful. Baldoni are taught such secrets in the cradle. "Can you pass a message to a man who understands that?"

Can I even use that sign? Is it forbidden to someone running from a sworn vendetta?

The woman finished the fine polishing of the apple, set it in a basket, and chose the next. "Might be I could. Might not." Her expression was compounded of slyness and greed.

"If you have work more important than carrying my message . . ." She held up a shilling. "I'll find another messenger and leave you in peace."

"I'll send it. I'll send it. Didn't say I wouldn't." The apple seller made a grab for the coin.

The shilling stayed in hand. "Here's my message. 'The old man in the red castle asks a favor.' "

" 'Man in a castle arsks a favor.' "

" 'The old man in the red castle.' Then say, 'I need four trustworthy and discreet men for three days.' "

"Keep going on, don'cha? I ain't the bloody post office."

"Twenty words." Because she was tired, her mind started turning the words into the simplest of substitution ciphers . . . *URW HGCKN* . . . before she stopped herself. "That's not heavy as messages go. Say it back to me."

"You want four men and they keep their gob shut."

"That's not the message."

The apple seller fingered across the basket, apple to apple, with a surprisingly delicate touch and repeated the message, word for word, without flaw or hesitation, catching the original accent and intonation. "I don't forgit things." She smiled sarcastically. "And I don't go to that part of town in the dark. After it gits light, then I'll carry it."

"Good enough." She flipped the coin and watched it disappear into layers of rags. "Where can I sit for three or four hours, out of sight?"

The Coach House taught many lessons. Nobody died of being tired was one. One can sleep sitting up was another.

Even three hours of sleep would improve this coming day no end.

The rags rearranged themselves. Another apple came out of the basket to be shined against the skirt. "I'm not a bloody inn. Try the man what sells beets and carrots up that way. Fowler, his name is."

"Where should I wait for a reply? And how long?"

"Dunno. Go where you please. They'll find you when they wants you."

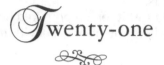

Twenty-one

Know what a man lies about and you know the man.

A BALDONI SAYING

"SO THAT'S THE MERCHANT."

"A reasonable likeness." Pax smudged white into the black line of the underjaw, pulling three dimensions out of the shadow. Then thin charcoal to define the chin. This was the seventh copy he'd made. He was fast now, sketching.

Hawker said, "I've seen him."

"You chased him from the Moravian church."

"Not that. I know the face from somewhere."

The finished drawings were spread out over the tables, still damp from the fixative. Hawk studied the copies, then helped himself to one of the quills and stroked it back and forth between his fingers, pacing fireplace to window and back, crossing between two of the big, shabby leather chairs. Finally he stopped at the window and looked out, keeping well back so he couldn't be seen from the street. "It'll come to me."

"France, maybe."

Hawker shook his head. "Somewhere. He doesn't look like a Frenchman anyhow."

White chalk brought the bridge of the nose out. "He passed for French sometimes." Making copies of a face meant catching the little tricks of the likeness again and again. Not easy. "I don't know where he came from. He told different stories."

"Handsome fellow." Hawk came to stand behind him and watch him work, not blocking his light.

"People find him charming. He uses that." He'd fought the temptation to reveal the monster. He'd forced himself to set down only the surface of the man. The shape of the eyebrows, the width of the nostrils. The face he drew was just a face, absent arrogance and cold disdain. Absent the evil.

He sharpened his lead and etched thin pencil lines at eye and mouth. Added a touch of white to the eyelids to show the first puffiness. He hadn't seen these details in that glimpse in the Moravian church. This was his guess of how age had changed a monster.

Done. Anything else was just playing with it. With chalks, you had to know when to stop.

Hawk was right. This was a pleasant face. The Merchant smiled and smiled and was a villain. *My mother wasn't the only woman he destroyed.*

Hawk leaned next to him, across the back of the chair. "You're damn good. He almost breathes." With one finger, not touching the surface of the paper, he circled the calm eyes, the mouth with the almost smile on it. "You think this Caché woman of yours finds him charming?"

"Not in the least."

"She's working for him," Hawk said.

"If I thought that, I wouldn't have let her get away."

"Or else you would have." Hawker shrugged. "We make mistakes about women."

"I don't."

"You haven't before. Doesn't mean you won't now." Hawk shifted to view the sketch from a different angle. "The whole of the city of London's full of women harmless and beautiful as kittens and you consort with Death's Handmaiden."

Laughter welled up out of his chest, surprising him. "Cami's not a kitten, thank God."

"More like . . ." Hawker frowned. "What was the name of that Greek chit who chased men down and drank their blood? Head of a woman, body of a snake. If Doyle weren't downstairs organizing a search of Soho he'd provide the Classical allusion."

"I cut that knife wound on myself. That's not her work."

"You are a man of deep mendacity and I already figured it out about the knife cut."

Of course Hawk had known. Doyle probably did, too. "That's only one of the lies I'm telling. Hawk, I'm going to . . ." He couldn't finish that. "I'm in trouble with the Service already and it's going to get worse. You will keep out of it."

"I doubt that, somehow. It's a novel experience, trying to keep you out of trouble instead of the other way around. You've annoyed Galba in ways even I don't attempt. Hard to believe you're being stupid over a woman. I thought you were an island of sanity in a sea of rutting dogs. You aren't going to let go of her, are you?"

Nobody like Hawker for the delicate approach. "I'm using her to—"

"She's using you. And you're not going to see that till it's too late."

"We're using each other." But it didn't feel like that. Nothing calculated had happened between them. Nothing wise and thin and careful. He'd swear she was no more able to stop what flared between them than he was.

He dropped the last chalks into the box and closed the lid.

Hawker went back to the window and pushed the curtain aside half an inch. "I was barely out of bed this morning when I got my orders. I'm supposed to see you don't kill the Merchant when we get close to him. That and some other minor injunctions." Hawk's attention remained fixed on Meeks Street. "I am to be the voice of reason. I told Doyle that was not my forte."

"That must have amazed him."

"I'm supposed to follow you today when you leave, sticking to your trail through the byways and alleys of London. The theory is, you won't do anything suicidally stupid if I'm there to be a good influence. Yes, I thought you'd find a chuckle in that."

That was the deft hand of Doyle, ordering Hawker to do what he'd do anyway. Doyle sent a flanking column of artillery and the light infantry, when he sent Hawker after him.

He wiped his hands on the damp cloth, getting the last of the charcoal off, rolled his cuffs down, and buttoned them. He was stiff from sitting so long. He stood and linked his fingers and stretched.

A horse stopped outside the house. There was a low murmur of voices on the steps. Visitors.

"He's back." Hawker's voice held relief and amusement in the two words. "Grey. And he's brought his French spy with him, tra la. Just what we need, more French spies about the place."

Grey, Hawker, and Doyle. All the men from that last mission were home now. "They were worried about you three, in Paris. When I left, they weren't sure whether any of you were going to make it to England." That was one last man to face and admit treason to. Grey, Head of Section for Britain. The man he'd worked for these last six years.

"Grey's dallied and been lackadaisical in returning from France, for which no one shall blame him, considering the company he keeps." Even before knocking sounded below, Hawk was away from the window and out the door of the study. At the top of the stairs he stopped short and held his arm out to block the path. "Wait."

They stood overlooking the hall. Below, Giles came at a run and unlocked the door to the front parlor. A minute later, Grey came through, grimly determined, pushing a young, dark-haired girl ahead of him, protesting, lovely and panicked and fiercely courageous. The two passed without looking up, headed for the back of the house, toward Galba's office.

"We got her away," Hawker said under his breath. "And she has not given him the slip, despite having some skill in that activity. They're safe. Both of them. Sometimes we get lucky."

"Who is she?"

"Not one of your Cachés, so you don't need to fabricate complicated lies for her. How nice to deal with French spies who aren't Cachés." Hawker spun on his heel and strode back down the hall, stripping off his coat as he went. "I have to get down there and see she isn't bullied. The shirt's good enough, but I need a different waistcoat. A different coat, too. I need clothes." He swung into the second-floor staircase and took the steps two at a time.

"Hawk, if there were ever a man not in need of clothes—" He caught the coat Hawk threw at him from the top of the stairs.

"My baggage is strewn around the German countryside. Long story. That was my eventful July. I barely touched foot in England before they sent me to Paris. Then I escaped France with the clothes on my back, which were not improved by immersion in seawater, thank you very much. I've been borrowing from Giles, who dresses like a schoolboy."

"He is a schoolboy."

"No excuse. You, however, left a trunk of clothes up in the attic, in the slops chest. I recall one waistcoat and jacket. It's not one of your usual shades of mud color, and it's well cut."

"I was pretending to be a very bad artist. Hawk, I hate to be the one to tell you this—"

"But they won't fit?" Hawker turned back and grinned. For about ten seconds he looked his age. "They're clothes from before you got so unnecessarily tall. Pax—" He stopped, hand on the newel post.

"What?"

Hawker's face didn't change at all. "I'll be five minutes, getting into a waistcoat. Then I'll go to Galba's office. No telling how long I'll be there. Plenty of time for you to just walk out of here."

"You're determined to get yourself into trouble, aren't you?"

"I think of it as my area of expertise."

If Cami goes to the Merchant alone, he'll kill her. The Merchant didn't leave witnesses alive behind him.

He stared at the wall for a minute, seeing the exact color, the tiny imperfections in the plasterwork, the hard, unbreakable reality of it. There was no way out of this choice he had to make. He said, "I'll be in Berkeley Square at noon, meeting Cami. Follow her when she leaves. If I'm not there to keep her alive, it's your job."

"I'd just as soon not."

"Hawk . . ."

"Yes. Yes. I'll keep her breathing. I am continually doing work I don't enjoy."

And so he gave Cami to the Service and pulled Hawker neck deep into this mess. "If they ask you where I am, don't lie."

Hawker said, "I'll make sure they don't ask me."

Twenty-two

Do not forget there is evil in the world.

A BALDONI SAYING

THE COACH WAS STURDILY BUILT, A LITTLE SHABBY, and entirely anonymous. It could have rolled down any street in London without attracting a second glance. Soon, it would.

They'd hidden it in the yard behind the cabinetmaker's shop, between high stacks of wood, in the narrow space used for deliveries. The simple modifications needed had taken three days because the cabinetmaker, Moreau, could not be set to work at night. His neighbors would find it unusual to hear hammer and saw past the setting of the sun.

"Almost done." The man called the Merchant spoke encouragingly. "There are only—Jacques, how many?—only a half dozen still to go."

He listened, with every appearance of sympathy, to the boy's complaint that no more kegs would fit.

"They must," he said. "We have measured very carefully. Come, you can do this. I expect no less of you."

He'd placed himself where he could watch the small kegs being carefully fitted under the seats. The boy was nimble enough to reach into every corner. He would accomplish this task.

It was not necessary to threaten. The boy was well aware

that his parents and young sister and the servants of the household were already locked in the cellars.

"You see. And now just three more. Shift everything to the right, only an inch. You are almost there."

Soho was a busy, noisy quarter of the city, with many men making deliveries to many workshops. The business here would be done before men passing by took interest in the ordinary task of unloading a wagon on the street.

Jacques and Hugues carried kegs of gunpowder in through the shop, out to the yard, and handed them one by one to the boy to put in place under the seats.

The Moreaus' son was a brave boy, steady with his hands. He barely cried while he worked. In many ways, a child this age was the most satisfactory of all assistants.

"That is the last of it. See, it all fits neatly. I told you it would. Go with Jacques now. You have served France well, and no harm will come to you, I promise."

The last delicate manipulations, he performed himself, checking every inch of the long fuse line that snaked back and forth, attached to the underside of the seat.

Jacques returned and stood outside the coach, waiting. "Do you want them dead?"

"None of them have seen my face, except the young boy. It's better they live for a time." Because it would do no harm to explain, he added, "Dead men begin to smell."

Jacques nodded, understanding the principle.

He gave the connection of fuse to keg his intense concentration, then double-checked his work. Most mistakes are made in the small, easily skimped tasks.

"You are wondering why I leave matters unfinished? The Moreaus will continue to serve us. I have arranged for a letter to be posted in three days, accusing them of complicity in this outrage . . . of exactly what they have done, in fact. The authorities will find them in that cellar and discover the evidence we shall leave behind. They will doubtless hang at least some of them. They will be martyrs to the Revolution."

He closed the cushioned seat top down and secured it in place with a padlock. Two inches of fuse emerged through a drilled hole, ready to light.

"A good reason to keep them alive," Jacques said.

"Let us hope they die bravely when the time comes. You may leave them some water. We are not needlessly cruel. And reassure them that they will be safe." The Merchant climbed from the coach and set the door closed behind him. "There is no more deeply satisfying work, no higher cause, than the Revolution." He patted the side of the coach as if it were a great horse. "I feel honored sometimes."

"We are very lucky," Jacques said.

wenty-three

A wise man is unwise in love.

A BALDONI SAYING

BALDONI MAKE GRAND GESTURES. THEY PAINT A
broad canvas, as it were. They drink deeply of life and frequently do not live to a great old age because of that tendency.

Cami carried misgivings and a loaded gun as she walked
toward Gunter's Tea Shop. Neither of these was likely to prove
useful.

Last night, she'd kissed a man and been shaken by the sud-
denness and intensity of her desire. What she did not know
was whether this came from fear and excitement and, frankly,
a certain lack of clothing. Or was it because he was a friend
and she'd never kissed anyone she cared tuppence about?

She only knew that it had not happened to her before, and
if she turned away now, it might never happen again. That
was why she came to Berkeley Square. Not because she was
foolish or because she calculated a use for Mr. Paxton of the
British Service. She came because she was Baldoni.

Berkeley Square was a huge green space, surrounded by
the great houses of the very rich, full of trees and benches and
children playing with hoops or balls. A peaceful, pretty place.
She'd come within sight of Gunter's Tea Shop an hour early to

sniff out traps and ambushes, but she was not surprised to find Pax there before her. They'd been trained by the same men, after all.

He must have been aware of her the moment she entered the square, but he gave no sign. He sat on his bench, sketching in a small book. He wore a coat, as drab as yesterday's, and the same slouched and vaguely disreputable hat. His hair was drawn back neatly. His hat cast a crisp slice of darkness across his face. One did not see the jutting, emphatic bones of his face that hinted he was not English, exotic in this London square.

He'd made himself prosaic enough, with his legs stretched out before him into the path, holding the sketchbook in his left hand and a pencil angled in his right. He presented the appearance of one absorbed in his task. Anyone looking saw a thin, brown scholar, just on the edge of being shabby. A schoolteacher or young cleric. A man of intellect rather than action, ordinary and harmless.

What she saw was a canny, lean predator, at rest merely because this was not the moment to strike.

If she'd fallen into a British Service trap, it was already too late for her to escape. So she walked toward him and sat down by his side, touching almost. That was a good distance for exchanging confidences. Also, she would not mind touching him.

He tucked his sketchbook into the pocket of his coat and settled back, putting his arm around her shoulders, along the back of the bench. He did it as if they always sat together side by side in this intimate and easy way. Once, they had.

"I'm being followed." She started in the middle of the conversation, without the preliminary social niceties. She'd been thinking about him so much in the last dozen hours it was almost as if they hadn't been apart. "I point this out because you'll notice and worry and possibly injure someone if I don't."

"Even now, I don't kill people without a good reason." He was gravely polite or deeply satiric. One could take a choice.

"Observe the boy over there, pretending to be fascinated by that carriage horse. Brown hair and blue smock. Do you see him?"

"I see he's keeping an eye on you. Not making a secret of it, is he?"

"He is one of Nature's open and honest souls. Did you hurt yourself badly last night, being chivalrous and letting me escape?"

"As you see." He lifted the arm that rested behind her back and turned it, demonstrating a lack of pain. She would have believed this from another man, perhaps.

"You should let me do any further stabbing of your person. I'll be more careful than you are."

"I'll bear that in mind. Your boy's been joined by another. There, coming up on the other side." A minute nudge to her arm. "See?"

"There are three of them, taking turns." They were her best assurance of safety this morning. Those who had business with Lazarus were sacrosanct till he finished with them. The King of Thieves didn't tolerate men interfering in his criminal livelihood. Lesser thieves and killers would keep their hands from any prey Lazarus had marked as his own. "They send children, who are thus assumed to be harmless."

"You weren't a harmless child."

"Nor were you," she said softly.

"There's the third. I almost didn't spot her."

"They are not without a certain naïve competence. Right now, they want me to see them."

Pax's hand closed firmly on her shoulder. His voice, by contrast, was entirely calm. "You've aroused the interest of someone powerful. You're not frightened, so you know who it is."

She shrugged. How much to tell him?

"There are only a few men and a few reasons you'd let attention fall on you. I don't like any of the guesses I'm making." He released his hold. "Let's walk. I'm not comfortable sitting here. I don't like all this empty space at my back."

"No one's going to attack us in broad daylight."

"Once upon a time, on a day very much like this, I killed a man twenty feet away from Braddy Square at three in the afternoon." He stood and turned and offered a hand.

"I imagine he deserved it."

"One of the Tuteurs. Jean-Emile Cambert."

"Ah. Many of us would have enjoyed ending that life." She let him pull her to her feet and he drew her arm through his. The wool of his sleeve was rough under her fingertips. He smelled like pepper and snuff and, in some way, himself.

That had been the smell of him last night. That was what she'd tasted on his skin and breathed in his mouth when he'd kissed her and she had kissed him back. The scent that snuck past her defenses and struck wanting into her flesh.

In the daylight, on this open path, in the midst of children rolling hoops and pigeons chasing bugs through the grass, madly and stupidly and immodestly, with great exactness and specificity, she wanted him. Her body was not wise.

"I don't think the Service is setting street kids on you," he said. "Doyle might, I suppose. You remember Doyle."

The air had become transparent as glass after last night's rain. Shade lay on the path, patched with irregular sunlight. The fabric of his coat, where she held his arm lightly, showed hard use. There were fine pulls of thread and tiny worn spots. Under this disguise, Pax seemed likewise worn. Seen close, by someone who knew him, he didn't look vague and amiable. He looked like a panther on a long hunt. Weary and wary.

She wanted to stop, right in the path, and kiss the corners of his mouth and the line between his eyes. She'd have to stand on tiptoe to reach his forehead or he'd have to lean down to her. Then she'd kiss the lobes of his ears.

Apparently she was going to lead a lively and interesting life in her imagination.

She said, "I'm not likely to forget William Doyle. He came from London with questions and scared me to death. Twice, in fact. The first time when I was shaking with fever and they'd barely washed the seaweed out of my hair. He was suspicious of me because I was such an unexpected addition to the Leyland household. But I looked woebegone and afflicted and very young and I fooled him handily."

"It's what we were trained for."

She watched her shoes and the gravel path. "I was lucky to get away with it. After that, for all those years, when the Leylands visited London I avoided Meeks Street like the plague.

If I hadn't I would have run into you sometime or other, which would have been awkward for both of us."

Pax said nothing, which was tactful of him.

They strolled toward Gunter's, matching steps. She let herself enjoy the little pleasures she could distill from this brief time. Small dogs ran in circles and barked. Grass grew docilely between the pathways. Sun warmed her face. Ardency and heat glowed between her legs. It was also simple enjoyment to keep pace with deadly, masculine grace that stalked beside her, pretending to be a scholar. It was his joke on the world. Her joke that she could see through it.

Desiring him awakened every sense, made the sun brighter and the grass a deeper green. She could feel his attention on her, in that same way, with that same awareness. If they'd been friends, they could have spoken of it and laughed together.

Coaches lined up along the pavement across from Gunter's Tea Shop in the shade of the big plane trees of Berkeley Square. Waiters hurried in and out, carrying trays to barouches and landaus so My Lady This and Her Grace of That need not deign to enter the shop and mingle with the populace. The Fluffy Aunts always made tart comments about that, trading aphorisms in Greek and Latin, over their macaroons and tea cakes. They were such radicals.

Pax kept a light, alert touch on her as they passed between two of those coaches and into Berkeley Square. The urchins who worked for Lazarus crossed, too, pretending to play games around the horses, getting chased off by the coach drivers.

At the front window of Gunter's, they stopped. She said, "I'm not here because of any threats you made."

"I know. You're here because I kissed you. We'll both have to deal with it. You couldn't walk away from that. I can't walk away either."

"It made everything complicated." She had seldom employed the art of understatement to such good effect. "I'm here for practical reasons, too." She watched Berkeley Square and Pax and the three children who followed her and belonged to the King of Thieves. Probably there were others taking an interest. As she'd said, it was complicated. "I need help. You were right about that."

"We have lots to talk about, in short. Gunter's is a good place for it."

"It is the quintessence of all that is frivolous and innocent. We must face grim realities, so naturally we go to Gunter's to do it."

She'd lured Pax into a grin. He said, "The day I got to London, the day I walked into Meeks Street, Doyle took me to Gunter's and bought me chocolate ice cream. I sat there the whole time, worried I'd make a mistake and give myself away. Couldn't even enjoy it."

"My aunts—" The stab of pain was getting familiar. She could almost ignore it. "I mean, the Leyland sisters—took me to Gunter's when they brought me to London the first time. The Tuteurs had tipped me into the cold ocean to introduce me to England and I acquired pneumonia. I wasn't recovering fast enough so the aunts wanted a London doctor to listen to me cough. The ice cream was a treat afterward." Irony. Irony. Life was full of small, ridiculous coincidences. "It was chocolate."

"The indulgence of choice for young spies. Or old ones, like us. Come. I will ply you with sweetmeats and we will discuss serious matters."

She might come to like Pax, as well as Devoir.

"The first of which . . ." He pushed the door of Gunter's open and stood aside to let her walk in before him. "Is Mr. Smith."

wenty-four

Three things a man must have to live well—good bread, good wine, good friends.

A BALDONI SAYING

THE FLOWERED ICE CREAM CUPS STOOD EMPTY AT the side of the table, the spoons sitting in them like upright flags. Pistachio ice for him. Bergamot water ice for her. Gunter's was open and airy, the windows full of light. Waiters in white aprons lingered at the tables to flatter old women and be indulgent to the children who kicked the chair legs and whined and were arrogant with their nursemaids.

Cami watched steam gather on the surface of her teacup and wondered what to do. It was an unusual sensation, this being uncertain. She didn't care for it.

Pax had left his tea untouched. His hair fell across his temple to his cheek, straight and emphatic. She wanted to lift that pale line and stroke it back, behind his ear. It was very distracting.

"You aren't drinking," she said. The tea was excellent. Everything at Gunter's was excellent.

"I don't want to leave you to go piss. You might decide to not be here when I get back."

"How well you know me." Since she wasn't going to arise and flee, she drank some tea. "Are you quite certain this is the

Merchant? There was universal rejoicing when he died. There was no doubt."

"Now there's no doubt he's alive," Pax said. "I saw him."

"He didn't show himself to Cachés. None of us knew what he looked like."

"I do."

Such coldness when he said that. It was as if shadows flew in thin ripples between her and the sunlight. She was left with no doubt Pax knew the Merchant very well indeed.

At a table nearby, under the benevolent eye of a governess, two beautifully dressed little girls giggled together, licking ice cream from their spoons, innocent and greedy as young goats. Beyond them, a boy of thirteen or fourteen sat alone, reading Latin, giving his ice cream and the book equal attention. That could have been Pax, when she first knew him, if the scholarly boy had been white haired and starved thin and knew fifty different ways to kill somebody.

Revolution and war seemed a long way away.

Pax watched her without seeming to do so. "I don't know why the Merchant is in England, but he's going to kill people. Will you tell me when and where you're meeting him?"

She sighed. "When I was walking from Brodemere to London, I made extensive plans to deal with a blackmailer and I felt very clever."

"That sounds like you."

"I had intended to hire four men with guns and conduct a simple ambush. It would seem I underestimated Mr. Smith's ruthlessness and his resources by several orders of magnitude. I am now very afraid."

She stirred her tea. They fell silent while a waiter came to remove the empty ice cream cups.

Pax watched the street outside, the waiters, the long counter where men and women entered the shop to buy pastries and carry them away. He'd be able to sketch any of those people if someone asked him to.

The British had acquired a good spy when they'd been infiltrated by Pax, though it was possible they didn't see it that way.

"Whatever he has of yours," Pax said. "Whatever you want from him, it's not worth your life. Walk away."

Which was good advice and, like most good advice, difficult to follow.

She blew out a long breath and watched it ripple on the surface of her tea. "I wish it were that easy. I wish I could stand
up and walk out of here straight to the docks and take the first
ship leaving England. I'd go somewhere very far from here."

"And never look back."

She'd been talking to her teacup, because she wasn't going
to see anything useful on his face anyway. Now she turned to
the harsh, ascetic profile. "Remember the night we planned to
run away to a tropical island? We were all going to break out of
the Coach House and steal a ship on the Seine and sail away."

"We were going to become pirates."

She remembered a long, cold night in January with
everyone huddled together, sharing blankets, whispering
back and forth in the dark. "That was one of the days they decided not to feed us. They'd whipped . . . it was Guerrier. We
had him in the middle of us, still shaking."

"He'd made some mistake in his English."

"The Tuteurs were in a bad mood. I told Guerrier about the
island we'd find, far away from everywhere. It'd be warm and
we'd dine upon pineapples and oranges every night and keep
a monkey for a pet. I'd just read *Robinson Crusoe*."

"I would have eaten the monkey if I'd got my hands on
one." Pax's bony wrists rested on the edge of the table. His
hands were half-curled, as if he held something carefully.
There were ink stains in three or four places. It plucked at her
breath, seeing something so familiar. Devoir, with ink stain-
ing his hands. Pax with the same ink marking him.

She said, "They bite, you know. Monkeys do. At least, the
squire's aunt had one with a bite like a bulldog."

"Then I won't buy one."

"Just as well. I can't picture you with a monkey." She
smiled at the thought. "There are no more desert islands in
my dreams. If I walked away from here right now, I'd go to
New Orleans or Baltimore, or Kingston and set up a shop to
make hats for dowdy colonial matrons. Or maybe I'd become
a jewel thief. I'm temperamentally suited to be a jewel thief."

"Now, there's a practical plan."

"If I were practical, I'd—" *I'd let Camille Besançon die. The Fluffy Aunts would never know.* She buried the thought. She unthought it. It had never been in her mind. "I'd be in Barbados, selling hats. I wouldn't be here, feasting on ices, getting more and more afraid."

"You should be afraid. You stand between the Merchant and something he wants."

"And he is deadly."

"Perhaps the most ruthless man you will ever meet. Mad in a way. When you face him, you won't see death coming. Most men give some sign before they kill. He doesn't." Pax's fist twitched on the table next to his cup. "Don't make me step across your dead body on the way to killing him."

Across the room, a small crisis took place with raspberry syrup and a pink dress. Napkins all in a flurry. Three waiters and the promise of sugar cookies.

Innocent people leading harmless lives. Lucky children who knew nothing about the world that existed beyond their safe garden walls.

The Merchant killed innocents like these.

Pax followed her glance. "You won't leave the Merchant loose in London. When and where are you meeting him?"

"You complicate my life."

"Good. You complicate mine. Infinitely." His smile flickered by so fast she might have missed it. "You can't do this alone. I can help you. I understand how he thinks. When and where, Cami?"

She tilted her teacup and looked at the pattern. Bone china. The light showed through. It was fragile, delicate, beautiful. Easily broken. The Leylands' niece could be just as easily destroyed by men who hunted the Merchant at all cost.

She set it down. "My family—my birth family, not the Leylands—have a saying, 'In the history of every disaster, there is a moment when someone says, "I trust you."'" We've arrived at that moment." She spread a hand palm up, fingers wide, to show the ineffable perversity of life. "I think I'm about to trust you."

"You already do." Pax's eyes found hers and didn't waver. "You didn't come to me because I made threats."

"I disregarded them."

He reached to her hand where it rested on the table and ran his index finger over her knuckles. "You came to me because of this. You feel it between us."

She twitched away from that little scrap of contact.

"And because I kissed you," he said.

"Lots of men have kissed me."

"Lucky men." He kept the touch between them. One tiny hot island of heat there on the back of her hand. "I want to kiss you here, across your knuckles. I want to bite a little here, here, here." He applied his nail, lightly, up and down the cusps and valleys of her knuckles. "I've never done that to anyone. I want to do it to you."

Heat exploded inside her. Shocking. Unexpected. Breath devouring. She was half-blind with it.

"That's why you came to meet me," he said. "Not because it was sensible or because I made threats. Not so we could concoct a plan to deal with that murdering bastard. You're here because when I kissed you, you kissed back and everything changed. We didn't expect any of that."

"I didn't anyway," she said.

"A shock to both of us." He turned her hand over and touched the center of her palm, holding all her thought, all her intention and awareness, right there, in that spot.

She closed her hand around the sensitivity, around the little fireball of excitement. Her voice was rock steady. "I don't have time to want you."

"It won't take more time than we have. We'll plot the death and downfall of the Merchant during the day. Give me the nights."

She looked away when she made her decision. "As long as you understand I'm not doing this because you seduced me into it."

"I didn't let you go from the bookshop because you seduced me."

"I didn't—" She hissed impatiently and batted at the words. "Forget it. We're both making mistakes. Points about even."

And she told him about Camille Besançon.

"Cami." He interrupted after only a dozen words. "There's no chance that little girl survived."

"I saw her. I think she's genuine. And genuine or not, she's going to die if I don't get her away from the Merchant. The Besançons died so I could be placed with the Leylands. I won't have another death on my conscience."

He didn't argue. Maybe that said everything she needed to know about the deaths that had placed him in the British Service.

"We rescue the woman," she said.

"If it doesn't get you killed and doesn't let the Merchant escape."

She shook her head. "The Leylands are as close to being Service as makes no difference. Get their niece out of the line of fire."

"No promises."

She hadn't expected any. "Then there's the aunts. The Merchant will go after them next." Her mouth felt dry. She drank tea. "The Leylands must be protected."

"Done. The Service will take care of them."

"And finally, if I hand you the Merchant, if I play bait in your trap, will the Service give me a head start before they come after me? One week."

"I'll ask."

Every one of those answers was the truth. He dealt honestly with her.

She closed her eyes. Opened them. "Semple Street, Number Fifty-six. Monday, eleven in the morning. I have to walk out and show myself before he'll come."

"That's not much time. Do you—" He broke off.

He was looking at the door of Gunter's.

She saw nothing there. Nothing happening. But Pax did. She quivered alert, every sense open, but saw nothing unusual. A big man in simple, respectable clothes had just walked in. Somebody's coachman, large, square, reliable looking. The clerks behind the counter sprang to take his order, so he must work for some important family.

Pax, beside her, became invisible.

It had always been one of his skills, this trick of becoming part of the background. He acquired the stillness of an animal in the forest. But it was more than that. In some way, he simply wasn't there. If she hadn't seen it many times before, she would have been disconcerted.

Very quietly, he said, "Keep your hands on the table."

She did. The shop continued its calm, well-ordered clockwork. The cheerful buzz of conversation didn't waver. Waiters simpered and glided under their trays. The nearest people, two women eating tea cakes, talked about Scotland and the best soil for growing roses.

The coachman wanted a package prepared. Everything to be settled deep in shaved ice. This ice cream and that one and that. For a young girl on her sickbed, who had no appetite and was in pain. The man made payment in pound notes, peeled off a large roll.

The countermen conferred deferentially. "This will take a few minutes. Would you take a seat? Tea? Coffee?"

"No." It wasn't even arrogance. It was beyond that—an indifference that reduced this shop and the men who worked here to nothing at all. The coachman's eyes skipped past fashionable women, past elegant men, and came to Cami. "I'll find a seat."

Pax murmured, "So. That's who had you followed. I thought it might be."

The man crossed the room and stopped at their table, in front of her. "You sent me a message." He sat, without invitation.

This was someone senior in London's hierarchy of criminals. Close up, he had the cold eyes of a banker.

"Please join us," she said, feeling no temptation to sarcasm. "A cup of tea or coffee?"

"I can't stay long." He considered Pax. "Mr. Paxton. Always a pleasure."

Pax didn't answer and never took his eyes off the man.

"And you" the man ran his eyes over her, weighed her up, measured, assessed—"claim to be a Baldoni. Explain to me why they've never heard of you."

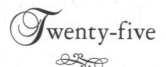

Twenty-five

We're all just labyrinths of deception.

WILLIAM DOYLE

"Six men headed for Soho," Hawker said, "armed with a copy of this." He shoved aside an unlit lantern, three letters, and a pair of driving gloves to unroll the sketch on the hall table. "The Merchant, looking ordinary."

"Many deadly men look ordinary." Galba was already dressed for the street, meticulous in overcoat and hat. He frowned at the face that looked up at them from the table.

"I prefer it when killers show a little murder on their countenance," Hawker said.

Doyle said, "It's there. You see it in what's missing."

Galba put a glove on, finger by finger, stiff and emphatic about it. "I know this man."

Doyle touched the corner of the paper. "You met him in France?"

"At Cambridge. Bring it in here."

The downstairs study was empty, all the traffic of the early morning having run itself off to another part of the house or out to Soho. A dozen agents left a certain disorder behind.

In the study, Hawker laid the picture flat on the desk. Galba turned up the flame in the lamp, and they all looked at it.

Hawker said, "Cambridge?"

Galba narrowed his eyes, studying feature by feature. "This is Peter Styles."

"Styles . . . Styles." Doyle visibly shuffled through his memory. "The Honorable Peter Styles, who turned out to be somewhat less than honorable after all. That Foreign Office theft . . . it must be twenty-five years ago. He was the second—maybe third—son of one of the earls up north."

"The Earl of Cardinham. I believe this Peter is now the heir. He took a First at Cambridge."

"Before my time," Doyle said. "Hawk, if you're standing around idle . . ."

"I am never idle, Mr. Doyle. I am always preparing for the next stroke of brilliance."

"Right. Do that while you put these in the dumbwaiter." Doyle passed over coffee cups and hooked up a pair of ale tankards deftly in one hand, betraying some experience in that activity.

"I don't know why everyone is determined to make me a waiter." Hawker was not silent with the plates and cups. "So the Merchant is an Englishman."

"This man is." Galba picked up the sketch.

"I am casting my mind back a good ways now. Styles made a great noise at Cambridge." Doyle rubbed the back of his neck. "I heard about it even in my day. He was leading around a band of noble radicals who were going to reform the world. A brilliant mind, but something wrong with him even then. Hawk, get that last cup on the windowsill, will you."

"We would not wish to leave it behind, all forlorn without its fellows."

"We would not wish someone to break it up and use the edges to attack," Doyle said. "I don't remember much more about Styles. He left behind nasty rumors and unpaid bills when he shook the dust of Cambridge off his boots. They say he crippled a man in a duel. They say he seduced his landlady's daughter, age fourteen."

"A charming fellow," Hawker said.

"And a credit to the Foreign Office, which is where he went next. A year later he went through the offices and helped himself to every secret that wasn't nailed down and a pile of money intended for bribes in the German states and took the packet from Dover."

Hawker brushed his hands. "I have frequently asked myself why I don't do the same. If you don't have any more menial work for me, I will depart. I'm supposed to be following Pax."

"Follow him," Galba said. "Stay close. The Merchant knows his face."

"And that she-wolf may cut his throat in a fit of pique. Maybe I can eliminate one or the other of those threats."

"Don't kill anybody," Doyle said.

"You are tying my hands as an effective agent. You do know that." The rest of Hawker's commentary disappeared down the hall with him.

When Hawker was gone, Galba and Doyle stood in silence for few minutes.

Galba said, "Do you see it?"

"What?" Doyle said.

"Look closely." Galba was doing just that. "Forget who it is. See it as if it were hanging on the wall in a country house."

Doyle took the sketch. "I'd think it was good. I'd wonder who the artist was. I'd think the man looks familiar. I never saw Peter Styles, so I can't—" Doyle stopped. Stared for another moment. Whispered, "Frogs and little dancing fishes. I don't believe it."

Galba said, "The resemblance is unmistakable."

wenty-six

Family is everything.

A BALDONI SAYING

SOME ACTIVITIES ARE UNSUITED TO GUNTER'S. NEGO-tiating with criminals was one. Any reference to the Baldoni, root and branch, was another.

Cami said, "Let's leave," to the criminal who sat across from her. "I don't want to talk about this here."

"Now, why is that?" the man said softly.

She stood. "We can be overheard, and I'm cautious."

"Happens I'm cautious myself. Why don't we continue our discussion elsewhere?"

Pax dropped coins on the table and picked her cloak off the back of the chair and pulled it around her shoulders. He said, "She's protected."

"You're not doing a notably good job of it, Mr. Paxton, if she's face-to-face with me."

"That's her choice," Pax said calmly. "It's all her choice."

"I'll bear that in mind."

She led two very dangerous men out of Gunter's, greatly reducing the level of lethality within. Pax followed last, keeping an eye on things.

Sunlight struck bright after she'd been inside. There were

more thugs on the street than she was comfortable with. She walked a dozen feet down the pavement to put some space between herself and the door of Gunter's, observing which people noted the movement and which ignored it. Separating the sheep from the goats.

She selected a spot twelve feet down because it seemed more promising than the rest. A staid, self-important stone house on her right, every window closed. No one stirring. On her left, a black coach she'd seen drive up, curtains drawn, horses and driver profoundly uninterested in the passing scene.

A nice, tight, defensible space where no one could sneak up on her. "We'll talk here."

"As you wish." Her criminal beckoned one of his attendant thugs, but it was just to send him to take charge of the ice cream when it was packed and ready. That chore completed, he gave his attention back to her. He was as frightening in the open air as he'd been sitting across a table.

She was something of a judge of brutality. The Baldoni had never entirely renounced the practical, everyday side of criminality. She could appreciate graded and careful intimidation.

Pax stood a pace behind her, at her left shoulder, probably thinking along similar lines. She didn't have to turn around to look at him. She could feel him there, the way she'd feel a fire burning in a cold room.

There were a number of large, roughly dressed men on the street.

She said, "You've brought an audience. I don't like that," to the man she must parley with, seeing whether he'd make a concession.

He did. He made some signal, negligently, with his right hand and the three ratlike children who'd followed her since Covent Garden disappeared into the greenery of Berkeley Square. They would doubtless run about, playing children's games unconvincingly. Dangerous-looking men up and down the street revealed their allegiance by strolling off to loiter in a more distant place. The visible menace faded away, except for a large black man who'd exchanged the wall beside Gunter's door for the closest lamppost. That one leaned against the iron pole, arms crossed, face blank.

Behind her, Pax spoke softly. "The Service will be deeply annoyed if anything happens to her."

"I have no quarrel with the Service," the man said. "She came to me. I didn't go hunting her."

Pax, having made his point, went back to being enigmatic. He didn't mention that the Service interest involved interrogating her and locking her up indefinitely. Or hanging her if that seemed most useful.

She'd come to London prepared to negotiate with villains from the rookeries of London. This held a certain danger, but, as the Baldoni so wisely say, the safest place is in the grave.

She folded her hands. "I've come to buy a service. I'm told anyone who does this is given safe passage."

"None of them use a century-old signal to get my attention."

His attention. Fear wrapped like a cold cloak, prickled her skin, seeped inward. This was no lieutenant of anybody. This was the King of Thieves. The ruler of London's underworld. This was Lazarus himself.

Pax was a waiting silence behind her. He knew.

Endings grow from the seed of their beginning. Six days ago, trying to sleep in tall brush in a field in Cambridgeshire, she'd made her plans. It was too late for qualms.

She said, "Does it matter what sign I use? I could walk into the middle of a street and shout. You have eyes everywhere."

She was immeasurably glad of Pax's presence behind her, ally and friend, solid as rock, subtle as water, edged sharper than a knife.

Lazarus looked amused. "You've made me curious." His gaze slid past her. "You don't have any intention of explaining this, do you, Mr. Paxton?"

A shift of dark and light at the corner of her eye. Pax had made some motion. Maybe a head shake. No words from him, though.

Lazarus said, "Your lot was on the street last night, up and down the town, keeping an eye on her. But she hasn't been to Meeks Street. I'd say you don't know what she's up to, either."

No response from Pax this time.

She was the descendant of many generations of powerful, dishonest men. The problem in dealing with master criminals— one of several problems, actually—is that they don't need the money. They like it, but that's not the principal reason you are face-to-face with them. You are an antidote to boredom. A curiosity. A puzzle. It is not good to negotiate with someone who wants to be entertained. "I'm delighted everyone is so interested in me. If you have questions—"

"I like to know who's buying my services. A foible of mine." Lazarus half turned, looking expectant.

The black coach they stood beside was not empty, as she'd assumed. The door opened. A man emerged and set an elegant, well-shod foot on the step of the carriage. He was perhaps sixty years old. His long dark hair, combed back from his forehead, had gone white at the temples. He was nattily and expensively dressed in black and carried an ebony cane. In a hundred subtle ways, he did not look English.

She'd have said this sort of man would have nothing to do with business transacted by the London underworld. But Lazarus was waiting.

The old man's face . . . Out of her childhood memories, across a dozen years, past deaths and revelation and the torment of the Coach House, she remembered him. She'd made a grave mistake using any password of the Baldoni.

The old man said, *"Cosa abbiamo qui?"* What have we here?

The voice reached back to a time beyond memory, to her cradle, to tumbling on the floor in a melee of dogs and cousins. To being pulled from her perch on the roof of the chapel and spanked soundly and hugged just as soundly. To warm milk at bedtime and warm laps in front of the fire.

Pax said quietly, "Who are you?"

The man said, "A man with a certain interest in anyone who claims the privilege of a Baldoni."

When was the last time she'd let herself speak Tuscan, the language of home? She could name the day and the hour. It

had been in Paris, when they'd arrested Papà, and she'd gone
to her cousin to beg for help and been refused so utterly.

*"Run away or the vendetta will take you, too. Go away.
You are not one of us."*

Tendrils of a sort of madness twined through her brain.
She knew him. Uncle Bernardo—her great-uncle Bernardo.
She refused to lower her eyes. She said, *"Ho il diritto, pro-
zio."* I have that right, Great-Uncle. And with that she claimed
the family that had turned their backs on her. Claimed the
vendetta that had killed her parents.

He whispered, "Sara? *Piccola* Sara?"

She inclined her head fractionally. Barely at all. Barely
admitting it. Those who said women and children weren't
part of vendetta lied. Her mother had died in *la place de la
Révolution* with her father, both of them denounced to the
Committee . . . by a Baldoni. The doors of Baldoni protection
had remained closed to a child who cried there and beat on
the gate with her fists and pleaded. No one came to rescue her
from the Coach House.

Uncle Bernardo came closer and stretched out his hand to
touch fingers to her hair. She didn't flinch. He whispered, "Sara?
It is Sara."

Too fast to predict or avoid—he'd been a great swordsman
in his day, with reflexes like lightning—he pulled her to his
chest, against the black wool and the starched ruffles of his
old-fashioned neckcloth, into the memory of lavender and
starch and eau de cologne. "Sara. *Sei tu? Sei viva?* You live?"

Old anger cracked inside her heart and loosened and disappeared, as spring breaks the ice on a stream and carries it
off. "I thought—"

She was held at arm's length and inspected minutely.
Clasped again. "We thought you were lost forever. We thought
you were dead in that French madness. *Grazie a Dio.* How
does this happen?"

In Tuscan, with catches in her breath, words tumbling together, she told him about Paris and the riots. About Mamma
and Papà, executed. "I went to Cousin Francesco and they
sent me away at the gate. I sent message after message. No

one answered. No one came." She took a deep breath. "It's been so long, I didn't know you."

The elegant long face twisted. Then he shook his head, as if dislodging a memory. "I have become old."

"Never."

That got her a hearty kiss on her forehead. "But you . . . how you have changed." His laugh was a Baldoni, Tuscan laugh, unbounded, full of feeling. "You have grown up. I would have passed you on the street and not named you." He took her left hand and raised it. "You are not married. You have no husband?" A dark look ran over Pax. "I cannot imagine why not. Wherever you have been, someone should have seen you married."

Lazarus watched with interest but without comprehension. Perhaps he didn't understand Italian. Perhaps.

"I've been busy," she said.

"We will fix that." The door of the black coach hung open. Uncle Bernardo put his hand under her elbow. "Come with me now, Sara. Whatever business you have with these English cutthroats, you may forget it. Your family will serve you. I have many years of neglect to make up for." He switched to English. "You have no need of such men."

Lazarus said, "She's yours, then? A Baldoni?"

"Not merely one of us, but my own niece. You have restored the lost sheep to our fold. The Baldoni owe you a debt."

Lazarus said, "The service she wanted?"

"Will be negotiated. Or she may not deal with you at all. She has the resources of the Baldoni at her back. And our protection."

"I will keep that in mind." Lazarus nodded.

Uncle Bernardo switched to Italian. "Come, Sara. Come home. That which was lost has been found. The one who was dead is restored to us. Your cousins will get very drunk tonight, celebrating."

Pax—no one was better than Pax at going swiftly and silently—held the door of the black coach with the air of a first-rate footman. She let herself be ensconced within, on the velvet cushion, three hundred thoughts whirling over the brim of her mind like froth in a stirred pot.

Pax swung into the carriage last and took the backward-facing seat. In a coach one noticed the length of him. He had to fold his legs up to fit.

This is the first time I have ever been in a carriage with him.

"You. I give you no permission to accompany me," Uncle Bernardo snapped. "Stay with Lazarus, who owns you."

Lazarus was leaning in at the window of the coach. "Paxton isn't my man."

"Then what is he doing here?" Uncle Bernardo was disapproving.

"Paxton belongs to the British Service." Lazarus smiled, as a great mastiff dog might smile, showing teeth that looked like they would bite very hard. "You have a senior agent of the British Service in your coach, about to go home with you. If the Service makes a claim on your niece, Mr. Paxton would be the one enforcing it." He tipped his hat. "Good day to you."

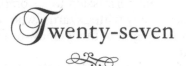

Twenty-seven

*An ordinary man may keep a promise. A
ruler—never.*

A BALDONI SAYING

"SO YOU WON'T TELL US WHERE SHE IS." LILY LEYLAND
removed her gloves and, with them, much of the vagueness of
her manner. She was still a frail old woman, swallowed by the
chair she'd taken beside Galba's desk—Doyle's favorite chair—
but she didn't look the least silly or dithery.

Galba centered the decoded note on the desk between
them. "I do not, in strict fact, know where she is."

"I don't suppose you're trying very hard to find out," Lily
said. "If you knew where she was, you'd have to bring her to
Meeks Street."

"Which you do not wish to do." Violet blinked at him
owlishly.

"It would present you with the most appalling dilemma."
Lily dropped her gloves in her lap.

"One we hoped would never arise," Violet murmured.

Lily said, "When I retired—forgive me for oversimplify-
ing in the interests of brevity—I did not expect bloody revolution in France."

"And ten years of war," Violet added.

"*Dis aliter visum.* The gods saw it otherwise. But we're all aware that if Cami appears at Meeks Street—"

"As an enemy spy," Violet added quickly.

"—she becomes prey of Military Intelligence. And Military Intelligence is populated by nincompoops and swine."

"Besides, she hasn't been spying."

"He's well aware of that," Lily said. "Aren't you, Anson?"

"Unfortunately, I am." Galba sighed and ran his hand through his hair. "My life would be simpler if I were dealing with a straightforward enemy agent instead of your pet."

"Pet or no, she's not a French agent. No, dearest," she hurried on before Violet could speak, "Anson is well aware Cami isn't selling codes to the French."

"She's not even French," Violet said. "She's Italian. Tuscan."

Lily shot a sharp glare at Galba. "Did you know?"

"I had no idea. But then, I only found out she's an impostor," Galba glanced at the clock on the mantel above the small hearth, "thirteen hours ago."

"When she came to us . . . when that unconvincing clergyman dropped her on our doorstep—"

"He brought her all the way from Folkestone, but hadn't bothered to wash the sand out of her hair," Violet muttered. "Or wrap her warmly. He was the most callous man. That's someone I would have enjoyed shooting."

"Yes, dear, but we had other concerns at the time. Cami was in a high fever by the time she came to us. Of course we knew she wasn't our niece—"

"No resemblance to Hyacinth." Violet shook her head. "Nor to the Besançons. She was so miserably unwell and so terrified, poor child. So obviously a fraud."

"We knew, then, finally and with certainty, that Hyacinth, Jules, the baby, and our niece Camille were dead. It was a great shock."

"A sadness we've learned to accept. This woman the blackmailer writes of . . ."

"Is an impostor. Cami shouldn't spend a minute pursuing that chimera." Lily nodded toward the bookcase. "I've refused your tea, Anson, but I wouldn't say no to a brandy."

Galba took three small, plain glasses from the side table. He didn't pour from the decanter on the table, though. He reached up to the high shelf and brought down the bottle that had no label on it. They waited while he poured, then lifted glasses together and gave the first sip of brandy the silence it merited.

Violet spoke first. "We didn't take Cami in without considering the matter carefully."

"We're not sentimental simpletons," Lily said. "That first night, when her fever rose, she began to babble in Italian. It was revealing in every way."

Violet took another delicate sip. "A lovely dialect. Pure Tuscan."

Galba said, "That's when you should have sent for me."

"To do what?" Lily snorted. "Drag the North Sea for the bodies of my sister and her family? Scour France for the fanatics who killed them? Should I have given you that little girl lying in a bedroom upstairs out of her head with fever? Do you imagine you would have gleaned the least scrap of useful intelligence from a ten-year-old?"

"Of course not."

"You would have taken all that courage and brilliance and dropped it in some orphanage." Lily rested the glass of brandy on the arm of her chair.

"I would have found her a place in a comfortable girls' school, somewhere very far from the centers of power. Cardiff comes to mind."

"Which would have been a great waste of an excellent codebreaker," Lily said.

"At that time she would have been a solvable problem." Galba took a sip of brandy and sighed. "Now she is not. Lily, you can't take in French spies like stray kittens."

"She is not a French spy. If anything, she's a British one. Here." Lily leaned to tap the note that lay open on the dark wood of his desk. "She is reporting to the Head of Service. I've had charge of Cami since she was a child. I know how to select and train agents. Even cocky little lordlings who think they know everything."

"For which this little lordling will be forever grateful."

Galba held his glass between both palms and rolled it slowly. "Your Cami isn't some child the French picked off the street. She came to you a trained spy. She's a Caché."

"We know that." Lily tapped her glass impatiently. "As soon as the Caché business came out, we knew that was what Cami had to be."

"It explained so much," Violet said. "Iniquitous to use children that way. Truly evil."

"There was an incident that convinced us she was not loyal to France. An unpleasant man showed up looking for Cami. The man the Police Secrète had put in charge of her."

"A bumptious little man," Violet said. "Watching the house. Interrogating the maid. Leaving notes under rocks."

"We thought we'd have to deal with him. Fortunately, it turned out to be unnecessary."

"Cami stabbed him," Violet said. "Very quietly, by the hollyhocks in the back garden, during a thunderstorm."

"Difficult for her to dispose of the body."

"Raining, you see."

"He looked heavy. We were tempted to go out and offer our help," Lily said. "Fortunately, she'd arranged to have a wheelbarrow handy."

"She put him in the millpond. With rocks and burlap bags and rope. Quite an efficient job for one so young. Though I never could bring myself to fancy fish from the millpond, after that."

Galba closed his eyes. "I see."

"What you should see, Anson, is that she's not a spy or a threat to England." Violet's nose turned pink with indignation. "As if we would harbor traitors and spies under our roof."

"The situation in France became confused shortly after that," Lily said judiciously. "The execution of Robespierre and his followers, the suppression of several factions of the Police Secrète . . . we assumed Cami's connection with the French had been lost in the shuffle. No one else has ever shown an interest in her. Certainly Cami never approached the French."

"She is our niece in everything but the small matter of blood," Violet said.

Galba set his hands on the desk, making two temples of them. "Vi, much as I might like to hand her over to you and return to the status quo, you can't simply take her back to Brodemere in a handbasket. There are serious matters at stake. And a major complication."

"Which is?" Lily raised eyebrows.

"She has attacked and seduced one of my agents."

"Has she?" Lily said.

"It can't be much of an attack if he was in any state to be seduced afterward," Violet observed.

Lily murmured, "It seems so unlike her."

"The attacking or the seducing?" Violet asked.

"Neither." Lily frowned. "But doing it to an agent. So odd of her to become involved with a Service agent while she's fleeing . . . whatever it is she's fleeing. One does not seduce agents in the middle of a desperate enterprise. I don't understand at all." She turned to Galba. "Which agent? Not Hawker, surely. I would regret doing something violent to Hawker."

Galba said, "Paxton."

Lily exchanged glances with Violet.

"Matters are a bit more serious, then," Lily said. "One expects someone more light-minded to be part of a seduction."

"He's not at all what I expected," Violet said. "So . . . self-contained. One sees the attraction, of course. The artistic temperament. There is that intense concentration."

Violet discovered her glass was empty and held it out for a refill. Galba obliged. She said, "He seems a responsible young man."

"He's an Independent Agent." Lily pursed her lips.

"Which vouches for his usefulness."

"He was polite when I talked to him about Moldavian. At length. That's a good sign." Violet leaned back comfortably in the chair. "And, really, he has quite a nice body."

Lily coughed. "That's hardly to the point."

"That is exactly to the point, Lily."

"When one is young, perhaps. You and I are no longer young." She turned sharp, cynical blue eyes to Galba. "Tell us everything."

Twenty-eight

Do not drink deeply at the table of your enemies.

A BALDONI SAYING

PAX KNEW LONDON. NOT AS WELL AS HE KNEW
Paris and Florence, but better than most men who'd lived here
their whole lives. The carriage let them out on Carnet Street.
He'd walked this street with Doyle and Hawker seven or eight
years ago, Doyle talking about the history of the place,
Hawker discussing the best way to break into the upper-story
windows.

A few houses to the north, one of those windows opened, a
small rug emerged, flapped vigorously, and retreated.

The big houses had been broken into flats when the fashionable moved farther west, to Mayfair. This was what he'd
call half-shabby, a neighborhood where ambitious tradesmen
climbing up the social ladder lived cheek by jowl with old
gentility, slipping down. Bricks crumbled, the woodwork
needed painting, but the front windows were almost painfully
clean, glinting in the sun.

The Service had a file on the Baldoni that went back two
hundred years. He'd be adding to that later today, if some
boatmen didn't fish his body out of the Thames.

Cami let him help her out of the coach, holding on to his

shoulder longer than was necessary. She looked around and gave judgment. "They're playing the Struggling Emigrée, I think. Or the Prisoner's Wife. Something like that."

"The Struggling Emigrée," Bernardo said. "Your aunt Fortunata is a French widow from Nîmes with a small Rubens hanging upon her wall and no idea what it is. Fortunately, a wealthy baronet has offered to take the worthless picture off her hands, merely as a favor, from the great respect he has for her. He comes to tea and offers more money each visit."

"The benevolence of mankind," Cami murmured.

He pitied any baronet who wandered into this nest of Baldoni.

The Baldoni camped in London like a tribe of nomad raiders, taking short forays out to pillage. They were a family of long-established tradition. When north Italy hosted a shooting war, the Baldoni sent their hotheaded young men and women, their children and the old, out of range of gunfire. They scattered their next generation and their movable wealth as far as they could.

Amsterdam, St. Petersburg, Vienna, Paris . . . he'd run into Baldoni, always in inconspicuous corners, always lingering a whisper outside important events, profiting, knowing everything.

"The baronet is a connoisseur of art, you see, having made the Grand Tour."

Bernardo Baldoni climbed the front steps and opened the door with a key. He led them along the central hall, dim and painted a dispirited green, down a flight of stairs, to a closed door at the bottom. It opened to a big kitchen, legacy of finer days when this had been somebody's mansion. This was a high-ceilinged space, well proportioned, with pale, whitewashed walls. The curtains hung in folds of five or six different whites depending on how the light came through. Polished pans hung, a line of copper, above the sideboard. Vermeer would have used this as a backdrop for jewel-colored clothing.

Cami hung back at the door for a moment, pressed against him.

There were four women inside the kitchen. Three at the table dealing with vegetables. One, dressed in black, leaning over the fire.

Bernardo said, "Look who I have brought home, at last."

They were on their feet in an instant, staring, wondering. The oldest of the three, very old, very thin, took a step forward. "Sara?"

Bernardo pushed Cami forward. "Our Sara."

"It cannot be."

"How did you find her?"

"Little Sara? In England? After all this time? How could this happen?"

Baldoni closed in from every side and Cami was swept away from him in a tide of questions and exclamations.

She didn't seem to be in immediate danger from these family members. He stepped back, put his shoulders to the wall so nobody could get behind him, and watched.

They were babbling in Tuscan, the language of Florence and surroundings. He'd spent months in Tuscany so it was easy to follow.

The old woman, tiny, energetic, white haired, with a nose like a scythe, held Cami's face between her hands, looking, searching. "Truly, it is. I see Marcello in her. She has his eyes."

"*Sia ringrazio il Cielo.* Thanks be to the saints."

"Where have you been? Why didn't you write? One letter. If you had sent one letter . . ."

It should have been easy for him to step back and become nothing but eyes and ears to observe and evaluate. But this time he couldn't make himself detached. The cool shell he'd lived inside seemed to be permanently cracked. Cami had done that.

She was passed from woman to woman, embraced, kissed, and—yes—scolded. The matron with rolled-up sleeves and hands white with flour kept muttering, "England of all places. England! A Baldoni hiding in London. It is unnatural."

"You should have come home. All these years."

"We thought you were dead, along with Marcello and Giannetta."

"*Ma abbiamo cercato dappertutto!* We looked everywhere. Everywhere! There is no corner of Paris we did not search."

"Why didn't you come to us?"

The door slammed back. Two men strode in, alert, tense,

pistol in hand. Young men with Baldoni faces and cold Tuscan eyes. Florentine bravos, right out of the Renaissance.

Gun barrels came up, swung around. One to Cami. One to him.

He didn't twitch. Cami went just as still.

The men—barely men, men one step up from being boys—kept their attention tight on him, on Cami. Fingers ready, but not on the trigger. They were idiots to pull guns in a crowded room full of women and children, but they had either training or good instincts.

And they were just as wary of Cami as they were of him. Excellent instincts.

The old woman snapped, "*Attenti!* Be careful, *idioti.*"

"*Aspetta!*" One man grabbed the other's arm.

Bernardo gestured impatiently and both guns were lowered, uncocked, and put away into deep pockets of the coats. The old woman—Aunt Fortunata—stalked over to cuff the young men and tell them they were fools. They would make Sara think they were outlaws, Bulgars, barbarians, *briganti.* They would frighten her away, tearing in here like madmen. It did not matter what they'd thought. They did not think at all.

Five or six conversations in rapid-fire Tuscan resumed as if nothing had happened. The pair hung their heads sheepishly and let themselves be poked in the waistcoat by a long skinny finger, soundly abused, and marched across to meet Cami.

A glimpse of the Baldoni at home. A year ago he'd led a gang of hotheaded boys just like these, from Lombardy and Piedmont and Tuscany, making raids on the French. He eased his fingers off the hilt of his knife but left his hand tucked casually into his jacket.

Baldoni arrived from the rest of the house, pushing past him with quick, sidelong, surreptitious inspections. A man of middle years, dressed like a well-to-do merchant. A woman carrying a baby. A younger man with ink-stained hands. Anywhere else, that would make him a clerk or accountant. Here, he was probably a forger. Two girls, thirteen or fourteen, dark-eyed and graceful as fawns. Scouting the fringes of the main army, keeping behind a cover of skirts and chairs, were roving skirmishers, children not yet waist high. Uncle Uberto, Cousin Maria, Aunt Grazia, Cousin Amalia, another Cousin Maria—all indiscriminately related.

Cami folded in seamlessly among them, as if she'd always been there. As if she'd returned from a routine mission to cheat the good folk of Birmingham or Bristol and everyone was glad to see her back. As if they'd saved her a chair by the fire.

This was family. Unshakable bonds and unquestioning acceptance. He'd never had family, but he knew it when he saw it.

This was what she'd lost when the Tuteurs brought her to the Coach House and made a spy of her. She'd slept on the mat next to his in the long attic dormitory the Cachés shared. Most of them cried when they first came. Not Vérité. Night after night he'd seen her lying in the dark with her eyes open and her face empty, not crying at all.

Emotional reunions didn't change the fact they'd misplaced a nine-year-old girl. He wouldn't let them just reach out and snatch her back.

Bernardo Baldoni planned to do exactly that.

Cami was having the dramatis personae explained to her at length. ". . . the son of your cousin Catarina. She married an Albini, Geragio Albini, who was the great-grandson of Alrigo Baldoni, your great-grandfather's cousin. Catarina is also a cousin on your mother's side through the Targioni."

Cami kept saying, "Yes," and "I see," looking dazed and pleased.

The noise rose, echoing off plaster walls and the stone floor. Uberto—called "uncle" by everyone, but apparently a distant cousin—retrieved wine bottles from a cabinet in the far corner. One of the Marias brought glasses. The pair of shy young girls shook out a white linen cloth together and pulled it across the table. A happy family scene. What made it ironic was that any of these laughing, gesticulating Baldoni might kill him, if they came up with a marginally sufficient reason. He was counting the women in that, right down to those two doe-eyed girls.

Nobody looked at him directly, which said exactly how much everybody was watching him.

"... your cousin Emilio's wife's niece, Maria-Angiola. The one from Pisa ..."

The two men who'd come in carrying guns had transformed into smiling, charming, handsome dandies. "Is it really you? The Sara who was lost? I'm your cousin Antonio."

"Antonio?" Cami blinked up at him. "Tonio? You used to chase me with frogs."

"I was toughening you up, like a good Baldoni woman."

That was a Baldoni to keep an eye on. "Cousin Tonio." Dark, lean, no more than twenty. But older men detoured around him, deferred to him, watched him. He was important in this family.

He threw an arm across the shoulder of the man at his right. "This fool is my baby brother, Giomar. He was this tall—like this—the size of Nicolo over there—when you left. He won't remember you at all."

"I remember her. When we had sweet rolls on Sundays she'd give me the raisins out of hers."

"... Catarina's mother was Baldoni. That was Luisa, the daughter of Jacobino Baldoni, your great-great-uncle. Luisa ran off with a Frenchman, but her second marriage, after they dealt with the Frenchman, was to a Rossi."

"... counterfeit ducats from the Grisons into France. Everybody knows how it's done. But, no, they decide to be clever ..."

"A good wine. Very nice. I'll bring up another bottle."

"She is the picture of Giannetta. The image of her."

"... idiots decided they'd save money by not bribing the ..."

"The mortadella from Prato. That one."

The kitchen was lit with expressive faces, warmed with bright dresses, punctuated with the impact of ink black hair pulled into a knot at the nape of the neck, plaited in a long dark river of a braid, or tousled in curls. They all had the tawny gold skin of Filippino Lippi angels. The young ones even looked like angels. They must find that useful.

Cami was so unmistakably one of them. Her features, her

skin, her hair were Florentine as any Renaissance Medici. *I'm supposed to see faces. Why didn't I see that?*

". . . so I'm playing banker. Me!" Cousin Antonio threw his hands up, protesting, in the easy athletic gesture of a fighter. "A banker. I wear dull coats and pontificate on the pound sterling and the volatility of India bonds."

Cami murmured something.

". . . one of Old Paolo's schemes. We were going to abandon it, but there it sat, making money. Every year, more and more money. We can't give it up just because it's legitimate."

The band of children seethed underfoot, aided by three—no, four—dogs. A baby howled. No one paused in the crowded dance of bodies going to and fro. They touched in passing, put an arm around a cousin—everybody seemed to be a cousin—handed the baby back and forth.

This was how Baldoni lived when they weren't playing roles, in this din, this confusion, this breathing in each other's breath. Nothing could be further from the cold expectations of the house he'd grown up in.

"I do this in my office"—Antonio made a motion of moving stacks of coin—"and suddenly money is in the Austrian branch. Then I charge as if I'd shipped gold in a pouch, with a fee and bribes for every border."

"We will make *ribollita* from yesterday's soup and chicken *alla cacciatore.*"

"The real profit comes from changing currencies. When we buy and sell it's like coins falling down from the sky." Antonio shook his head. "There has to be something wrong with that being legal."

Bernardo Baldoni came across the room toward him, carrying a glass in each hand, and offered him one.

Baldoni bearing gifts. He took the wine and raised it to his lips and didn't drink any. Baldoni all over the room would make note of that and know what it meant.

"It's a happy occasion that brings Sara back where she belongs." Bernardo drank from his own glass. "I thank you for your part in this."

"She's Camille now."

A tiny hesitation. "She has changed," Bernardo agreed. "But she's still our Sara. Still Baldoni."

He said, "Of course," in a voice that meant just the opposite.

Cami had acquired a glass of wine, Aunt Fortunata, and a pair of young matrons, one at each ear, talking, one with the baby on her hip. That was the baby that had been passed from Baldoni to Baldoni till there was no telling who it belonged to.

"She hasn't forgotten her Italian," Bernardo said.

"That's good. Though your English is excellent."

"We learn English from babyhood. Something of a family tradition."

"Is it?"

"Tuscany has always been full of the English—travelers, mercenaries, exiles, artists, madmen . . . spies. We've found the English profitable over the years. Our relationship with our French masters is less satisfying." Without any sign he was changing the subject, he said, "How is an agent of the British Service concerned with my niece?"

"We've known each other awhile."

"And how does that come about?"

"It's a long story. And not my story. It's Cami's."

Bernardo waited, gravely polite, for more comment. When that didn't arrive, he said, "You respect her privacy. That is admirable."

"I respect her skill with edged weapons. Let's go outside. You could float an egg on the noise in here."

A nod. "We must talk, Mr. Paxton."

Cami looked up to see them leave, but it was Antonio who followed him out. Antonio and three Baldoni walking at his back. He didn't like it that Antonio looked thoughtful. Thoughtful men were more dangerous than angry men.

Twenty-nine

By his actions, you will know the man.

A BALDONI SAYING

BY THE TIME SHE DISENTANGLED HERSELF FROM cousins and aunts and a small child inexplicably wound around her legs, Pax was gone. She found him in the hall, almost to the front door. Her path to him was complicated by Tonio and the stiff-legged fighting cocks who swaggered behind him, playing at being dangerous, and didn't want to share the game with her.

Or—it was no game. These cousins of hers were most certainly deadly. They were simply much less deadly than Pax.

They were three tomcats trailing a tiger. Who was in a bad mood, most likely. And everyone was heavily armed. It is almost impossible to hold reasoned discussion once pistols enter the conversation.

Bernardo opened the front door politely and stepped through first. Baldoni politeness. One does not force a guest to present his back to a possible enemy.

Bernardo was saying, ". . . considerably more joyful than I expected when Lazarus sent word someone had used an old, old recognition signal. I assumed I would be dealing with a fraud."

"A reasonable expectation."

"It would not be the first time a stranger has claimed to be Baldoni," Bernardo said. "Briefly."

Pax took the front steps, his back insouciant, his step deliberate, his hand—she could tell by the angle of his arm—on a knife. He was ignoring his tail of escort. Tonio would find that annoying.

She pushed past cousin, cousin, cousin, and cousin and went to where Pax and Uncle Bernardo had stopped to confront one another at the low iron railing that separated the house from the pavement.

When she hurried up, Pax looked down at her with his calm, serious face and the smile that didn't escape from deep in his eyes. To Bernardo he said, "Do you think she's an impostor?"

"She is my nephew's child. There was never a moment of doubt. I know her as I know my own sons."

Tonio and his fighting tail of bad judgment arrived. She said, "He's my friend," and clarified that with, "If any of you touch a gun, I'll break your fingers."

Uncle Bernardo said, "There is no question of welcome, Mr. Paxton. She is one of us."

It was early afternoon. The street was without shade and almost empty of people. The few men and women going about their business showed no interest. If attentive eyes peered at them from hidden corners, they were discreet about it.

Her cousins slipped away, one gliding casually down the pavement, others out into the street. They were not spectators at a coming fight. They intended to be participants. She did not bother to point this out to Pax, who was perfectly capable of seeing for himself.

Baldoni men, and many of the women, prepared themselves for adventurous lives. Antonio would have taken lessons in boxing and fencing. He'd be a crack shot. He'd traveled in dangerous places. The three men at his back were young, strong, and equally well trained.

But they faced someone outside their experience—a man who lived in the cold shadows they occasionally passed through on their way to a profitable venture elsewhere.

Pax didn't fight for sport. His calculations didn't include shaking hands afterward.

She didn't say, "Pax, my cousins would very much like to rescue me from something and you are handy. Don't hurt them."

Antonio stepped into Pax's path and said, in English, "Go back to Lazarus and tell him we'll settle whatever claim he has on Sara. She is Baldoni. Ours. Run tell him that, *figlio di puttana*."

"He's not from Lazarus," she snapped.

"All the better," Antonio said. "Nothing to stop me from cutting his bollocks off."

"You will leave his bollocks precisely as they are."

"I am your closest male relation—"

"You are my closest male idiot. No one removes any man's balls on my behalf. I will do whatever castrating is necessary among my acquaintance."

"Children," Uncle Bernardo said mildly, "he speaks Italian."

Pax wasn't revealing a knowledge of Italian on his face. That meant . . . "You know him, Uncle."

"I know of him," her uncle said. "Antonio. You and the others . . ." He motioned to the cardinal points of the compass. Without comment, her cousins separated to take up positions at the distant edges of sight, guarding, watching, and not hearing whatever Uncle Bernardo was about to say.

That left her standing between Pax and Uncle Bernardo as one might stand between unfriendly wolfhounds.

"You did not know Mr. Paxton had lived in Italy?" Bernardo said.

She could have filled libraries with what she didn't know about Pax. "It doesn't amaze me."

"Or that he killed men there? Many men. Not openly in the duello, not in battle. He came as a sneak thief in the night and murdered."

She didn't answer. Decoders learn many secrets. She'd coded messages in and out of Italy. One agent sometimes received orders to kill.

Uncle Bernardo continued to speak mildly. "We are realists in Italy. France and Austria fight their battles across our countryside, as they have for centuries. We are the bosom friend of whichever army is closest. When Monsieur Bonaparte marched so swiftly and destructively around Italy, many nations followed events with considerable attention. Including the English."

"As they would," Pax answered, speaking the language of Florence, of Tuscany, of the Baldoni family.

"One man who concerned himself particularly was named Il Gatto Grigio—the Gray Cat, so called because it is said all cats are gray in the dark."

"A melodramatic name," Pax said.

"We are a melodramatic people, we Italians," her uncle replied. "It was said that Il Gatto came and went among the French armies, unseen, like a cat. Where he passed, munitions dumps exploded, supply trains were lost to landslides, donkeys could not march because their feed was tainted, and prisoners escaped before execution."

"Sounds like a dozen men at work," Pax said, "and one man taking the credit."

Uncle Bernardo nodded. "It might be so. It was also said that Il Gatto did more than harass and harry the French. French soldiers who committed atrocities upon unarmed villages died at his hands. Il Gatto found them, no matter how well they guarded themselves. And that, I think, was the work of one man."

"Possibly," Pax said.

Uncle Bernardo said, "He struck alone, at night, silently. The country people said he walked through walls. Il Gatto was mist that blew away. The whisper of leaves."

"A nuisance to the French," Pax said.

She had known Il Gatto Grigio was an English agent. Until now, she hadn't known it was Pax. In a world filled with brutes, the British Service had chosen Pax for that work. Damn them anyway.

"He was said to be a Piedmontese. Or a man of Venice. Or a Florentine. He was black haired and swarthy. He had light brown hair and a scarred face. He was dark haired and walked with a limp. He was an Austrian spy, pale and light haired under his disguises."

"A gray cat indeed."

"And like a cautious cat, he trusted very few men. Many claimed to know him, but the real number was only a few dozen. I was most fortunate to have one of my own in his inner circle—the boy who led the donkeys and hid with Il Gatto in the hills was a Baldoni. So I knew the Gatto was pale under his disguises and almost certainly English."

"There are no secrets." Pax might have been having a conversation that bored him.

"The boy showed me Il Gatto once, in Mantua, drinking coffee at a café on the other side of the square. I was surprised and not surprised to find the man who so annoyed the French was a thin brown scholar no one would notice, harmless and unmemorable. You were reading a book at the time. I was told later it was Virgil."

"A scholar's choice of reading."

"I think, if you rolled up your right sleeve I would see a scar on your forearm."

Indifferent, Pax said, "And if you did?"

"Then I would know you for certain." Uncle Bernardo looked left and right, to study first one end of the street and then the other. "It happened that once Il Gatto was stealing arms in the town of Varallo. It was typical of him that he paused to empty the guardhouse as he left. One of the men he saved from execution was the friend of a Baldoni."

She was tired of standing between men being subtle and unrevealing and both of them very good at it. *Enough.* "Then you owe him a debt, Uncle."

"Which I acknowledge. I suspect I owe him several. I will think upon how to repay them." Her uncle looked from her to Pax. "Mr. Paxton, we will speak again someday. You will not find me ungenerous. Call upon the Baldoni in any need and we will answer. But, for now, it's best that you leave and do not return. There is nothing here for you."

Good Lord. He's protecting me from Pax.

"He stays," she said. "Or I leave with him."

That brought Uncle Bernardo's attention to her with an almost audible snap.

"You haven't asked why I'm in London." For a little space

she'd almost forgotten the Merchant, who planned to kill her and had experience in such matters. "Or why I need someone like Lazarus."

"Whatever difficulties you face, your family will serve you." Bernardo frowned and gestured. "You have no need of Lazarus. Or of Mr. Paxton. Sara, what is this man to you?"

"A friend."

"He is British Service. To befriend the police is to lay your hand in the mouth of a rabid dog."

"I knew him before he was British Service. Long ago."

Her uncle looked on her soberly, obviously searching for the right words. "There is much to admire in Mr. Paxton. He is a hero in Italy. When the French offered extravagant rewards for his death, there was no farmhouse in Piedmont or Tuscany where he could not hide and be sure of safety."

"I'm not surprised." And she wasn't. She had seen him gather the Cachés around him and transform them into a band of brothers and sisters.

Her uncle, with almost visible reluctance, went on. "He is an assassin, Sara. He has killed many times. There is an emptiness in the soul of such men." Uncle Bernardo paused. "What is he to you?"

Pax gave no sign he was being discussed in this depth. He stood in that relaxed fighter's stance that meant he might pull out his watch and consult it for the exact time or he might attack, without warning, in any direction. He had his hand negligently on his knife and was exactly one lunge from Uncle Bernardo's waistcoat buttons. He was also keeping an eye on her cousins. Who could blame him?

She said, "He is a friend."

"Friend" was wholly inadequate to describe Pax. He was bastion, shield, and implacable protection. He was a friend as a stone castle is a house.

"Baldoni use the word 'friend' carefully," Bernardo said. "It is an obligation second only to family. We do not—"

"I understand what that means." It is at such moments one chooses loyalties.

"Whatever this Paxton has been to you—"

"You cannot imagine what he has been to me, Uncle Bernardo. When I was alone in Paris, without family, abandoned—"

"The family never abandoned you. It was Francesco. Only Francesco pursued your father."

"Vendetta."

"Not vendetta. Never vendetta. My child . . . My child . . . Cesare sent your father into exile to prevent a bloodbath that would have destroyed us all. Francesco acted in evil madness, in unforgivable betrayal." Uncle Bernardo was pale, breathing heavily, his voice harsh with suppressed anger and pain. "When you knocked on the gates and begged for help, every Baldoni was gone from Paris. Francesco sent lying words to you. Lies. An hour later he hanged himself inside the house."

Pax said, "She was a child. She was alone. With all the resources of the Baldoni, you didn't find her."

"We shook that city like a rug, street by street. A dozen of us, for weeks."

"You didn't find her," Pax said.

"For which there will never be sufficient recompense."

"Then pay her back now," Pax said. "She doesn't need a hearty convivial dinner or more cousins with babies. She needs . . ." He faced her. "What do you need, Cami?"

She started with the blackmail letter delivered in Brodemere and ended with the address on Semple Street. Some secrets—the Mandarin Code, the Fluffy Aunts' profession—she omitted.

Tonio and the cousins returned and drew in close, listening.

She ended with, "If I can't find where the Merchant has hidden Camille Desançon and free her, I will walk alone on Semple Street into the hands of the Merchant. With your help, I am hoping to do that and still live." She looked from one face to the other. They were so intent, so eager, she could smile.

"I'd like to kill the Merchant." Giomar said that. "I'd like to be the man who did that."

"You will be the man who holds the horses. I'll do the killing." Tonio suddenly didn't look much older than when she'd known him in Tuscany.

Pax, in a voice of calm reason, said, "The kill is mine. My choice whether he lives or dies. This is not open to debate."

They were all speaking Tuscan. This, in itself, was an incitement to extremity. From the Medici onward, she could not begin to imagine the number of murders that had been planned in that language.

Cousin Alessandro suggested drawing cards for the privilege.

Pax cut him off. "The British Service wants him taken alive. That's a good deal harder than just shooting him."

Tonio grinned, all but rubbing his hands together. "This sounds like fun."

"We do not undertake a hazardous game because it is 'fun.'" Under half-closed lids, Bernardo regarded Pax, then her. "Nor do the Baldoni annoy the British Service unnecessarily. So long as someone destroys the Merchant it does not matter which hand holds the knife. Cami, let us come inside and you will tell us your exact plans. Mr. Paxton, join us. Perhaps you will feel safe in drinking wine with us this time, having been declared a friend."

hirty

If you do not have the rope to hold your ass, do not weave a halter to catch him.

A BALDONI SAYING

MAYFAIR BELONGED TO THE DECOROUS, WELL groomed rich and their deferential servants. The City of London was public buildings, the mint, the great banking houses, and many boring, self-important men.

Soho was considerably livelier. It housed most of the French of the city, rich and poor, royalist and radical, a congregation of every sort and condition of French humanity. If the Merchant wanted to be inconspicuous, this was where he'd come.

Cami visited Soho Square when she was in London with the Fluffy Aunts. This was another neighborhood of bookshops, Italian and French. It occurred to her, as she walked past familiar shops and cafés, that she knew London chiefly by its bookshops.

Pax walked beside her. He slid his thumb along the brim of his hat, turning it downward a fraction of an inch, perfecting his disguise. He'd made himself look entirely French, somehow, by putting on an artist's neckerchief and a faint smell of turpentine. He carried a large sketchbook—borrowed from her cousin Maria—against his chest.

The half-pleasant, half-uneasy buzz of desiring hadn't left her. If anything, it was growing stronger as they went about this workaday task together. He distracted her. Part of her attention was stuck to him like glue, pulling significance from every ordinary gesture. She looked at his careful, clever fingers wrapped around the book and wanted them on her skin.

"You should dye your hair darker," she said.

"I will in a bit, when I get back to Meeks Street."

"My cousin Maria would have done it for you. She's good at things like that." After a minute she added, "You're safe with my family."

He made a noncommittal noise.

Perhaps he had a point. She'd eaten the *piccolo convivio* with her family, reveling in cheeses, fine olives, and bread pulled quickly from the iron pan on the coals of the hearth. But she'd taken her wine from the bottle Pax drank from and made sure nobody slipped anything in his soup.

She trusted her family implicitly. She simply didn't trust them with Pax.

She said, "It's only for these next two days. After that you won't have to meet them again. When I finish dealing with the Merchant, I intend to run from England like a scalded cat."

"To a desert island with coconuts?"

"To Tuscany." She supposed she was happy to be going home. The thought of leaving England—and Pax—was a squirming bundle of worries and hopes and fears. She didn't even try to sort it out. She just carried it around with her and took it out now and then to shake her head over it.

Here was another hat shop. The sixteenth hat shop. She was keeping count. "Two minutes," she said and accepted the sketchbook from his hand and ducked inside.

Pax watched her through the plate glass window while she opened his sketchbook to the milliner's assistant, the milliner, and two women from the back of the shop. He'd drawn Camille Besançon's hat right down to the last cherry from her description.

But—No. Not their work. No one had seen one like it. No one knew who'd made it. Sorry.

They were also unacquainted with the Merchant and the

Merchant's henchman when she flipped over the next page
and the next and showed those sketches.

Back on the street, she shrugged. "I wish they wouldn't try
to sell me bonnets. I'd never noticed how many hideous hats
there are in London. She says there's a milliner's in the next
street."

"We'll head that way, then."

They walked on, side-by-side, studying every face they
passed. She said, "There are more hat shops in Soho than I
would have guessed."

"It always seems that way, whatever you're looking for. I
once carried a bit of cake around Vienna, trying to find who
made it. Lots of pastry shops in Vienna."

"If this is being a spy, I'm glad I gave up the work. It's
boring."

"This is being a spy," Pax said.

He was a spy, honed by years in the mountains of her
homeland, killing men and avoiding the French army. He
looked particularly harmless when carrying a sketchbook.

She'd have Pax with her when she went to meet the Merchant. The knot in her stomach loosened a little, remembering that.

There were plenty of Frenchmen to look at in Soho, men
washed ashore by the Revolution and the wars. Old Frenchmen wearing wigs and shabby brocade coats from the Old
Regime. Young Frenchmen wearing the sober black and long
hair of the French radicals. None of them were the Frenchmen she needed, however.

"The man has to be in Soho." She wasn't trying to convince Pax. She was coercing the world into doing her bidding.
"Soho is close to Semple Street. Close enough to the church
in Fetter Lane. Everything fits. Everything about Soho makes
sense."

"A good reason for him to be elsewhere."

"I know." She felt grumpy about this truth.

They turned the corner, both of them taking the opportunity to assess the streets in every direction. They were still
being followed by the street rats who belonged to Lazarus.
One of her cousins—young Lucia—had attached herself to

them when they left the Baldoni kitchen. It was considered good training for the young to follow a friendly family member about the streets. The dark-haired man, Pax's friend, brought up the rear, insolent and open about it.

Pax took the sketchbook into the next tavern while she inspected the tiny shop window next door. Behind dusty glass, it displayed many shades of silk thread. She thought about the supply needs of a small band of murderous Frenchmen based in Soho. It made a sort of grid pattern in her mind, relating importance and frequency. Wine was near the top left. A hat with cherries on it was relegated to the bottom right. Small corners of speculation and conclusion filled her brain. Pax, in the taverns, had more chance of success than she did.

From time to time she half turned to the street, taking inventory of the pack that kept an eye on her, studying the faces of men going past.

She was seen in return.

A man driving a one-horse cart suddenly dropped the reins, vaulted down to the street, and ran. She caught the flash of movement but not one single impression of his face. If he'd kept driving and looked away from her, she wouldn't have noticed him at all.

Too short and stocky to be the Merchant. It had to be one of his French minions. Someone who'd seen her and knew her.

She dove into the street, offending the horses of an oncoming carriage, already startled by the Merchant's henchman running under their noses, already clattering and snorting, dancing in the traces. A man on horseback skittered sideways and snarled words she didn't catch.

She dodged all that. Followed an outraged shout ahead of her, wove past one dark coat and another. Her quarry looked back over his shoulder and now she recognized him. It was the man of large ears and poorly cropped hair that she'd tracked from one Soho tavern to another. The man the Merchant had set to following her.

A second chance at him. A second chance at everything he knew if she could catch him, bring him down, question him.

Thirty feet ahead, he shoved a woman aside. Her

companion—a stocky, pugnacious middle-aged fellow—objected. Grabbed him. The two men grappled back and forth across the pavement. Then the henchman kicked out and hit groin. Broke loose and plunged ahead.

She ran after him, dodging the idiots who blocked her way. Too many of them—

Somebody yelled, "He's got a gun!"

Men scrambled back. A space opened in front of her. The Frenchman held a pistol in his outstretched hand. Raised it.

Hard muscle crashed into her. Knocked her sideways, stumbling, off balance. The pistol fired with a huge crack and a flash of light.

For an instant, everything was eerily silent.

Pax's body crushed her to a rough brick wall. His strength, his miraculous speed, had knocked her out of the line of the bullet.

His face, hard and angry, was inches away. He ran his hands over her, roughly, fast, up and down both her sides. Over the back of her neck. Looked at his hands and didn't see blood.

One sharp nod and he was gone, running in a long stride, bent low, a spear cast through the confusion, unstoppable, headed straight for the Frenchman.

Who saw him coming, threw away the useless pistol, and drew a knife. Swung to meet Pax in a wide-legged defensive stance.

He'd have done better to run. None of these people had ever seen Pax on the sparring field of the Coach House.

Pax didn't meet the Frenchman head-on. At the last moment of the headlong charge, Pax flipped his knife to a reverse grip, flashed past on the right, avoided a strike, and slashed the inside of the man's forearm.

Classic Pax. That was a permanent disarm, if done right.

The Frenchman gasped and dropped his knife.

The kill stroke for that attack was an immediate upward jab to the right kidney. But Pax just raked across the jacket as he went by, leaving it slit and hanging, the shirt exposed, and a line of bleeding red across the man's back.

From everywhere, all at once, men closed together in a

circle and started shouting. One could count on the enthusiasm of the Englishman for a fight. Any fight.

She headed in, considering tactics as she went. Pax could do a kill on his own. A disable-and-capture was hard as the devil. An easy way to get killed. It needed two fighters, not one.

Slash. Slash. Pax forced the Frenchman back toward a shop front, avoiding the knife the man brought out left-handed.

Corner. Control. Disarm. *We have him.* She slipped between bystanders to join this endgame. *When we have him, we have the Merchant.*

Then some idiot hurried into the fight, squawking orders. A wide little man, well padded, waddling with importance. "See here. See here, now. There'll be no public brawling in the streets. I am Sir Henry Clitheroe, Justice of the Peace for Roxingbury and Upper—"

Of all the fools—

Every other soul in the crowd—man, woman, beldame, and toddling baby—had sense enough to keep away from the edge of those knives. Sir Henry stepped right between Pax and the Frenchman, waving his hat as if chasing off chickens.

Was there ever a greater invitation? The Frenchman grabbed Sir Henry, pressed his knife to the flapping wattles of that chin, and backed away, dragging along the Sir Henry and all his protests.

Pax began talking in French, soft and calm. "Let him go. You haven't hurt anyone yet. It's easy now, because nobody's hurt."

She slid through the crowd, closer and closer to the Frenchman's back. A man at the curb fretted and poked his cane in the direction of all the drama, asking everyone around him what was going on. As she passed, she appropriated the cane because it was going to come in useful.

Faster now because she used the cane to clear her path, she came in behind the Frenchman. He didn't see her. Pax, though, did. He crossed, light-footed, left to right, edging the man between them. He made the handsignals they'd used when they fought as a team at the Coach House on the training field.

Sir Henry, bleeding from shallow cuts at his throat, threatened transportation and hanging.

She swung the cane like a club, whacking the Frenchman's elbow. The knife jerked away, dropped, and stopped threatening that throat. Pax pulled Sir Henry—protesting, squirming, yelling—out of the way.

The crowd howled like a single animal. She jammed the cane between the Frenchman's legs. He kicked at her and missed, kept his footing, spun, and ran into the jumbled wagons, horses, and carts of the street.

She threw the cane away and went after him. To her left, Pax ran flat out to circle around and cut him off.

And in the street a sporting rig and high-stepping pair pranced along, two wheels on the pavement, avoiding the brouhaha, making good time.

The Frenchman pelted out in front of them. The horses reared and came down with iron hooves and the Frenchman fell. The driver fought, pulling the reins, and the horses screamed, a terrible sound. Rose up on their haunches and came down again. Impossible to stop. Impossible to control. The light carriage rocked and tilted, about to go over.

Frantic men came to help, grabbed at the halter and straps, trying to contain the plunging, squealing carriage horses.

In the gutter, the Frenchman died without a sound. When the white-faced, terrified young driver backed his horses away from the red bundle on the street, life had been gone for a long time.

Thirty-one

"YOU TOOK IT FROM ME. YOU STOLE IT. EVERYBODY saw that. Theft. Outright theft." That was the man whose cane she'd borrowed. He talked at her from one side, then tap-tapped around to the other side and said much the same thing there.

A very dead man lay in the road. Pax stood behind her, his arms wrapped around her. He was wonderfully solid and she let herself lean back against him just the smallest amount. She would rather have been with him somewhere they weren't looking at dead people.

Far down the street, some merciful souls had taken the horses to the street pump to wash them clean. The driver sat on the steps of a house a dozen yards away, his head in his hands. Every once in a while he'd get up and go into the alley to the side and empty his stomach.

She hoped Cousin Lucia had left. She didn't see the girl anywhere in the circle of avid faces. Lazarus's apprentice thieves were at the front, showing an intense, professional curiosity.

Pax's friend, the angry, dark-haired one, knelt and searched the corpse from his hair to the soles of his boots, efficiently and with no sign of distaste. His findings—a handful of coins and two keys—were piled on the pavement at his side. The dead man hadn't carried a scrap of paper. There was no maker's mark in the hat that lay, brim upward, next to him.

"A careful man," she said quietly. "He never put anything in his pockets."

"Carry nothing when you're working," Pax said, quoting the Tuteurs at the Coach House.

"My family has a similar motto. We say, 'Everything in your pocket gossips about you.'"

"You have an interesting family."

"Thank you. We pride ourselves on our collected wisdom." She leaned more strongly against him. She shook in her muscles, fine little trembles that came and went. Just the tiniest shaking. It was from being shot at, she thought.

"I'll report you." The man she'd deprived of the use of his cane, for a very few minutes, brandished it in her face. "I'll have you arrested. There's a Justice of the Peace here."

At the edge of all great events, there will be some fool who has no idea what's going on. Who makes a nuisance of himself and gets in everyone's way. She kept her eyes on the grim, careful search of the body and said, "If you don't put that stick away, I'll ram it up your posterior till it comes out your nose."

She continued to not look at him. After a minute, heels, interspersed by the tap of his cane, clicked away rapidly.

Pax hadn't released his arms from around her. She felt his amusement playing back and forth in his muscles.

"I'd better look at the body," she said. "Your friend knows what he's doing with the dead, but I might see something."

"The more eyes, the better." He tucked her arm through his as if they were strolling across a park. Where they went, however, was to the corpse.

She knelt beside the limp bundle on the pavement, careful to keep her skirts out of the widening pool of blood. The man's eyes were open and staring. That was the worst part of those dead by violence. The eyes were always open and always empty.

"I suppose you can improve your sketch," she said to Pax, "now that you have the model in front of you."

"I can."

She didn't really look at the body for a while, though her eyes were pointed in that direction. Her mind seemed stuck in place, like a wagon spinning its wheels in deep mud. Finally, stupidly, she said, "At least we killed the right man."

"He needed it," Pax said. "He worked for the Merchant. See anything?"

Only death. This sort of thing was what she escaped when she chose the quiet life of Brodemere. Pax's friend rolled the body to this side and that to unbutton clothing and methodically go through pockets.

She put out a hand. "Stop."

He glared at her.

"On the trouser leg. There." She pointed. "What is it?"

"Stable dirt." He dismissed her.

She pinched some up. Smelled it. "Sawdust . . . wood shavings. Oak maybe. It needs an expert."

Annoyance flickered in the young face and was gone, leaving a sort of dark amusement. "Maybe he visited a coffin maker. He'll need one." Pax's friend plucked out a new handkerchief—he seemed to have several—spread it on his open hand, and brushed shavings and wood dust into it. "I would have come to that part of him in a bit. See anything else?"

She shook her head and stood up. "I'll look at the wagon."

Someone had led the Frenchman's horse and cart out of the middle of the road, where he'd abandoned them. She ran her hand over the horse's back. This was a piebald horse, short legged and unlovely, matched with a sturdy, short cart. Everything utilitarian and well cared for, from the wheels to the hooves of the horses. This was a jobbing cart from a reliable yard. When she made a circuit of it she found, burned into the wood on the back right side, the words *McCarthy, Nibb Lane, Soho*.

"Six streets that way." Pax indicated with a little jerk of his head.

"The Merchant is in Soho."

"Or he wants to make us think he's here."

"Then he's succeeded. I think he's in Soho."

The little horse was of a placid, urbane disposition, calm in place and incurious. She went over the harness, which was wholly ordinary and recently cleaned. The horseshoes held the usual collection of city detritus. They'd been cleaned recently. "He hires a small cart, not a coach. He needs to shift something he won't carry in a coach. Something dirty. Something bulky. Secret. Stolen. Something that attracts attention."

"A body," Pax contributed.

Was Camille Besançon already murdered, and her body disposed of? "Or a prisoner, bound and gagged."

Pax might have turned the pages in her mind and read them. "He has no reason to kill that woman before the meeting." Pax squatted beside the front wheel and took out a two-inch magnifier. "He plans ahead. He leaves people alive while there's any possible use for them."

They worked in tandem, silently, for a few minutes. She said, "There's nothing by the driver's seat. Not a speck. Not a crumb."

She looked at every crevice of the frame and springs while he went over the four wheels. After a while, she said, "I haven't killed very many men. Those people in the Coach House were the first. And then, one man who came to Brodemere. And now the Frenchman."

Pax said, "You didn't kill this man. Those horses did."

"I've also never been shot at." A tarp covered the surface of the little wagon. She took a corner and waited for Pax to take the other. "I don't think I like it."

"Getting hit is worse."

"Strangely, that is no comfort at all." She nodded and they pulled the tarp back, uncovering the bed of the cart.

She knew the smell. Would have recognized it earlier if a whiff of it hadn't already been floating in the air.

Pax said, "Gunpowder." He was not informing her. He confirmed what they'd both realized.

"Guns?" She shook her head slowly. "An attack on something? A riot?" Twenty years ago, the Gordon Riots had torn the town apart, threatened the rich and powerful.

"Not riot." The dark-haired man, Pax's friend, came up behind her. "If the French were brewing civil insurrection, we'd have heard about it. We have well-paid informers. Informers on informers." He asked Pax, "You want to see a collection of dull coinage? No? Can't say I blame you." He tucked away a bulky handkerchief. "And that is the delicate odor of gunpowder."

"We noticed," Pax said dryly. "Cami, this is Hawker. Hawk, this is Cami."

She ignored the introduction, as did Mr. Hawker. She'd heard of Hawker from the Fluffy Aunts' gossip. She could only hope he knew far less about her than she did about him.

The planking of the wagon was gray-brown, dry, and clean. She paced two steps sideways, watching the light on the wood's surface. She said, "Not guns."

Pax was looking at the same thing. "No oil."

Guns live in a light film of oil, or they rust. Everywhere they're stored, they leave smears of gun oil. Even wrapped in burlap, they'd leave the distinctive smell of the oil behind. None of that here.

She swept her fingers into the crevice between boards and came away with coarse black powder under her nails. She smelled it, rubbed it between her fingers, and confirmed what she did not want to know.

"Gunpowder," Pax said. "A wagonload."

The young man, Hawker, murmured, "We are in big trouble."

This was suddenly no longer a spy game played with secrets and codes. The lives to be lost were no longer counted in twos or threes.

In the dust at the side of the wagon, she made out a curved mark, most of it already brushed away. Then another curve next to it. Wordlessly, she followed the lines with her fingers.

"Kegs," Pax said.

"Kegs. Kegs and kegs of gunpowder." She felt sick in the pit of her stomach. "They must have been lined up all the way down the cart. You could blow up Parliament with this much powder. Or a dozen ships in harbor. Or London Bridge." *Or anything you wanted.* Who would die? Where? When? How many lives?

"Ten or twelve kegs. God help us," Pax's friend said.

"Sixteen." She counted out the places with her hand, showing him.

"You can't just buy this much." Hawker peeled the last of the canvas back, careful not to disturb the dust, doing the same thing she had, studying the faint circles left behind and the thin trace of powder. "We have a traitor somewhere in military supplies."

"It's naval stores or artillery." She tested the texture between thumb and forefinger. "Not for guns. There's a different feel to this. Larger grit. This is for cannons."

Hawker glared at her. "Of course you'd learn that, out in Brodemere, between studying Babylonian and German."

She said, "I don't actually speak Babylonian. No one does. I learned the distinctions of gunpowder when I was eleven or so."

"Cachés," Hawker said in disgust. "Gunpowder and sawdust. Probably Babylonian, too. I'm going to Daisy's."

Pax said, "We'll join you. I have to make sketches." He waved two men out of the crowd and talked to them, fast, with gestures that said it was about moving the wagon somewhere.

Someday, there would come a point at which her life could become no more dangerous and complicated. She hadn't arrived there yet, apparently.

Thirty-two

A man ruled by old hatreds is like a tree nourished upon stone.

A BALDONI SAYING

PAX SAID, "HAVE YOU EVER BEEN TO A WHORE-house?"

They'd come to a big, solid house that fronted on one of the narrow passageways in which Soho abounded. Hawker, who had stalked the whole way, ten paces ahead, ignoring them, trotted up the stairs, knocked, and was admitted. The maid who answered the door, a neat black woman of middle years, waited patiently for them to catch up.

Cami climbed the stairs beside Pax. "I find myself desperately wishing I could claim to have been a frequent visitor to brothels instead of bookshops and botanical gardens and bootmakers and that nice man in Terne Street who sells magical herbs. I'm perfectly certain female British Service agents spend more time in brothels than in hat shops."

"I'll have to think about that." As they entered, Pax got not only smiles from the black woman keeping the door but a kiss on the cheek and whispers of welcome that were not meant for Cami to hear. He was obviously much at home.

He said to the woman, "Give us a few minutes. We'll come upstairs."

They were left alone in a long, luxurious hall scattered with Persian carpets. The sideboard held an explosion of expensive lilies, roses, and irises arranged in a red Chinese vase. On the landing above, a naked bronze nymph was caught in the act of covering breast and pubis from public view.

She'd do better to just put some clothes on.

Pax had bedded the women here. Some of them. All of them? She pictured him upstairs in some . . . would there be vulgar, red-velvet coverlets? She could almost see his large hands, sensitive, assessing, responsive, on a woman's white flesh.

It would be easier to chat with the Merchant than to face these smug women who knew the secrets of Pax's body. She would be very cool and—

"I don't use whores." He interrupted her imaginary conversation with several dazzlingly beautiful courtesans. She was being polite to them. "Not the ones upstairs. Not the ones on the street."

"They know you here." Before she finished saying that, her brain had raced ahead to various logical conclusions and she knew. "You draw them. You go to brothels to sketch nude women."

"Only because women don't walk around the streets nude in this climate."

She considered whether she wanted to walk upstairs and meet the women Pax had studied in great detail, nude. Then she decided that, yes, after all, she would.

He untied the string that held her cloak and tossed it behind him, over the stair railing. "It's not that different from drawing flowers, Cami." Her bonnet was held by a simple slipknot, easy to loose. He removed it and let it fall to the smooth wood of the table, beside a vase of flowers.

"You used to draw me, when we were in the Coach House. You drew my face all the time and then you burned the sketches, because the Tuteurs would have taken them."

"You had an interesting face. You still do." His hand was on her face, his thumb, blunt, rough skinned, and gentle, slid across her lips. "Why did you tell the Baldoni you'd go with me?"

"Because I'm a grown woman and they have no control

over where I will go or who I'll see. Because I want to be with you." *The sands run out between my fingers. I have a day and a little more. Not quite two days. I am very afraid.* She said, "Could you hold me. Next to you, I mean. In your arms."

"Just what I was going to suggest."

She went toward him and folded herself into him as she would have pulled a large, warm blanket around her. His chest was the right height to lay her head upon. His shirt was soft. His coat, rough textured under her cheek. His sternum had no padding on it at all. When he put his arms around her, she felt straightforward bones and hard muscle. The knife sheath on his left forearm was bumpy and obvious. Had she ever embraced a man carrying weapons? She didn't think so. Her lovers had been comfortable country gentlemen. Unarmed.

Pax said, "For that four minutes when we were all discussing whether you were going to stay with the Baldoni or go off with me, I was wondering where to take you."

"I know a good bookshop," she said against his chest.

"I would have brought you to Daisy's. I don't have any better place to take you."

"I like to try new things. Life is a vast banquet."

"That's more of your family wisdom, isn't it? But I don't think they mean taking you to whorehouses."

"They might. We lead adventurous lives." The living presence of him, breathing and solid, was intensely real. He wore the simplest of cravats and the trailing ends of the tie hung down to press into her forehead.

Pax said, "Daisy's is a sanctuary of sorts. A neutral place. The Service hides people at Daisy's every once in a while. Lazarus does, too. The Foreign Office isn't above dropping some tricky Polish exile in here for a while. Nobody bothers anybody else. Dangerous men visit this house and they like it quiet."

"An interesting establishment."

"You'd be safe here if you don't want to go back to the Baldoni. Hawker owns part of the place. He calls himself a sleeping partner."

He took a while and kissed into her hair, again and again, as if he planned to start there and kiss every inch of her body.

He was aroused. She felt that as a hard warm thrust against her belly. A demand. A promise of sorts. When they were naked together he would be unyielding and very strong. She very much wanted to carve out a time and place to be naked with him.

Her lovers, both of them, had been country gentry, strong from hunting and husbandry. Pax was strong from fighting for his life and surviving in dangerous places. It was the difference between the hound that lives in the manor and the lean wolf that prowls the woods.

One feels very safe in the arms of a wolf. Or at least, she did.

"Your relatives are right not to trust me," he said. "I would have ignored every decency and brought you to a whorehouse. I'd have wanted to take you upstairs and make love with you."

She would have agreed. She would have taken his hand and led him upstairs herself. "You're about to say that isn't going to happen. I can read that in your tone of voice. Or maybe it's the fact we're not racing upstairs at this minute."

He said, "I won't sleep with you under a roof where women sell their bodies."

"You have scruples."

"I have none," he said flatly. "Don't misjudge me. There's no crime I haven't committed. Your uncle was right about that."

"We're graduates of the Coach House. We—"

"I was lost before I ever set foot in the place. Cami, my mother was a whore."

She couldn't see his face. He held her, breathing down into her hair, tense as strung wires. "Tell me."

"She didn't work in a brothel or get paid in coin." He'd already decided what he'd say, she thought. Already prepared the words in his mind, the way a cook gathers her ingredients out on the table before she starts mixing and chopping. "The man she lived with gave her to his friends and to men he had a use for. He was . . . frightening when she didn't do what he wanted."

"I'm sorry," she said.

"Sometimes he hurt her. I think she wanted him to hurt her." He'd become so still she couldn't feel his breath going in and out, only the iron control that locked every muscle. "He destroyed her, bit by bit. I watched him do it."

"You were a child. What—ten? Twelve?"

"Younger than that."

Pax, who'd been the strong one for all of them at the Coach House, had been a child who couldn't protect his mother. "Then you couldn't have changed anything."

"He abandoned her in Paris, in the riots of the Revolution. I kept her in the house when I could, but she'd get out and go looking for him. After a while she just stopped, like a clock that isn't wound. Didn't sleep. Didn't eat. Didn't move. I sent a message to Denmark and her family came and took her away."

"But not you?" She tried to say it neutrally.

"They had no place in their house for her bastard." His arms closed tighter and tighter around her. She felt no part of him that wasn't stone. "I don't use whores. I don't care whether they've chosen the life or been forced into it or do it for money."

She said, "Your father—"

"He's not my father!"

His anger cracked like a lightning strike. Scorched like fire.

Breathing hard, leaving not an inch between them, holding on to her as if he'd press her into his skin itself, Pax said, "He lived with my mother. He's nothing to me. I am no part of him."

She was no trained artist, like Pax, but she could see the likeness of blood, the resemblance between Pax and her blackmailer. There was no escaping that bond. Even the vehement denial, the rage, told her that man was, indeed, Pax's father.

The blackmailer and Pax, bound together inextricably. "The man who lived with your mother is the Merchant."

"That's one of his names." Pax didn't let go. She heard his breath rasp in and out of his chest. "The Merchant of Shadows. For what he did to my mother, I'm going to kill him."

Thirty-three

For advice, go to your oldest friend.

A BALDONI SAYING

A HOUSE LIKE DAISY'S DIDN'T ATTRACT MUCH GEN-eral notice. The neighbors deplored it and were avidly curious, but did no more than grumble. Daisy did her shopping for the house up and down these streets close by and confined the noise in the evening to a dull roar. When they weren't working, her women looked like anyone else. They didn't go onto the streets without hat and gloves, respectably dressed. The watchman and the beadle got their accustomed bribes. Lazarus collected his pence. Everyone knew she had powerful protectors. The house was tolerated.

Hawker followed Daisy up the stairs to the second floor, along walls painted pale yellow. There was soft carpet underfoot and a statue of goddesses getting up to some naughtiness at the turn of the stairs.

"I'll show the sketches to the rest of the girls, but they haven't been here," Daisy said.

"Wouldn't think so. They're what we might call unappreciative of the finer things in life. Not your style."

"Which is an excellent style, these days." Daisy ran her hand along the banister. "Véronique will ask here and there, with the sketches. The Frenchwomen in the trade have their own little society, close as inkle weavers."

"That's companionable." He climbed a bit more. "You got a new girl."

"Sally. She's going to be Selene in the house."

"Who left?"

"Annie. She's gone back to the wilds of Ireland to marry into the gentry. 'To marry above myself,' as she put it." At the turning of the stair, Daisy looked over her shoulder to grin. "God help the man she has in her sights."

"Poor cove don't 'ave a chance."

He checked for worn carpet, for handprints on the wall, chips in the mopboard, the smell of cabbage or stale perfume. Not that he needed to worry. Everything at Daisy's, from door knocker to attic, was prime, clean, orderly, and sweet. The whores, too.

"She'll make a good wife," Daisy said.

"She's had lots of practice, anyway."

"I like the woman Paxton brought. Interesting to talk to. She said she'd send us her cousins, which is not what we hear from most of the guests."

He made one of those noises that don't mean anything in particular. He didn't want to talk about Cami Leyland. She was another of those deadly women who could turn on a man at any moment. Pax wasn't seeing that.

Daisy's room was at the end of the hall and locked, because she wasn't an idiot. She found the key, opened it. When they were inside and less apt to be overheard, she said, "You move like something's broken. Your ribs? Or something wrong with your arm?"

Trust Daisy to see that. "Nothing much." He eased his coat off and let it drop on the table beside the door, the way he always did. There was a pair of those fussy china dogs she set such store by on the table, yapping at each other for all time to come.

She said, "Show me."

"I've cut myself worse shaving."

"Then stop using those black knives of yours to shave. Show me."

"It's practically healed." Because she wouldn't let him be till she saw the wound, he untied his cravat and began unwinding.

"Let me do that." She brushed his hands away and took over. She didn't stop at the cravat. The waistcoat was next to go, unbuttoned down from the top. Took only a second and she was pulling that off. Daisy had lots of practice undressing men.

Three buttons at the neck and she had his shirt open. Push the shirt aside and the bullet wound was revealed in all its ugly glory.

Not a sound from her, but her face froze.

"I told you it weren't much. A professional hazard, you might say. And it's healing." He'd taken a long inspection in the mirror this morning when he unbandaged and tossed out the wrappings for good. The swelling and pinkness on his chest was about gone. There was none of that disgusting exudate everybody kept deploring. Its absence was fine with him. He owned a coin-sized red mark with some scar radiating out, like a little red sun. "I feel very manly and professional. All my cohorts have impressive scars. Now I do, too."

Daisy left her hand on his collarbone, not touching the wound but lifting the shirt away from his skin so she could see. "I can see it hurts you from the way you move."

"Tortures of the damned, that's what I'm suffering. I'm just being stoical."

As usual, Daisy ignored most of what he said. "Is this all?"

"You don't think this is enough? I come back with an actual bullet wound—this is me first bullet wound, by the way. It's a good one, as these things go. Something I can show off without being indelicate. I like to think it's artistic." It was an identifying mark he could have done without.

"What happened?"

"Well, I got shot, diddin I? One bullet. Lost a piece of skin and a couple pints of blood. Oh, and a waistcoat. I've been having bad luck with my wardrobe lately."

"What happened?" She held his shoulder lightly and waited.

He'd been interrogated by experts, but Daisy had 'em all beat. She could always get him to talk.

"It was her," he said. "My Frenchwoman. She shot me."

He felt tired suddenly. It hit him every once in a while.

Daisy looked at him for a bit and didn't say anything. She made him sit on the bed so she could take off his boots. When she'd done that, she pushed at him some more till he was flat on the bed, still in his clothes.

"I don't have all that much time," he said. "There's evil men to chase up and down Soho this afternoon. You've seen the sketches. And I'll have bodies to get rid of, most likely. Pax has only accounted for one so far, but the day is young."

She pulled a blanket over some of him. When she took the robe she wore up over her head, she didn't have a stitch on underneath it. She got into bed and she was there with him, warm and soft, and she held him. She hadn't said a word.

After a minute, he rolled over and pulled her in so they were facing—more than facing—so close there wasn't any space at all. He grabbed handfuls of her hair and put his head down into it. His breath broke into chunks, cold and sharp, like ice, and fought its way in and out of his chest. There was no way anyone could tell his eyes were leaking.

A long while passed. Daisy stroked the back of his head and down his back. He hid his face in her hair and let himself shake. He could do that because this was Daisy. She knew him from the beginning, from before they joined Lazarus's gang, back when they curled up together in corners and kept each other from freezing.

At last, she said, "So you won't go back to your French-woman. Your Justine."

"No."

"That's the end of it, then."

It wasn't even the end. It was what came after the end. Not the cliff edge, but the sound you made when you hit the bottom.

"You want one of the girls?" Daisy said.

Damn. He hadn't planned to snuffle, not even in front of Daisy. "I got—" He lifted himself up on his elbow so he could wipe his nose on his sleeve. "I got the prettiest girl in the house in bed with me already."

"Do you want a girl to fuck?" she said.

Trust Daisy. Trust Daisy to know the right thing to say. "No." He flopped back and looked up at the ceiling. "God, no."

"I thought you might make an exception today."

"Fucking's the last thing I need, even if I'd do it here, which I don't."

"You want to get drunk? There's gin in the cupboard. Or brandy."

One last swipe of his arm across his face. "Not that, either."

They lay side by side looking at the ceiling as if it might do something interesting. A nice enough piece of plaster-work. A central medallion with scrolls and wreaths looping around. When he bought the house, Daisy wanted to give this room to the best of her girls to impress the customers. He'd had to argue her into taking it for herself.

They'd come a long way from picking pockets on the street, him and Daisy, with Daisy being his stall, bumping into the pigeons to give him that opportune moment.

She filled up her room with little china dogs. Stupid things. Sometimes he brought one back from a mission. He'd been crossing the border once near Salzburg and the guards found one of those bloody dogs wrapped up in his shirts and about laughed themselves silly. Laughed so much they missed the papers hidden in the false bottom of the trunk.

Vienna had been a good operation. He and Justine had—

No point in remembering. He said, "It was her duty to put a bullet in me, her being French and all. I don't blame her."

"How nice for her."

"She didn't enjoy doing it. Give her that much." It was a while before he could think of anything else worth saying. He said, "It hurts."

"So I imagine."

"Not this." He tapped his chest where he had his hand-some new bullet scar.

"I know."

Funny how he couldn't even laugh at the china dogs. Usually they cheered him right up. "And here's Pax downstairs doing the same thing. Got himself involved with a woman who'll turn into a cobra and bite him, given the least inducement."

"Seems nice enough," Daisy said.

"They do. Women like that. I was looking right at Justine when she shot me and I didn't think she'd do it."

"You still love her."

"Hell, no."

"Yes, you do. You used to be smarter than that."

Him and Pax. Both stupid. "I'll stop doing it pretty soon." He rolled over on his stomach, being careful with his shoulder. If he broke it open, he'd start bleeding and ruin Daisy's bedcovers. "So. Give me some advice, then. If you were French and mad as a rabid dog and wanted to blow up a bit of London, what would you pick?"

Thirty-four

Every small venture may be the last. Attend mass frequently.

A BALDONI SAYING

"HE'S DEAD," JACQUES SAID. "I DIDN'T SEE THE BODY, but I talked to men who had."

The Merchant was silent for a long time, thinking. Then he said, "Édouard died at once? He said nothing?"

"The woman who owns a shop directly in front of where he died said he was dead when they pulled the horses away."

"It was an accident?"

"I heard a dozen stories. He ran into the street. He was shot. He was stabbed. He was in a fight over a woman. He fought a German. He fought a Norwegian. He attacked a judge from Antwerp. He was a jewel thief carrying a fortune in rubies." Jacques shrugged. "I could look at his body. The magistrate took it away."

Sharply, "No. If there's interest in the death, you may already have been noted."

"I was one of a hundred curious fools looking at bloodstains. I listened. I let other men ask questions."

A careful man, Jacques. Reliable. It was unlikely he'd made mistakes. The Merchant acknowledged it. "You did well."

"He was carrying a gun."

The Merchant considered. "It may have been given to the magistrate or carried away with the body or stolen. It's an English gun with no ties to us."

"The woman from the shop said his body was searched and robbed by a gypsy."

"Even better. Theft will break any possible small link to us. What else did you see?"

"A pool of blood beside the road. The cart and horse, gone, probably back to the livery stable. Chatter from a dozen English mouths, but no one asking official questions."

"The mission is not endangered. No harm done," the Merchant said. "We will remember Édouard tonight, in a toast. He died doing his duty to the Revolution."

"There is no better death," Jacques said.

The Merchant showed no impatience, no anger. Nothing. "There is almost no chance they will trace us here. But we will advance our plans." He sifted details in his mind. "Hugues and Gaspard will take that woman to the cabinetmaker's shop and guard her."

"Now, instead of tomorrow night?" Jacques said.

"Now. We will spend this night and tomorrow at the cabinetmaker's. A small change of plans. And on the day of the operation, you will perform Édouard's tasks as well as your own. Do you see a problem with this?"

It was a measure of Jacques' long, careful experience that he didn't agree until he'd thought deeply. "Only the woman."

"Who is always a problem. Tell Hugues and Gaspard to persuade her if they can. Tie and gag her when she becomes noisy. They need not be gentle."

On the far side of the inn parlor, Camille Besançon sat in the most comfortable chair in the room, wearing the crimson silk robe that had been the price of peace for today. She'd let her long, black hair free over her shoulders to comb it in front of the fire.

The Merchant said, "After she is removed from here, you will pack our bags and cleanse these rooms. Dispose of her clothing and all this . . . trash she has brought in." What useless, pointless things women were. At least this one was pretty.

"My one small regret is that I didn't give Édouard that woman to enjoy. He asked, last night."

Jacques shook his head. "You were right to refuse. We are warriors. Women are for after the battle, not before."

"It's a waste, though. After the battle that one will be dead," the Merchant said.

Thirty-five

Hope for the best. Expect the worst. Plan for both.

A BALDONI SAYING

"WE'VE FOUND THE HAT SHOP," CAMI SAID. "MILES of walking the streets and the clue is here. One of the women recognized that . . . masterpiece. She saw it in a window and thought it looked good enough to eat. She did not, understandably, buy it to put on her head, but she also didn't forget it."

Cami propped her chin in her hands, her elbows on the table, and watched Pax create a map. He swiped flour together into a pile on the tabletop, took it between the palms of his hands, and let it sift down from left to right. He did it the way a man sows fine seed mixed with sand, evenly, scattering a thin film.

They were at the big dining table in the front room of the whorehouse, sitting on Chinese Chippendale chairs, surrounded by paintings of women in various stages of undress. She recognized some as Pax's work.

She said, "It's Lilith who knew the hat."

"Trustworthy source." Hawker paced the room, side to side, aiming annoyance at Cami every once in a while.

Perhaps he was irritated at being called from the bed of the brothel owner, Daisy.

It was late afternoon with the sun at a long slant into the room, but breakfast had just been cleared away and the table polished. Supper would be laid out at nine or ten tonight, when the men began arriving. The women of the house lounged about the parlor and front room in pretty négligée. They wore quite respectable dresses in the evening, apparently.

"Men who visit early gets a bit of a thrill, see," Lilith had explained. "Makes 'em feel all naughty, seeing us dressed like this." She was the oldest of the whores in this house and not particularly beautiful, except that she radiated warmth like a stove. "One gentleman comes here regular to watch Luna—that's Molly over there—put her clothes on."

Cami knew more about expensive whorehouses than she had this morning. Any day one learned something new was a day well spent. That was a saying of the Fluffy Aunts, not the Baldoni.

"They leave the kegs of gunpowder . . . somewhere. Then the empty cart goes north." Pax drew a line in the flour on the table with his finger. "Up this street, headed back to where it was rented. That's here." He touched a spot. "Livery stable." More strokes to show more streets as he named them. He held his breath when he leaned over to study the lines, not disturbing the lines in the flour. Straightened. "Crown Street, Sutton, Denmark, Rose. Those are all possible lines of approach to the livery stable. But he doesn't take them."

She let her open hand hover over the rough map. "He comes this way." That was the streets south and east of Soho Square. "Through here. By way of Moor Street." She took her hand away and went back to staring at the table. "They left the gunpowder somewhere south and east of Moor Street."

"Well, that doesn't leave much to blow up, does it?" Hawker, tightly, sarcastically polite, stopped striding up and down the room and came over to frown at the impromptu map. "Maybe three-quarters of London. I'd start with the mint, myself. Then maybe the royal family. Or London

Bridge. I've always had a fancy to blow up London Bridge, myself."

"London Bridge is falling down," she said softly, to annoy him.

Pax ignored this little byplay. It was not the least of his many fine qualities that he felt no need to protect her from his deadly young friend. He made a square in the center of his map, empty of flour. Soho Square. "The man we followed yesterday when you left the Moravian church."

"Now dead," Hawker muttered.

"The man I followed on a long tour of Soho," she agreed. "Drink to drink, tavern to tavern. One of those boring afternoons."

"Not boring for somebody with his eyes full of poison," Hawker snapped.

Hawker was one of the several men in London who'd be happy to lock her up indefinitely. His eyes were full of iron doors shutting behind her and the keys sent to problematic and distant storage. No bonhomie in that direction.

"I lied," she said. "I wasn't bored. I had curs yapping at my heels. Now look at this . . ." She held her hand out flat, palm up, knowing Pax would understand what she wanted.

He did. He slapped the hilt of his knife on her palm. She said, "If you will pay attention . . ." to Mr. Hawker and began marking alleys and side streets, gently, precisely, with the tip of the knife. "The man we followed went like this. And this. And this." She looked up and smiled at Hawker as one might smile at a large, mean dog who was safely on the other side of a fence. "Look at where he crosses his own path."

"Staying in territory he knows," Pax murmured.

"That's good. I see it. Yes." Hawker, the trail in front of him, forgot to be angry. "We have more. Wait." He swung away from the table and came back with two of the china comfit boxes. One with small violet pastilles. One with lemon drops. "We have early reports from the men out walking sketches around."

Pax said, "Anything solid?"

Hawker shuffled a dozen pastilles into his hand. "It is a wonder and an amazement how many shifty-eyed Frenchmen were lurking around this city last week. Doyle sieved out a few reports from the dross. And these are . . ." Rapidly, Hawker set seven pastilles in place. After a pause he added another two, further south.

"The henchman died here." She took a lemon drop and set it in place. "The livery stable where someone rented the wagon . . . here." More lemon drops. "The taverns he visited."

"The alleys he stopped to piss in." Hawker started placing more lemon drops down.

She said, "I doubt—"

"Men don't just use any old alley."

Pax sprinkled flour and drew in streets and alleys ahead of them. They were wandering off the map a bit, outside Soho proper.

"It's not simple." But there were patterns. Men always made patterns.

Pax drew back and watched them place the last markers. There was a concentration about him now, a driving, intent focus. She imagined him in some Piedmontese farm kitchen, surrounded by rough, hardened men, all of them tired and dirty, armed with a mix of old muskets and new rifles stolen from the French. She could see him listening to reports. Pax was a man who'd listen more than he talked. He'd be totally absorbed, seeing every detail, the way he did now.

Maybe he'd make a map like this on the farmhouse table, using corn meal that could be scattered and erased in an instant. Maybe he'd stand and stare down at it and his men would get quiet.

"This"—she set down her last marker—"is the hat shop where Lilith remembers seeing that hat."

Pax stood frowning.

Patterns. She let herself stop thinking. When her mind wasn't yelling at her, she could see them. "Look here. The man we were following didn't go here. He went around it." She circled a space on the map.

"Inns? That's what he's not going near." Hawker was talking to himself. He leaned close, absorbed. "The Angel? But you have to go through the central court to get to the rooms. Everybody can see you. The Boar's Head?"

"Fielding's Inn," Pax said suddenly. "Large, rambling, dis-organized. That's what he'd choose."

Hawker said, "They may already be gone."

Pax was already running for the door and didn't slow down for them to catch up.

hirty-six

We know what we value by what we spend to purchase it.

A BALDONI SAYING

WHEN PAX CLIMBED THE STAIRS AT MEEKS STREET, Grey was waiting for him. Grey held the door open, not saying anything.

The Head of Section for England didn't answer the door at Meeks Street. Pax followed him through the ugly front parlor, where none of the reds matched, into the white, calm hallway.

They went six paces in silence. "The Merchant got away," Pax said. "We found the rooms he'd been using, but he was gone. We missed him by an hour."

Grey said, "Hawker told us."

"The Merchant has a woman and three or four men with him. Stillwater and Tenn are asking questions, house to house, up and down the street. We haven't found where he stored the gunpowder. Probably a good ways from where he was living."

Grey turned and blocked the hall. "You lied to me. From the beginning. Every day."

There was no part of returning to Meeks Street that was easy. This meeting was harder than most. "For years."

"You lied to men who trusted you. Any hour of the day or

night you could have walked into my office and told the truth."

"I have no excuse."

Grey had been a major of infantry before he came to the Service. He didn't smile much. He wasn't smiling now. He looked like a man about to convene a court-martial.

Grey said, "I didn't think you were a coward."

"I did it to stay in the Service." *The Service was all I had.*

The fist came out of nowhere. Pain hit like lightning—big, bright, white, and sudden. Black spilled down over everything.

When the world came back, he was on his arse, his back against the wall. His jaw stabbed agony. His head was solid pain from one side to the other. He leaned his head on the plaster and waited for the hall to stop tilting sideways.

Grey said, "Is there anything else you're lying about?"

"Yes. At least, there's things I'm not saying."

"Damn you for that. But at least it's honest." Grey reached a hand down.

He took the hand and got pulled to his feet. The trick was keeping his head level. His brains would stay in the braincase if he kept his head level.

"If you ever lie to me again," Grey said, "I will kick you into Northumberland. You're holding on to a place in the Service by the skin of your teeth, Mr. Paxton. Don't repeat your mistakes. And now we have kegs of gunpowder to deal with. Galba's office. Now."

Grey walked away and left him holding on to the wall.

That clears the air, doesn't it? He'd been dreading the meeting with Grey. Turned out he didn't have to say much of anything at all.

He'd take a brief rest against the wall here. *Yes. That's the ticket.*

He didn't open his eyes when boots came down the stairs. That was Doyle's walk.

Doyle said, "Galba's waiting for you."

"Grey told me." It hurt to talk. He fingered along his jawbone, but nothing seemed to be broken. Grey was an expert when it came to unarmed fighting. "I may be just a minute getting into motion."

"Grey's annoyed."

"I have figured that out."

"He's kicking himself he didn't notice one of his agents was in trouble."

"We're spies. We're secretive." The edges of his sight were no longer fading into black. Now he'd walk down the hall to Galba's office. That was next on his list of challenges for this afternoon.

"A senior officer's responsible for his junior officers." They started walking the hall. Doyle was in no hurry. Just as well. "It's the army way."

"Another reason to stay out of the army." He tasted blood, but when he swiped across his mouth none came off on his hand. No split lip. Grey had delivered a clean, precise blow, making his point with skill and economy. "I lost the Merchant."

"You found him in the first place, with all of London to sieve through."

"We won't find him again. He's in his final retreat, safe and secret. And the gunpowder's somewhere safe. He may already have planted it. We have one more chance at him. Hawk gave you the details?"

"Semple Street, Number Fifty-six, eleven in the morning on Monday," Doyle said. "I tortured it out of him."

"I hope you used thumbscrews." They passed the framed map of medieval Florence. He liked Florence. For a while he'd kept rooms over a bakery there. "I need five or six men, preferably men the Merchant won't recognize."

They'd come to Galba's office. Doyle set his hand on the doorknob. "Pax, the planning for Monday is no longer your job."

A lifetime of control kept his voice calm. "Whose job, then?"

"Mine. You won't be there. You won't be in England. Giles is packing a trunk for you."

"You're taking this operation away from me?"

"Galba's decision."

"Why?"

Doyle paused fractionally. He didn't open the door. He seemed to come to a decision. "How accurate are your sketches of the Merchant?"

It came to this. Again. The unbreakable, unendurable connection with the monster. "Very."

"Pax, is the man your father?"

"No." And then, "Maybe." It was as close as he could come to admitting it. "He claimed to be sometimes. He lied about so many things, he could have lied about that, too."

"You look like him," Doyle said.

And the mirror here at the end of the hall said the same thing. He'd watched his face become the monster's face, year by year. "If it's the truth, it's a random accident. A dark joke of the gods. A technicality."

"A significant technicality," Doyle said, very quietly. "Galba's not going to send one of his agents to perform heinous actions."

"He's not sending me. If I kill the Merchant, it's because I've been planning it since I was ten years old. It's taken me this long to get close to him with a gun in my hand."

"Makes no difference. A man doesn't kill his father."

"He's not my father." He said it too loud. Galba and Grey would hear it inside the office. "I purged his blood from my veins. I repudiate him."

"It's not that easy," Doyle said. "God knows, a lot of us wish it were."

"Then I accept the blood guilt." He forced himself to meet his own eyes in the mirror. Then Doyle's eyes. "I'll kill him and let the Furies do their worst."

"Then you and Galba are going to disagree on some major decisions over the next couple of days."

Doyle opened the door. Galba and Grey were inside. Galba, at his desk. Grey, standing by the window, studying one of the sketches of the Merchant.

Doyle said, "Did you know the Merchant's real name is Peter Styles? He comes from Northumbria and he has a title."

"He attended Cambridge," Galba said calmly. "Come join

us, Mr. Paxton. You will not be permitted to kill the man, whatever good cause you have to do so."

"Lots of people want the Merchant dead," Doyle said.

Not as much as I do. He followed Doyle into Galba's office.

Thirty-seven

VIOLET LEYLAND LAID THE SPYGLASS ACROSS HER lap and stretched as well as the low roof of the hackney coach allowed. She straightened her legs and rolled her shoulders. "I'm not as young as I used to be."

Lily said, "Neither of us is young," without moving or opening her eyes. She was curled on the opposite seat with her coat rolled under her head, dozing. In a long and varied career, they'd spent many days and nights like this, on duty, on watch, taking turns sleeping.

Violet said, *"Morte magis metuenda senectus."*

"Old age is indeed more to be feared than death." Lily sighed. "There was a time Anson would not have sent us off to mind our knitting."

From where she sat in the hackney, Violet could see the whole length of Meeks Street and everyone who came to the door of Number Seven. It was not a perfect way to understand what was going forward at headquarters, but it would serve.

"He's protecting us," Lily said.

"He's making sure we won't interfere in his operation."

"That, too. Oh, look. There's Mr. Paxton just going up the

stairs," Violet said. "I would say he looks calm, but determined. He has a forceful stride, I think. Matters must be developing."

"He'll be in the center of it."

"Yes."

"Then we will follow him when he leaves," Lily said, pleased. "I haven't followed a handsome young man for ever so long."

"The life of the mind, dear. We have chosen the life of the mind."

"Of course. And very satisfying it is." Lily lay down on the seat again, making herself reasonably comfortable.

"I hate getting old," Violet said.

"I do, too. But the alternative is worse."

Thirty-eight

*Find peace and prosperity in a house and you will
find a woman ruling.*

A BALDONI SAYING

THE FAMILY GAVE HER A SMALL, PRETTY ROOM AT
the back of the house. The clothing bundled onto the seat of
the chair would fit somebody about twelve and the handwriting in the half-finished letter on the desk was the hand of
a young girl.

She told them, "I don't mean to push someone—is it
Maria?—from her room. I can sleep on a trundle bed somewhere."

"For this first little time, you are guest as well as kins-
woman." Great-Aunt Fortunata herself stuffed a feather pillow into a clean pillowcase.

"Maria is beside herself with excitement to give you her
room. 'Puffed up,' as they say in English." Aunt Grazia, comfortable and maternal, made the bed and pulled a coverlet
over the top. "I sent her to the park with a clutch of children
so you may bathe in peace. The house will be quieter for a
while."

"Sleep if you can," Aunt Fortunata said. "Sleep through
supper. There will be food in the kitchen even in the middle
of the night."

They keep feeding me. "I'll be fine." A fire the size of a spaniel dog burned in the grate, lit there as much for company as for warmth. Tea was made and set upon the table. A kettle vibrated on the hob. At the edge of the mantelpiece, little cakes were neatly stacked on a plate. There seemed nothing they would not do to welcome her here.

"The boys will be back late," said Aunt Grazia, "clattering in, talking at the top of their voices, and starving. You need not worry about waking the household. They will do that."

By "the boys" she meant Tonio, Giomar, and Alessandro, who'd gone out to wander the neighborhood of Semple Street in picturesque guises.

"I won't even hear them." Her heart and mind were stretched tight as twisted string, yet she must sleep. She was so desperately tired. Maybe, in dreams, she'd see a way to close her fist around the Merchant and snatch the human bait from the trap he would set.

I renounced the lessons I learned in the Coach House. I resolved that I would not kill. I would not spy. Maybe I became too ordinary.

The curtain at the window was pulled back to show sunset, a high wooden wall, and the three large sheds in the complicated kitchen yard. The roof of the nearest shed was directly below the window, a nothing to get to. Perhaps young Maria wriggled out this window and went wandering London at night. There was a certain look of devilment in Maria's eye that argued the possibility.

Aunt Grazia held up a night shift. "You're much of a size, you and Amalia. We're making this for her trousseau, but there's plenty of time to make her another. The embroidery is not quite finished."

"Because Lucia does not tend to her needle." But Aunt Fortunata sounded indulgent.

Aunt Grazia draped the night shift over the back of a chair, absentmindedly stroking it smooth. "Amalia has a blue dress she will lend you for tomorrow. It will be most becoming. And for Monday, a dark green, inconspicuous and easy to run in. Would you like a gun? A second gun, I mean."

"One cannot carry too many guns when going to meet an

enemy." Fortunata plumped the pillow on the bed and centered it carefully. "There."

"Let me lend you one of mine," Grazia said. "A lovely little Austrian cuff pistol my oldest brought back from the battle of Millesimo."

"After having been told to keep well away from the fighting." Fortunata clucked her tongue. "Headstrong."

"The payroll funds were simply too tempting." Aunt Grazia laid a round ball of soap in the dish beside the towels. "She is Baldoni, after all."

$\mathscr{T}$hirty-nine

Before a great enterprise, talk the plan over with friends.

A BALDONI SAYING

". . . NOT SO DIFFERENT FROM THE WAY YOU PLACED your men in Italy. Your street is an ambush in a ravine. Those houses have upper stories. That means snipers."

Always good advice from Doyle, Pax thought. "If he wants Cami dead, he can reach out and do it. A sniper won't stop him."

"Sniper fire from our side closes off an escape route. Traps the Merchant in that canyon of a street," Doyle said.

"Good point." *If I let him live that long.*

Deep midnight and the smell of the Thames. Pervasive damp and the rustle and slap of water against the pilings. Doyle and Hawker didn't hurry in this stroll along the night-time docks of London, down to the ship that was supposed to take him to Italy. They were lax and lackadaisical guards. It was clear they expected him to escape before they got to the *Pretty Mary.*

"Complication with fighting in a city, though," Doyle went on, "is you got civilians popping out of every doorway, just asking to be taken hostage."

Cami would be a hostage the minute she stepped out onto the pavement. No comfort to know she'd be armed.

"Or they're leaning out the windows trying to get themselves shot." Hawker had helped himself to a handful of gravel a few streets back, stealing it out of a potted plant on somebody's front steps. He'd been shying it, stone by stone, into the street as they walked along, hearing it skip and clatter, watching it when there was light enough from some lamp in a window. "I don't know why they do that. If you asked a hundred citizens of London, 'What should you do when people start shooting off guns?' not one of them would say, 'Go stand at the window and pretend to be a pheasant.' "

The last house they passed was a tavern with a light at the door and noise inside, even at midnight. The inns and public houses were busy all night at the docks, working to the change of the tides instead of the time of day.

The dock was dark, the uneven succession of long planks treacherous underfoot. Down at the end, an open boat was being loaded by three men under the light of a single lantern. Baskets of bread, more baskets—those might be eggs—and what looked like milk cans. The pile to the right was probably his luggage.

On the Thames, every ship on the water was slung with lanterns to keep thieves at bay. Light repeated in the water, rippling, broken into pieces. The *Pretty Mary* was one of those ships.

Doyle said, "You could just go to Italy and simplify matters immensely. I hear the light's good for artists."

"It's good light."

"I'm not new at this business. I'll take the Merchant for you." Doyle was in outline against the river. "I'll take him alive because we need him for questioning. But he will die. It's just a squabble over who gets to kill him."

"He's worried about the woman," Hawker said.

"I know that." Doyle watched the loading at the end of the dock. "We all know she's walking into a trap. Whether she lives depends on what the Merchant wants and whether we can get to her in time." He turned back. "When she walks onto Semple Street, I have as good a chance of keeping her alive as you do."

Hawk said, "He's not listening. He's thinking about taking

a dive into that dirty river when he's about halfway between here and that boat out there."

"Ship," Doyle corrected. "The big ones are ships. The small ones are boats. Pax, I can't promise to keep her alive or get her safe out of England. I can't promise to keep her out of prison. She's a spy and I don't know what she's done—"

"The difference is, he doesn't care what she's done," Hawk said.

"But if it's possible, I'll keep her alive and loose on the streets," Doyle said. "I have influence and I'll use it for her. Will you go to Italy and spy on the French and Austrians and leave her to me?"

They already knew his answer. He gave it anyway. "No."

"You're disobeying direct orders. You know that."

"I don't have any choice."

Waves slapped the mud under the dock. A metallic cold rose up from the expanse of water. Even if these two didn't force the issue, even if they let him walk away, he knew he'd be walking away from the Service.

"I hope you're not expecting me to tie him up and haul him out to that ship." Hawker still had a few pieces of gravel held in reserve. He skidded one out across the water and listened to it splash. "He'd stab me, being in thrall to that devil bitch of his."

Might as well make it clear. "There are two of you. I can't win without hurting you. And I'll fight. I don't think you're willing to hurt me."

"We're not going to do it that way," Doyle said.

"Good." Hawk threw his last piece of gravel and waited for a splash. "Because I'm bloody well not pulling a knife on Pax. Last time I did he almost gutted me."

"I sliced your forearm. One cut," he said.

"It is only by my supernatural agility that I escaped that encounter alive. Now I'm going to wander down the nearest alley to relieve myself against a wall, leaving Pax to disappear into the cool of the evening or take ship to Italy, whichever strikes his fancy. Mr. Doyle, if you want to stand between Pax and his murderous woman, I leave you to it."

A dark chuckle. Doyle said, "I'm not that stupid."

Hawker became silence and darkness, walking away.

Galba sent Doyle and Adrian to put him on the ship because he knew they wouldn't force the issue. Galba had left him the choice—obey or disobey—and all the consequences.

He called, "Hawk." He felt, rather than saw or heard, Hawker pause.

"Hmm?"

"I'll be at the Baldoni's, off and on, starting in the morning. It's not my operation—"

"It's your operation," Doyle said. "I'll send Hawker over about noon. Tell him what you need from the Service and I'll see you have it." He paused. "You will get me the Merchant. He killed an old friend of mine."

It was like flame, the unwavering, burning cold inside him. "I will bring him down."

Hawk had become invisible. The trailing edge of his voice drifted back. "Galba's going to kill me for this."

Doyle aimed his reply in that direction. "Cheer up, lad. Likely somebody'll beat him to it."

Forty

With a small decision, we change all the future.

A BALDONI SAYING

THE ROAD BACK TO CAMI FELT FAMILIAR, EVEN though he'd only walked it twice now. It was all in the anticipation.

At the end, almost there, Pax went motionless in the dark at the doorway next to the Baldoni house. Men approached behind him on the street, walking without reservation or wariness. Two . . . three of them.

He breathed shallowly. He was too old a hand to hold his breath in a situation like this. Tense the forearm, shake the knife down across his palm. A seven-inch blade, long enough to get through clothing and into a vital organ. Silent weapon. Silent death.

Laughter. The cadence and intonation of Italian. He was listening to the approach of some Baldoni. Soon enough he could recognize the voices. That was Cousin Tonio, who was too good-looking and confident to be quite reliable on a job. Maybe. Or maybe Tonio enjoyed playing the likable rogue. The English branch of the Baldoni's well-respected and meticulously managed Banca della Toscana had not been placed in the hands of a fool.

The other voices must be Alessandro and the young Giomar.

They strolled past him, not seeing him. They were dressed in cloaks of invisibility themselves, the patched, secondhand garments of the poor. Groom, hod carrier, mason's apprentice, bootblack, stevedore, butcher's boy . . . they could have been any of those. They wore poverty and an exuberant vulgarity as if they'd been born to it. Anyone who saw them on Semple Street would know they were up to no good, poking and prying about, hoping for some trifles that weren't nailed down.

But, if the Merchant saw them or heard them described, he'd never suspect them of scouting out the territory. All the cold intelligence of the Merchant, and he had no sense of humor. He'd never understand the Baldoni appetite for exuberant gestures.

They passed, laughing, talking about music, climbed the front stairs, and pushed into the house.

His opportunity. Any attention would be on them. He went over the high wall to the side of the house and into the garden. Ran to the back garden and entered a slice of shadow he'd picked out the last time he was here.

The Baldoni, enterprising crew that they were, left a lantern burning at the back of the house in the window beside the kitchen door. Somebody might want to get in, quietly, at an odd hour.

One of the household dogs scented a stranger on the wind and whuffed a warning but the boisterous entry to the kitchen and demands for food covered that up. It wasn't repeated. Perhaps the dog was one of the ones he'd snuck food to earlier.

He breathed quietly and waited. Ten or fifteen minutes passed. Behind the brick and mortar, in the kitchen, voices lowered to sober conversation. A dog whined and Alessandro's complaint quieted it. A woman's voice spoke. The windows up and down the house stayed dark. They must be used to feeding their young men at midnight.

He remained undetected, but there was watchfulness in the Baldoni household, a sense of somebody awake besides those men in the kitchen. He'd snuck into army camps that were less alert. Whatever quarrels he might have with the

Baldoni in the future, tonight he was glad Cami rested in her bed with a couple dozen dishonest, competent, cynical Tuscans between her and harm.

Upstairs, over the kitchen, one window was lit by more than the red light of a banked fire. Somebody'd left a candle burning in the window in the corner room at the far end.

That would be Cami, waiting for him. He hadn't asked her to wait. He hadn't expected to come to her. Yet, here he was.

A wooden shed backed to the house directly below the window. It was no challenge to hook his boot into a rough board and draw himself up to the shed roof, which was embedded with broken glass. Somebody'd spread a wool blanket over some of it. That could be some enterprising young Baldoni sneaking in and out. It could be Cami's fine hand.

He scrambled across without noise, hands and feet spread to support his weight.

She'd thrown the sash up. A slit in the curtain showed a bedroom of tidy whitewashed walls and a dark, shiny wood floor, with a rag rug in front of the hearth. The dressing table would belong to a woman. The framed paintings on the wall, to a young girl.

The candle he'd seen from below was in a glass chimney on the dressing table. Another was at the bedside.

He pushed aside the curtain with the back of two fingers. Cami lay on her back in bed, eyes closed, her hands clasped behind her head on the pillow. She'd pulled the sheets and coverlet as high as her heart. Her breasts were covered in a chaste white night shift, made of linen so thin her nipples showed through. Her hair lay in curls on the white of the pillow like the first ink on clean canvas.

She showed she wasn't asleep, and provided a reason it would be unwise to be a burglar entering this house, by opening her eyes. A knife had found its way to her hand that hadn't been there an instant ago.

If he'd been less certain of his own skill, he might have thought he'd made some sound climbing up. He hadn't. Cami just knew.

He pushed the curtain back all the way. "I was passing and I saw your light."

"I hoped you would. I'm glad it's you."

"I'm glad it's me, too. I'd be stepping over a corpse, otherwise."

"Another man would have set the dogs barking."

"Sausages." He put his hands on the windowsill, swung across, and put his boots to the floor. "While we were eating, I slipped them sausages under the table."

"Everyone slips them sausages under the table. Baldoni children in medieval Florence slipped sausages to the ancestors of those dogs."

"They trust me because I smell like you, from kissing you over the last couple days."

"They're canny dogs." She sat up as he crossed the room to her and dropped her knife carelessly on the bedside table.

I'm wearing more clothes than she is. I have to get out of them. He sat on the bed beside her and leaned to take her head between his hands. He kissed her, not reverently. Not like the prince waking Sleeping Beauty. He kissed her like a man taking his first drink of water when he's dying of thirst.

She pulled herself upward and put her legs underneath her till she was kneeling on the bed, pressed against him, solid and urgent. Her lips tasted like mint pulled right out of the earth, still warm from the sun.

He said, "I have to get my coat off. I want to touch your skin with my skin."

Her tongue came inside his mouth and he stopped worrying about what he was wearing or not wearing. The world closed in till it held one sensation, one thought, full of the knowledge of her mouth.

His cock, huge and sensitive, rose, moved of its own accord, demanded. He gave a little of his mind to controlling that. The rest, he gave to her.

She withdrew from his mouth. Her arms still around him, she laid her head to his chest and breathed onto his neck.

His. She was his. For this one moment, she was his.

He closed his eyes. This was what he wanted, no light, no color, no shapes and angles. Only the dark velvet of her breath against his throat. The silk of her hair under his chin.

Where did he put his hands on her? What did he touch?

I can get this right. I speak six languages like a native. I know how to fight. How to kill. How to march ten men across a mountain range in winter. Twenty-four years old and I don't know where I can put my hands.

I'm supposed to know what to do next.

None of the books he'd read said anything useful.

He opened his eyes, looked down at her head, resting on his chest, and kissed into the tender, soft cluster of curls.

Touch her. That's what she's saying. She's saying I can touch her anywhere. He put his hands on her shift, under her breasts, holding that soft curve. Her rib cage was full of breath and the fast pound, pound, pound of her heart. He held life, warmth, breathing, vibration, all the miraculous complex whole of her.

I will never hold a woman's flesh again and not remember this.

He lifted her and she lifted herself, pushing down upon his shoulders till her little, perfect breasts were at his mouth, ready to be kissed. His cock held a hunger so huge it was pain. "I want to make love to you." His whisper came out low and grating.

She laughed, deep in her chest. He felt the sound of it in his bones. She pushed a little away so they could see each other better. "I want you back."

"I'd better set about seducing you."

"Oh, yes."

She was playing with his hair, drawing it through her fingers. An ache spread from his groin and filled his whole body. He was going to die of this. Practical matters. Deal with practical matters. "I need to take my clothes off but I don't want to let go of you."

"A problem." Her face was bright with laughter. Lit from inside with it. Dancing with it. "I'll help."

She wriggled to a more comfortable position. Torment. He was rigid for her, hard and heavy with wanting her. He was going to . . .

No. He had himself under control. Deep breath. Another deep breath. "Don't move. Give me a minute."

"I will give you an entire night." Her hands went to his

cravat. She worked on that, her eyes downcast, absorbed in drawing the knot apart. "We're in no hurry."

His cock was in a hurry.

She wasn't naked, but she might as well have been. The shift showed her breasts as if she were naked. He didn't need years of experience to tell him she was lovely.

I can live through this. He'd be inside her in a minute. Two minutes. Ten minutes. A century. "You have very beautiful breasts. I've seen many breasts and those are a fine example." He was babbling.

So he held her shoulders, thin shoulders all bone and soft skin, and a body filled with fire. Fire like the first fire taken from the hand of Prometheus, clean, vital, unending. That was what he felt under her skin, inside her, where his hands rested on her shoulders.

She unwound the cravat from his neck and pulled it away, long and long, and tossed it over her shoulder. She didn't look to see where it landed. She said, "You're worried. You don't have to be worried. I'm not a virgin."

"That's good." His voice was hoarse. Thank God there weren't two virgins in this bed.

"There were two men, back home in Brodemere. One, when I was seventeen. The other—"

"Doesn't matter." Another thought came, breaking through the madness that filled his brain. "Unless I have to kill somebody." His hands tightened. "I can do it next week. Just tell me who."

"You don't have to kill anybody. They were fine men. I liked lying with them. It was . . . pleasant."

"Pleasant. Good. I'm glad. Let me get some of this clothing off me."

Pleasant wasn't good. He'd have to do better than pleasant. His hands didn't quite shake when he unbuttoned his vest, but they weren't steady either. He pulled his arms from jacket and vest together and tossed them on the floor beside the bed. He managed to do that without dislodging Cami.

She said, "I think I would have liked lovemaking more if my lovers had not had to hurry so much. They always worried we might be caught."

Sounds like a couple of selfish bastards. "I'll try to go slow." His shirt now. He'd get out of his shirt. He undid the buttons at the collar. "We might be caught. You have a house full of cousins. Uncles. Aunts."

"I locked the door and wedged paper in so it won't open. If anyone comes you can flee through the window as if this were a bad play."

She was teasing him. Laughing. Everything that was Cami, all her spirit, all her courage, all her wild embrace of life, was under his hands.

He fell into her grin. He wanted that on canvas. He wanted everything of her. Everything of Cami. Wanted to draw it, taste it, see it again and again. He was caught by the planes of her face. He ran his fingertips there and there as if he were light falling on her.

She said, "Love me."

He held her hips and pressed her down onto the raging hunger of his cock and kissed her. On the soft, pulsing temples, on her cheeks, under the curve of her throat.

She was the one to shudder now. The one to breathe faster.

Not her mouth. Not yet. That would have undone him.

He licked the curve of her ear. Took her earlobe and bit down on it and let himself drown in madness.

Forty-one

Seize the moment.

A BALDONI SAYING

THEY SAT IN RUSH-BOTTOMED CHAIRS IN THE kitchen in front of the long hearth—two old people, brother and sister. They were rich, back in Tuscany, in land, farms, and vineyards. Rich in power, which was more important.

If they chose to sit in the kitchen with their feet at the fire, if they dabbled in fraud and bamboozlement, if they raised a pack of noisy, larcenous grandchildren in London or, barefoot, in the big villa in Tuscany, it was because a wise man does not forget his roots.

"The boys"—Giomar, Tonio, and Alessandro—had eaten hugely, downed a pitcher of red wine between them, and gone off to bed.

Bernardo drank hot watered brandy. Fortunata, a tisane of mint and cloves from a flowered teacup. "He's upstairs now," she said.

"Admirably silent." They'd heard no sound when he entered the window on the floor above. Bernardo cradled the terracotta cup between his palms. "An Italian would serve as well, a family from Piedmont or Sardinia. One of the Rossi in Milan. We could find someone who would not meddle in politics."

"A milksop."

"He would be more welcome."

"Not to Sara." Fortunata was very sure. Two brown dogs sat at her feet, alert but silent, knowing there was a stranger upstairs, sensing he was to be tolerated, intrigued by this.

"To give her to someone so far from home, on this cold island, among the English . . ." Bernardo said what he thought of the English with the sweep of one hand.

"It is familiar to her. Confess, Bernardo, you agree with me. In all ways, she's better off with an Englishman who will command some respect and keep her safe, but who will play no politics in Italy."

"Or play only to British interests."

"Which are our interests," Fortunata said comfortably, "in the long run. They have no imperial ambitions in Italy. Next year or in ten years or thirty, this man or his sons will help us oust the French and the Austrians from Italy. He has made his start with his band of killers and idealists in the mountains. We will shine in the luster of his exploits when it becomes known the daughter of the house of Baldoni married Il Gatto Grigio."

They sat, listening to the still of midnight and the small sounds of an old house on a cool night. They were not so old they could not remember what a man and woman would do in bed.

"Is he worthy of Cesare's grandchild?" Bernardo looked into the cup he held. "We know nothing of his family, or even if he has one. I will investigate."

"Do so. Though it would be a pleasure to acquire a spouse for the family who does not come with a horde of rapacious relatives."

Bernardo set his cup on his knee and looked into the fire. "He is a warrior. A subtle, cunning man. Even-tempered. Ruthless when necessary."

"Almost a Baldoni."

Bernardo smiled. "Almost a Baldoni."

Forty-two

If one is not honest in bed, one is honest nowhere.

A BALDONI SAYING

CAMI WANTED HIM. WANTED HIM WHOLLY, ALL THE many virtues and lethalities of him. All of the man.

He was admirable in so many ways. There are sorts and degrees of adventurers. Some men were too wise to break and enter a dwelling inhabited by armed Baldoni. Pax took this risk in his usual imperturbable way.

She touched his hair where it fell over his forehead and the curve of his eyebrow, the sharp bone at the top of his cheek, wanting to memorize the bones beneath his skin. Or deeper than that—wanting to know the thoughts in his mind.

He said, "We have time. Time to taste each other."

She wanted to taste him. He brought the smell of the night in with him, on his shirt.

He wasn't wearing a knife sheath on his arm or fixed at his back. Perhaps he'd tucked that deadliness into his jacket before he tossed it aside. He was tactful as well as lethal. One does not wear a knife to a romantic assignation.

"I won't let my cousins kill you," she said, "in case you're worried about that."

"Getting knifed by your relatives is one reason I shouldn't

be here. There are others." He fumbled at his cuff buttons and didn't take his eyes from her face. "I can't think of a single one right now."

She found it exquisitely endearing that he wanted her so much he had become too clumsy to undo a button. "Let me do that."

He held out his wrist in a gesture, deceptively tame and domestic, so she could slip buttons from their moorings and free him. This was a symbolically satisfying chore, freeing him from the bindings that held him. They sat on the bed and she enjoyed every nuance of undressing him for the first time. There could be only one first time, though there would be many other times, if they lived.

The shirt was good linen, soft with many washings. She smelled the faint, clean scent.

"I was lying awake," she said, "looking at the cracks in the ceiling and seeing maps of Scotland and hoping you would come to me."

His hold around her became adamant. "Let me get the rest of these clothes off." He lifted her away from his lap lightly, as if she weighed nothing. Then he held her a minute longer as if his hands were reluctant to let her go.

At some point since parting from her he'd darkened his hair to brown. When he was above her and inside her, she'd reach upward with her mouth and taste his hair, damp with sweat.

He leaned to pull off his boots and tossed them to the side of the bed. When he stood to unbutton his trousers, he pushed his sleeves back in folds up his arms. His shirt fell in long, loose folds from his shoulders to his thighs. His upright cock jutted, clearly visible, nudged hungrily against the cloth. His eyes were full of heat.

And she . . . she was suddenly too restless to sit still. She swung her legs around and stood up to walk to the window. Her skin prickled with the cold and the floorboards were chill under her feet. She'd be grateful for the warmth of Pax's body in that bed.

She closed the slit where the window curtains had parted when Pax came through, excluding even the last small crevice of darkness, tucking the edges together.

There are explanations to be made when one is a woman of some experience. She began, "The men I lay with—"

"You don't have to tell me," he said.

"It's not an apology. I just wanted to say, those men didn't know me. I opened my flesh to them, but not my mind. This is the first time I have made love with a man who is my friend."

"I couldn't do it at all," he said. "I couldn't take a woman to bed with me and tell her lies with every breath. Not a woman I cared about."

"There were no good choices for us, were there?" *He's known only bought women.* "The Coach House poisoned us both." She rubbed her upper arms. Her shiver was not entirely from the chill in the air. It was excitement rising in her belly. "This will be different for both of us. I feel naked with you. Naked inside my skin because I have no wrapping of lies around me." She shook her head. "I'm being dramatic."

He crossed the room. Each step was set with care, deliberate as if he approached her across a lake, insecurely frozen, and any misstep might plunge them into the dark water beneath.

He was, of course, silent. That was the least of his skills.

They stood a few hand spans apart. Touching distance.

He said, "Truth. Lies. There's probably a Baldoni saying about that."

"Several. We say, 'Telling the truth is planting coins in a field, hoping to reap bullion.' You're still dressed. Let me remedy that."

He bent and let her take his shirt in handfuls of linen up, over his head. He came from her hands naked, beautiful, wholly at ease without clothing. That was another legacy of the Coach House, one of the more harmless.

The Greeks carved statues of their athletes and of their gods. Pax could have been one of them—an Olympic runner, stripped to lean muscle for speed, or the god Hermes. But the Greeks did not depict their gods in a state of arousal. Pax was most supremely aroused.

The sight of Pax, rampant in all his demanding sexuality, buffeted her like a fierce wind. Her breath built inside her and would move neither in nor out. Her skin heated.

The cloth of his shirt felt heavy and significant and warm

as she held it. She wanted to take it to bed with her and hide it under her pillow, to keep the smell of him with her when he went away in a few hours. It was with reluctance she let it drop. That left no barrier between them, really, except her shift.

She said, "The first time, I was seventeen. He was the squire's son."

"Cami—"

"This isn't about him. It's about me. Let me tell you. He was very handsome and I hungered to fall in love and be foolish. Instead, I was mortifyingly sensible and calculating and clear-sighted. I was a French spy and could never marry anyone. He had to marry money. The daughter of a shipbuilder, as it turned out."

"He sounds like a selfish popinjay."

"He was a nice young man."

"That condemns him absolutely. 'A nice man.' " Pax shook his head, smiling. "What would you want with a nice young man? You scared him to death."

"I don't scare you."

"Oh, yes, you do."

Her lovers, both of them, had been dark, with wiry thickets of hair upon the body. She liked it that Pax was wholly different, pale as the moon reflected on a steel blade. That he was swift, precise, and austere as the blade itself. When she ran her hand across his chest, she felt smooth springing hair, invisible to the eye.

At seventeen, she'd longed to be overmastered by passion. Tonight she would be. There would be no careful exchange of pleasure in that narrow bed.

She was halfway mad already and Pax was shaking with the need to control himself.

She said, "I like your hair better when it's white."

"Disguise. I'm supposed to be sailing to France. About now, I'd guess."

"Tonight? But—"

He set a finger on her lips. It was a shock, a vehement thrill. "That's a long story." His eyelids were heavy and half-closed. "I'll paint you naked, if we both live. I'll paint you in red silk and rose petals."

She had never, not once, considered the possibility of being covered in rose petals. Her voice became husky. "You hollow me out until I'm full of wanting you. I can't hold anything back. This is no light moment for me."

"It isn't light for me, either. There's been no one else. No one but you." She watched him follow his own fingers as they journeyed from her mouth, down her neck, to the pulse in the hollow of her collarbone. He said, "You hold me in the palm of your hand, Cami."

To be told, so simply, that she had such power. That she was the first woman he'd felt this for. It left her without words.

He said, with stark simplicity, "This isn't comfortable for either of us. Tonight, we'll feel too much." He slid her shift off, down her arms. "Let me unveil you. Let me see."

Cloth slipped over her. She felt individual threads of embroidery brush by. Her breasts held back the glide of the linen for a moment, then let go. It whispered across her belly, down over her hips, till the hair between her legs was uncovered and cloth piled around her feet. Her mind tumbled and danced like a kite in a high wind.

He said, "I don't deserve this." Maybe he didn't know he'd said that aloud.

She felt shy suddenly. "It's not so much. A body. They sell them on the streets—"

"This isn't about your body. It's you. The body just comes along for the ride."

He swept her up, easily, and carried her to the bed. He'd always looked frail, with his thinness and the keen, intelligent face. That was deceiving. Pax was distilled strength. Any weakness in him had been burned away in fire after fire his whole life.

He laid her on her back on the sheets, among the crumpled coverlet and blankets. The bed creaked under him as he climbed in to kneel between her legs. His body was dense. Solid. Hands smooth as soft leather stroked her thighs and opened her knees.

Not simply to take. Not to fall upon her, heavy and hurried. Her lovers had not been crude men or uncaring, but they'd been in a hurry, worried every moment they were with her, afraid of being discovered, of being forced to marry her, of public shame.

She'd thought all men were like that, grabbing for sweets like greedy children. Clumsy.

Pax was not clumsy.

The bedside candle lit his familiar, sharp-edged face. His pupils had become huge. Behind him, dimly, the cracks in the ceiling became and unbecame maps of unknown countries.

This was the man she had chosen in so many ways. This analytical mind. This disciplined body. This man with no softness over the stark frame of him. She ran her hands over the tendons of his neck, over the muscles of his back, tight with suppressed need, that stretched like whipcord across long, clever bones. His cock prodded her thigh and that was long and hard and clever as well.

He kissed her mouth and his hair fell and tangled with the kissing. He gave a low growl of need—of hunger—and began kissing his way down her throat, down between her breasts, down to where her ribs rose and fell, pumping breath in and out. She could lift her head and see him loving her skin with his eyes, his fingers taking in the ridges and valleys of her rib cage. Kissing each one.

He raised his head and met her gaze. "You taste like a color."

"I do?"

"Rose madder."

"That's one of the reds, isn't it?"

"Mouth color. Earth color. Color of that blossom between your legs. One of the oldest hues. Intense, and it doesn't fade over time."

"You're making me a"—she drew in a shaky breath—"compliment."

"You taste like sunrise." He licked around her breast.

She jerked madly when he came to the nipple. Her body jangled like a hundred bells ringing and she curled around a pleasure so intense it was pain.

Slow as a kestrel hovering in the sky, his hands shaking, Pax stroked down her belly, staring and wondering. Stroked the insides of her thighs, under her buttocks, and around to cradle her hips in his hands. He lifted her, kissing down the long bow she made of herself. Kissed her between her legs, spreading the tangle of hair with his tongue. Lapped his tongue into her.

She choked out a gasp. Desire poured across her. Sweet. Honey sweet. She arched toward it.

Her lips formed "Oh, my," without saying it. She'd read about this. In Latin. The aunts had an extensive library. *But I didn't know men actually did it.*

Obviously men did.

He lifted from her to look into her face. "Even your shadows are red and gold. It's like falling into a painting to touch—"

He jerked in surprise. Went completely still.

He looked over his shoulder. "There's a cat biting my ankle."

A cat?

She drew her elbows behind her back and propped herself up to look.

Where the sheets were thrown back in disorder, a ball of gray fur was wrapped around Pax's leg, attacking the foot with single-minded intent.

She said, unsteadily, "It's a kitten."

"With teeth and claws." Pax shifted to see better. The cat fell into a frenzy, growling, drawing little beads of red blood.

"It could be worse. He could have attacked . . . elsewhere." She fell back on the bed, sputtering into laughter.

"I was thinking that." He twisted free from her and detached the kitten, paw by paw, till he held it up by the scruff of the neck. He stood with it, magnificently naked, hugely erect, looking frustrated. He and the cat glared at one another, man to cat, cat to man. "A Baldoni watch cat. I should have expected this."

She giggled like a schoolgirl. "A gray cat. *Un gatto grigio.*"

"I hated that nickname." He gave a grin. "I'll evict him." He held the cat against his chest, stroking its head with one finger, and padded over to the door to undo the protections she'd placed there and put the intruder out.

Because she laughs at me, Pax thought. *Because she's*

never had a lover who gave a damn about her. Because we
both may die soon. Because she's beautiful.
I have to make this good for her.

Cami curled on the bed, biting her knuckles to keep
laughter inside. Her breasts were pebbled up. The lithe, strong
muscles of her thighs shook in fine tremors, thrusting a little
toward him. Wanting. Ready.

He'd known the mechanics of this. He hadn't known how
he'd feel when he threw himself into this maelstrom and let it
pull him under.

"If I don't have you soon, I'm going to die," he said.

"Come between my legs." She opened her arms to him.
Opened her knees. "Now."

"Now," he agreed. "Before Fate calls up hellhounds and
vultures as well as cats."

She drew him down to her. It wasn't so complicated. Not
when he wanted her this much. There, at the center, she was
slick. She pressed against his hand when he stroked her hair
aside.

When he entered, she rose to meet his cock. More than
meet him, she thrust herself against him. He was inside her
and she was smooth and beautiful, warm as rose madder. She
closed around him and closed tight.

With everything he was, he drove into her. Again. Again.

Hard, he drove into her, felt her thrust back to him. Return
everything he gave. Delight in it, need it, glory in it. All her
strength answered to his.

She sobbed in a way that was also laughing. Her fingers
clawed into him and she groaned deep in her throat. She
tightened everywhere around him. Her entire body stiffened
and thrashed hard, suddenly, once, twice, again, again.

The pleasure was like exploding everywhere, helplessly.
He was in time, barely, to withdraw from her and spend
against her thigh.

She shuddered one last time and softened under him and he
collapsed on her, sucking in air. It smelled like lovemaking.

Men didn't talk about this part, about holding a woman
afterward, both of you plastered together, damp everywhere,
your bodies somehow melting into each other.

I'll keep you alive, Cami. I swear it.

He said, "I'm glad one of us wasn't a virgin."

The blankets and sheets were everywhere, but he laid his hand on one and pulled it up to drag over both of them. There didn't seem to be any more hidden animals.

Cami lay perfectly limp. When he pulled her in next to him, she poured into the space like water. His cock stirred. Soon they'd make love again.

She opened her eyes. "What did you say about virgins?"

"Not anymore," he said.

Forty-three

One must sometimes invite the wolf to the table.

A BALDONI SAYING

IN THE EARLY HOURS OF THE MORNING, WHEN the Crocodile tavern in Covent Garden was filled with petty tradesmen and laborers on their way to work, William Doyle took his ease at a narrow table in the dark corner, engaged in quiet conversation, eating breakfast, collecting information. He wore a leather vest and plain shirt, and around his neck, a Belcher neckerchief. Anyone glancing in his direction would assume he transported wagonloads of bricks for a living or sold cattle at Smithfield Market or, if they got a closer look, that he routinely committed theft with violence.

The young man across from him might have served in a draper's shop or sold expensive gloves or pounded Latin into the heads of reluctant schoolboys. He was, in fact, a freelance seller of secrets. A collector of errors in judgment. An entrepreneur in other men's moral failings. A blackmailer, in season.

"I need to know by tonight. Noon is better," Doyle said.

"You give me very little time."

"Nobody has any time," Doyle said. "Give me hints, rumors, a whisper . . . anything."

"I make no promises."

"Do what you can." Doyle slid a folded banknote across the table. It was covered smoothly and instantly by a slender, well-kept hand. The younger man rose from his bench and left like an amiable snake setting off to swallow barn rats.

At the tavern door he brushed past Bernardo Baldoni, entering.

Bernardo stepped to one side and stood with his back to the window, letting his eyes adjust to the dark, giving Doyle a long moment to look him over. Then he threaded his way around two tables to the shadowy corner behind the bar.

He sat on the bench recently vacated and set his hands in plain view. Bernardo was not a large or imposing man. He looked even less so when sitting across from the mass of muscle that was William Doyle. He said, "Mr. Doyle," and it was a statement, not a question.

Doyle frowned. "I know you."

"We met once, ten years ago, in Paris, over cards. I was a corn factor from Marseilles. You were a German count."

Neutrality settled over Doyle's ugly face. "Right."

"The card game was at the Palais Royal. The play was high. We were both cheating."

"That's ordinary enough. Cheating." Doyle took up his mug and drank ale, wiped his mouth with the back of his hand, and waited.

"So I thought. Until I noticed you were cheating to lose."

"Looked that way, did it?"

"I sensed a complicated scheme in play, and it was not one of my own, so I withdrew with all prudent speed. Paris was full of political plots and plans at that time. Most of them ended badly for someone."

"Still true," Doyle said amiably.

"There was a murder in that club that night. A political murder. I was sufficiently intrigued that I made inquiries and discovered who you are."

"Did you, now?"

"The British Service remains impenetrable. Your Military Intelligence is less so."

"I've been told that."

Bernardo motioned the barmaid closer and ordered coffee. "The military are a great trial to us all."

The two men sat, measuring each other, till the woman returned to swipe at a patch of table with her apron and slap down a mug.

When she was gone again, out of earshot, Doyle said, "The coffee's a mistake."

Bernardo sipped. Grimaced. "So it is." He set it carefully aside. "A reminder that I am among the English. No other nation would call this coffee."

"We're an imaginative race," Doyle said.

Bernardo leaned back in his chair. For a while they watched the other patrons of the Crocodile eat and drink. The tavern collected a mixed bag of workmen connected with the theater, laborers, market vendors, and women of various degrees of respectability.

Bernardo said, "You may know who I am."

Doyle made no comment.

"So." Bernardo turned a hand palm up. "I am Bernardo Baldoni, brother to Cesare Baldoni." He paused. "I see that you knew."

Doyle didn't acknowledge that but didn't deny it, either.

"I have come to deliver a message to the British Service." Bernardo's voice became less genial. "You take an interest in the woman called Camille Leyland. This must cease."

"Why?" The single blunt word from Doyle.

"She is ours. She is Baldoni. She is my great-niece."

Doyle closed his eyes. "I see." A minute passed in silence. "Tell me she isn't also Cesare Baldoni's great-niece."

"She is his granddaughter. His only granddaughter. I think it is best that the British Service know this."

"Hell."

"She is also Ernesto Targioni's granddaughter. Add to this that she is Scipione Zito's first cousin and closest blood relative. You know what he is. I have not even begun to list the families she is tied to by blood and marriage across Tuscany. The Minutoli. The Scribanos . . ."

"In short, related to everybody but the pope."

"There is a distant connection to—"

"Damn."

"As I say, you should know this."

Doyle hissed out a long breath of impatience. "What the devil was a Baldoni child—*that* Baldoni child—doing unprotected, getting scooped up by the Police Secrète and put in the Coach House? Why the hell weren't you keeping watch on her?"

"Disorder beyond belief, and one man's unforgivable villainy. It is a family matter." Bernardo set the tips of his fingers together and looked down at them. "It is the family matter of several important families, in fact."

"And again, I have to say damn it to hell."

"You have an understanding of the politics of Tuscany. Cesare declared there would be no vendetta with the Targioni. We all assiduously covered over that ugliness. Now, unless it is seen that my niece is most abundantly cared for and happy, the old scandal will emerge into daylight."

Doyle closed his eyes and pressed thumb and forefinger to the bridge of his nose. "Accompanied by a certain amount of bloodshed."

"It is Tuscany," Bernardo said. "And it is family."

"The bloodshed happening in French territory, when our peace treaty with France is shaky as hell. It's going to look like England's making trouble on purpose."

Bernardo said, almost apologetically, "You are not the only one who finds this a difficult situation. You see the implications, do you not?"

"I see the implications."

"For the Baldoni, for all the old Tuscan families of power, she is a lit candle tossed into a powder magazine."

"Which the French will blame on us."

"The small blessing of this day is that my great-niece is under my roof again, instead of in a British prison, accused of spying for the French. Or dead at British hands."

Doyle looked past him, at a blank spot on the plaster wall. "We wouldn't kill her."

"Of course your Service would not," Bernardo said. "Perhaps

the blundering Military Intelligence of England also would not. But I am Tuscan and Florentine and we scent intrigue in the lightest breeze. No one in Italy will believe she spent ten years in England and the British Service did not know who she was. If my great-niece trips over a stone, or is struck by lightning in Hyde Park, or walks in the rain and catches pneumonia, the English will be blamed. That one death will drive the great families of Tuscany into the arms of Napoleon."

"We'll have to keep her alive, then, won't we?"

"With the aid of various saints. *Con l'aiuto dei santi.*"

The two men looked at each other for a time.

Doyle picked up his mug. "I'd suggest the ale in this establishment, but I imagine you don't drink it. Has she told you what she's doing tomorrow?"

"She goes to face Il Mercante di Tenebre. I do not stand in her way. Baldoni women have always fought. She honors us when she goes to face that beast."

"But it would be best if she didn't get herself killed on English soil."

"Very much so. Your Mr. Paxton is in my kitchen, where the coffee is somewhat better than this," he tapped his cup, "plotting to keep her alive." He pursed his lips and continued, "It has occurred to us that Mr. Paxton may present a solution to another problem."

Doyle waited. It was impossible to know if he suspected what was coming.

Bernardo said, "My Sara is heiress to inheritances in two great families—possibly the Zitos as well. She will have also the dowry of her grandmother, who was Maria Vezzoni . . ."

"There is just no end to this, is there?" said Doyle, looking sour.

"She must marry, and soon, to a family who will not cause troubles with this great inheritance. Someone tied to neither the French nor the Austrians. It has occurred to us that an Englishman may be the solution to our problems."

Doyle didn't give anything away on his face. "It might."

"I will not force my Sara—Cami, as I must call her—into anything distasteful to her. Not with the least feather of persuasion. But she seems fond of your agent Paxton. He spent last night in her bed."

Doyle didn't say anything.

Bernardo made himself comfortable in the chair he had taken. "Tell me about Thomas Paxton."

Forty-four

Do not have a good escape plan. Have three.

A BALDONI SAYING

QUIET, ORDINARY SEMPLE STREET SAT COMPLA-
cently in the morning light and provided no clue as to why
the Merchant had chosen it for their meeting.

Pax wore a gaudy brocaded waistcoat and a jacket of
exactly the wrong shade of blue. Uberto Baldoni had
unearthed this outfit from some vast Baldoni clothing hell.
The jacket didn't match the buff trousers, which didn't match
the boots. The hat had ugly proportions. Everything was too
shiny, too new, too bright, and of the shoddiest construction—
the visual equivalent of chalk shrieking on a slate.

He caressed the wide lapel of his jacket as if he considered
it a thing of beauty. In a way, it was. This was the perfect disguise. He was invisible because he was so apparent. Men
tracking the Merchant didn't strut the streets in strident, flam-
boyant blue.

His hair was dull brown. He hadn't shaved that morning.
He swaggered along with a bold, searching eye, looking like
somebody who'd steal washing off a line.

Cami strolled at his side. The Baldoni had decked her out
in a blond wig, flowered hat, and fussy yellow dress that made

her stand out from the sober matrons of Semple Street like a canary in a flock of sparrows. She carried a yellow parasol. Her walk was a paean of availability. The tilt of her head, nicely vulgar. A pretty little cake of a woman.

Of course, if you bit into her, you'd find steel underneath the icing.

"I'm not a vain man," Pax said, "but I hate you to see me dressed like this."

Her bonnet swung in his direction. She gave a broad and bawdy grin. "I like this Paxton. He looks disreputable."

"I look like a pimp. Not my preferred disguise. Every eye on the street is on me."

"There are many ways of hiding. If you look like a pimp, I look like a woman of pleasure. Not an expensive one. Do you think the Merchant set somebody to watch the street?"

"It's not his way. Before he told you Semple Street was the meeting place, he'd cut all ties to it. He's left nothing here that leads back to him."

"Unless he's set a trap for me." Cami dawdled, entirely the woman of leisure. No one would see her studying from window to window, looking behind the glass for watchers. Looking in reflection after reflection for anyone following. "He knows I'll come here. When I do, I'm easy to kill. Easy to capture. Why not grab me off the street today and torture the Mandarin Code from my flesh?"

"If he wants to capture you," he said, "he won't waste time watching Semple Street day and night. He'll grab you tomorrow at eleven o'clock in the morning. He'll have a couple of men with him when he picks you up."

"Three men. You flatter me."

"He underestimates women. I'd bring five well-trained minions and a supply of weapons."

She peeked under the frilled edge of the yellow parasol and batted her eyes at him. "So many compliments."

"You are in all ways admirable."

They'd reached Number Fifty-six. She stopped and he made a pantomime of retying the ribbon of her bonnet. It gave her time to take in the street, up and down, from this point.

She said, "I'll stand here to wait for him, tomorrow." She

chose a section of gray-brown pavement at her feet. "This spot." Her eyes were dark and thoughtful, pupils dilated.

He didn't look down. It was too easy to imagine blood and Cami's body curled on the ground and him too late to do anything but murder the bastard. "It'd be easier for me if I were the one walking out to meet him."

It was his job to face the Merchant, not Cami's. It had always been his job. Now it was his job to stand back and let her take the risk.

"Next time," she said, "I'll save the hard part for you."

He smoothed the wide yellow ribbons of her bonnet and let go.

On both sides of the street, windows and doors gleamed under the bright sky. Cami considered them. "Before I became entangled with you, and thus with the British Service, I had envisioned a relatively simple exchange with a blackmailer, enlivened by a slight chance of dying." She managed to make the parasol express irony. "Now I have the same chance of dying, but also the British Service. I'll walk down this street under the gaze of five, six, seven British Service agents—however many of them. Their first objective will be to capture the Merchant. Then they'll come after me."

"I won't let that happen. If I'm not here, Hawker won't let that happen."

"You mean, if you're dead, putting it in frank and simple terms. If that happens, I won't trouble Mr. Hawker, who will doubtless be busy. I'll go—Look over there at the grocery. You've passed it, I imagine, on your tours of Semple Street. That's my escape route"—she touched it with her attention, just a moment—"when I run from the Service. That track beside the grocery that looks like a delivery way to the yard in back. It goes to an alley that runs all the way to Tallison Road. It's not shown on the ward maps."

"I walked it last night before I came to see you."

"I'm surprised you and Antonio didn't run into each other. It's a dim, grim alley, according to Antonio—high brick walls on both sides. We'll block it just on general principles. Giomar and Alessandro will bring the pony cart in there just before dawn and overturn it and wait with a couple of guns each. It's an escape for me and a trap for the Merchant, if he's stupid enough to go that way."

He pictured them. Boys really. "They're young."

"No younger than some of the men who followed you in Italy." She grinned. "My family gossips. This morning they gossiped about Il Gatto Grigio and a third cousin of mine who went into the hills with him. He was fourteen."

He wanted to tell her he hadn't led boys that young. But he had. He'd used them as lookouts, scouts, messengers, information gatherers, guides. Some of them—men, boys, even women—the ones who'd come from the gutted, burned-out farmhouses they passed, walked right behind him up the mountain passes, to lay ambush.

She said, "Antonio wishes he'd been with you in the hills. He's tired of playing the respectable banker while everybody else is roaming the Piedmont alps, shooting at the French." Cami looked at him from under her hat. "I told him it probably wasn't as much fun as he thought."

"It wasn't."

She became more sober. "You don't need to worry about Giomar and Alessandro. We're an intensely traditional family. Baldoni children go out with the gold shipments when they're thirteen. Those two have shot mountain bandits."

"Then they're old enough to defend an alley. I'll talk to them this afternoon. Speaking of guns . . ." He twitched his hand, indicating a house in the row behind them. "I'll put a sniper there. Second floor, third window from the right. Your cousin Antonio found the place for us."

She examined the house and the window unobtrusively, taking it in, judging angles. "It's odd, considering my many skills, that no one ever taught me to shoot a rifle."

"I'll teach you someday. I didn't learn to do it right till they sent me to Italy." Five years back, before he sailed for Genoa, Grey had taken him out to Doyle's big house in the country. For a week they'd spent every daylight hour shooting rifles and every night drinking and talking with some of Grey's old army friends about scouting and ambush.

Nine of his kills had been long-range shots with a Baker rifle. He said, "There's a straight line from that window, down the whole length of the street, from corner to corner. If the Merchant gets that far, the sniper will stop him."

"At that distance?"

"He can notch a man's left ear at that distance. Or hit his left knee."

"And leave him alive to chat with your Service. I'll be annoyed if they kill him by accident. Especially if London Bridge blows up the next day and falls into the Thames. I'm very fond of London Bridge."

"The River Police are watching the bridges."

"They can't watch everything. The mint, Brooks's club, the shoppers on Bond Street . . . That's enough gunpowder to topple Westminster Abbey like a house of cards. With people inside." Her voice cracked a little around the last words.

She took a deep breath. "We have to trap him here." She took one last glance at Number Fifty-six. "I was hoping to see . . . something. But it's just a dull house of nothing in particular." She shrugged. "I'm done. We can walk on."

"Hawker's told me what the service knows so far," he said. "The vast resources have heaped up a pile of trivia. Shall I pass it along?"

"Do. I dote upon trivia."

"Number Fifty-six. On the ground floor is an old man who tailors suits on Jermyn Street. The basement, two brothers who work in a blacking factory. Both floors upstairs are leased to a solicitor's clerk and his numerous family."

"There's a baby. I heard it crying. And the window with bars must be the nursery."

"Our clerk copies legal briefs, most recently for a case concerning inheritance of a woolen mill in Yorkshire. Servants in the attic. Next door, at Fifty-eight . . ." They walked, and he organized what he knew and laid it out for her. "Across the street, at Number Twenty-nine, the house belongs to a sea captain's widow who lets rooms. We have an old woman who feeds cats in the basement. The ground floor is a retired nanny. One floor up . . ." House by house, he matched windows to inhabitants.

They came to the corner, where Semple Street ran into Medwall Street. Cami sighed and tucked the parasol under her arm, evidently feeling it had served its purpose in establishing her role. "We Baldoni say, 'One insight is worth a hundred facts.' But I have no insights, except to say the men and women of Semple Street are ordinary as rocks. It's as if somebody went to the warehouse and bought dull people as a wholesale lot."

Cami's mind saw patterns when the facts were still scattered like stars across the sky. "There's something we're not seeing."

"We will continue to not see it, no matter how long we linger in this vicinity." Cami shook her head. So strange to see her in these bright, frilly clothes with such a serious expression on her face. "I'll go home and take out a map and stare at it till the very writing crawls away to hide from my intense scrutiny." Impatient now, she turned and started down Medwall Street. "It's my turn to be informative. I'll show you where the Baldoni will be busy. If the Merchant gets this far, they'll deal with him. It should be safe. The Merchant will doubtless have discharged his pistols somewhat before he gets here."

"Cami . . ." There wasn't anything to say. The stark fact that she would probably be dead within minutes of meeting the Merchant lay between them. Neither of them wanted to say that in simple words.

"I'll wait for you tonight in my bedroom. Come to me," she said.

Everything—daylight, the street, house sparrows hopping on the pavement, people walking by—receded. He was overwhelmed by the memory of her body, laid back on white sheets, her legs open to him.

"To love you again," he said.

She said, "To talk and for the joy of your company. Also, I expect to have trouble sleeping."

"That's a prosaic reason for inviting me."

"I'm lining up the next twelve hours and filling them with simple things. Chocolates and good red wine and you. Will you come?"

"Yes."

Last night, in the coldest hour before dawn, he'd left her

bed and climbed down from her window. No dog barked, nobody stirred, but he slipped away from the house with the uneasy certainty his presence had been known. Instinct had set the hairs prickling on the back of his neck.

He'd climb up to her room again tonight. Instinct be damned.

Cami said, "And there is Mr. Hawker, leaning against a horse. What a surprise."

Hawker waited for them at the corner, his shoulder against the flank of a bay mare, the hoof curled up to rest on his thighs. He was cleaning the hoof with a little pick. Nobody had to get close to see he was cursing.

"He does that well," Cami said.

"He's putting something in there to give himself a lame horse to walk slowly past whatever he wants to look at."

"A coin, probably, under the shoe. It's very convincing and does little harm. Do you think a Baldoni ever worked for the British Service at some point? You seem to know a lot of the family secrets."

"I wouldn't be at all surprised."

When they got close enough, Hawker looked up and was amiable, pretending to a slight acquaintance. The hoof was returned to the pavement. The hat was tipped. Hawk was gallant in Cami's direction. Cami smiled and twirled her parasol and was bitingly sarcastic.

"Next street up," Hawker said, shaking his head as if he were handing over bad news about the horse, "the hackney's pulled over to the curb. Tenn's on the box. Doyle's waiting for you inside. Last-minute advice."

Beside him, Cami constructed a tight little smile. "I will excuse myself, then. I have no wish to meet Mr. Doyle again."

Hawker said, "Leave her here with me. I'll take care of her."

orty-five

*If you do not teach your son to be a thief, you make
an honest tradesman of him.*

A BALDONI SAYING

CAMI WAITED TILL PAX WAS OUT OF HEARING
range. Then she turned to this Service agent, Mr. Hawker.
She said, "If you have something to say to me you don't want
Pax to hear, this is as good a time as any."

He leaned against the horse, arms folded. They had patient
horses in whatever stable the British Service used. She wondered what the stable owners thought of all the horses lost and
injured by Service agents over the years. Did the British Service come up with excuse after excuse or did they change
livery stables with some frequency?

Hawker said, "There's a puzzle that's been bothering me.
That house—Number Fifty-six—means nothing. Semple Street
means nothing."

She said, "That is a brilliant summation of my own views."

"But the Merchant wants to meet you there. Why is that,
Miss Baldoni?"

"Because life is not tediously predictable, Mr. Hawker.
Maybe his tailor lives there."

"Or maybe you were told to lure Pax out where he'll be
easy to kill."

That hadn't occurred to her, not once. "You think I'm setting a trap for Pax."

"Who tells us what the Merchant said?" Hawker stepped toward her suddenly, ignoring the horse sidling behind him. "One person. You can say anything you want, can't you?"

She stood with him, eye to eye. Not a tall man, Mr. Hawker. "More than that. I can say anything I want and be believed. I'm Baldoni."

"And a liar from the cradle."

"I sucked it in with my mother's milk." She faced him and waited.

"Pax moves around a lot and he works on his own. Hard to trace. Hard to predict. Maybe your job is to bring him out in the open tomorrow for the Merchant to kill."

"A bit overelaborate, Mr. Hawker. Why would I do that?"

"You're a French spy."

"Not French, Mr. Hawker. Tuscan." She rolled her shoulders in a shrug and turned away. "And I don't spy for the French."

"You're Caché." Hawker's voice was sharp as thorns. "That's close enough. The only reason I don't use this"—the knife was a blur of black that whipped toward her till it was a cold prick at her jugular—"is that Pax wouldn't like it." The knife stayed where it was. He leaned closer and whispered, "If you hurt him again, I'll carve that pretty face of yours into ribbons."

She said, "Look down."

A second passed before he dropped his eyes. He'd already figured it out.

Her pretty yellow parasol with the delicate flounces now ended in a six-inch steel spike, sharpened to a dagger point. It touched his chest, right below the heart.

Baldoni don't let their eyes talk about what their hands are doing. Whoever had spawned this dangerous boy held the same views. Nothing at all moved in his eyes.

He let the knife drop from one hand and caught it with the other. He stowed it away in the inner recesses of his jacket, point downward. He said, "If I came after you, I'd pick a moment when you're not armed."

"You're a bloodthirsty fellow." She slid the catch of the

parasol back into place and retracted the spike. "If I ever decide you need killing—and I might make that decision any minute now—I'll do it with a rifle from some distance. From behind."

"Like a good Baldoni."

"No. A good Baldoni would do creative things with your organs of generation while you were still breathing, then mutilate your corpse and leave it for your friends to find. Baldoni don't waste a death." She tapped the parasol lightly, making sure the trigger mechanism was locked.

"You're good," Hawker said. "If you wanted to kill Pax, he'd be dead. If you wanted to blind him, he'd be blind."

"He's safe from me." Lifting her head, she saw Pax coming toward her in long, loose strides, looking neither left nor right. Coming to her. She said, "And I'm safe from you till I bring the Merchant out of hiding. After that . . . I fear I may suffer some unfortunate accident. Maybe you'll get that job. You seem suited to it."

"Is that what you think?" Hawker watched her steadily. "But you'll be there tomorrow, won't you, to do your dance with the Merchant?"

"Yes."

He nodded once, as if he'd proved something. "Then I'll get you away from Semple Street if the Service decides to arrest you. Be ready."

Forty-six

Do not attempt to change the course of a river.

A BALDONI SAYING

MIDNIGHT. PAX MADE HIMSELF A SHADOW DOWN the alley and along the back wall of the Baldoni household. It was a high stone wall with glass on top. He slung his coat over to ease the way. He was soft and silent landing inside the yard.

The yard looked empty. The lantern hung at the kitchen door still left big pools of dark to hide in. No dogs came sniffing to investigate him. To all appearances, the Baldoni household slept, peaceful and unguarded . . . tonight, when the Merchant was loose in London and Cami lay in bed upstairs.

No. He didn't believe it.

Somebody was awake in this yard, watching and waiting. More than one, probably.

And his instincts said he, in particular, was expected. So he'd arrive, as expected.

He didn't bother being surreptitious through the yard. He passed the old stable—the beasts needed for tomorrow were breathing in the stalls. By some family tradition, youthful Baldoni males slept separate from the house, above the stable in what had been the grooms' quarters. Beyond that, the long shed held a pony cart. They'd be rolling that out before it was light.

Usually he didn't make a lot of noise walking. Tonight he clicked his boots down enough so he wouldn't surprise anybody. Other nights, on other forays, into other strongholds, he'd take an hour to cross thirty feet. He'd locate the guards and dispose of them, one by one. He'd ease his way by unexpected routes past them, around them, behind them. Tonight he didn't have to bother with any of that.

He walked into the center of the . . . he was calling it a courtyard in his mind. The Baldoni stamped their opinion so firmly on the yard that it struggled to be orderly and beautiful, even in the dreary climate of London.

Cami's window was lit softly, glowing with only a hearth fire inside, no welcoming lamp. But she was waiting for him.

Bernardo Baldoni stepped out of the oblong darkness of the kitchen doorway. It was no surprise to see the old man. No surprise at all.

"You've chosen an unusual place to take the night air, Mr. Paxton," Bernardo said.

"You as well. Were you waiting for me?"

"Let us say I came outside for one last smoke before retiring." Bernardo came forward till they stood a few feet apart. He carried a cheroot—a small, neat, expensive one—cupped in the hand that held it so the red glowing tip didn't show. He held it up. "May I offer you one?"

"I never acquired the habit."

"The life you lead affords few indulgences." Bernardo raised the cheroot, breathed in, held the smoke a moment, and breathed out. When Bernardo spoke again, it was to change the subject. "I saw your sketch of the Merchant. You're a very good artist."

"Thank you."

They seemed to be alone. At least, he didn't feel any other watchers. No itch between his shoulder blades. No tug at his attention from one window or the other. The night felt empty, except for him and Bernardo.

Bernardo said, "Your work is particularly impressive for a man who has had so little leisure to practice the arts of peace."

"Chalks and ink are portable. I find time to sketch."

"Your lethal skills are also portable." Bernardo gestured, leaving a thin line of red on the night where his hand passed.

If Bernardo was taking a roundabout route to warn him away from Cami, he was wasting his time. "Cami knows what I am. If you want to warn her about me, wait till after tomorrow. She has enough on her plate."

"We will not disturb her peace of mind tonight, of all nights." Bernardo was silhouetted from the side as he glanced toward the window where Cami slept. "The Baldoni have a long memory, back to the days when the great Medici ruled Florence and made it the most beautiful and dangerous city in Europe. The Tuscans understand the man of action who is also an artist. The man of death who also creates beauty."

Nothing he could say to that. A light Italian shrug seemed the appropriate answer.

He understood the intertwining of art and violence. There'd been days in the mountains when he and his men paralleled the advance of the French, walking through the burned-out villages the invaders had left in their wake. He'd sit in an empty stable or lean against the wall of a goatherd's hut, lost in drawing some small, everyday thing—a broken mug, an old man's left hand, a pair of boots. Maybe it had kept him sane.

"You come to visit my niece," Bernardo said bluntly. "At night."

"Yes." Nothing to do but admit it. This wasn't a conversation he wanted to have with Cami's uncle, on a dark night, twenty feet from her bedroom window. "If there's fault to be found, it's mine."

Bernardo took smoke again, held it, blew it out. The fire-breathing dragon, guarding the tower where Cami slept. "My niece, my little Sara, the child who sat on my knee in the Villa Baldoni in Tuscany, is gone forever. I will miss her. But I am coming to be quite fond of the woman who has returned to us." He said softly, calmly, with easy dignity, "What do you intend with my niece, Mr. Paxton?"

A Baldoni threat didn't need to be laid out more plainly. It was there, stark and obvious as the bricks of a wall.

Truth? He was going to get into her room and make love to

her. He'd be with her tomorrow. Then he'd be with her the next day and all the foreseeable days after that. He said, "I plan to keep her alive tomorrow."

"I hope you will." Bernardo spoke in the same deliberate way. Unhurried. "The Baldoni will be there in our roles and our places. Your plans are well considered. But in the end it is she who must face the Merchant, and you who must be there to protect her." He grimaced and tossed the cheroot down on the cobblestone and ground it out. "If you live to be an old man, Mr. Paxton, you, too, may someday send others to do work you would wish to do yourself. I give you the task of defending our Cami."

"I intend to."

"You will remove her the minute that snake is taken and give her to us. She will not be put into the hands of the Service. Not for an hour. You understand that."

"I'll get her out of there."

"She must leave England. I have considered where in Europe she will be safest—"

"She'll be with me."

Bernardo looked once more in the direction of Cami's room. "Are you going to marry my niece, Mr. Paxton?"

"If she'll have me. Yes."

Bernardo nodded. "In my youth, men requested permission of a woman's family before asking her to marry. Like many customs and traditions it has been disrupted by these years of war."

"I haven't asked her." He hadn't said the words. The hour of eleven o'clock, tomorrow, lay like an insurmountable cliff, blocking off the days beyond. He wasn't planning past tomorrow.

"Fortunata and I approve, standing in the place of her grandfather. But it is, of course, Cami who will decide. We do not live in the Middle Ages."

He had a feeling the Baldoni still lived in the Middle Ages.

"We will discuss settlements at some point," Bernardo went on. "The legal documentation will be complex, as she owns property in several nations."

Cami had money? That was going to complicate things. If

it was any great amount, he hoped she liked managing the stuff. He sure as hell didn't want to.

"You do not ask what property or how much," Bernardo said.

"I'll worry about that when the time comes."

"Very wise." Bernardo began walking, beckoning him along to his side. "You are wondering whether you can come to her in her chamber tonight. The answer is no."

That, he answered with another Italianate shrug that said everything and nothing. He'd acquired a selection of such shrugs on his travels.

"Since you will so soon be one of us," Bernardo continued, "we have prepared a bed for you with some of the young men. Bachelors' quarters, you might call it." Bernardo indicated the stable they were walking toward. "We are crowded in our accommodations here in London, but we've doubled up again and emptied a bed for you. It's the last bed in the row upstairs. Don't disturb the others going by."

"I thank you for the hospitality."

He didn't have to see Bernardo to imagine the ironical smile. "Good night, Mr. Paxton. Sleep well."

Forty-seven

We are young only once, because God is merciful.

A BALDONI SAYING

A CANDLE NEXT TO THE DOOR SHOWED SIX BEDS lined up against the long wall under the slanted ceiling. Five beds held young men and boys, asleep. Pillows and blankets gave a glimpse of Baldoni faces, hard to tell apart in the weak light. Most of them looked old enough to shave. Barely. He'd probably been introduced to them.

These and some others would be the gang of laborers who would soon be taking furniture from a house one street south of Semple. They'd be the men who would hide in a load of hay being delivered to an inn on the southern corner of Semple and Medwall.

A dog, sleeping between the first two beds, woke and looked at him, accepted him, and resettled its head between front paws and closed its eyes. It was a well-trained Baldoni dog and didn't bark when familiar smells came and went in the night.

That was the dog saying, "You belong here. You're one of us." It was strangely heartening to be approved by a dog.

He wove between chairs piled high with coats, stepping over shirts bundled and thrown on the floor. Found footing

among books, empty wine bottles, and cricket bats. Passed a
table playing host to three rather fine throwing knives. The
empty bed was at the end of the room. He lay down fully
clothed, booted, and armed. The snores, the rasp of bodies
against blankets, the smell of men together in a close space
were all familiar. It felt like being back in the hills in Piedmont, with his men under cover and safe for the night.

He let go of wariness. He was deeply asleep in three
minutes.

HE woke himself an hour later to the same dim light and reassuring small sounds. He rose from the bed in the same silence he'd taken it and walked the length of the room and out
the door without disturbing anyone.

In the dim yard behind the Baldoni house, a lantern still
burned at the back door. Cami's window was lit only by the
fire on the grate, still no welcoming lamp.

He needed a cold, empty room.

He took a while, going up and down the obstacles of wall
and shed and alleyway, looking at all the windows, till he
picked his entry point. If he had to, he could cut fingerholds
and go up an unbroken plaster wall. But this front door was
furnished with pilasters and an ugly pediment and the window directly above the peak of the pediment was dark as a
well.

It could be a trap, of course. Always that to consider.

He toed one boot into a tight corner, set the other in the
next crevice. Fingerhold by fingerhold, toehold by toehold,
his cheek flat to cold stone, he climbed. A minute later, he
curled his fingers over the lip of the lintel and pulled himself up.

No curtains blocked his view into the room. Light leaking
under the door at the far side showed a small bedroom with
the clutter of somebody's possessions. The bed was empty.
Good.

The locks in a Baldoni household, he wasn't surprised to
find, didn't slide away tamely to a knife edge. But where
there's a glass window, there's a way through. He braced

himself against the sill and slowly, patiently scraped putty from one of the windowpanes with the point of his knife. If anybody heard, it would sound like a mouse gnawing away at the woodwork.

He'd entered a lot of houses, planning to kill somebody. Nice to break and enter for the purpose of loving a woman.

A little prying and the glass pane fell into his hand. He reached through and pulled back the dead bolt that held the window in place. The sash lifted silently. He climbed into a faint smell of perfume and soap.

A woman's bedroom, then. He laid the pane of glass aside. By touch and the smell of soap, he found the washstand, brought the soap ball back to the window, and ran it over and over the edges of the putty. He fit the pane of glass into the empty square, tapped the edges in, and it held. That would do for now.

The bedroom door wasn't locked. He eased it open.

On the rug in the hall, in a line, three dogs sat and looked up at him.

The Baldoni favored a breed of ugly, brown-and-white dogs with a calm, deliberate temperament and a well-toothed underbite.

He squatted down, murmured, *"Signora,"* and offered the rightmost bitch his fingers to sniff. *"Buonasera, dolce mia."* He pulled the soft ears. Scratched the high-domed head.

He went down the line, doing the same for Caterina and Lucrezia, giving a few words to each. Curved lower fangs gleamed in the light of the little candle at the end of the hall. He didn't let himself imagine what that trio would do to housebreakers.

When he got up and walked away, not looking back, the three padded off in the opposite direction, patrolling, doing their job.

Cami's door wasn't locked. He stepped into the room far enough to see her in bed, awake, looking at him. The trundle bed beside her held one of the children—Lucia—asleep.

He slipped back into the hall and waited.

Her door opened and closed noiselessly. She threw herself into his arms as if every inch of her would cling to every inch of him. Cami's body—warm, breathing, holding everything important, alive with promise. He closed his eyes and took her to him.

She didn't say anything, just held him as if he might be torn away in a storm. He lifted her face, still by touch, still with his eyes closed so he could feel every density and softness of her skin, and found her mouth with his and kissed into her.

Knowledge of what was coming tomorrow swept around him like turbulent water. The islet of safety they stood upon eroded by the minute. They had so little time.

He kissed her over and over again, every feature of her face. The darkness around them made this a moment of touch only. Of shapes emerging into the darkness, disappearing into the dark again.

"Not here," she whispered.

She was wearing only a night shift. She'd be cold in this open hall. They needed a room.

"Downstairs," she said.

She took his hand and led him down the hall to the stairs. The warmest thing in the night was her hand. The kitchen, when they came to it, was a haven with the good fire on the hearth and the order of well-used, accustomed shapes and shadows. Square of the table, circles of pots hung on the walls, golden bronze in the light of the fire.

Cami wrapped herself around him and he pushed her back against the wall. So much warm skin everywhere. He wanted to kiss it all. Suck it all. He wanted to be inside her.

He devoured her with his mouth. Couldn't think. Couldn't formulate a plan. Couldn't force his brain away from the manic desire to push her shift away and open his trousers and get into her.

A man doesn't take his pleasure. He gives pleasure. Damn, who said that to him? Doyle. Doyle said that once, in the offhand way he said important things. A man gives pleasure to a woman.

Hair the black and silver of volcano glass. Endless depths of color in it and the heat captured there forever. He stroked her forehead, her eyelids, and followed that, kissing. The memory of contour and color turned to sensation in his mouth. The tiny strands of her eyebrows gritted between his teeth. Her skin smelled like the lavender in the sheets she'd been sleeping on.

She reached up and dragged her fingers into his hair and held him. She said, "You shouldn't have come," and kissed him. "They know you were here last night. Nobody said anything but after dinner Fortunata and the aunts started talking about"—she kissed him again and shook her head—"stupid things. Money, land, politics. Marriage."

"Marry me," he said.

"Yes. Of course. We'll do that."

"Fine. Work out the details later."

"Yes," she said and stopped his mouth with kisses.

He slid his hand between them, over the cloth of her shift to the hard bead of her nipple and the soft breast. He felt her gasp into his mouth. She gasped again as he explored the nipple between his fingers, gently, then harder. She liked that. He'd find everything else she liked.

She took her hands from around his neck, stroked in under his jacket and down his body. She fumbled with the buttons at the fall of his trousers.

Too much. Too much. He threw back his head and groaned. His hands clenched reflexively where they held her, on her shoulder, on her breast. He was going to hurt her. He was going to grab her and push her against the wall so she couldn't escape. He was going to ram into her and use her like the bastard he was. He shook with the need to do that. Every muscle tightened, tightened under the vise.

Cami freed his cock from his trousers. It sprang up between them, hard as hell.

He gritted out, "I don't think I can go slow."

"We'll go slow next time."

"Have to please you first. Make you happy." *Don't let me disgrace myself.* "Have to do things to you."

She pushed herself to him. Her hands guided him inside her. "We'll do things later."

He was almost sure that made sense. He gripped her buttocks and drove into her.

She arched back with a strangled cry, her face turned upward, beautiful as a mad flower, eyes blank, mouth open and gasping. Her fingernails dug into his back and it was lines of fire that should have hurt but didn't.

"Do things like this." She panted that out.

She was silk inside. Warm velvet. He shoved into her, pulled out. Into her and out. Hard. Avid. Her throat was milky white and vulnerable. He caught her earlobe with his teeth, licked and bit his way down her throat. "Supposed to be in a bed. Damn. We need a bed."

"Find a bed later."

"Right." He pulled her to him tightly, lifted her off the floor to take her breast in his mouth. He growled—yes, growled—in his throat and consumed her.

The throbbing center of her clenched around him with every nip, lick, suckle. She answered what he did to her with shocks that ran through her, with sharp gasps, with the thrashing of her whole body, writhing and ecstatic.

Her response stunned him. *I did this to her. I made her feel this.*

She dug fingers into his shoulders, steadying herself, and thrust to meet him. They rhymed. They matched. They were one motion. One dance. *This is how it's done.* He took her mouth and breathed in her breath.

She gave a cry like pain and joy and her teeth bit down on his lips. Beyond control, beyond thought, he slammed into her and slammed into her and lost himself in her.

The world was dark and full of pleasure. Somewhere in the madness he remembered to hold her tight so she wouldn't slip down on the floor. The hard, cold floor. He held her and held her and maybe they both fell asleep for a minute, standing up.

Bernardo Baldoni awoke from the light sleep of the old and heard various small noises in the house. He considered and discarded possibilities, decided what those particular sounds must be, turned over, and pulled the covers higher over his shoulder.

He was a romantic at heart, as any good Tuscan and especially any good Baldoni must be.

It would seem Mr. Paxton was amenable neither to practicality nor threat. He would do very well for Sara. Very well indeed.

Cami, he reminded himself. Very well for Cami.

orty-eight

*Trust in God, but remember He does not plan for
you to live forever.*

A BALDONI SAYING

CAMI DREW OUT THE WATCH UNCLE BERNARDO
had given her a few hours ago. It was gold, enameled in indigo flowers, very pretty and very old, smooth and cool in her
hand. Uncle Bernardo said it had belonged to her grandmother. She clicked it open. "Twenty minutes. Then I walk
out and play the tethered lamb."

Pax said, "The tethered tiger. You're nobody's lamb." He
smiled. "You should check your powder."

She did, to please him, and because it gave her something
to do in these last long minutes. The powder was dry. It was a
warm and sunny day for London.

She put her pistol away carefully—the dress she wore had
several spots for concealing such weapons.

They stood in the rough track beside the grocer's. She
didn't bother to hide because she was expected. Pax kept
himself against the wall, in the lee of a drainpipe, where he
was inconspicuous. He was so close she could have stretched
out a hand and touched him. But there were already many
eyes on her so she didn't.

They could see Number Fifty-six from here. When she

crossed the street and went to her appointment, Pax would be watching.

"Everyone in place?" Pax turned his head to say that to a space farther down the alley.

"Ready and accounted for." A man emerged, unaccompanied by any sound. Hawker. He wore a blue workman's smock and carried a basket under one arm, where a few sheets of window glass were packed in straw. "They're placing bets whether the Merchant will show up at all."

Pax said, "We'll find out."

Hawker set the basket down at the mouth of the alley. "The guns are on top." He shoved straw aside to show a line of pistols, nose down in the straw. "Don't cut yourself on glass."

She said, "Several guns. Do you think we'll need them?"

"Hard to have too many guns," Pax said.

"I use knives myself." Hawker shifted his gaze to her. "A more elegant and reliable weapon. I'll teach you to throw knives when I get a chance."

That was unexpected. "Thank you."

"You're going to be with Pax, looks like. He'll need somebody who can watch his back. Today, we'll watch yours. Now I will blend into the passing scene by repairing a window." He inspected a small, dirty window that led to some cellar room. "This one, I think."

"It's not broken," she said.

Hawker's sideways kick was too fast to see. There was little noise and most of the glass fell inward.

Hawker said, "Now it is."

"I don't suppose you actually know how to fix a window," Pax said.

"No idea." Hawker was already taking a sheet of glass and a half dozen miscellaneous tools out of the basket. He squatted to inspect the window. "That is why I am just going to pretend to fix it."

Her watch fitted into one of the little pockets sewed into the sleeve of the dress. She took it out again, as much to hold it as to open it and read the time.

"How long?" Pax said.

"Fifteen minutes." Now that the time was so short, she

wished it would hurry by. "This'll be over, one way or the other, in an hour."

"We'll go back and eat afterward, I imagine. What are they cooking?"

"Cooking?" Her mind seemed perfectly blank. She knew someone had talked about this. "I don't—Fish. We're having fish. Whatever they found at the market. And soup with sausages. I'd forgotten how much I missed soup with sausages."

"Then we'll eat soup, and revel in it." Pax held her in his complete attention. He also watched Semple Street with that same complete attention. As did Hawker.

As did she. Semple Street looked almost unreal. Like a stage setting waiting for the actors. "There'll be something with apples for dessert. There was a big bowl of them beside the sink."

A portly citizen—he was completely a civilian and bystander in this matter—emerged from his house and turned left, walking briskly, leaving the scene and the interesting events to come. He lifted his hat politely to a pair of women who stood at their door, chatting and wearing particularly ugly bonnets.

Carriages passed, but none of them contained the Merchant. Not yet.

Pax said, "I like apples. I remember the time we went over the wall, hunting them."

At the Coach House.

They must have been mad. Thinking back, that was the only explanation. But the two of them used to slip over the wall and go stealing in town. They stole food. The Cachés were kept hungry.

The apple expedition had been especially satisfying. They'd stolen a few dozen from vendors in the market on the quai de la Tournelle and sneaked a basket back over the wall. Then all of them had gorged on apples—two apiece, an amazing feast—in the back of the practice field behind the targets and bales of hay and old benches. Not a scratch on anyone. No one beaten for it. A wholly successful operation.

A good thought to carry with her today.

Reluctantly, she opened the watch and turned the face to Pax, silently. She felt cold inside and strange.

"It's time," Pax said.

She'd planned to walk away from him, calmly and bravely, as a soldier parts from a comrade to go to battle. But he took her wrist and pulled her to him and kissed her, strongly and thoroughly.

He said, "I love you. Be careful. We'll move in when you give the signal."

She'd been cold, so cold, inside. Now she carried that fire away with her, in her belly.

PAX returned to his selected piece of shadow where his choice of clothes made him invisible.

Hawker went on repairing the window, looking knowledgeable, using the tools pretty much at random. "It's not the code," Hawker said, just loud enough for him to hear. "It's her."

"I know." It had been obvious from the start the Merchant was after Cami. "She knows."

"There's about no documents to decipher from Mandarin yet. It's too new." Hawk tap-tapped at jagged glass. "And we'd stop using it the day she disappeared from Goosefat-on-Tweed anyway. She could hand the real code over this morning, down to the last orange pip, wrapped up in a red bow and stamped by the post office. Everybody's warned. It's worthless."

"If he wanted codes, he would have kidnapped one of the Leylands and beaten it out of an old woman. This is too elaborate for that. He's wanted Cami, and only her, from the beginning."

"Now he's got her." Hawk went on calmly scraping putty. "He's brought Cami to this street, this morning, at this hour. We can assume that's exactly what he wants. I'm glad somebody's pleased with this morning's work."

"We've handed her over to him." But that wasn't quite true. Cami had handed herself over to the Merchant. She walked toward him now, without hurry or any sign of nervousness. The wind was strong enough to pull at the curls of her hair. Grey would have to compensate for that wind when he shot. She wore no cloak, no bonnet to get in the way if she had to fight or run.

Carts, horses, and the occasional carriage passed. Men and women went about their business on Semple Street. A child rolled a hoop down the street. The background hum of London filled the air. It was a bright day, an hour short of noon.

Hawker said, "There are a number of us keeping her alive. And she's deadly competent all on her own." He picked up a small trowel. "Good choice, by the way."

"I think so."

"Probably kill you on your honeymoon, but you'll die happy."

"I agree. Hand me that pistol, will you? Is it loaded?"

"Why do you ask questions when you know the answer? Of course it's loaded."

He didn't care how careful and wise and deadly Cami was. A piece of lead the size of his fingernail could take her from the world forever. One bullet. Break the goblet, and life pours out.

Forty-nine

*It is not necessary to be brave. The pretense is
enough.*

A BALDONI SAYING

CAMI LEFT THE ALLEY AND WALKED OUT INTO
the open, feeling Pax's eye on her. In these last hours he had
become a vessel, filled with purpose, solid and dense in his
concentration. All for her. That knowledge burned like a
flame in the back of her mind, giving off warmth. She was not
alone.

She picked up her skirts as she stepped into the street,
glancing left and right. The sniper was set up behind that window. Baldoni—her blood, her family—waited at both ends of
the street, armed and ready, none of them in sight. Service
agents practiced their form of well-armed subtlety behind
some of the closed doors up and down the street. There were
seven of them, six men and a woman.

Pax was one of them still. He didn't believe that, but it
showed in every word they spoke to him. In their faces. The
fraternity of the Service had closed ranks around him.

This motley, disjointed, powerful, and clever crew was
going to take the Merchant alive. It would be done. Had to be
done. It was too late to wonder if there'd been better choices
along the way. It was far too late to back out now.

She narrowed the world to here and now. Semple Street took on vivid clarity and color. The shadows had contracted to nothing, this close to noon. Birds chittered on windowsills. Voices leaked from open windows. Somewhere to her left she heard the sound of a broom sweeping. A fragment of newspaper rolled end over end in a gust of wind. A cat sat, artistically arranged on its doorstep. Women in black, heads together, talking, had settled in for the duration. A window opened and a small rug took an airing, shaken out.

She came to Number Fifty-six, to her own particular square of pavement, the exact cobbles, and set her feet firm and a little apart, ready to run or fight or be shot by one of the many men who might do that. It was taking her post as a soldier on the battlefield does, resigned and scared.

She could sense eyes on her, like the faintest itch on her skin. She felt Pax's steady regard. She could have Pax's attention out of the whole mixed brigade of watchers.

Let Pax live through this. If you'll just let Pax live . . .

She caught herself bargaining with God, promising to light a hundred candles in gratitude. She knew better than to haggle with God like a fruit seller in the market. God expected her to pay attention to the business at hand.

But she'd light flocks of candles if Pax lived.

She slowed her breathing. Tensed and released the big muscles of her body a few times. No point in burning up all her courage and strength before the game even began.

Forty-seven coaches, carts, gigs, and carriages passed. Twenty-two people. One dog. Then the Merchant.

"I probably could put glass into this." Hawker turned his head and considered the broken window. "It doesn't look that hard."

Pax said, "Planning to change professions?"

"Never hurts to be prepared. One of these days I'm going to push Galba just an inch too far and get booted out of the Service."

"That day has come and gone." Pax rested the pistol on the nail he'd driven into the drainpipe and sighted down the length of it. It was a Mortimer and he'd had the barrel rifled to give it some accuracy. At this range, it would work as well as a Baker.

Hawker was turning over the sheet of glass, holding the edges through folded rags. "I'll bet you could throw this, if you added some heft to it." He weighed it in his hands. "Who are they going to let torture the Merchant when we catch him? Not you."

"Doyle, I imagine."

Hawk nodded. "Then Doyle will be the one to kill him at the end. Or Galba will come in and do it, being Head of Service."

"You're counting your chickens before they're hatched."

"I'm wringing their necks, plucking, and stewing them before they're hatched." Glancing into Semple Street, Hawker added, "Just concentrate on sighting your gun. Our girl's holding fine. Calm as a pudding."

SHE knew it was the Merchant before she saw his face. The plain black landau, anonymous, secretive, with the curtains drawn, announced him like a blast of trumpets.

The Merchant was driving himself, which she hadn't expected. He dressed like a coachman and counterfeited the bored competence of a hired driver. He'd come to this meeting without his henchmen.

He was five minutes early. She'd have thought he was a man to be finicky about unimportant details.

She wiped the back of her hand across her mouth. That was her signal to all the neighboring deadly people. It said, *This is the Merchant.*

A hundred feet away, in a second-floor window, the curtain drew back. That passed her message to everyone who couldn't see her directly.

The closed coach told her he'd brought something or someone with him. He could fit two or three henchmen inside, ready to kidnap her. Or he could have Camille Besançon in there.

The carriage stopped level with her. The leather curtains

of the windows didn't twitch. Up on the box, the Merchant took a lungful of the cheroot he carried, set the brake, and wrapped the reins around it.

Close up, he was a deeply unconvincing coachman. That pallid face gave him away. He wore gloves too fine for a driver. His boots were gentleman's boots, smooth, glossy, well fitted, and soft. He made mistakes all over the map. The cheroot was another one. She'd never seen a driver carry anything in his hand but a whip.

The Merchant shed his gloves, matched them palm to palm, and dropped them on the seat. He shrugged out of the driver's coat, which was a thick, well-worn, authentic garment of many capes that had been made for a fatter man. He climbed down to go to the horse's head.

When he took the halter, he held the cheroot out to the side where it wouldn't annoy the horse.

"I am glad you decided to come. You brought the code?" He ventured that as one would hope, politely, that a borrowed book was about to be returned.

"I have it." She touched the bodice of her dress. That wasn't where she'd hidden the fake code. One tells many minor lies to hide the great ones. "Show me the woman."

"In a moment."

"Now."

"Patience. All in good time." He might have been a very nice man, saddened and hurt by her suspicion. He smiled at her and his eyes were most perfectly empty. "I have her inside the coach. Let me . . ." The horse was an orderly and placid mare, but she shuffled hooves and shook her great head at the smell of tobacco and fire. The Merchant waved largely. "You, boy! Come here."

She'd been aware of a rattle and click along the pavement behind her, but in a situation that held a choice of threats, she'd concentrated on the nearest and most deadly. She glanced over her shoulder, keeping the Merchant in view at the same time.

The boy approached, bowling a hoop, letter perfect in his role of Child Playing on the Street. He was dressed exactly as a loving mother in Semple Street would send her son from the house.

Carlo Baldoni. He was what—twelve? A child in the line of fire. Damn the Baldoni anyway, and damn her for not expecting this.

Carlo propped his hoop against the railing, a convincing, well-used hoop that he'd doubtless stolen. Respectful, curious, he approached. "Yes, sir."

The Merchant dropped the halter, navigated in his pocket, and found sixpence. "You like horses?"

Breathless and high voiced, with exactly the right accent, Carlo said, "Oh, yes, sir."

"Then hold mine. This is Dolly. She's very gentle." The Merchant sent the coin riding over and under the back of his fingers. Sleight of hand. Pax could do that, too. This might be where he learned it. "You'll have another like it when I come back."

When Carlo came to pick up the reins, the Merchant clasped his shoulder in a friendly way and gave him the coin. One could almost see nephews and nieces gathered about the knee of this genial man as he handed out sugarplums. "What's your name, son?"

"Tommy. Tommy Goodall."

"Tom. A fine, strong name. Men with that name have been great fighters for great causes." The Merchant smiled down into the innocent, upturned face. "You'll do something important in the world, Tom."

The Merchant's voice was like the sweetened cream that topped iced cakes. Sweet, cloying, full of wind, amorphous. She heard an inhuman emptiness whistling beneath.

He showed no inclination to reveal his larger plans to her. Not why he needed the Mandarin Code. Neither the purpose nor the location of the gunpowder.

She would make certain this woman in the coach was safe, then let the British Service have him.

Every moment she delayed was an invitation to disaster. Pax stood in the alley with a pistol pointed at the Merchant's heart. Mr. Hawker would be lethally equipped. Innocent-looking Carlo was Baldoni and thus old enough to carry a knife. There was a sniper three houses down. She was armed herself, for that matter. The potential for death was strewn across the Semple Street landscape like brown leaves in September.

From inside the coach came a faint knocking sound, as if an animal were trapped there. Or as if a woman, bound and gagged, tossed herself back and forth on the seat.

The Merchant walked a little ways from the landau, to smoke his cheroot.

Why was he smoking? Her mind skittered off, pursuing that oddity. A clumsy disguise? A weapon? A signal to his men?

She said, "Show me that woman."

Amiable as a basking snake, sincere as bread, he held out his hand and made curled beckoning with his fingers. "You will see the woman when I've examined the code. Give me the paper, Cami Leyland. Come, I think we must trust each other a little, at this point."

Horribly, sickeningly, when he wore that expression of grave reason on his face, he looked like Pax.

Like Pax . . . and not like. The Merchant had the square jaw, the lean cheekbones, the long, mobile line to his lips. There was the shared blood, plain to see.

Pax had said, "I am no part of him."

Different men had been poured into the same vessel—one clean, one unclean. They were nothing alike, Pax and his father, not in the least grain or particular.

She said, "What are you going to do with the code?"

His eyelids drooped. "You know I can't tell you that."

"I have to know what I'm risking. I have to know whether they'll trace this back to me."

Something ugly curled behind his eyes. His voice held condescending amusement. "I promise they'll never know it was you."

He lies. To a Baldoni.

The Merchant was one of those who protected his great lie with many small lies. He lied with the exact opposite of the truth instead of a slight twisting of it. He promised most when he was about to betray. A Baldoni five-year-old would be ashamed to lie so badly.

She furrowed her brow as if she were thinking furiously. "Are the Leylands involved? I can be traced to them."

"This is nothing to do with the Leylands. The code won't be connected to them at all." He scarcely bothered to hide the mockery, he was so certain of her stupidity. "We won't use it in England."

Lies. The truth is the opposite. The kegs of gunpowder were in London so his operation was in London. What connected the Mandarin Code, kegs of gunpowder, Camille Besançon, Semple Street, and her? How did they intersect?

"You'll take this code overseas?" she said.

"I leave for Austria at once. This is nothing to do with England." With his mouth, with the muscles of his face, with his skilled voice, the Merchant conveyed reassurance. Not with his eyes, though. Never with his eyes. "I promise you will escape harm."

He plans to kill me. Fear and anger shivered through her. Why hadn't he already done it? What was he waiting for?

The Baldoni said, *To know the purpose of a lie, look at the results of it.*

The Merchant's lies had brought her to Semple Street. So far, they'd accomplished nothing else. Maybe the Merchant wanted her here.

She kept her hands still, not giving the signal. Up and down the street, she was watched through field glasses and gunsights. Two dozen men waited to move in.

He's stalling for time. Something's going to happen.

She could sense Pax as if he stood beside her, his finger on the trigger, his eyes on the Merchant, in his belly the ice-cold hatred of a lifelong vendetta.

Don't kill him, Pax. Not yet. Not yet.

A rider passed, sitting his horse in a sloppy, preoccupied manner. In the house behind her, a baby had been crying for a while. That continued. And down the street, out of sight, a wagon, or maybe a carriage, approached. Four well-paced horses, light on their feet. A coach, then. The noise of their hooves slowed as they approached.

"This gets us nowhere." The Merchant blew out an impatient breath. "One of us must yield. Come. Look at the woman and be convinced." He turned on his heel, abruptly, and pulled open the door of his coach.

She could see a human form bundled on the bench seat of the landau, tied hand and foot, gagged.

He said, "Behold the offspring of the counterrevolutionary Jules Besançon, traitor to France, and the Englishwoman Hyacinth Leyland. Poisoned fruit of those poisoned blossoms."

He leaned inside and fumbled about in the dimness. The stairs flipped down. He drew back.

She said, "I see a woman. Not necessarily Camille Besançon."

The Merchant flicked his cheroot away, into the gutter. "Question her. Satisfy yourself of her bona fides. I'll wait at the corner and give you privacy." He motioned in that direction.

"And the Mandarin Code?"

He'd already turned his back on her and taken the first steps away. He didn't pause. He just said, "Later."

The coach she'd heard approaching pulled up outside Number Twenty-nine, the house opposite Fifty-six.

With the arrogance of the servants of the very rich, the coachman stopped in the middle of the road, directly beside the smaller landau. Between them, they did a fine job of blocking Semple Street altogether.

It was a big, rich, well-shined coach with a crest on the door and a team of four black horses. A ridiculously expensive coach for this neighborhood. A coach with a guard next to the driver and a footman behind.

"You there." The coachman waggled his long coach whip at Carlo. "You there! Move up. Move along. Nobody can get past with you blocking the road."

She couldn't see the man inside the coach. Didn't know who he was. But she knew the kind of man he had to be. Somebody important.

"Damn. Oh, damn." She understood everything. Saw it all, beginning to end.

It was already too late for her.

She raised her hand into her hair—that was the signal to close in and take the Merchant—and screamed out, "Carlo, run!" and scrambled into the Merchant's carriage, where she would die.

Fifty

Life obeys no plans.

A BALDONI SAYING

PAX PUSHED OFF FROM THE WALL, RUNNING. BEFORE he saw Cami's signal. Before the bloody Merchant took off down the length of the street. Before he knew why.

Cami clambered into the coach. A thousand alarm bells rang in his mind. He could feel death hovering over her like a vulture, claws stretched out.

Hawker snapped, "It's Addington."

The Prime Minister. The big black coach had the Prime Minister in it? That was the Merchant's target. Assassination and the chaos that would follow Death.

He yelled, "Get him out of here," in Hawker's direction and dove through the door of the landau.

A woman, bound, gagged, thrashing, was tied flat to one seat. Cami crouched on the floor of the coach, prying at a hasp on the other seat.

"The gunpowder," Cami snarled. "It's here. That's what he did with the kegs. He lit a fuse and it's gone under the seat. I can't get to it."

The seats were built for storage. Lift the lid to toss a coat or blanket in. This one was locked. A blackened string of fuse hung over the edge of the seat and disappeared underneath.

"Back!" He pointed the pistol.

Cami threw herself over the wriggling woman on the seat, giving what protection she could in case the slug went wild in the coach.

The crack of the gun slapped his ears. The bullet hit the lock and ricocheted out the door.

It didn't hit Cami. Didn't hit Cami.

The coach shuddered, tilted up, and tried to throw him to the floor. The horse shrieked. *Nobody's holding the horse. We're going to go over.*

No time to think about that. He'd hit the padlock dead center, shattering the mechanism. In the rocking coach, he reversed the pistol, grabbed the hot barrel, and slammed the butt down, once, twice. The bar snapped open.

The landau thumped down level again. Somebody had hold of the horse. Not Hawker. Hawker was on the street, yelling and throwing rocks. Addington's coach clattered away to the squeal of horses and the shouts of the coachman.

He threw back the seat and the cushions. The space below was filled with kegs and the smell of gunpowder. The smell of a fuse burning.

Behind him, Cami cut the woman's feet free, flapped the door open, and pushed her, yammering and limp, out into the street. "Run, you idiot."

A fuse was nailed to the wood on the underside of the seat, back and forth, back and forth, then down into the keg at the end. A jagged point of flame raced along the course of it. He couldn't pull the fuse out of the keg. When he tried to pinch the flame out, it just raced between his fingers.

He spat on his fingers and tried again. Again. Searing hot pain and no effect on the white tip of fire. Nothing stopped it. Sparks flashed and fell on the kegs, any one of them hot enough to set everything off.

Cami reached across him with her knife. She slipped the blade under the line of fuse, inches ahead of the flame, between the last two bent nails that held it in place. She sawed at the line. The fire ate its way under the last nail. Inches left before it got past her. Breaths left before it reached the keg.

She cut through.

The line of fuse parted. The fizzing white fire curved down to the hanging end. It burned there for an endless moment. Then, abruptly, blinked out.

One tiny orange spark drifted lazily onto the top of the wooden keg below and went dark.

Silence. Cami's breathing. His own. A woman screeched outside the coach. There didn't seem to be a second fuse. He didn't hear one.

He could notice the pain of burns on his thumb and fingers. "Cami . . ." He took the knife from her and opened her hands to show red burn lines where she'd tried to snuff the fuse before it snaked under the seat.

Of course. Of course. He said, "Good work."

"You, too." They were both breathing like bellows.

Somebody started shooting on the street.

Fifty-one

Blood cannot be washed away.

A BALDONI SAYING

THREE REGULARLY SPACED SHOTS ECHOED OFF THE brick fronts of the buildings. Rifle fire. That would be Grey, shooting from his sniper roost.

Pax swung out of the coach, hit the cobblestones, sidestepped the woman on the ground, drumming her heels and screaming—Camille Besançon—and ran for the end of the street.

Cami was a step behind him, keeping pace and guarding his back. He didn't have to see her. He knew exactly where she was. Lately, he always knew.

Maybe the Merchant had expected to slip away in the shock of the explosion, in the pandemonium of fires and screaming horses, houses collapsing, and men and women dying. As it was, he made it less than a hundred yards. He lay on his side on the cobbles, twisted in pain. A pool of blood seeped out under his leg from where he'd been shot in the knee. He wasn't going anywhere.

The Merchant had been brought down at the outermost edge of rifle range. Grey had held his fire till the last possible minute. He'd fired two warning shots, then placed a hit to the knee. Grey stood in the window, reloading one of his rifles. Another leaned beside him, muzzle upright.

A mixed bag of Service agents and Baldoni stood over the Merchant, making sure he didn't crawl off and watching for any attempt at rescue. They'd searched him. A wallet and notebook, two pistols, a trio of nasty-looking steel spikes, and some small soft pouches lay on the pavement to the side.

There'd be time to sort it out later. He knelt briefly to check the guns. They were well-kept, expensive pieces, probably Prussian. Neither had been fired. The bastard had been shot himself before he could take hostages or loose a shot at anybody. He cocked one and slipped it carefully into the deep pocket of his greatcoat, holding the grip, his finger beside the trigger.

Men fell back to let Cami and him through into the quiet in the center of this circle. The Merchant lay there, pasty white, sweating, daubed in blood. Nothing redder than blood. Somebody'd tied a rough bandage on his knee.

The Merchant turned his head and looked up. "You."

It had been ten years since he'd met the Merchant face-to-face. He still had nothing to say to this man.

The Merchant said, "You've come to gloat."

"I've come to clean up this mess."

Down the street, at the landau, Doyle held the horse steady. Hawker and Stillwater slopped in that direction, carrying buckets to wet the gunpowder down. The Baldoni boy sat on the curb, head in his hands, bleeding from his nose. Householders poked heads out their windows to see what was happening.

Cami came to stand beside him, close enough that her shoulder brushed his arm. She held her gun in both hands, cocked, but pointed to the ground. She was intent and deadly, legs braced, ready to run or fight, ready to raise that business-like gun and shoot. His Cami, at her natural work.

The Merchant dragged himself to sitting. "So. The British Service sends my son to destroy me. My sweet butcher of a son. There's irony in that."

I'm not your son. "I sent myself."

The man in the dirt at his feet could have been a stranger. He felt no connection with this Peter Styles, born to privilege,

well and expensively educated. Brilliant fanatic of the Revolution. Cold-blooded murderer. A man-killing dog to be
tracked down and shot.

Fifty yards away, the woman they'd freed from the landau
knelt on the dirty ground, sobbing. A yapping dog in one of
the houses provided a tinny antiphony. Men crossed back and
forth with buckets, climbing the stairs of one of the houses.
Water dripped from the bottom of the landau onto the street
and fingered its way into the gutter.

Addington's coach had already disappeared around the
corner. With luck, the Prime Minister would never know how
close he'd come to death.

"He scuttles away to save his miserable life," the Merchant
said. "A pity. Going up in flame would have been his finest
hour." He hacked out a laugh that turned into a cough. "Do
you know why your Prime Minister comes to Semple Street
every week? Not to visit a mistress. He comes to make a
mawkish visit to his old nanny. You are led by a milksop sen-
timentalist. I leave England in his bungling hands."

A crowd was gathering. People had come out of their
houses, being curious. The grocer's boy and the grocer. A
housemaid from Number Thirty. At the back, peeping from
behind everybody else, two old women in black. Nobody got
close, being wary of the guns, but everybody watched avidly.

Down the street Hawker was half in, half out of the carriage, pouring out buckets, laying down the law about something. Boys ran by the coach windows, peeked in and pointed,
and ran away shouting.

"Political murder," Cami said softly. "This wasn't about
codes or the Leylands or Camille Besançon. It's me. He needed
me here."

The final pieces of the puzzle had fallen into place as he
walked from the landau to this bloody corner of the street.
"He needed Vérité from the Coach House."

Cami had made the same calculations and come to the
same conclusions. "None of this is about killing Addington—
who cares what happens to Addington? It's someone from the
Police Secrète killing Addington that is significant. Me, killing him."

"You, yourself, are nothing." The Merchant hunched inward, holding his knee. The little smirk stayed on his lips. "You are my puppet, not remotely worthy to play the role I assigned you. You were trained and nurtured by the Revolution, and you betrayed it. But you came to this place, tame and obedient, as I planned."

"I didn't die, however, which pleases me." Cami made an eloquent shrug. She slowly lifted the gun she held, till it pointed at the Merchant's heart. "I would have felt very stupid when I found myself scattered in small bits from one end of Semple Street to the other, interlarded with scraps of coded paper."

He touched her arm with the hand that wasn't in his pocket, holding a gun. Just to feel her being alive. Just to know she was here. "You would have made a convincing French spy."

She considered this. "To be fair, I am a spy. I'm Caché. I've been an interloper in the household of the Leylands. I've befooled and befuddled the British Service for years. No one is better suited to be the linchpin of a French assassination plot than I am." She grinned suddenly. "I would have been admirably silent if questioned."

She could laugh, because that was the way she was made. Pure courage. When he thought how close he'd come to losing her forever, it made him want to knife somebody.

He cupped his anger inside and let it sit there, waiting. "A month ago, men tried to kill Napoleon and make it look like an English plot. This is the same. The Merchant's fingerprints are all over both of these schemes."

"It's a pity no one's killed this man." Cami sighted down the barrel of her gun at the Merchant. "It would improve him."

"Napoleon dead at English hands. Addington dead at the hands of a French spy. The peace would break. The treaties wouldn't hold. It would mean war."

"We've had enough war to last us into the next century," Cami said.

"Revolution is born in the storm of war." The Merchant's breath hissed between clenched teeth. "It demands the blood of martyrs."

He knew the words. They came from the bleak lessons of his childhood. "There are no martyrs here."

"Death is the purest revolutionary act." The Merchant wrapped his arms into his coat, ignoring the smears of blood. "If I die, a hundred other men will finish my work. The revolution will come."

"It won't come today."

He was finished here. And the Merchant was finished.

Rough wheels clicked on cobblestone as Tenn led the pony cart out of the alley toward them. The sooner they took this show off the street and out of sight, the better.

"He expects you to kill him, Pax. Will you?" Cami could still disconcert him when she became cryptic and Baldoni.

"What? No. I'm—"

"Pax, let me say this before you do. One thing. It is a great and ancient evil to spill the blood of your family. In every place and time, it has been a horror beyond speech." She frowned earnestly. "My father killed his cousin, you know. It was by accident, but he never felt clean of that act."

"Galba agrees with you. He thinks it'll give me nightmares."

"It will," she said. "Give you nightmares, I mean. Killing doesn't lay devils, it raises them. That's not a family saying. I just made it up."

"I like your sayings."

He'd expected to feel cold rage when he finally confronted the Merchant. He'd expected the old pain, despair thick and black as night, spikes of ice in his belly. That was the way it'd always been when he thought about his father.

The moment for revenge had come and gone. He'd felt nothing. "I don't need to kill him. He doesn't matter enough."

"Ah." After a minute, Cami nodded and lowered her gun. "That's a great relief. I was ready to do it for you."

Incongruously, in the middle of the street, while he kept one hand on the gun in his pocket and dozens of people watched, he wanted to smile.

When he'd loaded his pistol this morning, he'd held the lead bullet and imagined it stopping the heart of the Merchant. Old habit. He'd done that when he went hunting one man in particular in Tuscany and Piedmont.

He had no orders to kill the Merchant. The need to do it had drained away.

"He can live long enough to hang." A cold truth. The greatest revenge was sending the Merchant to the gallows.

"You've suckled the bourgeois morality of the British Service." The Merchant grimaced and leaned inward upon himself, arms wrapped under his coat. "Do you think you've become one of them? They *use* you to do their dirty work. You are their perfect, stone-cold assassin. You are their monster."

Maybe once he had been. But Cami had changed him. The empty man who'd come to London was filled. He didn't even recognize that Paxton anymore.

The Furies could go home. There'd be no patricide today. "We all have a monster inside us."

"When I go to trial, I'll tell the world about my son, the French spy in the British Service. The bloody killer. The aristocrat who joined the revolution."

"The bastard of Ilse Dalgaard, Danish subject. Father unknown." It felt good to say it. "The flotsam and jetsam of Europe. Nobody cares what I do."

"The legitimate grandson of an English earl." The Merchant, hoarse and whispering. "I married your bitch of a mother in Amsterdam. When I stand trial, you'll be beside me. We'll give them a crime they can't sweep under the carpet."

The Merchant's eyes found Cami. "You will be my martyr for the cause. My loyal revolutionary, shot by the British Service as she tried to assassinate the Prime Minister." He jerked his hand from hiding. Something glittered in the sunlight. A thick silver pencil case, smeared with blood.

No!

A gun. A trick. A toy for idle gentlemen. A tiny pistol, good for one shot only. Pointed at Cami.

She snapped her pistol up.

She has no time. His own finger was on the trigger. Without drawing, he shot through the pocket of his greatcoat.

His bullet hit the Merchant square in the middle of his forehead. The man fell backward, already dead. He looked . . . surprised. As if death had refused to follow the plans he had for it.

He had to push Cami's gun aside so he could pull her to him, breathe in the smell of her, kiss her face, eyes, ears, nose. Her hair. Her mouth. It wasn't enough. Cami was alive. He'd never be able to hold her close enough.

ON the edge of the small, excited group that had gathered to comment upon the first shooting and was now expounding upon the second, two old women craned their necks to observe events.

Violet said, "He appears to be dead."

"There is a hole in his forehead. Ipso facto," Lily said.

"I cannot help but feel this is the simplest solution to several difficult problems. *Mors omnia solvit.*"

"As you say, death solves everything." Lily had been holding a small gun hidden in the folds of her skirt. She returned it to her reticule. "The business of shooting one's father is fraught with social and moral implications. One cannot like it."

They were both silent while they considered the complications of a man shooting his father.

"Paxton's actions are . . . unfortunate," Lily said. "On the other hand, one would not have wished that task to fall upon dear Cami."

"A sensitive girl. More so than one would think," Violet said. "Young Paxton, as well."

"A young man of some complication. Not really suited to be a patricide."

"We must see this hushed up a bit," Violet said.

"It can't be silenced." Lily waved a thin, blue-veined hand across the collection of British Service agents and Baldoni. "Everyone saw. Gossip and rumor will scatter to the four winds. No stopping it."

"We will shape the official story."

More thought. Lily said, "We could say that I did it. By accident, of course."

"You tripped."

"While I was examining the gun."

"The man was shot twice," Violet pointed out.

"Not the sort of thing one would do inadvertently. A pity we can't just drop the body in the Thames."

"Heir to an earl. So necessary to prove the succession has passed."

Lily said austerely, "It is more than necessary to demonstrate the Merchant is actually dead this time."

"Perhaps . . . a robbery. In St. Giles."

"Or Hampstead Heath."

Violet said, "I'm tempted to have him dropped in an alley in Soho. It adds a French flavor to the death."

"Soho. Yes. Excellent."

Another minute passed. "They should remove the body," Violet said. "It's unsightly."

"They're waiting for those two to finish." But Lily's voice was indulgent.

"So romantic." Violet applied her elbow ruthlessly to the kidney of the man in front of her, gaining a better view. "I do admire an enthusiastic man."

"Eventually, they'll have to come up for air," Lily said.

"There is nothing, absolutely nothing, more attractive than a man who's just killed on your behalf."

"They should clear away the body, though. And find privacy for that."

Violet sighed. "*Amantes sunt amentes*, as Terence says."

"Lovers are lunatics." Lily sniffed austerely. "I'm not surprised Paxton overlooks the matter. Men are not naturally tidy. But Cami has always been neat in her habits. It's not like her to leave a body lying about."

"They are distracted," Violet said. "And who shall blame them?"

Over the rumble and jabber of the crowd, in the background, where the landau was still being drowned in buckets of water, the sound of sobbing continued.

Violet said, "We should see to her, I suppose."

"She very likely is our niece."

"She does sound exactly like Hyacinth in one of her *crises de nerfs*. Hyacinth did have a delicate spirit."

"This one, too, apparently," Lily said.

They turned to walk toward the sobbing. "I think," Violet said judiciously, "we should find her a French husband."

"Soon," Lily agreed.

They glanced back, one last time, to Cami and Pax, madly kissing, surrounded by a circle of interested spies and criminals.

Lily said, "That's taken care of."

Violet nodded. "I do like a happy ending."

Fifty-two

*Drink, dance, laugh, love. A man who does not
enjoy the pleasures of life is poor indeed.*

A BALDONI SAYING

SHE KNEW HE'D COME TO HER WINDOW. NOT A
sound in the night, but she knew he was there.

It crossed her mind that he had come to many windows
this secretly. The deaths that haunted him had begun this
way. It would be healing to him to use his skills on such benign purposes.

She got out of bed in her shift, slipped on shoes, and padded
along the blue carpet to the window, which was open, even
though it left the room chilly. She carried a knife with her,
being prudent, but laid it aside on the table when she looked out
and saw him below.

His hair was perfectly white under the moon, disheveled
and unraveling from its tie. He was outside the window, sitting on his haunches, keeping an eye on the empty backyard
and maybe studying London.

She said, "Have you come visiting, or did you climb up to
enjoy the view?"

"I promised Bernardo I wouldn't go to your room tonight."

"Did you, now?"

He would not come into her room, only this close. Close enough, maybe, to hear her turn in her bed or sigh in her sleep. He wouldn't lightly break his word, once given.

"I'm not sure why. It had something to do with your great-aunt Fortunata fixing me with an unwavering stare."

"You are wise to be terrified of her."

"That's what I thought." Pax tilted his head back to look up at her. He looked natural and at home, standing on a bit of roofing in the night. He was, maybe, being the Gray Cat right now.

She leaned out the window and reached her hand out to him. He reached up to take it. They could just clasp hands.

He said, "You're beautiful."

"You can't see me."

"I don't have to see you to know you're beautiful. Moonlight become woman. Light and darkness. Chiaroscuro, painted on the night."

She wasn't certain what "chiaroscuro" meant. With luck, a month from now she would be living with him in a studio in Florence, pretending to be his model and his lover, spying upon the French and the Austrians. She'd best acquire the language of artists.

But not tonight.

The kitchen rumbled with voices and rattled with the clanking of pots. The women of the house—the men, too—were cooking for tomorrow. Every spy and swindler in London and a surprising number of quite respectable folks would be in this house to witness her wedding.

Everyone acted as if a solemn and significant merger of great houses was going forward. Perhaps it was. Uncle Bernardo had explained matters to her at length, involving at least a dozen families and much of the north of Italy.

Aunt Lily had been more succinct. "You have an obscene amount of money. I'll put my man of business on it. He's used to dealing with obscene amounts of money."

She'd signed a marriage contract two inches thick, in English and Tuscan. Frankly, she'd rather not think about it.

As he sometimes did, Pax followed thoughts she hadn't

spoken. He said, "When I asked you to marry me, I didn't know you were rich."

"I didn't know you would be an earl, so we're even."

"I'm not going to be an earl." Flat words, holding a heavy cargo of annoyance.

"A dozen men heard the Merchant say you were legitimate. Eventually it'll get back to your grandfather."

She felt a little nerve in his hand twitch. "Who will ignore it, the way I do. Just lies. The Merchant spitting a last drop of venom. There's no proof, in Amsterdam or anywhere else."

But most likely there was. That would be the Merchant's long, subtle vengeance—to give his family a French spy as the next heir. The proof, when it turned up, would be watertight. Pax would find it difficult to escape the Royal College of Heralds.

"In any case," she said, being tactful, "we won't be around to argue the succession to minor English earldoms. We'll be in Florence, living in a garret, spying on all and sundry."

"A garret with good light and a big bed."

If they were going to talk about beds, she was too far away from him. She couldn't see his face in this romantical dimness. She hooked her hands onto the windowsill and spilled forward into the dark, making her careful way down the slope of the roof. Soon, he would be holding her.

He stood before her. His big, warm hands cradled her at her hips as she slid close. He stretched out, long and easy under her hands, taking his coat off. He held it so she could get her arms in. The sleeves ran long and she had to fold them back twice.

"This marriage won't be legal." He found her hands and took them in both of his and settled the two pairs in the space between them. "We'll get married again somewhere in France. A dull civil ceremony."

"And once more when we get to Italy. I think my grandfather will insist on it, and another huge celebration. We'll be very thoroughly married before we're through."

"I don't know why they're letting me have you. Your family." His thumb indicated the voices in the kitchen. She felt it where their hands were locked tight. "Maybe it's about making you Danish. The French will leave Danish property alone."

"So will the Austrians, when they next invade. Denmark is a small but useful neutral country. But this has nothing to do with Denmark. My cousins approve of you."

The angular planes of his face were sharp and dark. Slowly, he freed his hands from her hold and took them to lie heavy on her shoulders. "They think I shot my own father to save your life."

"You did. They are shocked, but approving. This is the meat of tragedy and romance to the Baldoni. Fifty years from now, grandmothers and aged aunts will tell stories about you and pity you and praise you for a grand heroic gesture. If there were an initiation to be a Baldoni, you passed it this morning."

"You know it wasn't like that."

"Nonetheless, they believe it. You are one of us now. They like the scent of vengeance about this, too. It consolidates your reputation among the young men. We're a ruthless lot, we Baldoni."

"Not vengeance." Pax's eyes, which saw the world with such pitiless clarity, were turned inward. "All the evil that old man had done, all his schemes and plots . . . but all I thought about when I pulled the trigger was keeping you alive. There's no meat for the Harpies to sink their claws into. No unclean horror. No sacrilege. Now all I feel is relief that you're here, alive, under the sky with me."

She had to smile. "I'm relieved, too."

"It felt inevitable," he said. "When I took off after him on Semple Street, I think I already knew I'd kill him."

"Somebody had to. I'd have disposed of the matter myself if I'd been faster. The Fluffy Aunts were sneaking around the outer fringes of that mob with the same intention."

He shook his head. "I'm his son. He was my problem to clean up."

She could imagine how hard it was for him to say, "I'm his son."

She reached up to the long-fingered, rough-skinned hands that grasped her shoulders and pressed them tighter to her. "He wanted death, you know."

Pax looked past her, out into the night. "I know."

"You saw it, too. He wanted death at your hands," she said. "So he left you no choice but to kill him. There was nothing ahead for him but humiliation, trial, and execution, so he bought a quick martyrdom. And he made you suffer."

"He tried," Pax said.

"If you feel the Furies breathing on your neck, he's won. If you think these"—she squeezed his hands, tight, to make perfectly clear what she meant—"are stained with blood—"

"They are."

"With his blood. We're not children, you and I. Our innocence was problematic at best. If you look at your hands and see unclean blood, he's won. If you—"

"I can see what he tried to do. None of it worked." Pax's mouth closed over hers. He freed himself from her grip and slid his arms around her to nestle the two of them together. He set his forehead to her forehead. He whispered, as if he were telling secrets. "I've done worse things than rid the world of that bastard. I'm not going to lose sleep over it."

He would, though. His Service had chosen him for terrible deeds because he was honorable to the core of his being. She'd chosen a man who would do whatever was necessary and pay for it afterward in bad dreams. The best sort of man.

In their married life, she'd try to do whatever killing became necessary, as a loyal wife should.

"I'm glad you're untroubled," she said, softly in his ear. "I begrudge that man even a small victory over you. Can we leave this damp and windswept roof and find better shelter in that shed? That one. Do you see? One small pony quarters there at the moment and he won't object to our visit. A huge heap of hay was delivered this afternoon and piled into the back corner. It's quite clean."

"That's coincidence, I suppose. Not connivance from your cousins and aunts."

"Entirely coincidence," she agreed.

Slowly, carefully, giving it all his attention, he kissed her. And kissed her. Warmth grew between them, and then heat. Clouds covered and uncovered the moon.

After a while they left their chilly perch and sought more privacy.

Keep reading for a mesmerising excerpt
from Book One in the Spymaster series
by Joanna Bourne

The Forbidden Rose

Available soon from Headline Eternal

"YOU HAVE NOT BEEN FOOLISH," SHE SAID. "BUT YOU have been unlucky. The results are indistinguishable."

The rabbit said nothing. It lay on its side, panting. Terror poured from it in waves, like water going down the steps of a fountain.

Her snare circled its throat. She had caught it with a line of red silk, teased and spun from the torn strip of a dress. It could not escape. Even when it heard death coming toward it through the brush, it didn't struggle. Being sensible, it had given up.

"The analogies to my own situation are clear. I do not like them." Marguerite de Fleurignac sat down and pulled her skirts to lie smooth over her knees. The grass was slick and sharp-edged on the bare skin of her ankles. Behind her rose the ruins of the chateau. She did not look in that direction if she could help it. "I am starving to death, you know. Not as one starves in stories, nobly and gracefully. I starve stupidly. I scrape up oats from the bottom of the feed bins and pick berries. I pull wild carrots from the earth and gnaw on them in my cave under the bridge. None of this rests easily in my stomach. It is very sordid. I will not share the details with you."

The rabbit's eyes stared beyond her.

"Life is not like the fables. No magical bird alights on the rooftop, bearing messages. You do not offer me three wishes in exchange for your life. No prince rides up on his white horse to rescue me."

Rabbit fur was a brown made of many shades, like toast. The guard hairs were darker than the down that clung close to its body. Inside its ears was a delicate velvet, pale as cream, and she could see the pink skin underneath. Its eyes were fringed on top with a row of short, thick hairs. It had eyelashes. She hadn't known rabbits had eyelashes.

Terror terror terror.

It had been a mistake to look so closely at the rabbit. She should not have talked to it.

When she was five or six, Old Mathieu, the gamekeeper, had let her tag along behind him through this wood. He set snares and made great slaughter among the rabbits and put them in a big leather game bag to carry home.

He had been dead fifteen years. In his last illness, she'd visited him every day in his dirty, crowded hut by the river. She'd brought him the best brandy from the chateau cellars to ease the pain.

Uncle Arnault, who was marquis then, had scolded and given orders, which she had ignored. "You spoil these peasants. You make pets of them." Papa had pointed out that spirits were not good for the humors of the body. She should take the man seawater and a mash of beets. Cousin Victor sneaked after her and pushed her down and spilled open the basket and broke everything inside.

Uncle Arnault was long dead, having discussed politics with the guillotine. Papa was marquis now, inasmuch as anyone held the empty title. Victor had joined the most radical of the revolutionary groups, the Jacobins. The casks of brandy had exploded in a ball of blue flame when the fire fingered down to the wine cellar. It had never mattered a bean that she had given brandy to a dying man.

Old Mathieu's sons had been in the mob that came to burn the chateau. She'd seen them with the others on the lawn in the light of torches.

A pulse rippled in the rabbit's throat, under the fur. That fluttering beat, in a hollow the size of a copper sou, was the only sign of life.

"I make up stories in my head and I am always remarkably heroic in them. When men actually came to destroy me, I ran like a rabbit, if you will forgive the comparison." She wiped rain from her face. Her forearm was gritty and smelled like crushed grass and sweat. And smoke. "You are doubtless stultified with boredom to hear my problems. One's own disaster is of compelling interest. The disasters of others, less so."

Clouds hung flat and close overhead, the color of old bruises. A few sharp tiny points of rain hit her face when she looked up. Even this far from the chateau, thin black flakes of ash had caught in the leaves of the trees. The rain fell with ash in it.

"Here is the story, if you wish to read it." She caught drops on the palm of her hand. "This," she lifted one speck of black onto her forefinger, "came from the destruction of curtains in the blue salon. And this," another bit of ash, "was a page from a book in the library. A mathematics text. This . . ." She picked a fleck of ash from her forearm. "This is the period at the end of a sentence in one my notebooks. That was the only copy of an old tale of the people. It is lost now."

She let the drops of water run away. She was very tired. She had been up all night, two nights in a row, walking the last shipment of sparrows to safety. She had taken three men, three women, and a child through the dark fields to the deserted mill that was the next waystation. She'd waited with them till Heron's son came to take them onward. Then she had trudged the long way back. Because Crow—careful, reliable Crow who never missed a meeting—had not yet come. He was late, and she worried.

The sparrows had complained a great deal that she had no food to give them. No one had asked what had happened to her in the burning of the chateau.

They would go to London, those sparrows, and tell everyone how brave they had been and what dangers they had undergone, fleeing France. None of them would speak of the bravery of Heron's young son who came at night, alone, to lead them onward. Or of Jeanne, who was the Wren, who risked death to smuggle them out of Paris. Or of Egret and Skylark and the others who hid them along the way. The sparrows would take it all for granted.

She shivered, which was what she deserved for sitting on the ground in this small rain, talking to a rabbit. "I will tell you what I should do. I should go deep into the woods, carrying—you will forgive me for being blunt?—carrying your dead corpse, and light a fire and put you on a spit and cook you. Then I should begin my walk to Paris in the dark of the night." Rubbing her arms did not make them any warmer. "Crow is more than wise. I should leave him to take care of his own sparrows and go warn the others."

The rabbit's fear was like the whine of iron on a grindstone. *Terror terror terror.*

The wind coming from the chateau pushed at her back, smelling of smoke, ugly and somehow metallic. "Do not expect pity, Citoyen Rabbit. I am without a heart. It was the first thing I ate when I became hungry."

The rabbit did not flinch when she laid hands upon it, but inside its fur, it shivered. The knife in her pocket was sharper than it had been four days ago when it lived the placid life of a letter opener. She worked a finger into the snare of silk that held the rabbit. "Instead of being sensible, I will chew on parched grains that do not agree with me and let you go free." She cut the red thread. "You will not be grateful. I know. You will come back tonight with a hundred rabbits and burn down the bridge and me underneath."

It did not move.

"Go. Go. You annoy me, lying there. Go, before I change my mind and eat you with wild onions and watercress."

The rabbit shook from end to end and wobbled to its feet. It lurched off into the drab grass of the drainage ditch. The waves of terror departed with it.

It was a relief to be free of that. "It would have made me sick, I think, to eat something so afraid."

Don't miss the first exquisite novel
in the *Spymaster* series

The Forbidden Rose

A glittering French aristocrat on the run.

England's premier spy with a score to settle.

The lies, scandals and madness of revolutionary Paris.

*When deception and desire intertwine,
can love surface and survive?*

'Intriguing, refreshing and rewarding'
Library Journal

Don't miss the enthralling second novel
in the *Spymaster* series

The Spymaster's Lady

An elusive French spy known only as the Fox Cub.

A British spymaster who might finally be her match.

Two enemies thrown together to forge an uneasy alliance.

In desperate times, is a forbidden passion possible to resist?

'Love, love LOVED it!'
Julia Quinn

Don't miss the spellbinding third novel
in the *Spymaster* series

My Lord and Spymaster

A father wrongly accused of selling secrets to Napoleon.

His daughter kidnapped on the hunt for the traitor.

A valiant captain who swoops in to the rescue.

In a game of love and lies, will passion mask the treacherous truth?

'An undeniably powerful
new voice in historical romance'

All About Romance